I0763517

Pit Planet

Books by David Dvorkin

Fiction

The Arm and Flanagan
Budspy
Business Secrets from the Stars
The Cavaradossi Killings
Central Heat
The Children of Shiny Mountain
Children of the Undead
Damon the Caiman
Dawn Crescent (with Daniel Dvorkin)
Earthmen and Other Aliens
The Green God
Pit Planet
The Prisoner of the Blood series
- *Insatiable*
- *Unquenchable*

The Seekers
Slit
Star Trek novels
- *The Trellisane Confrontation*
- *Time Trap*
- *The Captains' Honor (with Daniel Dvorkin)*

Time and the Soldier
Time for Sherlock Holmes
Ursus

Non–Fiction

At Home with Solar Energy
The Dead Hand of Mrs. Stifle
Dust Net
Once a Jew, Always a Jew?
Self-Publishing Tools, Tips, and Techniques
The Surprising Benefits of Being Unemployed
When We Landed on the Moon: A Memoir

Pit Planet

David Dvorkin

First hardcover edition published by Betancourt & Company in 2003

ISBN: 978-1-7345636-2-7

Dedication

To Leonore

CHAPTER ONE

Benton's work hours increased because of the contract with The Jacksonite Corporation, but his social life improved.

It was starting from a low baseline, though. He had always been of a solitary nature, had always concentrated on his work, had never made friends easily. His older coworkers were married and very settled. They didn't socialize with each other and had never shown any interest in seeing him outside the office. Their families occupied their time after work.

This new batch he was hiring for the Colliery project were different, though. They were younger and livelier, and partying was much more important to them than building software. All of a sudden, Benton found himself being invited to parties every weekend. True, he would be introduced by some deferential subordinate as "the boss," and that was dampening. In fact, some of these subordinates were older than Benton, but they all treated him as though he were older than they. Sometimes he wanted to protest that he was still young, less than thirty in Earth years, but he had to admit that the automatic respect had its appeal, too.

Once the novelty wore off, he began to find the frequent parties pleasant but not involving in any way. They provided a break from the hours of work and pressure, but little else. The conversations tended to stay safely shallow.

At one party, it all turned very serious very suddenly.

Benton was chatting with a girl who seemed to know as few of the other guests as he did. She was short and slender, with a nervous intensity that bothered him even while it attracted him. In a period when most young women on Farandhazy were changing their appearance, and especially their hair, every other day and using everything cosmetic technology offered to disguise their true appearance, this girl was remarkable for being so obviously undisguised. Her straight black hair, cut simply just below her shoulders, was obviously her own. No lenses changed the dark brown of her eyes, and her face, perhaps too thin to be considered attractive by most men, was innocent of cosmetics.

Her name was Augie Syen. When they were introduced, not able to think of anything else to say, he said, "That's an unusual name." She grimaced and said, "I had unusual parents."

She was Benton's physical opposite, and he supposed, looking into his drink to avoid her intense, searching stare, that that explained his sudden, strong physical attraction to her. Nothing like this had happened to him since he had come to Farandhazy five Earth years earlier, fresh from college, to work for Contco.

Was it the physical difference, or that intensity of hers, the way she concentrated on one thing to the exclusion of everything else? A touch neurotic, perhaps, but right now she was concentrating on him and he was having some difficulty breathing. Unfortunately, she insisted on talking about Colliery and the contract he was working on.

"It's immoral," she said. "If you help The Jacksonite Corporation in any way, that's immoral. It'll just increase their stranglehold on the Galaxy."

"No, I don't think that's right," he insisted, hating the argument, or rather hating arguing with her. He hesitated, not quite sure how much of this he should talk about to a stranger. But then he looked at his less–than–sober subordinates around him and decided that it was probably far too late to worry about keeping any details of the project secret. There were bursts of loud laughter and slurred speech. Drinks were being spilled. Couples who had not arrived together were leaving together. Company secrets had probably been shared long ago. If any of them are thinking about company secrets, Benton told himself. "What we're doing for them has no connection with how they market the stuff. They contracted us to build a system integrating underground sensors, communications networks, computer monitoring and control, automated mining equipment, ventilation balancing..." He trailed off at her blank look. "Making things safer, that's all," he said. "And more efficient. We'll help them increase their productivity, and that'll reduce the stranglehold. Also, we'll help them raise their efficiency, and that's sure to bring down the price of jacksonite, which will be good for everyone."

Augie snorted derisively. "The demand for jacksonite is so high now, and the supply is so low, that what you're doing just won't have that effect. Better efficiency will just mean higher profits for those bastards, not lower prices. They're probably already as efficient as they want to be. How're you going to increase that?"

He had wondered about that himself when first discussing

the project with his boss, Charlie Gabbro. Surely The Jacksonite Corporation, with its breathtaking wealth, must already have in place the most advanced automation hardware and software. Its mines must be a technological marvel. Why did the Corporation need what a small, obscure company like Contco could provide?

But Charlie Gabbro's concern was with the project's success, or more accurately with the beneficial effect that success would have on his own career. Other concerns were beyond his ken. "Focus," Charlie liked to say. He also liked to call Benton "Jamie me boy," which Benton was sure he had picked up from watching some costume drama set in ancient Scotland. He referred to Benton as "head honcho" on the project—another term Benton assumed he'd picked from a costume drama. Charlie also liked to repeat "Ten billion barnards." That was the sum—more than ten times Contco's current annual revenues—being held out by The Jacksonite Corporation for the follow-on contract, should Contco's work on the current one impress them sufficiently. "Don't be tense, Jamie me boy," Gabbro said often. "Just do your work. You and your team. Ten billion barnards if you succeed. If you fail, we'll blacklist you."

Benton wrenched his mind back to the present moment. Augie was saying, "Even if you could somehow increase their production, so what? Just because they can dig more of the stuff out of the ground, that doesn't mean they'll send more of it to market. They already mine more than they market as it is. They keep the excess in safes somewhere. They release jacksonite slowly in order to keep prices high."

"You can't prove any of that," Benton said, feeling exasperated and even feeling a stirring of loyalty toward The Jacksonite Corporation. Ten billion barnards, after all. "I've heard those charges before. Hell, you sound as though you hate The Jacksonite Corporation personally!"

There was a long and awkward pause, as if they had both suddenly remembered that they were strangers, as if they were both embarrassed by the quick frankness and heat of their conversation, by its degeneration from social banter into argument, into something real.

Benton had been feeling involved, drawn in. He had thought there was a real connection. Now he suspected that had been an illusion.

"Except for you, this has been a boring party," she said suddenly. "I'd like to go back to my place." She waited expectantly.

And that's that, Benton thought. He said lamely, "Uh, well, goodnight then."

A look of great surprise crossed her face, followed by a flicker of anger. She spun about and headed for the door.

Illumination arrived, not quite a moment too late.

He charged across the room, pushing between conversing guests, oblivious to their glares. He caught up with Augie at the door. "Say, could I give you a ride?"

She was surprised again, but this time her surprise was followed by a grin. "You're a prize! Come on."

It was a wonderful night.

Benton kept congratulating himself on having done something right for once in the social realm. In the city, he was only one of tens of thousands of young, affluent, single, mobile technical people. He had often enough overheard other men discussing their frequent affairs, and he had always wondered why he had been left out of the wonderful game. Maybe be was finally learning to play it.

From Augie's reactions during the night, he assumed she was as pleased as he. Over their late breakfast, both of them deliciously exhausted, he said, "Now I'll be especially sorry to have to spend time away on Colliery."

Augie smiled and put her hand gently on his. "I know. How long will you be gone?"

He shrugged. "Hard to say." He thought for a moment. "It's almost a week's travel each way, so probably something like eight or ten weeks total."

"How long before you leave?"

"Four weeks from today." He smiled at her. "That gives us some time, anyway."

She grinned back. "And we can use every second of every night of it!"

They laughed together, almost shyly. The smile faded from Augie's face, and she frowned worriedly. "You won't have to go down in the mines there, will you?"

Benton shivered. "I doubt it. They don't seem to want anyone down there except their own people. We wanted to have own technicians install the underground part of our equipment, but they said no. They'll take care of all that. No outsiders allowed, I guess."

"Not in their precious mines," Augie said with a bitterness that puzzled him. "Or messing around with their precious jacksonite."

"Precious is the word." He didn't know why the tension had just crept into their conversation, but he wanted to chase it away. "It's fine with me. They can do that part, and I'll spend my time above ground, making sure the data's coming in properly and the computers are processing it correctly. I'm the head of the design team, so that's really more my proper area anyway."

He wanted her to admire him and suspected she wouldn't if he admitted to physical fear. He had no wish to go into a mine, whether on Colliery or anywhere else. He had once made the mistake of going underground with the technicians who were delivering some mining equipment, and he still hadn't gotten over the experience.

Mining wasn't made for men, as someone had once put it. He remembered vividly the ear–smashing noise, the dust and fumes, the shivering, vibrating rock floor and walls and his constant fear that they would collapse on him. Above all, he remembered the dangerous unmanned machines roaring invisibly in the dark. The machines had known where they were and where they were going, and where the other machines and the human intruders were, but the small group of men hadn't known where the machines were. Benton still had nightmares about it.

Later, after he had helped her clear away the breakfast dishes, Augie said, "Could you do me a favor while you're on Colliery?"

"Bring you back a shipload of jacksonite so you can get your own stranglehold on the Galaxy?"

She didn't laugh, didn't even smile. Instead, her face again took on that hint of neurotic tension and need he had noticed the evening before at the party and which had both disturbed and intrigued him. Now it was clearer, less disguised.

"Look someone up for me there," she said. "My uncle, Ben Coquina. He's really more than my uncle. He pretty much brought my brother and me up. Anyway, he went to Colliery with his wife a few years ago and never came back."

"Ben Coquina? I've heard his name somewhere."

"Yes. He's famous in his field. Geochemistry. Or was, before he disappeared."

"You think he's still there? On Colliery?"

"Of course he is!"

She was close to shouting. She bit her lower lip and turned away from him. When she spoke again, her voice was at a more nearly normal level, but Benton could hear the barely suppressed tremor in it that told how frantic she really was.

Still not facing him, she said, "Last time I heard from him was about three years ago. He was still on New Albion. He wrote to say he had almost succeeded in producing synthetic jacksonite, but the finishing touches would require some very expensive work, and the university refused to fund it. They couldn't afford to. The Jacksonite Corporation had heard of his work somehow and offered him whatever he needed if he would go to Colliery and do it under their auspices. He and his wife, Diori, would be leaving for Colliery in a couple of days and he would write again when he got there. But he never did write again."

"Perhaps he didn't get there," Benton said gently. He didn't know what else to say.

She spun around and clutched at his arms. "He must have! They made him a prisoner, or maybe they killed him. That's what they do, you see, to protect their damned monopoly. They wouldn't want anyone coming up with synthetic jacksonite."

This time, he could think of nothing at all to say. Of course the Corporation wouldn't want anyone to develop synthetic jacksonite. They had no reason to fear that anyone would, though. It was an illusory goal that eccentrics had been pursuing for decades, and none of them had succeeded. He had to assume that Augie's uncle was another such eccentric. From what she had said, the man's eccentricity had apparently risen to the level of severe self-deception, even of lunacy. How could Benton take this story seriously? He began to wonder if Augie Syen were delusional herself.

She said, "After I had talked to you for a while last night and found out you were going to Colliery, I knew you'd be willing to help me." She stared at Benton urgently, compellingly.

Understanding dawned at last. "That's why you did all this?" He nodded toward the bedroom. "Just to bribe me?"

"Oh, Jim, of course not!" She hesitated, then said, "All right, last night at the party I was mainly thinking about getting your help. But now you mean more to me than that."

He shook her hands off and looked at her coldly. "You were using me. Use someone else."

He stalked to the door. As he opened it, he heard her say in a soft and mournful tone, "There isn't anybody else. I need you. Please."

He hesitated for only a moment, then left, slamming the door.

During the following few days, she called him frequently. Each time, he shut the comm off as soon as he heard her voice with its undertone of insistent need. He took to leaving the comm at home, turned off, when he went out, even though that gave him an uneasy, isolated feeling. At last she stopped trying.

Benton threw himself completely into the details,

professional and personal, of preparing to leave.

On his last day on Farandhazy, just as he was about to leave for the spaceport, a small package was delivered to his apartment. The first thing he found inside the package was a picture of a serious, middleaged man standing next to a beautiful blonde woman perhaps twenty or twenty–five years the man's junior. On the back was written, "To our dear niece, Augie. From Uncle Ben and Diori." Furiously, Benton threw the picture in the trash.

Also in the package was a small, dark, heavy object, rectangular and attached to a chain. The greasy–feeling surface was characteristic of field–effect generators, but he could guess no more about it than that. A note taped to the object said, "Never mind what this is. Wear it around your neck like a good luck charm. It might be of use." It was signed *Augie Syen.*

For a moment, he almost threw the object and the note into the trash as well, but then he changed his mind, although he could not easily have said why. He put the chain around his neck and stuffed the gadget inside his shirt. It did indeed look like nothing more than a good luck charm.

And it was time to go.

He stood in the open doorway and looked around his apartment. How little of him was here! How little mark he had made on places or people, and how little he left behind. He had let others use him for various purposes but had not used anyone else. Those who had found him of use would forget him once he was gone. No one would have reason to remember him. He had passed and left no mark, like the faintest breeze drifting over desert sand without disturbing a single grain.

He sighed, picked up his two suitcases, and left, letting the apartment's computer shut and lock the door behind him with its cold and final–sounding click.

CHAPTER TWO

Choosing his words carefully, Benton said, "I have to disagree strongly with you, Miss Hornsfels. That's simply nonsense. It's already impossible to do without computers. The Republic has been almost totally dependent on them for decades, and the Empire used them even more heavily for centuries. You know, it was the sudden widespread loss of computer capability that really destroyed the Empire."

It would have helped, Benton thought gloomily, if Sadie Hornsfels had been ugly, or old, or at least pleasant. Instead she was stunningly beautiful and very aware of it, using her looks as a weapon to overwhelm men and cow women. She was condescending and conceited, and she was witheringly scornful except when she chose to turn on her charm. For the moment, she had decided that Benton was of sufficient interest to turn that charm on full force for him, and he was aware of a strong physical response in himself that he tried manfully to suppress.

Sadie opened her eyes a bit wider. Turning up the power, Benton thought bitterly, meanwhile gazing into her brilliantly blue eyes with fascination. "But I thought," she said, "that the Empire collapsed because it was so old and worn out. I also read somewhere that their computers turned against them and tried to take over the Earth."

"Oh, that stupid idea," he said in exasperation, "That just can't happen, either with our present–day technology or the way they built computers in the Empire. They're just machines. They're extremely powerful, but they're also very stupid, and they always do exactly what you tell them to." Just like men when you do the telling, he thought.

She pursed her lips. "I've heard that one before. But what did you mean about the loss of computers destroying the Empire?"

Benton felt remarkably intelligent, attractive, and strong. And willing to hold forth on any subject as long as it would keep the spectacularly beautiful Sadie Hornsfels so interested in him. For a moment, he suspected that she was playing a game, using him for some obscure purpose. Still, the longer he talked interestingly, the longer she'd stay there in front of him, letting him feast his eyes on her. A very different woman from Augie Syen. But Augie, he reminded himself, had been using him too.

"The Empire was an interstellar civilization, but they had achieved an extremely high technological level even before they spread out from Earth. Everything was computerized before they established themselves in space. Space travel was secondary. They never achieved our level of ability in interstellar travel. They didn't even have anything like the Arrastra Drive. Interstellar trips took tremendous amounts of time. I'll be at my destination in days. In Imperial times, it would probably have taken me months.

"We've taken a different route outward. Our civilization arose all over the place, on all the worlds that had been part of the Empire. Because we all knew that other human settlements were out there, we concentrated on space flight. Fortunately for us, the discovery of jacksonite gave us the Arrastra Drive and interstellar communications. Our civilization depends on that mineral.

"On the other hand, we haven't put much effort into computer capabilities because we haven't really needed to. So we're far behind the Empire there. They had some sort of organic compound in which circuits could be formed at the submolecular level. Formed and reformed, changed constantly. Constantly optimized for the task at hand. That's really why the Empire was able to reach such size and complexity, in spite of having a much more primitive technology than we have for interstellar travel. They made up for that with their amazing information-handling ability. All government power was highly centralized. In effect, computers on Earth ran the Empire." He shook his head. "Even if we changed our governmental structure and concentrated everything in the Barnard's Star system, we still couldn't do as good a job of it as they did, simply because we couldn't match their computer power. We have to stay decentralized."

"We also don't have to worry about our computers taking over and destroying us."

"But neither did they! Apparently what happened was that some anarchist group worked up a bacterium that fed on that organic compound their computer technology was based on. The imperial government collapsed overnight, disappeared, along with all the computers on Earth. All the computers everywhere else in the Empire were based on the same technology, so eventually the disease spread everywhere along with the waves of refugees, and all the computers were converted into useless junk."

"Yes," Sadie said coolly, "and in the overreaction to the garbled news from Earth, what little remained in the way of computer technology was destroyed during riots and short-lived local tyrannies." While Benton stared at her openmouthed, she went on, "A thousand worlds, half a million separate governments and sovereignties, and a new Dark Ages. Technology faded away, and here we are starting all over again. However, the bacterium is present on all those thousand worlds, so unless we can find a functional substitute for that organic compound, we'll never be able to duplicate their hybrid computer. How fortunate for us that jacksonite can't be destroyed the way that organic compound was. Thank you for a decidedly dull conversation." She turned on her heel and walked away.

Benton stared after her with his mouth open and his cheeks burning, his drink tilting so far that the liquid began to dribble out unnoticed and run over his hand.

He became aware of someone standing next to him and looked up to see a paunchy, middleaged man holding an empty glass and watching him with a cheerful smile—cheerful, but also cynical. As soon as he saw he had Benton's attention, he said, "Ah! Another victim of the magnificent Sadie. Don't worry about it. There have been and will be others." He glanced down ruefully at his empty glass and added, "I've been telling myself that all day, but it doesn't really help."

Feeling like a fool, Benton shut his mouth at last. He grunted noncommittally.

"Oh, sorry," the older man said, smiling even more broadly, "we haven't been properly introduced, have we? I'm Brook

Plasser, and you are?"

"James Benton."

Plasser looked at his empty glass again. Benton got the point at last and gestured to a waiter hovering beyond the crowd. When both their glasses had been refilled, Benton, feeling he was obligated to make conversation, said, "You know Sadie, then?"

Plasser took a long, deliberate swallow which drained half the liquid in his glass before replying. "Not before this trip. However, I've spent a great deal of time observing her. A pleasant enough preoccupation in and of itself, of course, but my purposes were, er, scholarly. She's a very accomplished mindpicker."

"A what?" Two drinks are too much, Benton thought. I'm hearing things.

"Some people pick pockets. She picks minds. You see, she finds herself making a long interstellar voyage, surrounded by very dull people like you and me. She's extremely intelligent, even more beautiful, and, if possible, still richer. For people like her and her friends, novelty—whether exotic experiences or new ideas and unusual information—is the only thing that provides excitement."

The room kept blurring out of focus for a second or two at a time. Bewildered, Benton said, "So I excited her?"

Plasser chuckled. "I rather doubt it. She thought you might provide her with something new and intriguing to tell her friends. Once she had picked your mind, she had no more use for you. She did the same thing to me on the first day out. Ah, well. I console myself with the thought that the existence of Sadie and her class is merely a symptom of the imminent decline of our civilization." He looked longingly into his glass, empty again, until Benton waved the waiter over once more. Benton was surprised to find that his own glass was also empty, and he had the waiter refill it, too.

Plasser swallowed a mouthful from the refilled drink, then licked his lips judiciously and said, "Each one is weaker than the last. I hope you're on an expense account. Otherwise I'd feel guilty at your having to pay for all those glasses of water. As for me—well, buying my ticket for this trip has consumed my available funds." He looked keenly at Benton. "What were you telling the divine Sadie that kept her interested?"

Benton shook his head, hoping that would clear away the fog that was filling his head. The effect instead was to create a small kernel of pain somewhere just behind the very center of his forehead, a kernel that grew slowly, pulsatingly, with every heartbeat.

Plasser repeated his question.

"Uh, sorry," Benton said. His tongue felt huge and stiff. Why was the alcohol affecting him so much? "I was telling her about computers. She wanted to hear about them, but then she turned out to know all about them already. Or it seemed that way."

Plasser made a face denoting distaste, as though his latest drink were indeed all water. "Computers! Awful things. They rob you of your identity, your uniqueness. Reduce a man to a number, so that wherever he travels, his past follows him electronically, the Furies in the form of bit patterns. Plug in his retinal pattern and DNA parameters, or whatever it is, and up pops his number. Presumably you feel otherwise. You're on your way to Wisteria because of computers?"

"No, no, I'm not going that far." The pain kernel had swelled until it filled his head. It was pressing outward against his skull—*press, press,* with each beat of his pulse—and he expected his head to burst at any moment. "I have a job on Colliery. I'll be getting off there."

Plasser looked surprised at the mention of the planet's name. "The Jacksonite Corporation hiring someone from outside! Now, that's unusual."

"Really?" Plasser's remark had scarcely registered. Benton's attention was focused on the pain in his head to the virtual exclusion of all else. He replied automatically, desperately trying to appear normal outwardly, to make conversation as though nothing were wrong.

"Oh, yes. Secrecy and security are the company's watchwords. Understandably, perhaps, since Colliery is the only world in the known Galaxy where jacksonite is found and the Corporation owns all of it."

"All of it," Benton repeated mechanically.

"Yes." Plasser looked at him intently. "You look quite done in. I'll bet you couldn't even make it back to your cabin on your own."

Benton shook his head.

"My, my. Come along. Let us leave the celestial Sadie and her friends to their jaded pleasures and get you to your bed. You may lean upon me."

Benton agreed inwardly with the wisdom of Plasser's suggestion. Sleep was what he needed. His legs wouldn't cooperate, though, and he leaned heavily on Plasser, stumbling from the room. He was vaguely aware of scornful laughter that sounded like Sadie's as he lurched past a group of which she was the center.

Plasser asked him for his cabin number. Benton barely managed to mumble it. "I think I can find that," Plasser said reassuringly.

Elevators, hallways, staircases. Benton had completely lost track of where he was. His greatest wish was to be allowed to lie down on the floor and sleep, or die. But Plasser kept hurrying him along, half carrying him.

Benton felt Plasser grasp his right wrist and press his hand against the plate beside the door. There was a long hesitation, as thought the computer dedicated to this job were signaling its disapproval of Benton's condition. Then the lock on his cabin door clicked and Plasser pushed the door open. Benton stumbled forward a few steps, fell onto his bed, and sank into unconsciousness.

When Benton awoke, it was morning by ship's time. His headache was gone, but he felt exhausted, as though he had not slept at all for days. There was an awful smell in the room that he couldn't quite place.

He sat up in bed and looked around, feeling confused. The place had been ransacked—drawers and suitcases opened and their contents scattered around.

Plasser, of course. He slipped something into my drink, Benton realized. That was why I got so drunk so quickly and then passed out. That gave him all the time he needed to search my cabin.

Benton forced himself out of bed and stumbled over to the dresser where he had hidden his small supply of ready cash. He'd not hidden it well enough. Plasser had found it.

What was that smell? It was awful. He had to do something

about it.

He realized for the first time that he was naked. He threw on a robe and made a quick call to the purser to ask that Plasser be arrested. The response somehow didn't surprise him. During the hours Benton had been asleep, a passenger's illness had forced the ship to drop to sublight speed and make an emergency stop at a settled world along the route so that the passenger could be transferred to a local hospital. The passenger, of course, was Brook Plasser.

"I can contact the authorities there and have them arrest him at the hospital," the purser said, looking professionally concerned.

Benton sighed. "Don't bother." By now, Plasser would no longer be in the hospital, would no longer be ill, would no longer be going under the name Brook Plasser, and almost certainly would no longer be on that planet.

I've been used again, Benton thought. I keep letting myself be used.

He needed to shower—to get clean, to wash it all away. He dropped his robe on the bed and walked into the bathroom.

The smell was almost overwhelming in here. He recognized it at last. He wanted to be wrong.

Words were written on the floor–to–ceiling mirror. The writing was a bright red–brown. The handwriting had probably been regular and smooth originally, but the letters were sagging and sliding down the mirror. Liquid rivulets, some brown, some clear, ran down the mirror from them. The words had been written in human feces.

Benton clapped his hands over his mouth and nose. Unable to tear his eyes away, he read, "Naïveté is charming but dangerous."

He backed out of the bathroom and tried to breathe.

I should call someone to come in here and clean this up, he thought.

Then he thought, No! I don't want anyone to know about this.

Fighting the constant urge to vomit, stopping frequently to go out into the cabin's main room and breathe, he wiped away Plasser's message and then wiped the mirror clean. He used the bathroom's disposable towels, the big ones meant for use after showering. He wadded them up and threw them down the disposal chute, hoping that they would be destroyed or recycled entirely by machines, that no humans were involved in the process at any point. He wanted no one to be aware of his humiliation.

Then, despite the lingering smell in the bathroom, he showered, scrubbing himself desperately, repeatedly, all over.

He still felt filthy when he was done. He also felt exhausted all over again.

He stumbled back to his bed and dropped almost immediately into a profound sleep. Although he dreamed, he remembered only one of the dreams when he woke, and in that one he was alone in a small ship, speeding through empty space, rushing away from the part of the Galaxy filled with men, away into regions which knew no life.

CHAPTER THREE

Benton was the only passenger disembarking for Colliery. He was waiting alone with his suitcases at a lock when the purser came hurrying down the hallway. The man stopped in front of him and said, "I just wanted to make sure you bore no ill will against the company for your unfortunate experience, Mr. Benton. We hope you'll be willing to travel with us again." He assumed his look of professional concern.

"Sure, sure." The man's concern was clearly professional, not personal, but it seemed silly to make an issue of that. Benton didn't want to make a point of anything. He wanted to forget the whole trip. "There's something that surprises me, though." Benton gestured at a nearby port, through which three quarters of a small sphere was visible, glowing weakly in dim sunlight. "That's not the way I expected Colliery to look. I also thought it was closer in toward its sun."

"Oh, that's not Colliery. We aren't allowed that far into the system. We're in orbit around the seventh planet in the system. Winze is its name." He grimaced at the awkward word, then quickly smoothed the expression from his face. "This is the port for non-Corporation ships. This is where we drop passengers off or pick them up."

Benton stared at the almost featureless ball. "Isn't that carrying security a bit far?"

The purser shrugged. "That's the way they want it. Who's going to argue with them? Well, enjoy your visit to Colliery, Mr. Benton." With a cheerful smile plastered on his face, the purser shook Benton's hand vigorously, wheeled about, and strode back down the hallway.

Benton watched through the window while the shuttle drifted into sight from behind the left edge of the port, killed its relative motion, and then began to drift closer to the passenger liner, moving toward the disembarkation lock. He felt the faint thud through the floor as the two ships made contact, and then the various noises and vibrations as the flanges of the mated looks were made secure and the new connection was pressurized. At last the red light above the lock winked to green, and he sighed in relief and picked up his suitcases.

The purser's voice came over a nearby speaker. "Passenger for Colliery, please prepare to disembark through Airlock B." Despite their recent conversation, it was as though Benton were an abstract, the passenger for Colliery, no longer Mr. Benton with a grudge against the company. The airlock door swished open and Benton stepped through quickly, glad to get away from the passenger ship.

The airlock walls were white and featureless. Sterile, he thought. Perfect. Just what I wanted.

One door slid shut behind him and another opened ahead. The forward door was two layers, composed of the joined outer doors of the two ships. He stepped forward again, into the shuttle's airlock, and the double door slid shut behind him. The thump of the closing was a relief to him. Now I'm cut off from them at last, he thought.

To his surprise, the walls of the shuttle's airlock were decorated. Pictures of lovely, pastoral scenes had been stuck up at random. It was out of place against the functional metal background, but he decided he liked it. This was really what he needed, not sterility. His mother had always complained about his inability to make up his mind. Perhaps she was right after all. Or perhaps not, he thought, smiling.

Finally, the last door opened, and he stepped forward into the shuttle proper.

He was met by a tall, beefy young man with close-cropped blond hair, a ruddy complexion, and an expression of nervous, eager friendliness. He stuck out a large hand and grabbed Benton's right hand. "Hi! James Benton?" He smiled uncertainly.

Benton smiled in response, feeling himself begin to relax at last. This man must be about his own age, but he exuded a kind of boyish eagerness that was charming. How unexpectedly refreshing to come across someone like this, a sunny and ingenuous personality, just when he needed it most—a real bonanza. "Yes, I'm James Benton. Jim." He shook the other man's hand warmly.

"Great! Harve Borrasca. That's me, I mean." He laughed suddenly. "Hell, I'm not doing this right at all. I've never done this kind of P.R. work before. I'm sorry. I'm supposed to impress you with our best side from the start."

He had an odd accent, unlike any Benton had heard before. Was it typical of Colliery? In any case, Benton liked it.

"You already have," Benton assured him.

Borrasca laughed again. "Fine. Let me help you with that." He picked up one of Benton's cases easily. Benton picked up the other one, trying to act as though he didn't notice the weight.

Benton was the only passenger on this trip and the only person on the shuttle beside Borrasca and the two pilots. They stowed his suitcases in an empty locker and then went forward to the cockpit to get a pilot's eye view of the entry and landing. Benton was fascinated. He had never seen an entry from this perspective before. "Entry" was the wrong word, though. There was no atmosphere on this world.

They were down and taxiing along a broad expanse of finely crushed rock toward a series of low, pressurized buildings, when Harve Borrasca said, "The ship that'll take us to Colliery should be ready to go in a few hours. I'm afraid there's not much to do out here at this base. It'll be dark soon." He pointed at the tiny disc glaring on the horizon. "Doesn't make any difference. There's no real scenery on this ball of rock. I'll see what I can dig up to keep us entertained."

Benton groaned theatrically. "I suppose I ought to be diligent and start checking out all my equipment right away to see how it survived the trip."

"Equipment?" Borrasca laughed. "Is that why your suitcase is so heavy?"

"No, that's all personal stuff. I mean the computer and the sensors and so on. All those large boxes in the freight hold."

"Boxes?" Borrasca said puzzledly. "There weren't any. The bill of transfer just says 'one passenger and personal luggage for Colliery.'" Despair washed across his face. "Do you mean I've fouled up again? Oh, Lord! Now I'm in for it."

"It's all right. Don't worry about it," Benton said. hastily, although in truth he felt pretty despairing himself. He paused, then said, "But it is what I need to do the job here, and I can't start without it."

By now, they were connected to one of the buildings by a long, flexible tube which was sealed to the shuttle's lock and had been filled with air. Borrasca jumped to his feet, his eyes blazing with righteous indignation. "Come on! Let's try and track this down." He was like a large child, boisterous, constantly eager to please, switching rapidly between joy, anger, and distress.

Despite his own distress at his missing equipment, Benton felt amused and wanted to reassure the other man and calm him down. "Just a clerical error, I'm sure. The boxes are probably here somewhere, just not recorded properly."

"You think so? Maybe. I hope so. Yeah, maybe that's it!" Borrasca led the way out of the shuttle and through the tube. He rushed ahead, seeming to have no trouble walking on the flexible, springy surface and in the low gravity. Benton swayed, bounced from side to side, lost his balance, and felt his stomach lurching. The closeness of the rocks and the airless surface, clearly visible through the almost transparent walls of the tube, didn't help.

They reached the building at the other end of the tube at last, to Benton's great relief. Borrasca pointed to a small room equipped with chairs, couches, and a vidscreen. "Look, why don't you just try to relax here," Borrasca said. "I'll get in touch with the shipping line and see what's happened."

Benton grunted his agreement. He was oddly exhausted already. He clicked on the vidscreen and sat down to watch idly. He had chanced upon a newscast concerning the latest political crisis in the Republican parliament on Lark.

Great, he thought. I need to escape news about those idiots.

He clicked through the channels. Most of them seemed to be

reruns of old programs, things he had seen years ago on Farandhazy. Unsurprising, he realized, considering the expense of providing transmissions to an outpost like this. The field discovered decades earlier by Franco Arrastra in his experiments with jacksonite could be used to send bursts of information at speeds much faster than the Arrastra Drive could transport mass, but at a far higher cost. "It costs more to send a message than a man," they said. Much more, in fact. But that money bought speed that would have been unimaginable in Imperial times. A message could be sent from one end of the Republic to the other in hours, if you were willing to pay the price. It did seem to Benton, though, that if anyone could afford the cost of such transmissions on a regular basis, The Jacksonite Corporation could.

Still, it would not have surprised him to see local programs in lieu of recycled programs from elsewhere, but even that didn't seem to be the case.

He did find one program that had originated on Colliery. It was a wildlife documentary, detailing the long, arduous, and finally successful attempt of a team of experts to reestablish a Collierite native species of birdlike animal, threatened with extinction by climatic shift. His interest aroused, Benton sat forward and watched the show to the end in fascination. This was a sort of care for native species and a dedication to their preservation that he had never seen elsewhere—certainly not on Farandhazy, where few people seemed to give a damn about animals, whether native or imported. Benton was filled with admiration for the wildlife experts, and for the government of Colliery which presumably employed them.

Only as the final, triumphant tones of the theme music

pealed out did he deduce from the closing credits that the scientists' employer was not the government but The Jacksonite Corporation.

Even more admirable, he thought. They're acting from real philanthropy, not political necessity.

He didn't even notice the passing of time, and he had forgotten entirely his reason for distress. When Harve Borrasca came into the room, Benton felt momentarily disoriented and had to remind himself why Borrasca seemed agitated.

Borrasca threw himself into an armchair. "Well, I think it's going to be okay. I've tracked your stuff down, and it'll be on its way to Colliery soon. It's the shipping company's fault, but what do you want to bet I'll get blamed for all of this, anyway?"

"What happened?"

Borrasca gestured in annoyance. "Seems some overly smart shipping agent on Farandhazy noticed what ship you were taking and just naturally assumed you were going all the way to Wisteria. Assumed, mind you, without even checking to make sure. How dumb can you get? Anyway, they were having space problems with the freight hold, so he bumped your crates and had them transferred to a slow freighter headed for Wisteria."

"With pressurized holds, I hope."

Borrasca looked horrified. "I didn't even ask! Does it matter?"

Benton sighed. "The crates aren't pressurized. If the freighter isn't, all we'll get is a bunch of metallic junk."

Borrasca cursed. "We'll sue the pants off them!" He brooded for a moment. "We'll find out in a couple of weeks, I guess. That's how long it'll take your stuff to get here. As soon as it reaches Wisteria, they're going to ship it out in our direction. I'd better call them back and make sure that at least that vessel is pressurized."

"And I suppose I ought to send a message to Contco to let them know what's happened."

"Don't bother. I'll do it for you. In fact, I just started thinking like a public relations man at last, and I have an idea about what to do during the next two weeks." Borrasca jumped to his feet, grinning happily. "I'll be back." He strode from the room, whistling jauntily.

Benton shook his head, smiling. Borrasca was almost too good to be true. He turned his attention back to the vidscreen. The channel he had been watching had gone blank following the documentary, so he switched back to the first one. It was still carrying coverage of the parliament on Lark, and, telling himself he ought to be a good citizen for once, Benton settled back in resignation and forced himself to watch.

The current crisis was due to a recent announcement by The Jacksonite Corporation that it was raising the price of jacksonite by ten percent, effective immediately. This was due, the Corporation said, to the decrease in the value of the barnard.

Benton shrugged. Since he had never yet had to travel interstellar on his own funds, any resulting increase in ticket prices wouldn't affect him directly. And as for other resulting price increases—why, so long as his salary kept reasonable pace, it wouldn't bother him. It seemed to Benton that it all balanced out in the long run, anyway, so what difference did it make?

The parliamentary argument struck him as more philosophical than pragmatic. The largest opposition party insisted that The Jacksonite Corporation's monopoly was immoral and should be ended, with military force if necessary. The speakers reminded Benton uncomfortably of Augie Syen. The government party responded that any official display of animosity, let alone active hostility, toward The Jacksonite Corporation was far from being in the Republic's best interests. At least, that was what Benton thought they were saying. The circumlocution and careful phrasing were hard to parse. The wrangling went on, but eventually Benton found himself growing interested, and soon he was caught up in the point and counterpoint, the thrust and counterthrust, of parliamentary debate.

Someone reached past him and clicked the vidscreen off. Benton looked up in momentary annoyance but relaxed when he saw it was Harve Borrasca, wearing the cheerful grin that never seemed to leave his face for long. "All arranged," Borrasca said. "And our ship's about ready to leave, so let's get moving in that direction."

Parliament will have to reach its conclusions without my help, Benton thought, and he followed Borrasca through a bewildering sequence of hallways. The trip recalled vaguely the faintly remembered journey to his cabin, led by Brook Plasser, on the passenger liner, but that was a parallel he tried to drive from his mind.

Harve Borrasca, striding along ahead, said over his shoulder, "I've got a good time lined up for you while we wait for your equipment."

At last they passed through a doorway into the by now familiar pressurized tube, and at the end of that, Benton found himself inside a ship again. The lock slid shut behind them and Borrasca laughed suddenly. "Don't worry, Jim. I know for sure that your suitcases are on board."

Benton chuckled dutifully. It didn't seem all that amusing to him, but he thought he should try to mimic the lightheartedness that he took to be standard with Collierites.

They climbed a short staircase to a comfortably furnished observation room. Floor–to–ceiling windows were spaced around it. Through one of them, they watched the barren world drop away.

"How long does it take to get to Colliery?"

"Two or three days, I think," Borrasca replied. "I'll ask the crew. Fortunately, Winze—that's the world we just left—is on the same side of the sun as Colliery right now. Otherwise it would take a lot longer, of course. Two or three Colliery days, I mean," he added. "That's roughly ten per cent longer than an Earth day. You'll have to get used to that sort of thing on Colliery. I know that in most other places, everyone still uses Earth time measurements, but we're very independent, and we do everything in our own terms. 'Years' means Colliery years, '1g' means one Colliery gravity. Et cetera." He grew very serious. "We feel that since the Empire's been dead for so long, there's no reason we should still be using archaic Earth measurements and other holdovers, when we have our own perfectly good versions instead."

"You still speak English," Benton pointed out.

"Well, sure! If we made up our own language, no one would understand us."

"That's why the rest of us prefer to use one system of units for time and gravity and so on."

"That's crap! I've heard that argument, and—" Borrasca caught himself and the anger faded from his face. "Hey, I'm not supposed to argue with you. That's bad P.R. for sure!"

"All right, then." Benton was happy to avoid any unpleasantness. "Tell me about what you've got planned for the next two weeks. Or am I really talking about 15.4 Earth days?" he added maliciously.

Borrasca laughed. "Okay, okay. Well, first of all, Colliery is the third planet of its sun." He held up his hand quickly. "Don't say it! I know—just like Earth." Both men laughed. "Anyway, that, plus the atmosphere, is the main similarity. It's a less massive planet than Earth. Lower gravity, slightly thinner atmosphere. Also much less water, which is just as well for all our mining. The mines are huge and all over the planet, and we're lucky that we don't have to worry much about pumping water out of them. Most of what water there is, is bound up in the poles. Most of Colliery is pretty much desert, except for a band around each of the polar ice caps. We call them the life-bands. About 200 kilometers wide in the north, and the one in the south is close to 300. It's due to the fact that the poles are retreating slowly and have been for thousands of years. It's all a long cycle, and in another thousand years or so the poles will start advancing again."

"And what will happen on Colliery then?"

"Dunno," Borrasca shrugged. "I don't plan to be around then. Anyway, those bands are where most of the animal life is and all of the farming used to be."

"Before jacksonite?"

"Yeah, before jacksonite." Borrasca grinned. "In other words, before the planet hit the big time. Well, when the big time did come along, the farmland was all converted to parks, wildlife preserves, and a few carefully monitored hunting areas.

Why, it's about the biggest and best vacation land in the Galaxy—and it's only for Corporation employees. And the Corporation's occasional guest. Right now, that means you, you lucky dog. You're going to have the time of your life, all expenses paid. And of course," he grinned again, "I've included myself in it as your escort."

"Does all of that mean that you don't use the desert for recreation?"

Borrasca grimaced. "Who'd want to?" He looked immediately apologetic. "Of course, if you'd like to go there, I could probably arrange it. There are a few areas in the desert that're restricted. Mostly, it's because the desert ecosystem is so fragile."

"That's admirable. All right, never mind. We'll forget the desert."

Borrasca's relief showed clearly. "By the way," he added slyly, "we also have two moons. One's little more than an asteroid, but even the other one isn't very big compared to the planet itself. Nothing at all like Earth and its moon."

"All right," Benton smiled. "Colliery isn't Earth. Got your point, and I'll remember it."

CHAPTER FOUR

The ship's lights were brightened and dimmed on a twenty-six and a half hour cycle, to correspond to the length of Colliery's day. Benton had far less trouble adapting to this than Borrasca seemed to expect him to.

Indeed, he had far less trouble than Borrasca probably would have had adjusting to another world. Borrasca mentioned that like everyone he knew, he had been born and reared on Colliery and had made only a few very brief trips elsewhere. The light-dark cycle on Earth or Farandhazy would probably have bothered him a great deal. Benton suspected that on his few trips to other worlds, Borrasca had experienced the days of disorientation, the inability to sleep when it was dark and to stay awake when it was light, and the digestive problems that were all common to people who traveled little. That was probably why Borrasca kept asking Benton worriedly if he was comfortable and if he was having trouble adapting.

Benton's life had been nomadic. Even though he had lived on Farandhazy for five years, that had done little to diminish his adaptability. He had been born on Earth itself, quite a rarity these days, but his parents had left there when Benton was three and he hadn't returned until it was time for him to go to college. His father had been an industrial psychologist of real ability, and his mother a commercial artist, but the true calling of both his parents had been wandering. In his father's profession, contracts usually ran for one Earth year, with a renewal option each year after that. The employers had always wanted to renew, but his father rarely had, and so after a year it was off to another city and frequently another world. In James Benton the boy, it had encouraged solitariness, introspection, and a shyness that often appeared to others to be aloofness and a cold nature. It had also nurtured a high degree of adaptability to different atmospheres, different gravities, and different periods of rotation and revolution.

While Benton was in college on Earth—the only world his parents had ever considered for their only child's advanced education—they had kept up their frequent moves. He was in his final year of college when he received notice that they had been passengers on one of the rare liners to vanish in interstellar space. The cause of those few disappearances was always assumed to be a malfunction of the Arrastra Drive, though what the malfunction might be and what it meant to the ship and passengers, no one, physicist or mathematician or engineer, had ever been able to say.

When at last they went into orbit around Colliery, it occurred to Benton how much of his life had been fashioned by jacksonite, that priceless mineral. His rootless past, even the loss of his parents—perhaps none of this would have happened if the existence of jacksonite had not made fast interstellar travel possible. Rather than dwell on this idea, he tried to watch the surface of the planet roll beneath the ship.

The ground far below was various shades of red and brown.

Benton saw no hint of water, neither reflected light nor the green of vegetation. The terrain seemed to be flat, although he couldn't be sure of this since they were passing roughly across the center of the sunlit side, so that it was about noon below and it would take a trained eye to pick out from the glare the few, short shadows uneven land might cast.

"Has it always been like this, Harve?"

Borrasca was sitting nearby, idly reading a magazine. "Hmm?" He looked up, then came over to the window. "Desert, you mean? Well, it was like this when the first settlers arrived, but there's animal life in both the north and south life-bands, and some of the species in the life-bands are related, so there must have been something other than desert here once."

"Maybe there used to be some sort of seasonal migration," Benton guessed. "Don't the, um, life-bands move with the seasons? They should grow and shrink."

Borrasca shook his head. "They don't move at all. Our axial tilt is very slight, so we hardly have seasons. Also, our orbit is practically a circle. The only effect is at the fringes of the life-bands, and it's slight. The long, slow warming of the atmosphere that I was talking about before is the important effect, and that cycles every few thousand years."

"I'm surprised life would even evolve under those conditions," Benton said.

Borrasca shrugged. "Don't ask me. I don't know much about that kind of stuff. Maybe I can dig up someone who does for you to talk to. Anyway, keep watching. The spaceport is on the night side now, so I told the pilot to come in on a polar orbit. That way, you'll get to see the day side of the northern life-band, and then we'll start our reentry over the ice cap and land in the dark.

That'll give you a beautiful view."

He was right.

With startling suddenness, the sterile, sandy surface changed to patches of green and then to deep, dark, solid green with no trace of the desert.

Borrasca pushed a button beside the window and the scene was replaced by an enormously magnified view of the surface below. Benton was delighted by the forests, lakes, parkland, and occasional small villages that reeled by silently. He caught flashing glimpses of herds of animals and of rare stands of some immense native trees, with huge, squat trunks and branches that must have extended outwards for hundreds of meters.

Borrasca watched him with open amusement. "Nice, huh?"

"Why, it's—" Benton said shakily, "it's the Garden of Eden."

Borrasca chuckled and swelled with pride. "It's even better when you're on the ground. Keep watching."

The trees grew stunted and then disappeared. Benton could see no more animals, only a stretch of low, dark foliage broken by patches of white. The white increased, the other colors dwindled, until they were passing over a scene of unrelieved, brilliant white that hurt his eyes. Borrasca touched another button and the scene returned to unmagnified size. Benton became aware of the faint vibrations of reentry.

"We must be just about over the pole now," Borrasca said. Ahead, the terminator appeared. They seemed to be rushing toward it. It swept by below them, and they were in the darkness of the night side. "Pity it's not full moon," Borrasca said. "Dolom, the smaller moon, is invisible all the time, and we don't get much light from the other one, Rheni. Still, when Rheni is full, you can see quite a bit of the night side of the ice cap and the life-band, and it's worth seeing."

By now, the planet below was utterly dark. The only light in the window was in one corner, where stars showed beyond Colliery's horizon. Then a glow appeared on the horizon, slid forward upon the black surface, and resolved itself into a landing field, almost frighteningly close. Because of the featurelessness of the dark side, Benton had been unaware of the steepness of their entry.

"The port is actually just south of the life-band," Borrasca said. "Pretty much in the desert. The normal entry orbits come in over the desert all the way, up from the south. That's so the incoming ships won't disturb the wildlife in the life-band. The trouble is that you don't get a good view of anything but sand that way. And since it's night here now, you wouldn't even have gotten that. So I insisted we be allowed to enter the way we did, so you could get the good view." He paused, then added, "Took me quite a while to get permission."

"Thanks. I really appreciate it."

"Maybe I'll be able to graduate from underpaid junior executive to overpaid, full-time P.R. man yet." He pointed to the runway lights whizzing past the window "We'll be stopped soon. Let's get your suitcases and get ready to leave."

Benton found himself moved through the port building quickly and efficiently by a handful of uniformed officials. It wasn't until they were outside again, shivering in the cold night air of the desert while they waited for their floater to be brought, that Benton realized just how quickly they had moved through the spaceport. "I'm surprised they didn't want to look in my cases," he said. "Other planetary governments are a lot stickier about their customs regulations."

"Planetary governments! Hah! We don't have one. Didn't you know that? The Jacksonite Corporation is the only government on Colliery, thank God. And you're the Corporation's honored guest. That's why they didn't give you any trouble. Just relax and enjoy yourself, Jim, and stop worrying about details. You'll have enough of that to do when your boxes finally get here. In the meantime, we're treating you to the finest playground anywhere. Enjoy it."

"I'll do my best."

During the trip north to the life–band, while Borrasca drove, Benton kept dozing off. Finally he was aware of the floater stopping and Borrasca saying, "Here we are at last. Come on. We'll want an early start tomorrow so you can get to your fun and games without wasting any time."

Borrasca opened the door and leaped out, seemingly as full of energy as ever. Benton groaned and forced himself to follow.

The fresh air and cool breeze revived Benton a bit. "Oh, that's nice," he said. He stood, eyes closed, smiling slightly, feeling the air on his face.

"Yeah, keeps the air clean in spite of campfires. The air tends to move from the pole toward the desert most of the time, so that breeze is always there. What I mean is, you can enjoy it at any time. You don't have to use it all up now."

Benton opened his eyes. "Oh. Sorry." By a single light shining nearby, he could make out a small cottage surrounded by trees. Borrasca, carrying both suitcases this time, strode off toward the front door, calling out, "This is home base for the next week. Hope it's been prepared."

It must have been. The interior struck Benton as the very model of what one would want in a vacation cottage, whether in the northern life–band of Colliery or anywhere else. There were two bedrooms, and Benton went into one of them immediately, turned off the overhead light, opened the room's two windows, stripped off his clothes, and crawled into bed. He tried to stay awake to listen to the faint night sounds of the forest and to enjoy the breeze from the windows as it washed over him, but within seconds he was deeply asleep. Not even the sound of Harve singing in the shower disturbed him.

CHAPTER FIVE

Now, take this for example," Harve said around a mouthful of food. He chewed rapidly, swallowed, then went on. "The only other planet where you could have this kind of pleasure would be a frontier world or some other primitive place, and there you'd have to do without the conveniences of civilization."

Between the two men, a small fire crackled pleasantly. Benton was aware that he did not feel the need to build up the fire in order to push back the darkness, for on Colliery the dark of night was completely unthreatening. With some difficulty, he held the leg bone he had been gnawing on in one hand, while with the other he wiped the grease and juices from his mouth. "There are hunting preserves elsewhere," he pointed out. "Even whole planets like that."

"Oh, sure," Borrasca said scornfully. "For millionaires. And civilization in those places usually consists of a fake hunting lodge, modeled along ancient African lines or something. And they have large predators that're dangerous to humans. Here, the civilization is real and convenient. We just keep our towns outside the life-belts. No large predators to worry about. Enough smaller ones to keep the small herbivores in check, and they stay away from people. So you get the best of everything."

"What about the large herbivores?"

"Low reproduction rates. There aren't any really large herbivores, anyway. The native plant life doesn't provide what they need for large body size or rapid growth. Also, I understand they never got much chance to evolve big because of the climatic cycles. Big animals couldn't survive the changes. Just as well, because the carnivores stay small, too. And you aren't slapping your neck."

Benton looked up from the leg bone, long shreds of meat banging from his mouth. "What?"

Borrasca laughed. "You should see yourself! I meant that there are no biting insects or insect equivalents, like there are everywhere else I know of." He tore a small piece of meat off and tossed it into the darkness. "That will be gone by morning. We call them ants for convenience, but of course they really aren't ants. They don't bite people, and neither does anything else. So that's another thing you don't have to worry about. You didn't know it, but when you left that passenger ship and stood inside the shuttle airlock, you were irradiated with all kinds of ultrasonics and I don't know what else. To kill off your fleas, just in case you had any."

"How hospitable!"

"You ought to see some of the visitors we get. Anyway, the process was repeated when you arrived on Winze, as an extra precaution. But now you can see the benefits of those procedures. Look at this place! You said it yourself—it's the Garden of Eden."

"Well, I think those ultrasonics I was irradiated with damaged my comm. It doesn't seem to be working."

"Your—? Oh, you mean the portable kind. We don't use

those here. We don't use the same comm system as other worlds do."

Benton was astonished. Comm technology was universal and standard. He was used to his comm working wherever he was. "You have a different system? That's really odd. Well, I guess I'll have to buy myself a local comm, then."

"I told you, we don't use that kind here. Ours are fixed in place. Every house or office building has a bunch of them."

"That's primitive!"

Borrasca shook his head. "That's independence. We don't feel the need to be connected to each other all the time, the way you offworlders do. We can go it on our own."

Sturdy pioneers in a tamed wilderness, Benton thought, but he didn't say it aloud. "What about emergencies? What if one of us breaks his leg or gets ill?"

Borrasca pointed over his shoulder with his thumb. "We can call from our flyer if we need to. Most flyers are equipped with a comm."

"Ah, I see now. You're strong and independent and you don't have comms around because you don't need them. But just in case you do need them, you have them around everywhere."

Borrasca looked briefly annoyed. "You know, just about every offworlder I've ever known was sarcastic and cynical."

"I guess that's what not living in the Garden of Eden does to you."

Borrasca laughed, his bad mood evaporating as quickly as it had appeared. "I can see through you. You really do love it here."

Benton nodded and, sighing with contentment, chucked the cleaned bone aside. "You know, they ought to send you to other planets to lecture on the wonders of Colliery. That kind of P.R. is your real talent. You could counter all the bad feelings about The Jacksonite Corporation."

"That could be fun," Borrasca agreed. "Trouble is, to do that I'd have to leave Colliery." He grunted, and his expression turned sour. "Anyway, if people want to have hard feelings about us, that's their damned problem, not ours."

Embarrassed and even vaguely ashamed, as though the Galaxy's enmity toward The Jacksonite Corporation were his fault, Benton turned away from the fire and concentrated on wiping his face and hands clean.

They had spent today hiking through the peaceful beauty of the life–band. Meadows, forest, gentle hills. Because of the high latitude, the sun stayed low but rose early and set late; this was nothing like the perpetual daylight at the pole itself during northern summer, but the effect was noticeable. The breezes were soft, the sunlight was gentle with a golden cast, and nights were mild. Lunch had consisted of prepackaged sandwiches flown to their cottage from some Corporation kitchen. Dinner the evening before had been at an elegant restaurant in one of Colliery's few, small cities.

These cities—towns, by the standards of other worlds—were scattered along the desert–ward fringes of both life–bands and contained a total population of under 200,000. Directly or indirectly, everyone worked for The Jacksonite Corporation, whether in the offices that controlled and directed the production and shipment of jacksonite, in a support industry such as the food–producing plants in each city, or as a merchant selling specialized goods or services to those who worked for the Corporation directly. No one seemed unhappy with the situation.

"That's because," Borrasca told him, "we are The Jacksonite Corporation. There are 500,000 shares of stock, and every one of them is owned right here on Colliery. Every citizen gets one share automatically at birth, meaning one vote. Even the people who don't work directly for the Corporation get a vote! The remaining three–fifths of the shares are divided among the Board of Directors. That way, a director or a coalition of directors can carry an important issue if they can get enough public support. That sort of thing takes a planet–wide vote, but you just vote in the morning when you go to work, and you find out the results usually by noon the next day. Even earlier, depending just where on the planet you work. Simple, smooth. We have real democracy here."

"Sounds like I should start looking for a job here." He was joking, he thought.

"Sorry, we don't allow immigrants. We'd be overwhelmed in no time. The system has evolved to exactly fit the population we have, except for short–term contractors like you."

"You must need to replace those who emigrate."

"No one emigrates. Well, hardly anyone. An insignificant number." He waved his arm in a gesture that took in the quiet, lovely forest around them. "Look at this! And last night you saw what our towns are like. Only an idiot would want to leave this world. Not to mention that if you do leave, you have to surrender your one share of Corporation stock. That alone would discourage me."

"Those very few people who do leave, do any of them come back? Tails between their legs?"

With a hint of malice, Borrasca said, "Nope. If they leave, they can't come back. Not allowed. That's the rule."

Banished from Paradise, Benton thought. The worst fate possible. "It all sounds remarkable."

"It works. That's the important part."

At the restaurant the evening before, they had been joined by a large group of Borrasca's friends. They were a pleasant, friendly bunch. At first, they reminded Benton of the new group of subordinates he had hired on Farandhazy to work on the Colliery project. However, he soon realized that the members of this dinner party differed from those young technical people on Farandhazy. These Collierites all seemed to possess the naïveté and ingenuousness he had noticed from the start in Borrasca.

On Farandhazy and elsewhere, the urban young seemed to become prematurely cynical and worldly-wise. Benton knew it was a pose, but it had always succeeded in intimidating him. However, these Collierites were all so simple, open, and relaxed that he relaxed too in their company. He wondered if all this were due to what amounted to their provincialism. Colliery was almost like a huge small town, with rare and limited contacts with more cosmopolitan mankind. A world full of innocents, Benton thought with some amusement.

But there were exceptions.

While the others were all chatting away animatedly about local places, people, and events—all meaningless to Benton—he noticed that Borrasca kept looking at the door. Finally, Borrasca's face lit up with a relieved grin and he stood up and waved his arms, shouting, "Galena! Here we are!" To the rest of the group, he said, "Here she is at last."

None of the others expressed pleasure.

Benton glanced toward the door casually, then stiffened, his eyes locked on the woman who was threading her way between the tables, heading toward them. He felt a distinct physical shock run through him. The feeling increased as she drew nearer.

And yet objectively there seemed no reason he should have been affected so strongly. She was striking, but no one would call her beautiful, or even pretty.

She was tall, remarkably so, he thought, though it was difficult to tell for sure as long as he was seated. She moved with the deceptive seeming clumsiness that masks the powerful grace of the athlete. Powerful. Yes, that seemed the word for her. She wore an ankle–length black dress or perhaps wrapping of some material that clung to her, revealing clearly the muscles in her thighs and hips, flexing and relaxing as she walked. He thought of a great female cat, gliding between the trees in search of her prey. She had jet–black hair, long, as seemed to be the current fashion on Colliery, but pulled back severely to expose her neck and jawline. Her dress left her shoulders bare but covered her breasts, unlike the clothes worn by the girls at the table with him. Broad, heavy shoulders, deep chest, strong neck, and prominent, strong facial bones. Trying to analyze her with detachment, Benton decided she was far too powerful, too masculine, for his tastes. He told himself that, but apparently he wasn't listening to himself. He was fascinated by her.

She had reached their table, and now she stood looking down at the group with an air of cool aloofness that verged on open contempt.

Cat at the water hole, Benton thought. Hasn't noticed any interesting prey yet.

Borrasca, still standing, had lost much of his earlier

ebullience and appeared to be a bit uneasy. "This is the famous James Benton," he said in a subdued voice. "Jim, this is my third cousin, Galena Hess."

"Jim. I'm glad to meet you at last." Her voice was deep, deeper than many a man's, and as powerful as the rest of her. Benton noticed fleetingly that she was taller than Borrasca, and Borrasca was a few centimeters taller than Benton. Her eyes were extremely large and as black as her hair. She stared at Benton with interest, her magnificent eyes catching and holding his gaze.

He mumbled something in reply. Third cousin? He'd never heard that sort of thing elsewhere. The small population, the lack of immigration or emigration, all of these must have resulted in a habit of keeping closer track of family relationships than was the case on other worlds. Benton realized that he had no idea at all who his own third cousins were or where they lived.

Galena motioned Borrasca to move aside, and she took the chair he vacated next to Benton. The power and intensity she radiated were almost overwhelming with her so close. Benton felt uneasy, even slightly panicked. She leaned toward him, and he was seized with the ridiculous fear that she intended to leap on him and crush him to death.

"I've heard a great deal about the work you'll be doing here," Galena said, speaking softly so that her voice seemed to enclose the two of them in a web of intimate privacy. "Has my cousin been keeping you entertained?"

For a moment, Benton's throat froze shut and he couldn't make the slightest sound. Finally, that passed and he was able to speak. "Oh, yes. We've been spending a lot of time in the life–

band, as well at theaters and restaurants here in the city. I have two weeks or so to kill, you see." He went on to explain about his delayed equipment, speaking too rapidly and unable to move his gaze from her eyes. You nitwit, he told himself. You're babbling.

When he finished, Galena smiled slightly and said, "I'd heard about your equipment not getting here. I'll be interested to see how well it operates once it's in place. Has Harve taken you onto the ice cap?"

"The ice cap? Why, no." Benton looked over at Borrasca, who was grimacing.

"No, of course I haven't," Borrasca snapped at her. "You know how I feel about cold."

Galena laughed, a low-pitched, dark sound that seemed to Benton to vibrate in his own chest. "When we were kids," she told Benton, "I used to threaten to lock him in a freezer if he got out of line. It always worked. He knew I could do it if I wanted to. I've always been twice as strong as poor little Harve."

Borrasca was looking determinedly at the table. "For God's sake, Galena," he said through gritted teeth, "lighten up." There was an embarrassed silence at the table, as the rest of the group finally caught on to the nature of the conversation between the cousins.

"That's okay," Benton said hastily, "I can live without the ice cap."

Borrasca grinned at him, though for once the grin seemed forced. "The ice cap should be part of every vacation, so they say. Listen, day after tomorrow, we'll be moving down to the southern life-band so you can spend a week seeing each place. Maybe I can work something out for then."

After that, the evening moved along more conventional

lines. Galena didn't stay with them for long after they had left the restaurant. Until she left, she had been right next to Benton all the time. Now she held out her hand and Benton took it automatically. Even her hand was bigger than his. She closed hers with a grip of iron, trapping his hand, and he found that it both excited and frightened him. "I'm sorry to have to leave so soon after we've met, Jim. But I'm sure we'll meet again before you leave Colliery. I have some arrangements to make this evening, and they can't wait. Goodbye." She gave his hand a slight extra squeeze and strode off. He felt that had she wanted to she could have broken his hand with little extra effort.

Beside him, Borrasca breathed a sigh of relief. "There, now. Family duty's done. She met you, which is what she wanted. Now let's get on with the evening's fun."

And they raced around the city sampling for free the intellectual and sexual pleasures for which ordinary citizens had to pay.

As the fire burned lower, both men stretched out on the ground to sleep. Only light coverings were needed at night in the life–band except when one drew nearer to the northern fringe and the ice cap. The next morning, they would hike back to their cottage, pack up, and fly south across the desert to the southern life–band for another week's worth of urban and wilderness recreation.

From the gathering dark on the other side of the fire, Borrasca asked suddenly, "What'd you think of Galena?"

"She's... hard to forget."

Borrasca grunted. "When we were kids, she decided at one time that she was going to marry me when we grew up." He laughed. "I was terrified for years until I found out that it's illegal on Colliery for third cousins to marry. Oh, man, can you imagine being married to that woman? Well, goodnight."

"Goodnight, Harve." Benton drifted off to sleep imagining what it would be like to be married to Galena. His dreams that night were almost frantically preoccupied with sex.

CHAPTER SIX

It was while they were flying low over the seemingly endless miles of desert that Benton suddenly realized that something had been missing from the start. He had not yet seen anywhere in the life-band or the towns any sign of what he had expected to see most prominently of all, the famous jacksonite mines. He mentioned this to Borrasca.

"The shaft openings are scattered around in the desert," Borrasca explained. "We try to keep the dirty side of mining out of sight. It means a couple of hundred poor souls have to work out here every day, to keep track of what comes out of the shafts, but fortunately I'm not one of them. If you work at a desk in the city, like me, you never have to even think about all those tunnels down there." He shivered. "And that's fine with me."

"You're lucky you live now, instead of on ancient Earth. In those days almost everyone who worked for a mining company worked underground."

Borrasca turned from the window through which he had been watching the desert and stared intently at Benton. Then he laughed suddenly. "Yeah, I'm pretty lucky, all right. You know, it's funny, but, that's just what my father used to say to me."

The reference struck a sudden and unexpected chord in

Benton. He should have realized, of course, that Borrasca's parents would live on Colliery. That went along with the general small–town nature of the planet. Elsewhere, few young people, once they were old enough to leave home and get a job, kept in touch with their parents at all. "Say, Harve, would it be possible for me to meet your parents before I leave Colliery?"

Borrasca turned back to the window. "They're... they're not around any more.

"I'm sorry." Inadequate words. A Collierite would also feel the loss of his parents more deeply and for many more years than would the mobile young people Benton had known elsewhere.

They fell into a not quite companionable silence. Benton turned to the window next to him and watched the desert moving by.

It occurred to him that all of the people he had met so far were office workers. Some of them were clerical, some were technical, and some were managerial, but he had not yet met a single person who actually dealt with what Borrasca had called "the dirty side of mining." Harve had mentioned the couple of hundred people who worked out in the desert, around the shaft openings, but Benton hadn't met any of them yet.

This must mean that no one needed to work underground at all. At first, this struck him as surprising. From what little he knew about mining, even the most advanced mines required at least some occasional human presence underground. There was always some sort of breakdown or malfunction that even the most cleverly programmed underground maintenance devices couldn't take care of without direct human help. Gangue's Law: The mishap that happens is the one you didn't provide for.

But the more he thought about it, the less remarkable it began to seem. As far as he knew, there was no other world in the Galaxy where mining was so important, where it was virtually the planet's only industry. Considering that, and The Jacksonite Corporation's stature in the Galaxy, the brightness of all the Collierites he had met, and the enormous and continuing demand for jacksonite, it was no surprise that Colliery had carried the automation of mining to its logical extreme. Obviously, it was never necessary, on this eternally amazing world, for humans to be subjected to the discomforts and perils of underground work. The Jacksonite Corporation must have long ago solved the major problem of automation, the one wryly summarized by Gangue's Law. Perhaps it wouldn't be much longer before even those couple of hundred poor devils Borrasca had mentioned would no longer have to work out here in the desert. Surely The Jacksonite Corporation, with its apparently superlative automation abilities, would soon automate their jobs as well.

In that case, he wondered, why do they need me? Either they're marvels at automation and computer software themselves, or they've bought equipment and software from the top companies in the field. Better places than Contco, surely. Probably better people than me, too.

That was an unpleasant thought. He shrugged it off. The answer probably had to do with internal Corporation politics, or possibly supply or maintenance problems with The Jacksonite Corporation's current contractors. He'd already seen, during the past week, how much spare money the Corporation had to throw around. So if they chose to throw some of it his and Contco's way, he'd best just keep quiet and do his job.

And he'd better start taking that job even more seriously. Obviously, the people who'd be judging the performance of his equipment and software knew what they were up to and would probably catch even the smallest error. Benton felt tension growing in him at the thought, but he told himself sternly that the best preparation for the work would be to throw himself even more fully and uninhibitedly into this last week of holiday.

Benton had unconsciously been expecting the drive from the landing field to the southern life-band to be much like the trip one week earlier into the northern life-band, and the differences took him by surprise. The change from desert to life-band was more gradual in the south. He thought it must have something to do with the greater width of the southern life-band and the greater extent and thickness of the southern ice cap, which meant that the boundary between the desert and the life-band was situated at a lower latitude. It probably also meant that more water was released into the desert during the summer and that the local plant life had been able to evolve to suit a greater range of humidity here during the current climate cycle.

Harve could probably clear all this up for him, but the Collierite had turned away, and Benton decided not to bother him. He glanced over at Borrasca a couple of times. Harve was clutching the steering rod of their flyer and concentrating fiercely on the too-infrequent directional signs. The set of his head and shoulders seemed to say, "Don't bother me." Benton shrugged mentally and turned his attention to the passing scenery.

This time, they arrived at their guest cottage—virtually identical with the one they had used during the previous week—well before noon. They moved their belongings in quickly and Benton made himself a light brunch in the well stocked kitchen.

While he was eating, Borrasca came into the kitchen looking shamefaced. "Hey, look, Jim," he said, "I feel pretty bad about the way I've been behaving. Personal problems. I really want to have a good time this week and forget about everything, so let's start with—Oh, hell."

A faint beeping sound was coming from outside. Benton realized it was the comm in the flyer. "What do they want now?" Borrasca said. He went outside. He returned in less than a minute looking depressed. "Now I really feel lousy," he said. "I've Just been ordered back to work for the next few days. Someone else is already on the way to take over for me here. I'm really sorry about this, but you know you can't argue with the boss. I suppose the other P.R. type they've assigned to you will be able to show you a good time."

Benton said conventional things to assure Borrasca that he wasn't upset about the change in plans. While he spoke, a sudden premonition struck him, and his heart beat faster. Borrasca retired to his bedroom to begin repacking and Benton waited with an odd mixture of uneasiness and eagerness for the hum of a flyer.

It was noon when he heard it. It dropped slowly down to the cleared space before the cottage, sending dirt and small stones flying in every direction before its engine was turned off and it settled quietly to the ground.

Borrasca emerged from the cottage, carrying a bag over his left shoulder and a small suitcase in his right hand, and stood watching glumly. Benton was right behind him, trying to remain outwardly calm and telling himself he was surely expecting far too much.

The door of the flyer opened and, while Borrasca uttered a curse and Benton congratulated himself on the accuracy of his premonition, Galena Hess stepped out.

CHAPTER SEVEN

She carried a small bag. She was wearing shorts, and the muscles of her legs looked even larger and more impressive than they had when Benton had watched her walking toward his table in the restaurant. She grinned at their surprise, a cocky, self-assured grin. "Morning, boys. Or noon. Harve, you'd better get on your way."

Borrasca glared at her. "What the hell are you doing here?"

Galena laughed at him. "I'm your replacement, kiddo."

"Did you arrange this whole thing?"

"Draw your own conclusions." Her smile faded and she strode up to Borrasca, standing almost against him so that he had to choose whether to crane his neck to meet her eyes or to step backwards. He chose a third route, one that was even more demeaning. He held his ground but looked off to the side and downward. Galena laughed again and then said, loudly enough for Benton to hear, "Don't push your luck, cousin. You know I can break you in both senses."

Borrasca turned toward Benton and gave him a look that combined apology with desperate appeal.

Wanting to say something kind, but not really knowing what words would be right, Benton said, "Don't worry about me, Harve. I can take care of myself." And yet at the same time he felt something approaching contempt for the other man for his cowardice whenever he faced this woman.

Borrasca looked at him for a moment longer. Then he walked around his cousin, went to his flyer, and climbed in. After one last look at Galena and Benton, Borrasca closed the door. After a moment, the hum began and the flyer lifted off and moved with increasing speed toward the north, quickly vanishing over the tree tops.

"Well, now," Galena said, her deep-pitched voice turned husky, "let's get started." She walked past Benton and into the cabin. Her shirt had no back to it, and he stood still and watched in admiration her alert, gliding walk and the shifting muscles of her legs and back.

When he entered the cabin, she was quickly emptying the contents of her bag into the remaining storage spaces in his bedroom. He stood in the doorway and watched her for a few seconds, then said, "You know, this is my room. Harve had chosen the other one as his."

She straightened up from her now-empty bag and said, "Of course I know that. You can move to the other room if you want to. Can you handle yourself?"

His excitement had increased, but he felt a flash of annoyance. "Women have never frightened me." A lie, but he thought he said it convincingly.

She raised her eyebrows in mock surprise. "How brave you are! I bet you've also never before met a woman who was stronger than you."

"You know, you seem to have a real fixation about that. Anyway, I still haven't."

Galena laughed. "Ah! A challenge! Well, let's put it to the

test."

By now, Benton's sexual arousal was giving way to hostility and combativeness. A small corner of his mind, though, was amused by the resemblance of this scene to a challenge in the schoolyard between two hostile young boys. Prompted by that corner of him, he said, "What's the test? A wrestling match?"

"Perfect!" Galena laughed again, and this time, as it had in the restaurant, her laugh resonated in his chest, leaving him momentarily breathless. "But in the buff." With a few quick movements, she stripped off her clothes, and then she kicked her sandals off.

This is the zaniest thing that's ever happened to me, Benton thought. Not that he was about to back out. His ego couldn't withstand that. This had nothing to do with sex. It was a challenge, and he had to win.

"All right." He stripped off his own clothes, feeling sillier by the moment. "And when I win, what's my prize?" He looked her nude body over, admiring the strength it displayed, but also admiring her sexuality. Paradoxically, unclothed, she looked both more powerful and more female. He felt his desire rising again.

Galena glanced at his growing erection and smiled. "The winner, whoever that is, decides what the prize is. Come on." She gestured him forward, at the same time falling into a wrestler's crouch. "I won't hurt you."

As it happened, she did, but perhaps it wasn't intentional. It could have been because he wouldn't give in.

Before long, despite his struggles, Benton found himself upon the bed, on his back, scarcely able to move beneath Galena's weight. Her thighs held his squeezed between them, immobile. She held his wrists in an iron grip, pressing them to the sheet above his head.

At least I made her pant, he thought. Almost as much as I am. Small victory.

Her rapid breaths washed over his face and he could feel her stomach moving in and out, drawing in the air and expelling it. Once again, his penis betrayed him and responded to her. He tried desperately to will it back to flaccidity, but without effect.

He relaxed under her, no longer straining for freedom. "All right," he gasped, "I've let you win. Name your prize."

Galena chuckled. She released his hands and slid her left arm under him, placing her hand against his spine. With her right hand, she began to manipulate his penis, guiding him into her slowly, a millimeter at a time. At last she thrust herself down on him, slid her right hand beneath his buttocks, and held his hips pressed tightly to hers. He tilted his head backwards so that he could watch her face. She leaned forward, her mouth opening. Her tongue filled his mouth, probing, pushing his tongue aside with ease. Her hips began to move slowly and rhythmically. He responded without conscious will, as though he no longer controlled his own body. He thought, This is perverted. She's being the man. I'm letting myself be used again.

As her motions became more violent, the bed began to creak and groan and sway in time with her heavy body. The embrace of her arms and legs became even tighter, almost painful, and her tongue seemed to grow and swell inside his mouth. He moaned and put his arms around her neck, surrendering entirely, letting himself by used by her, no longer caring.

It was an exhausting week. He saw less of the southern life–band than he had of the northern, but he saw a great deal of the inside of the bedroom. What he could never see, what was always barred from him, was the spirit that lay beyond Galena's strangely beautiful face. At times, he thought she was much like Colliery and The Jacksonite Corporation: possessed of intimidating strength and aura, doing what she wanted with him despite his desires, even forcing his desires to correspond with hers, carrying with her the sense that she could be as deadly as the planet's desert, yet hiding from him the inner truths of her soul as the placid beauty of the life–band must cover the endless tunnels of Colliery's vast mines, dark tunnels filled with clanking, roaring machines, single–purpose mechanical minds doing their work despite any obstacles.

They did some hiking, but their hikes were usually short. She would find one of those giant trees to hide them from the sight of any vacationers passing overhead, and, even if Benton wanted to go further, Galena would push him to the ground, tear off her clothes and his, and make love violently. He learned quickly not to resist, for that brought out the streak of cruelty never hidden far beneath her surface.

Only once did she stop before completion. Climaxing deep inside her, his face pressed to her shoulder, he mumbled, "I love you, Galena, I love you." She rolled off him suddenly and pushed him violently away. He turned to her and her face was suffused with fury. Then she began to laugh and lay for long minutes helplessly on the ground, roaring out her laughter. He never spoke any words of endearment to her again, but he found that, with his body under her control and manipulation, the incident did nothing to lessen his passion or his response to her.

They made only one trip to the ice cap. They wore special suits, lightweight, heated, with one setting that turned the fabric to an almost perfect insulator. Not using that setting, so that their skins could breathe comfortably, they rode across the glittering ice–fields on a small sled, skimming around vast mountains of ice and across frozen rivers that seemed to tell of an earlier and far different age, taking to the air to cross gaping chasms whose bottoms were lost in blackness.

Galena warmed more and more the further south they went, the further from the life–band, and the colder it became. She pointed out wonders he might have missed, laughed at his occasional jokes, and once or twice hugged him quickly and affectionately.

"Isn't it a bit dangerous to get too far from the life–band?" he asked.

"Not as long as our sled's working," she said.

"What if it breaks down?"

"We dig in and wait for help. Watch this." Galena touched the controls and the sled slowed and stopped. With the wind of their motion gone, Benton became aware of the ice cap's own wind, a steady, low, distant howl. The wind's tendrils crept into his suit eagerly through the small face opening. He shivered suddenly with a realization of how vast and truly hostile the ice cap was.

Galena stepped from the sled. She reached into a storage compartment behind him and brought out a small package. She placed it on the ice and pressed a red dot on its surface. With a hissing of air, it grew and billowed until it formed a silvery dome on the ice.

"Home for as long as we need it," Galena said. There was

gaiety in her voice, something he'd never heard in it before. "Come on."

She showed him how to use the double door—in effect, an airlock—without collapsing the dome. He expected it to be dark inside, but some of the dim sunshine filtered through the dome walls. He realized that they would not have to travel much further south to be in the region of winter-long darkness.

Galena had brought a small heater from the storage compartment in the sled, and she turned it on. In moments, the bitter chill had disappeared. "We don't want to heat up the air too much," she said, "because the walls of this dome are not very good insulators and we'd start to melt down through the snow."

Down, down, he thought, into the cold depths. He imagined the silvery dome with the two of them trapped inside it sinking slowly into the snow and the ice beneath it. How far? Kilometers? The two of them, lost forever far below the surface, frozen together.

"We just need enough radiated heat to take off our clothes," Galena said. She stripped her suit off and removed the light clothes beneath.

Benton shook his head in mock wonder. "Is there anywhere you don't want sex?" He took off his suit and the clothes he wore under it.

"Only in the grave, if I'm ever unlucky enough to find myself there." She picked up both their suits and with deft movements he could not follow combined them into a roomy sleeping bag. She increased the heating setting of one and the insulation setting of the other, then climbed inside and held it open for him to follow.

There was a difference this time. There wasn't the

undertone of brutality he had grown used to, or the feeling of being used without regard to his own needs or desires. This time, there was warmth and tenderness. Galena was on top of him throughout, as it seemed she must be in order to feel genuine excitement, and she was still the dominant member of the pair, but there was a sense of giving and receiving rather than of taking or manipulating. For the first time, Benton felt as if they were making love to each other. They concentrated on each other's pleasure, and they climaxed simultaneously. Afterwards, they lay side by side, arms wrapped around each other and legs tangled together, each half asleep, drowsing in the afterglow, drifting in the soft joy of remembered joy.

The ground trembled underneath them, heaved up and then fell back. They scrambled out of their sleeping bag and Galena quickly separated the suits. As they hastily pulled their clothes and suits back on, Benton said, "The ice must be cracking. We'd better get moving."

"No." Galena's voice was tired. The tenderness had fled from her face again and she was reserved, withdrawn, impenetrable. "It felt like a major tunnel collapse. There may be a new opening to the surface."

She refused to say any more than that. After a few more minutes they were back on the sled, the dome collapsed and stored in the compartment again, and headed back north, toward the life–band.

In a reversal of the earlier process, Galena grew colder and less communicative as the kilometers passed beneath their sled. Benton sighed and resigned himself to the loss. He tried to turn his thoughts to more impersonal matters.

For the first time, some idea formed in his mind of the true size and extent of Colliery's mines. Surely its tunnels didn't extend under the ice cap. If not, then the tunnel or system of tunnels that had collapsed must be many kilometers away—even hundreds or thousands—and it seemed almost inconceivable to him that the effect of the collapse could be felt over such a distance. The mines must be virtually geological in scope. In size, extent, and importance to the stability of the planet's crust, they must be comparable to a major geological feature. Why, they must truly be one of the Galaxy's great wonders and one of the mightiest of all Man's artifacts. The engineering skill and the audacity they represented were both awe inspiring.

What an amazing world this was! He could spend his life exploring it, he suspected.

When they reached the cottage hours later, Galena went in immediately. Benton followed and found her talking into a small comm much like his own.

So the devices did exist on Colliery! Borrasca had been wrong about that. Borrasca had not had one, though. Nor could Benton recall seeing anyone else use one here before this. He realized that Galena had left her comm behind in the cottage deliberately. She had wanted to cut them both off from the outside world, to find something more than physical with him. The planet itself had betrayed them, recalling her to her duty and to herself.

Galena put away the comm with a sigh and turned to Benton. He wanted to reach out to her and touch her, but that felt impossible. She forced a smile. "Just as well, anyway," she said. Her voice was cool, detached. "They said your equipment arrived a day or so ahead of schedule, so we would have had to leave now in any case."

This time, Benton did step toward her and reach out, but she pushed his hand aside and shook her head. "No. There's no time. For anything."

They packed in silence. When they were done, they carried their luggage outside and loaded it in the flyer, not looking at each other the whole time. Galena piloted the way she did everything else, taking off so suddenly that the acceleration drove the air from Benton's lungs, roaring away at the highest speed the flyer could achieve, stressing the machine and its occupants to their limits.

CHAPTER EIGHT

She left Benton and his luggage at an office complex, in the glaring afternoon heat of the desert fringe, and flew away without a goodbye. His crates were waiting for him there. So was Harve Borrasca, with his face carefully expressionless.

"This is where we'll install all your stuff," Borrasca told him. "It'll be the control center for the project."

"Right. How've you been?"

Borrasca shrugged and said nothing. They walked quietly down a cool hallway with subdued, indirect lighting, a welcome relief from the outside. A glass wall formed the end of the hallway, and a large, empty room lay beyond it.

Borrasca said, "So far, this is keyed to my pattern and yours only." He placed his palm against a metal plate built into the glass and the entire wall slid silently away to the right. Benton walked in and examined the room. Power outlets were abundant around the walls. There were some tables and desks and much open space. Through a doorway, he could see the edges of one of his crates in an adjoining room.

Everything I need to get to work, he thought, filled with reluctance. He shook himself, as though to shake that feeling away.

He happened to glance at Borrasca and saw sympathy in the other man's face. "It must have been a pretty gruesome week," Borrasca said gently. "I can imagine it."

Benton grunted noncommittally and went into the other room to look over the crates. He opened one of the smaller ones and looked over the equipment inside it. It was hard to be sure, but he thought it hadn't been subjected to vacuum. Perhaps he was in luck. He wouldn't really know until he had everything set up and running. "I'll need help unpacking this stuff and hauling it into place," he said to Borrasca.

"I'll have some muscle sent over first thing in the morning," Borrasca said promptly. "And anything else you want, just holler. I'm still your liaison man, you lucky devil, and I'll be here regularly to see what you need."

"What about the sensors that go underground and the communications equipment?"

"Right. I've been briefed on all that. There are a couple of teams standing by to put it all in place. The locations were chosen even before you got to Colliery. We'll get the crates unpacked and you can show us what's what, and then we'll get the underground teams going. Tell you what, though," He glanced at his watch. "We can start the unpacking tomorrow, as soon as the help arrives. It's too late to really get anything done this evening, so let's have one last evening on the town at Corporation expense."

Benton grinned. "I kind of expected you to say that."

"It's what I do best."

While they were exhausting themselves doing the town, eating and drinking too much with some of Borrasca's many friends,

Benton made a few unsuccessful attempts to pump him for information on a couple of items that particularly puzzled him. "Galena. How did she get to be so strong?"

"Yeah, she is, isn't she? It's her only talent."

I wouldn't say that. Benton kept that thought to himself.

Borrasca didn't seem inclined to say more on the subject, but then he laughed bitterly and said, "She always was, even as a kid, so it's mainly natural. It's also because of the kind of training she does all the time. She's... sort of a policewoman."

That was all Benton could get on that matter. He kept waiting for Borrasca or one of the people they were with to mention the other thing that preoccupied him, the tunnel collapse he had felt. But no one did. Finally, he mentioned it himself. One of the others waved it off with, "Oh, that. There was no damage aboveground, no opening, so there's no problem."

Galena had also mentioned the possibility of the tunnel collapse having caused a new opening. Why should that aspect of it be such a problem?

Benton had a sudden mental picture of a gaping hole appearing in the desert, clouds of dust billowing out, and up the slanting floor of the hole automated mining machines came roaring, frantic, directionless, out into the desert, chewing up the few plants and animals that managed to survive there. If it happened in one of the life–bands, the destruction might be even worse. That must be why everyone worried about the collapse opening up an exit to the surface. It was just another example of that admirable concern The Jacksonite Corporation showed for the native plant and animal life.

In the small hours of the morning, after the last of Borrasca's friends had given up and gone home, Harve took Benton to his house.

"My house?" Benton repeated, fighting to hold down the evening's food and drink. Borrasca's piloting of the floater had been by turns exhilarating and terrifying. Borrasca had finally brought the machine up against the front door of what was by Benton's standards a mansion.

"For the duration of your contract. Damn. Hold on. Gotta back up, or we won't be able to open the door."

"My house," Benton said again. "I've never lived in a house. Not since I was a kid, anyway." His parents had favored apartments precisely because of their feeling of impermanence. Nor had their incomes, excellent though they'd been, sufficed to even rent a house in most of the cities they'd lived in.

"This is Colliery, my friend," Borrasca said. His voice was slurred, but his good cheer was unaffected. It was possibly even heightened. "Everyone lives in houses here. Not like those barbaric other places." He shuddered theatrically. "Crammed together. Ants in a hive."

"Bees live in hives. Ants live in... ant heaps, I think."

"Yeah, well, Collierites live in houses, damn it!"

They wandered around inside for a while, Benton feeling lost in the enormous place. He admired the luxurious furniture and décor, but he thought the house was excessive for one person. Maybe I should live in one of the suites and then when it gets dirty move to another one, he thought. That would probably carry me through my contract here.

"It's okay," Borrasca said. "They stinted a bit, which I find pretty annoying. We should be treating guests better than this."

"Better than this? Is that what you said?"

"Sure. By our standards, this place is a bit substandard. We like our houses large and with lots of space around them."

Small, rich population, lots of good land, Benton thought. Makes sense, I guess. What a difference from everywhere else I've been! He yawned. "I should go to bed. Try to get a few hours of sleep, anyway."

"Yeah, right. I'll arrange to have a pilot and floater to take you back and forth to work. And entertainment, of course."

"How far is it from here to the office?"

"Nothing's all that far here. It's not a big town. Look." He walked to a window, beckoning Benton to follow him. "See that office tower? The five-story one?"

Benton suppressed a smile at the idea that a building that low could be called a tower. It did stand out, though, its lights gleaming against the night—towering indeed over the lower buildings around it.

"That's where we were earlier," Borrasca said. "Where your equipment is."

"I could walk that easily. Or is it unsafe to walk in your cities?"

Borrasca laughed. "It's always safe in the Garden of Eden! It's probably a pleasant walk. Just be sure to do it during the daytime. If you work late, call me and I'll have someone take you home by floater."

"Why?"

Borrasca hesitated. "I guess it really isn't entirely safe. Not because of people," he added quickly. "Collierites are all law-abiding and peaceful. We don't have any criminals. Sometimes animals wander in from the life-bands, though. So we have cameras in various places, to watch for them. If the police see something large moving around at night, they might overreact."

"They can't tell the difference between a human and an animal? They should have software that can take care of that."

Borrasca shrugged. "Don't ask me. I don't have any wish to walk around after dark, anyway." He shuddered. "I'd hate to give Galena or someone like her an excuse to come swooping down on me."

"There are others like her?"

"No, I guess not. She's one of a kind. Well, anyway, I'd better let you get to sleep. I'll stop by your office sometime to say hello."

Benton fell easily into a routine of walking to work early, before the heavier traffic began or the heat could filter into the city from the desert. He stayed late most days. Usually he did call Borrasca from the comm in his office and have a floater and driver sent to take him home. Occasionally, though, he walked. He saw no wild animals from the life–belt. He also saw no other pedestrians. Nor, to his regret, did Galena or anyone like her swoop down on him.

He spent his time working through the lengthy array of diagnostic test cases he had designed before leaving Farandhazy. There were no serious hitches. The hardware had not been damaged, and both hardware and software ran through his various simulations with so few bugs, and those so minor, that he found himself bracing uneasily for Gangue's Law to sneak up behind him and attack. But it never happened.

He could not have said as much for his personal, mental software. He felt isolated and alien again and had retreated into a cocoon. He ate breakfast alone every day, in an almost empty cafeteria in the office complex, and lunch in the same cafeteria. Sometimes he was joined by Borrasca or the two assistants The Jacksonite Corporation had assigned to him, but more often he ate alone.

He took to skipping supper, except for an occasional evening out with more of Harve's friends. He seemed unable to progress beyond the level of shallow acquaintanceship with any of these people. Always, he slept alone. During his lonely evenings in his house, he watched the vidscreen, read a small amount in the technical journals he had brought with him, or stood by a window watching the lights of the city and wondering what warmth of family life or sexual pleasure each one hid. He wondered, too, how these days of work could be so sadly different from his first two weeks on Colliery.

It was three weeks before he was fully satisfied that everything in his computer room was working as it should. What remained now was the final hookup of the computer with the underground sensors and another series of tests. Assuming those last steps went as smoothly as everything else had so far, that would presumably be it—the end of his contract and of his time on Colliery.

He contacted Borrasca to let him know the computer part of the system appeared to be ready.

"Great," Borrasca said. "Now, here's the idea. The sensors are all in place underground, and I understand the communications are all ready. During the night, tonight, they'll make the final connections to the computer. Then, first thing in the morning, I'll bring some Corporation big shots over and I want you to give them a demonstration. With all the bells and whistles."

Benton was horrified. "I can't do that! Once the hookup's complete, I'll need days more to check it out. The signals coming in may be garbage, or the connections to the computer may be fouled up."

"Forget all that. Listen, you can rely on those technicians. Everything'll be okay. But it really doesn't matter even if it isn't. Look, you're missing the whole point of this demonstration. All you really have to do is get pretty numbers and graphs and stuff on that great big screen you've got. Do you think the executive types I'll be bringing know anything about all this technical stuff? Just impress them, show them enough so that they're convinced all that money's being well spent, and they'll be happy. Then everyone else'll be happy. Don't panic now, Jim. Just relax and show them something with flash." He broke the connection and faded from the screen.

Benton jumped up and paced about the room, ignoring the goodbyes from his two assistants as they left for the day. What he was being asked to do—mislead executives who weren't technically competent to catch him out—was unethical. He was also being told that his long days of work on Farandhazy and here didn't really matter. Even ignoring that and being pragmatic, what if the damn hardware didn't cooperate tomorrow and he made precisely the wrong impression on these executives?

Another thought struck him. He had already convinced himself that The Jacksonite Corporation must include some people who were top-notch experts in just this field of automation and control. Why weren't they going to be here tomorrow for the demonstration? Perhaps they were and Harve simply didn't realize that not all the big shots he was bringing were technical idiots. This could be a disaster!

He stood in the middle of his office, sweating, his heart beating madly.

This is no good, he told himself. Harve was right. Try to relax. You're working yourself into a breakdown. Then you certainly won't make a good impression. Go home, go to bed, get some sleep.

He went home and he went to bed, but he didn't get any sleep. After tossing about in bed for what seemed like hours but was in fact less than one hour, he decided that he was far too tense to sleep. He got out of bed and walked about the house for a while before concluding that a walk outside might help. He dressed quickly, then realized that he needed some sort of warm outer covering because of the chilliness of the desert air that would by now cover this part of the city. All he had was a dark brown sweater, so he pulled that on.

As he passed in front of a mirror on his way out, he realized that his clothing, both sweater and pants, was all dark, so that he looked like a criminal out for a night of business. The thought amused him. He decided to complete the picture and make himself look even more like a vidscreen villain. He rummaged around in one of his cases until he found his dark woolen cap and put that on. He wasn't feeling sleepy yet, but the little masquerade had at least raised his spirits.

The streets were deserted in this suburban neighborhood. In some parts of the town, life and lights kept going almost all night. Here, however, sidewalks and streets were deserted and already most of the lights in the houses were turned off.

Once again, as so often on his walks after dark, he fell into wishing that Galena would appear, even if it was in her official guise. He missed her, he realized.

He was turning a corner from one quiet, dark street into another, heading back home at last, when he heard the sound of a door being violently opened somewhere ahead of him, and a grunt. Light flashed across a lawn and then vanished. Benton stopped walking and stood irresolutely for a moment. Instincts bred on more crowded and dangerous worlds came into play. He moved behind a tree and looked carefully around it. He heard voices and was grateful for the random impulse that had led him to dress in such concealing colors.

Now he could see two figures standing in the middle of the sidewalk, faintly silhouetted against the sky glow from a busier street some blocks away. Benton thanked the fates that there was no moonlight. One of the figures seemed familiar. It said something, took a step, and turned so that he glimpsed in silhouette the motion of long hair tied back. He almost called out her name, but some fortunate instinct stopped him.

Again there was the sound of a door. This time it stayed open. In the light shining out from inside the house, Benton saw two men emerge. One was enormous, centimeters taller than Galena and far broader, with a brutal, menacing face. He was dragging the second man, who was much smaller. He had the captive's arms twisted up behind his back. Ignoring his ineffectual struggles, the big man jerked him over to a floater parked nearby, pulled the back door open, and threw him in, slamming the floater door shut behind him. Then he went around to the front door on the other side and climbed in himself. During the short moments when the light from inside the floater had shone directly on the captive, Benton had seen that his face was bloodied.

The floater's front door remained open. In the light, Benton could see that Galena was talking to a short, slender woman dressed in a nightgown who looked up at her with evident fear.

Despite any possible danger, Benton had to hear what Galena was saying. Moving slowly and carefully, he made his way to another tree. He still couldn't hear. He held his breath and moved forward, hiding behind a third tree. He was close enough now to reach out and touch Galena, and part of him ached to do so.

"I'm telling you, you don't have to worry," Galena was assuring the other woman. Benton could hear the impatience in her voice. "You turned your boyfriend in, and we'll remember that. You're not in any kind of trouble. Stay away from people like that in the future, and you'll stay out of trouble."

Her companion called her from the floater and she stepped over to the vehicle and climbed in. The floater whooshed off down the street. Benton froze behind the tree until the floater had vanished. When he looked again, the woman had reentered the house and closed the door and all was dark and quiet again.

Feeling and acting now like some sort of criminal indeed, Benton scurried through the deserted streets to his own house. He locked the door behind him with a feeling of relief. He stripped off his clothes and climbed into bed, pulled the covers up to his chin, and lay in the dark, shivering, trying desperately to keep from thinking about what he had just witnessed.

CHAPTER NINE

Benton was up the next morning even earlier than usual. He had slept little. He hurried to the office complex and ate a scanty breakfast in the cafeteria, then went directly to the computer room. He didn't know just when Borrasca would arrive with the Corporation executives, but since he had gotten there so early himself, he hoped he'd have time for at least a short examination of the hardware and the work done during the night and that he would be able to perform a brief run-through.

Potentially the weakest link was the communications subsystem, the connection between the underground sensors and the aboveground computer. Benton would have preferred a simple physical connection—signal wires, land lines—for the sake of clarity and dependability of signal. Because of the distances involved, however, this was not feasible. Instead, the signals from each cluster of sensors were led to the surface over ordinary wires but were then amplified and broadcast via conventional radio beam to a receiver on the top of this building, then finally fed down to an interface hooked up to the computer. Benton had great faith in his company's sensors and in the software that was his own specialty, but it was clear to him that the connection between the two would be seriously unreliable.

He had asked about satellite relay and had been told that Corporation regulations did not permit the use of Corporation satellites for signals generated by non–Corporation equipment. This was "to prevent any potential compromise of Corporation security or equipment reliability." There were no non–Corporation satellites in orbit around Colliery. The same sort of security regulations were quoted as the reason the signals would have to be simple, unencoded, unpacketed analog ones.

All of this had been explained to Contco during the early stages of the contract negotiations—the stages in which neither Benton nor any other technical people at his level were involved. Those doing the negotiating on behalf of Contco could think of nothing but the huge amount of money the Corporation was dangling in front of them and so they were willing to promise anything.

For equally vague reasons, The Jacksonite Corporation had refused to provide any information about other, possibly interfering signals or anything about the propagation characteristics of Colliery's atmosphere. The only data on this that Contco had managed to dig up were left over from early Imperial surveys and were sketchy and incomplete. Benton recalled one of the communications experts at Contco throwing up her hands in despair and telling him, "We'll do our best for you, Jim, but you could get a garbage signal or a perfect signal or anything in between. Your guess is as good as mine."

Now he stared sourly and helplessly at the large, featureless metal cube that had been attached to the computer during the night and he wondered what kind of input it was receiving from the sensors a kilometer underground and so many kilometers away.

He should have been allowed to bring a team with him, of course. He considered his hardware expertise to be limited. He should not have so much resting on his shoulders, so much depending on him. He felt as overwhelmed by this responsibility as he had been by Galena.

He looked around the room. As far as he could tell, the technicians who'd been in there during the night to do the hooking up hadn't damaged anything. He clicked on the giant display screen, three meters high by five meters wide, that covered one wall. The device had had to be shipped tightly rolled up and packed diagonally in the largest crate, and now the lower right-hand corner still insisted on curling up and wouldn't lie quite flat against the wall. Benton thought for a moment and then pulled a chair over and set it so that it held the corner of the screen down. He hoped that the chair looked casually, rather than deliberately, placed and that no one would move it and spoil the effect of his demonstration.

He glanced at the figures displayed in rows and columns on the screen, and he breathed a sigh of relief. At least the display looked about the way it should—much as it had during his series of test cases. He didn't know if the numbers displayed were reasonable, but at least, even if the signals from the sensors were fouled up, the results on the screen looked reasonable to someone like him who didn't know any better. Perhaps the demonstration wouldn't be a disaster after all. He switched to a graphic display of those same variables. He nodded in satisfaction, his confidence growing. The curves of the graph changed continually as readings came in from the sensors. Now that has flash, he thought, feeling very pleased with himself.

Beneath that pleasure, awareness of something being not quite right nagged at him, but he couldn't pin it down.

It began to look as though he needn't have bothered coming in early after all. Everything was going so smoothly that it almost made him nervous.

Benton looked at the equipment cluttering the room and shook his head in renewed amazement that so much hardware, time, and money were being invested in what was really such a simple job. He sat down at one of his assistants' desks, since neither of them had yet shown up, and picked up a magazine lying on top. He settled back to read and wait for the official inspection party.

Benton's assistants arrived late, and Borrasca and the executives came in even later. This was far from being the "first thing in the morning," as Borrasca had promised. Benton's earlier nervous wakefulness had faded, and the effect of sleeplessness and of his strange, frightening encounter of the night before was telling on him. He felt drowsy and irritable. He had a nagging headache that was slowly but steadily building in intensity. However, he did his best to mask these feelings and to be both pleasant and amiable when Borrasca brought the inspection party in.

They were dressed formally and expensively. Benton, who had not even thought to dress differently today than on any other work day, felt shabby, poor, and at a disadvantage. He noticed some of the dapper men and elegant women looking him up and down disdainfully. All right, you bastards, he thought, smiling all the while. I've done my job, and that's all you hired me for.

Borrasca introduced Benton to the group, referring to everyone by their first names. "Well, Jim," Borrasca said heartily when all the introductions were over, "show us what all this pretty gadgetry can do."

I wish it could rise up on hidden legs and crush you all, Benton thought.

He reproached himself immediately for being so childish and launched into his memorized speech outlining the system from sensors through display screen. Some of his audience seemed interested, but the attention of others started wandering.

He dropped the rest of the prepared speech and summarized quickly, extemporaneously, and then drew their attention to the screen. He threw up various tabular and graphic displays, switching through the display options rapidly. This time he thought he had the complete attention of every member of the group.

"As The Jacksonite Corporation specified, this first phase monitors and controls ventilation balancing and power levels and does some modeling of geotechnical strains. We could have simplified things a bit by leaving out the ventilation module. If you'd like, we could do that in the next phase."

"No, no," one of them said, "we need it. Maintenance crews go down there occasionally. Machines break down, there are blockages of one kind or another. There are various reasons to have adequate air flow."

"Ah. Okay. Speaking of the next phase, you mentioned that you would probably want it to include control systems for your automated ore extraction and processing. When we're ready to begin design sessions for Phase 2, we'll have to have a good look at the automated system you're using now."

There was a long silence. Benton could sense their reluctance. Finally, Borrasca said, "Sure, we can talk about that when the time comes."

"Good," Benton said. "Okay. Note the movements in the graphs. This is very much real time. Displays change instantaneously each time new readings are received from the sensors and the models are updated. Note the speed at which our software is able to accomplish this." Probably child's play in the old days, he thought. "Contco is just about the only company nowadays whose software and hardware can provide you with this capability. Also," he typed a command quickly on the console, "you can request a historical display, showing the pattern in any selected variable—such as humidity or temperature—over any desired period of time. You can also compare the readings for specified sites, like this." He typed in another command and waited for the display to change. Before it did, he found himself staring at the historical display he had just created, showing the record over the previous hour of the readings of temperature and humidity from one batch of sensors. The unconscious alarm bell was ringing again, but before he could pin anything down, the computer responded to his latest command and changed the display.

One of the executives spoke up. He was an older man, tall and slender and obviously proud of his well-preserved condition, dressed in a flowing grey business suit with a black-edged grey cape which he swirled about at every opportunity. "This is excellent. I'm very pleased. Now, that historical display you showed us suggests something I'd like to see included in

Phase 2. Can you modify this system so that it models those patterns in the variables you displayed and predicts what the future changes will be?"

"Predict the future values? Well, I suppose that would depend on the smoothness of the patterns and the interrelation of the variables. And of course how well the underlying engineering is understood. But we have people at Contco who're experts in those areas," he added quickly. Or we will, he thought, as soon as we've hired them. He typed in the command to throw up the historical display again, using the discussion as an excuse, since his nagging unconscious wanted to look at it again. "I'm sure it would be possible." The curves for temperature and humidity he was now looking at covered the more than four hours since the system had been hooked up. There it was, what had been bothering him. The temperature curve showed strange peaks, sudden jumps at irregular intervals, and the humidity curve had peaks that matched them, occurring at the same times but starting slightly earlier, building more slowly and declining more gradually. "They're not regular at all!" Benton exclaimed. "What is all that stuff?"

He didn't notice the glances of concern the inspection team exchanged with each other. "Oh, it happens in mines," Borrasca said casually, but with a cautionary edge to his voice. "Gusts of hot, humid air can move through the tunnels sometimes."

Benton noticed the cautionary tone but ignored it. "Not repeatedly, surely. Anyway, where does it come from? Wait a minute, I just thought of something else I noticed on that other display." He typed quickly. "Look, here's a comparison between a few clusters of sensors all along the same tunnel, a few meters apart, for a distance of maybe half a kilometer. Now, it seems to me that a gust of hot, humid air like you described should spread out and diffuse along the tunnel as it moves through, but watch that display."

Everyone watched, and for the first time Benton became aware of the tension and air of hostility in the group crowded behind his chair. Would another gust of air never show up in the tunnel? If nothing happened on that display soon, he'd look like a prize idiot. Finally, it happened. A ripple moved along the twin curves, a sharp bump in temperature and a smoother, gentler bump in the humidity curve. It showed up first at one sensor, then disappeared at that location, and then showed up at the next sensor, further down the tunnel. The bumps moved along like ripples in water, and no one breathed until they had disappeared entirely from the display. Then there was a simultaneous release of held breath throughout the room.

"There!" Benton said triumphantly. "That was no gust of air. It was too compact and moved too regularly, smoothly. It was more like—" He groped for the thought, then laughed at the silliness of it when he caught it. "Like a knot of people trudging along the tunnel, passing each sensor in line. As a matter of fact," he said thoughtfully, making a rough mental calculation, "it was moving at just about walking speed." He turned back to the console and sat for a moment with his fingers poised above the buttons. "Let's see, it might be interesting to try the same sort of display for the other batches of sensors, too."

As he started to type, someone grabbed his wrist and pulled his hand away from the buttons. Benton looked up in annoyance. It was the man in the grey suit, his jaw set. Behind him, Benton could see the faces of the others, some of them angry, some hostile, some, like Borrasca's, bewildered.

"That's not necessary," the older man said firmly. "It's obviously some sort of sensor malfunction. We'll have our technicians go back underground and take care of the matter. Clearly, your system works superbly, and you are to be congratulated on a fine job. I think I can predict quite confidently that the follow–on contract will be yours, if you can do the modeling and prediction part I mentioned before." The others nodded vigorously and looked relieved.

Benton threw the other man's hand off angrily and stood to face him. "Wait a minute!" His feelings of alienation, his fatigue, his tension, and the gnawing memory of the previous evening combined to fill him with outrage at his treatment and fury with The Jacksonite Corporation. "I've had enough of this crap. Your secrecy makes it almost impossible for me or anyone else to do this job properly. You can send your technicians down to check the sensors, but I'm going down there too. And I want someone with me who's capable of measuring the temperature and humidity by hand. Then we'll take those readings back here and compare them to what the historical record shows for the same time. I want to be there to see that it's done and done properly." He stood glaring at the group, breathing heavily, his hands clenched.

Great, now I've done it, he thought suddenly. Now they'll tell me to leave Colliery, and they'll give the contract to some other company.

But he was wrong. These representatives of one of the Galaxy's mightiest economic entities wilted before his anger, and he realized suddenly what sort of people he was really facing. They're apparatchiks, he realized, and the thought filled him with contempt. They're part of their system, glad to go along with it and not rock the boat. If they kick me out, they'll have to answer for the whole incident to some higher–ups, and they're afraid to face that.

At first, he had assumed that these people were the higher–ups. If they weren't, where did the hierarchy stop? Perhaps not before it reached the Board of Directors Borrasca had mentioned.

The group retreated to a corner of the room for a quick, huddled conference. After a few minutes of this, the man in the grey suit and cape came over to Benton and said hesitantly, "You know it's against Corporation policy to let an outsider go underground, don't you?"

In for a mill, in for a million, Benton told himself. "Damn it, so what? You've spent a lot of money on this project so far, and I need to go underground to make sure that money wasn't wasted. *You* have to satisfy *me* that everything's working properly." And besides, he thought, astonishing himself, I'd like to see what's going on down there.

In the end, they capitulated, but they did impose some conditions. Time would have to be allowed for a team to go underground first and make certain unspecified preparations. "We can't have a visitor getting hurt," the older man explained. On this point, at least, they were adamant, and Benton resigned himself to having to put off his underground trip for a day or two. The group of executives, led again by Borrasca, retreated from the computer room. As they left, they watched Benton with a mixture of respect and trepidation instead of the disdain he had seen earlier.

When they were gone, he laughed with pleasure. The whole experience should have left him upset, but instead he felt buoyed up with self–confidence and purged of his earlier feelings of helplessness and resentment. For once in his life, he had taken control of a situation instead of caving in. It felt marvelous.

Then there was the prospect of going underground into an active mine. The idea made him slightly nervous, but mostly it filled him with excitement. Like the life–bands and the polar cap, this was going to be a great adventure.

Too bad Galena won't be with me, he thought. Although she'd probably just want to have sex in every tunnel there is down there.

Which was, he had to admit, an intriguing thought in itself.

It took two days before they were ready for him. He used the time to train his assistants in the operation of the system and to produce some additional documentation for the Corporation employee who would be taking over the system when it was finally operational. He also took the time to make some rough notes on the next step, the prediction of future values of the variables which the sensors measured and which were displayed on the screen. And throughout it all, he congratulated himself repeatedly for his dedication, his productivity, and above all his professionalism. I'll have to whip all these Collierites into shape, he told himself smugly, but they'll like the result when I'm done with them.

CHAPTER TEN

"Sure you don't want to back out? Last chance."

Benton shook his head.

"Okay," Borrasca said. "Climb in."

He was yelling, but even so, Benton could scarcely hear him. They were inside a small building that sheltered them from the desert sun. It also doubled as a cover for a shaft opening and a housing for an immense fan. The fan was rotating rapidly, its blades a circular blur about seven meters in diameter. The roar as it pumped air underground was deafening. The building shook with its vibrations. Benton was having trouble standing upright against the hurricane of air the fan was pulling in through the building's door. He squeezed his eyes almost shut against the wind, and it hurt his eyes anyway. This close, it felt as though the wind was alive and was trying to tear his eyelids off.

Borrasca sat in a small, four–wheeled vehicle. It ran on rails which followed the downward sloping floor of the shaft until they vanished around a curve far below. Borrasca's car was the last in line. Other cars were linked ahead of his, carrying a small team of technicians and, surprisingly, a couple of the executives who'd been at Benton's demonstration.

Benton climbed into the car and sat down next to Borrasca. He was sure no one would be able to overhear their conversation against the roar of the wind. Shouting, he asked Borrasca why the two executives had decided to come along.

"To watch." Borrasca's expression was sour. "You aroused their technical curiosity, so now we'll have them underfoot." He waved a signal at an operator on the other side of the fan. The operator acknowledged the signal and manipulated his control board. There was a series of loud, metallic clanks. With a jerk that almost knocked Benton's safety helmet off his head, the chain of cars began to move.

The cars moved down the slope, their speed increasing slowly. Benton turned his attention to the details of the shaft passing by. Rock walls pressed in from the sides and the rock ceiling was only centimeters above his head. The light from behind them had vanished, lost in the downward curve of the tunnel. The only light came from the lamps on their helmets. The ride turned bumpy, and he found himself bouncing out of his seat occasionally. When he looked up, he could see the ceiling was moving past rapidly. He started worrying about bouncing too high and crashing against the jagged rocks above him. His safety helmet would be little protection if that happened.

At least other lights began to appear, strung along the walls and ceiling. They must have been put there for us, Benton thought. They were dim and widely spaced, but they filled him with relief. If all this swaying, clanking, bouncing ride had been conducted in the dark, it would have been unbearable.

He tried not to think of that and to concentrate on the changing colors of the walls. It didn't quite work. Despite the interesting scenery and the presence of the lights, his incipient claustrophobia began to flare up. He was having trouble breathing and his heart was speeding up. He concentrated on the air rushing past his face. It seemed good, not stale at all. But it was already getting hotter and damper.

That's your damned imagination again, he told himself. We're not deep enough for that.

At last the slope eased as the shaft flattened toward the horizontal. The cars slowed gradually and the rattling of the wheels diminished. The roar of the fan had been left behind. The relative silence was a pleasant change. The lights strung along the shaft were much more numerous and powerful here. Benton said to Borrasca, "I'm really glad they put those lights down here. Much better than the helmet lamps. "

Borrasca leaned toward him and whispered, "The executives didn't want you to keep them in the dark." At least Borrasca seemed cheerful and to bear no ill will for having been forced to make this trip.

With a final series of clanks and clatters, the cars stopped. They banged into each other, bouncing back and forth until their momentum died.

The passengers climbed out of the cramped cars and stretched. Benton felt relieved that the ceiling was high enough here to do that without touching it. For the moment, his claustrophobic reaction receded.

One of the technicians said, "It's right down here, down this crosscut." They followed him into a smaller tunnel angling off the main shaft. This tunnel was strung with lights, too, to Benton's infinite relief. After a short walk, the tunnel opened into another one cutting across it at a right angle and only slightly wider. This was the location of the sensors, and it was where the manual measurements would be made. The lights here were even brighter and were strung closely. In the bright light, Benton could see a faint haze of dust in the air.

A man was standing in this tunnel, apparently waiting for them. As they entered, he came up to the two Corporation executives and gave a gesture that struck Benton as some sort of salute. He conferred with the two executives in low murmurs, pointing up and down the tunnel to draw their attention to something. They looked where he was pointing and nodded in evident approval. Benton looked too and saw that the lights stopped about ten meters in both directions, and that a group of men was standing where the darkness began at both ends. There was something about their manner, a wariness, that made Benton think of sentries on duty. He also noticed that the man talking to the two executives was tall and powerfully built. He reminded Benton unpleasantly of the man he had seen Galena with that night in the city. The man—saluted?—the executives again and strode off to one end of the tunnel, where he faded into the group standing at the shadows' edge.

Harve said Galena is a kind of policewoman, Benton thought. Is that what those guys are, policemen? In that case, where are the crooks?

The lights were much brighter in this tunnel. It would probably help their work. Unfortunately, rather than helping Benton forget he was far underground, the brightness reinforced his distress. Whatever softness the rocks might have seemed to have, whatever friendliness he could have tried to see in them as part of the friendly crust of Colliery, was banished by the harsh artificial light glaring on the ceiling. Every sharp edge, every hostile alienness of the rock was highlighted. Every little point or bump on the walls cast its small, inky shadow on the wall directly beneath it. Only on the floor of the tunnel, with the bright lights shining directly down on it, was there an absence of this startling contrast.

He noticed Borrasca standing at one of the walls and motioning him over. When he came up to him, Borrasca said, "I want you to see something. This tunnel is a drift. Look at this wall." Benton looked carefully where Borrasca was pointing, but all he could see was a layer of a slightly different color than the surrounding rock, perhaps half a meter thick, running parallel to the tunnel floor.

Benton shook his head. "What am I looking for?"

"It's this light. Wait a minute." Borrasca held his hands so that they shaded the layer from the harsh overhead lights. Suddenly it stood out against the drabness of the surrounding rock with startling effect. It was a soft pale yellow, and it seemed to glow with its own light from deep within.

Benton exclaimed at the beauty of it. "Is it gold?"

Borrasca laughed loudly. "Much, much better than that. It's a vein of pure jacksonite."

The parliamentary debate he had been watching concerning the increased price for jacksonite came back to Benton. One MP had been complaining because the Corporation had dared to break the "thousand barnard per gram barrier." More than a thousand per gram? He looked more carefully at the vein. A half meter high, it seemed to run the length of the tunnel, and he had no way of telling how deep it went into the wall. "My God," he breathed, "that vein must be priceless!"

Borrasca laughed again. "Scarcely that, but I bet there's

enough in this tunnel alone to cover that ten billion contract your company's hoping to get."

"Maybe when nobody's looking I can gouge out enough to make myself a millionaire."

Borrasca shook his head. "Try it. That stuff's harder than the rock around it. The whole wall has be practically dug away to free the jacksonite."

Benton looked closely at the vein and thought he could see marks where flakes of the mineral had been chipped away. Then this tunnel must still be worked. That made sense, considering the size of that vein. And yet the tunnel was too small for the frightening machines he remembered from his one other trip underground in an active mine. So they must use smaller, defter machines. Machines that could squeeze into even smaller spaces if they chose to chase him.... That image was even more frightening than the idea of clanking behemoths. Perhaps that explained the presence of a party of guards at either end of the tunnel—to alert the humans just in case some many–bladed mechanical monster decided to head their way.

He was dwelling on this unpleasant idea when one of the technicians approached him.

"We're ready to start the hand measurements, Mr. Benton. You did want to watch us, didn't you?"

"Yes, right."

He watched them take their measurements, making sure they recorded the right figures. They obviously knew much more about this sort of thing than he did, but he didn't want to surrender his temporary psychological advantage over the Corporation.

It was hard to pay close attention for very long, though.

These efficient, brisk young technicians in their bright yellow overalls didn't need him. They'd do a good job with no supervision. He felt both silly and unnecessary, standing behind them and watching them work.

He also felt bored. These details weren't really of much interest to him. The manipulation of the numbers by his software seemed almost more real than these actual measurements. More than that, he found the surroundings a lot more interesting than what the techs were doing.

Or maybe more alarming than interesting. The air felt stuffier and hotter all the time. Still not stale, thank God. He didn't need to worry about suffocating.

Nevertheless, his discomfort grew.

He looked around at the other members of the group. Except for the technicians, who were still busy scurrying about the tunnel taking their measurements, everyone was standing about, or sitting, or leaning against the walls, with expressions of the utmost boredom. Benton felt a wave of guilt wash over him. They're all here just because I made such a fuss, he thought. They're probably all blaming me for their being down here. I shouldn't have insisted on this.

The ground vibrated suddenly, sharply.

It's the cars we came down on, Benton thought. They're moving them along that other tunnel for some reason.

But the other men looked alarmed. They muttered to each other, and a couple of them started moving nervously toward the crosscut that led back to the entry shaft and the cars.

Did Benton imagine it, or did he hear faint, distant cries of alarm, voices calling out in some far part of these man-made caverns?

There was a roaring sound, faint at first, then suddenly loud. The men in the tunnel stopped moving, frozen with fear. Benton happened to be looking at one of the groups of guards at the end of the tunnel. They flew into the air as if some invisible monster had charged through their midst. With detached fascination, unable to move out of the way, he watched the men further up the tunnel being flung aside too, some against the walls and some against the ceiling. Then the mighty force reached him, he heard the roaring rise to such an intensity that his eardrums seemed to burst, and something vast and irresistible slammed him against the wall. He was floating, floating, and then the floor smacked against his face and everything faded away.

CHAPTER ELEVEN

The first thing Benton became aware of was twin aches—one high on his head, where he had hit the wall, and the other along his left cheekbone, where he had landed on the floor. The second ache was minor, little more than the sting of a bad scrape. The first, though, was awful, a pounding horror that made him wonder if his skull had been broken. At least it reassured him that he was still alive, although during those first timeless moments of consciousness he wished he weren't.

He reached up, took off his helmet, and gingerly touched his head. There was a large bump and some dried blood, but as far as he could tell the damage wasn't serious. Nothing moved when he pressed, at any rate. The helmet had probably saved his life.

Two of the lights were still operating, one directly above him and one at the end of the tunnel. Their color had gone from white to yellow, though, and they were flickering. His helmet light was dead. The helmet itself was split across the top. It looked ready to fall apart into two pieces. He got groggily to his feet, leaning against the rough rock of the tunnel wall for support. The haze of dust in the air had thickened. In some places, the walls, previously hard, vertical rock, had become gently sloping piles of rubble.

The vein of jacksonite alone was undamaged. Along the whole length of the tunnel, it gleamed beautifully in the shadows, converted to a jutting ledge where the wall containing it had fallen away.

What about the exit? Benton thought suddenly, frantically.

He stepped back from the wall he had been leaning on and looked it over carefully, but he could see no sign of the small tunnel, the crosscut, through which he would have to go to get to the shaft with the cars and rails. So it was covered up, possibly collapsed.

No way out!

Desperately, he tried to calm himself. Panic now could only make his situation worse.

"Jim!" It was Borrasca's voice. It was low and tremulous, like the voice of an old man near death. "Help me!"

Benton realized then how quiet it was. Before, he had been aware, subliminally at least, of background vibrations, the movements of machines transmitted through the rocks, the whisper of air moving past, the muttered conversations of his companions. Now all of that had vanished. All was silent. There was nothing to compete with Borrasca's weak cry, and even that seemed to be absorbed by the rocks.

Benton looked around, feeling confused. There were bodies scattered all over the tunnel. He was the only one standing, and he couldn't see Borrasca.

"Over here! I'm over here!"

"Keep talking. I can't see you." Benton's own voice sounded so calm and controlled that it surprised him.

He squinted, trying to penetrate the haze and the dim light. The two widely spaced working lights and the twisted, elongated shadows cast by the piles of rubble and the shattered walls made it almost impossible to recognize anything at a distance.

"I'm waving my arm. Can you see it?" A hint of panic had crept into Borrasca's voice.

Benton saw the feeble movement at last, on the floor a few meters down the tunnel. He ran over and found Borrasca lying with his head propped up against the tunnel wall. Borrasca's face was pale and his forehead was covered with sweat.

"Can you get up?" Benton asked anxiously.

Borrasca shook his head and pointed at his legs. His left trouser leg was soaked with blood below the knee.

When Benton leaned forward to examine it, Borrasca gasped, "Don't touch it! Rock fell on me from the roof." He stopped talking and panted, trying to regain enough strength to speak again. "I got the rock off and put on a tourniquet." Now Benton noticed the strip of white cloth tied tightly around Borrasca's thigh. "I've been waiting for someone else to move. Don't know how long. You're the first." He was weakening rapidly, his words coming in bursts. "How about the others?"

"I'll check them." Benton stood up and made a cursory inspection of the rest of the party. They lay strewn along the tunnel wherever the blast of air had flung them. Thinking again of that nightmarish rush of wind roaring through the tunnel reminded him of the possibility that their air supply might have been cut off by falling rock. He sniffed carefully. He could not detect any staleness or heaviness in the air. More than that, he was sure he could detect a faint breeze, as though a current of air were moving from the blackness at one end of the tunnel to the dark at the other end.

At least I don't have to worry about suffocation, he thought.

Food and water might be another matter.

And as for medical care... Benton turned his attention once more to the silent figures on the ground.

The guards at the end of the tunnel had caught the gust's greatest force. Sickened, Benton turned away from the pile of torn carcasses piled up there and the blood soaking into the rocks around them. By a freakish and horrible chance, the air blast had apparently picked up the two Corporation executives and ripped them along the tunnel wall near the ceiling. There were streaks of blood up there, and pieces of the two men were scattered the length of the tunnel, the elegant clothing which had set them apart from the rest of the party even underground reduced to barely recognizable tatters wrapped around unrecognizable body parts. Borrasca's idle joke about them being underfoot had turned into gruesome reality.

Other than Borrasca, none of the others was moving. Benton couldn't tell how bad their injuries were. He couldn't even tell if they were bleeding. Powdered rock covered everything, soaking up blood, disguising injuries. In the dim, confusing light, he tried to determine how badly they were injured, but he soon gave up. He had no idea what he was looking at or looking for. In the case of two of the technicians, Benton couldn't even tell if they were still breathing.

They could all have internal injuries. He had no idea what symptoms to look for. The only thing he felt sure of was that they all needed medical help, and soon.

What about Harve?

At least he was conscious, which was surely a good sign. But that tourniquet would have to be loosened regularly. Benton was pretty sure of that. Given the amount of blood he had seen on the ground underneath Borrasca's leg, Benton suspected that loosening the tourniquet would mean rapid, serious loss of blood.

Wasn't there any sort of emergency medical kit down here? He searched quickly but couldn't find one. Buried under some of the rubble from the slumped wall, perhaps, but he had no idea where to try digging, and it would be far too big a job for one man, anyway.

Benton returned to Borrasca's side and looked at him carefully.

Borrasca's eyes were closed. Even in the dim light, he looked paler. His breathing was fast, shallow, and irregular. Borrasca's condition alone was enough to convince Benton that he couldn't just sit still and wait for help to reach them. For Borrasca—and for the others—that help might come too late.

It's up to me, he thought. It's all on my shoulders.

He couldn't just wait here for rescue. That would probably mean waiting here and watching these people die. The people on the surface might not even know yet that they were in trouble, might not realize it for hours! He had to do something.

If he left this area, he'd be wandering around in pitch blackness....

He froze in terror at the thought, his heart pounding.

My helmet light isn't working, but someone else's must be, he told himself.

He steeled himself and, holding his breath to avoid breathing in the sweet stink of blood, he searched among their heaped up corpses. All the helmet lights were dead.

No separate power source, he realized. They obtained their

power from the general mine system. Broadcast somehow. However it worked, it was damaged by the accident. Stupid system. I'd never have designed it that way!

Almost hopelessly now, he kept searching. He was in luck. One of the guards had a small flash attached to his belt.

Or was this luck? If he'd been unable to find a light, he'd have had a perfect excuse not to brave the unknown tunnels.

Coward! he thought.

He tested the flash a few times, satisfying himself that it hadn't been damaged, and then he returned to Borrasca to check his condition one last time. To Benton's relief, Borrasca seemed no worse. Benton vacillated. Should he try to do anything for Harve before he set off?

As he stood there hesitating, Borrasca opened his eyes suddenly and looked up at him. He seemed to sense something of Benton's intent, for he said, "What... what're you up to, Jim?"

"I'm going to find help."

Borrasca struggled up onto one elbow. "Leave the area? No, you can't!"

Benton tried to calm him and get him to lie down again, but without success. Borrasca looked around nervously. He lowered his already weak voice and said urgently, "You *can't* go away from here. You mustn't! It's dangerous. They'll come for us. It won't take long." He paused as though trying to come up with a better argument. "You'll get lost. It's easier than you know."

Benton smiled reassuringly and spoke gently. "Don't worry about me. Look, the shaft is right on the other side of this wall. See? This must be where the opening of the crosscut was. Now, the tunnel is open on both ends, I think, because there's plenty of air moving. I'll just walk a short way until I find another connection into that shaft. Then I can just walk up to the surface and lead a rescue party back down. I'll probably be back down here in less than an hour." He stood up and started off toward the dark end of the tunnel, turning on his flash.

Behind him, he could hear Borrasca calling out weakly, "No, Jim! You'll get in trouble!"

Sudden annoyance crowded out Benton's earlier feelings of heroic self–sacrifice, and he walked away rapidly along the pathway created by the light from his flash, not slowing down until the light from the tunnel was no longer visible and he couldn't even imagine that he still heard Borrasca's voice.

Maybe Harve was right, Benton thought glumly. He was sitting in the dark, hoping against hope that his fading flash would regain its strength if he gave it a rest.

He had never liked wearing a watch. Perhaps that indicated some personality flaw. At any rate, it had deprived him of the comfort of glowing digits on the back of his hand and of the dubious satisfaction of knowing how much time had passed.

How long had he been walking? He couldn't even guess. He hadn't found another crosscut. Instead, he'd encountered a confusing series of branches and turnings. He understood the need to follow meandering veins of ore, but the ramblings of these tunnels puzzled him. What sort of randomized programming drove the machines that worked here and had cut these tunnels? To the best of his knowledge, the usual optimization for such a problem involved grids of perpendicular tunnels, like sheets of ordinary graph paper laid on top of each other.

All of which counts as much right now, he told himself, as

some metaphysical argument about the nature of good and evil.

What really mattered was that he was hopelessly lost. When he had realized that he had gone too far and had little chance of finding a way to the exit shaft, he had tried to find his way back to Borrasca and the others. It had proved impossible because of the complexity of the tunnels. He had neglected to mark his path, not even thinking he might need to retrace his steps.

Next he had tried to follow tunnels that rose, hoping that one of them might slope upwards all the way to the surface. But none he had tried had kept on rising, and he had quickly decided that their rising and falling was either random or else followed some law or logic that he couldn't determine and that would do him no good in any case. By the time he had realized that his flash was fading, he had no idea, not only where he was in relation to the group of injured people he had left behind, but even how much above or below them he might be by now. In the dim, narrow beam of light from his flash, even the slope of most stretches of tunnel was hard to determine, and for all Benton could tell, the desert floor might be one meter above his head or several thousand meters.

The dark pressed in on him.

His heart raced and he breathed in shallow gasps. He couldn't stand this any longer. He gave in and switched on the flash.

Giving its power pack a rest must have worked as he'd hoped, for the flash was brighter again. Or was that only an artifact of his eyes' adaptation to the dark?

After a few seconds, the light was definitely less bright again. He sighed and flicked it off. Perhaps he hadn't given it enough time....

The air was heavy and damp, but breathable. He argued with himself that he'd be dead by now if it weren't breathable. He had seen one of the huge fans forcing air through the mines. Even without Benton's software, the Corporation must be ensuring that air circulation was adequate. He didn't have to worry about breathing. He told himself that and tried to make his heart beat more slowly, tried to make his lungs work more regularly, tried to make the upwelling panic abate.

He closed his eyes and sat back wearily against the tunnel wall, hoping that closing his eyes would fool that primitive part of his mind and thus prevent panic.

But how would he stave off panic when the flash failed completely at last?

Benton opened his eyes and looked into the dark, this ancient enemy that he must find the courage to face. He realized that these next few hours or days would almost certainly be his last and he would have to spend them in that enemy's embrace. He sat still for long moments, wrestling with his terror, fighting to master it.

He might as well get used to the darkness. He didn't want to die with his eyes closed.

He opened his eyes and sat for a while, almost drowsing in the blackness.

Slowly he became aware of a patch of milky light glowing on the tunnel wall to his right.

Light from the outside! he thought. I've made it!

He jumped up and ran to the light, stumbling over rocks, banging against the tunnel wall and not caring.

But it was not, as he had expected, a shaft of sunlight shining through a hole in the tunnel roof and forming a patch on the wall. Instead, the patch grew only slightly brighter as he approached it, and what he found made him stop and stare in amazement.

At head height on the wall, a white, lobsterlike creature squirmed and struggled helplessly. It was at least twenty-five centimeters long, with antennae, eyes on stalks, and a pair of wicked claws that groped eagerly in the air. Its long, slender, segmented body ended in an even longer tail, which in turn ended in a globular organ that glowed steadily with the pale light that had caught Benton's attention. This lighted end of its tail was tied firmly and immovably to a projection on the wall. The animal twisted constantly, trying to reach the string that tied it to the wall. It wasn't quite flexible enough. Its claws snapped repeatedly a few centimeters short.

The light given out by the creature was very faint by normal standards. If Benton hadn't been sitting in the dark for so long, he might not have noticed it at all. Now that he knew what to look for, he could see other such patches scattered along the tunnel. Some of them wavered occasionally as the animals managed to twist themselves in front of their own light. He must have been passing these guideposts for some time, unable to see them because his flash drowned out their light.

Whatever these creatures were, it was obvious that they had been put there by humans for the use of humans.

I must be on the right track, he thought.

Benton's courage was restored. He started walking again, following the trail of the light-creatures. He put the flash in his pocket. He didn't want to lose the dark-adaptation that enabled him to see the animals.

Benton walked jauntily, cheerfully. Looking for the next light-creature, he turned a corner into a branching tunnel and came face-to-face with a group of men.

CHAPTER TWELVE

At first, he barely recognized them as human. There were about half a dozen of them, though it was hard to tell because of the faint light and because their dirty skin and clothes blended with the walls. A great deal of grimy skin was exposed. What clothing they had seemed to be barely identifiable remnants of conventional clothing used randomly as covering. One man had what looked like an old trouser leg draped over his left shoulder like a sash and was otherwise completely naked.

Benton looked them over, his mind racing. He saw that some of them carried light-creatures, their claws either lashed tightly closed or cut off. He leaped to the conclusion that these were the people who had hung the creatures on the walls. But who were they? And what were they doing here?

At the first moment, they had seemed as surprised as Benton. But their surprise faded much more quickly than his. Once it did, they seemed unhappy to see him there. They scowled, muttered among themselves, and glowered at him.

At last they came to some sort of decision. The man with the trouser leg over his shoulder came towards Benton cautiously. He raised his right hand, but it was not a gesture of peaceful intent. He held a large hammer in the raised hand.

Benton slowly drew out his flash. It was too small to be an effective weapon, but its hard, cold surface and substantial weight made him feel less defenseless.

The man said something, but Benton couldn't understand him. The language might be English, he thought, but if so, it must be some strange dialect. When Benton didn't reply, the other man raised his hammer higher and shook it threateningly, repeating what he had said before, but in a louder voice. By concentrating hard, Benton thought he could make out something like, "You're pretending to be a god!"

This made no sense at all. He must have misunderstood the man. Speaking soothingly, Benton said, "I seem to be lost. If you could help me—"

He got no further. The other man yelled something completely unintelligible and started toward him menacingly. The others crowded behind him.

Reflexively, Benton flicked on the flash, closing his eyes at the instantaneous pain from the intolerable brightness. Eyes still closed, he fumbled with the flash until he managed to turn it off again. He opened his eyes, but for long seconds he could see nothing but bright sparks floating in front of him. He felt a rising panic, expecting to be attacked while he was still blinded. He could hear voices murmuring, and he was sure it was the strange group, planning their attack.

At last the sparks faded and he began to be able to see in the faint glow of the light–creatures. The droning murmur was coming from his erstwhile attackers, but they were prostrate on the tunnel floor, saying over and over, "Sorry–sorry, sorry–sorry." The light–creatures they had been carrying lay unheeded on the ground. So did their tools, including the hammer with which Benton had been threatened. They were covering their eyes with their hands.

They're terrified, Benton thought. Of me!

The thought annoyed him. "Get up!" he said sharply. "Who are you?"

They scrambled to their feet. They looked bewildered. "We're undermen," one of them said deferentially.

Benton was finding them easier to understand, as though his ears were adjusting just as his eyes had. It was English, after all, but with an odd accent.

"You know, sir," the man said.

Another one said skeptically, "Gods know."

The fear was fading from their faces. They began to pick up their light–creatures and tools.

Tread carefully, Benton warned himself. He was in danger again. He had no idea why, but the air was thick with threat. "Why are you here?"

Now skepticism was appearing on more of their faces. The one who had answered him spoke again, but this time without deference. "To get more god–metal to send up to Heaven. Why else?"

The last words carried a definite challenge. He noticed that they kept glancing at his flash. It's not me they're terrified of, he realized. It's the flash. Or of the light. It hurts their eyes even more than it hurts mine. He clutched the flash more securely, wondering whether it would have the same effect a second time. "And where is Heaven?"

The answer came grudgingly. "The place of brightness, where you—Where the gods are." They were stirring about uneasily, muttering to themselves again. The man with the trouser leg over his shoulder had let the cloth fall off when he had prostrated himself, but now he had it back in place, like a sign of rank. He moved to the front of the group, as though to reassert his leadership.

A frightening suspicion was growing in Benton, even more frightening than the immediate threat he faced here, but it was so fantastic that he could not accept what his imagination was suggesting. He tried to speak firmly and commandingly. "Show me where Heaven is. Take me there."

They stared at him in utter amazement. Their faces filled with fear again and they began to back away. The ones at the back of the group turned about suddenly and scuttled away down the tunnel. Those in front hesitated when they saw they'd been left to face Benton alone. Then they turned and ran away as well. The leader with the trouser leg held out longest. He shook his hammer menacingly at Benton, but then he turned quickly and followed the rest.

Benton shouted after them, "Wait, you idiots! Stop!"

But it was futile. They vanished into the warren of branching and twisting tunnels. He cursed himself for having said something wrong and frightening them, but in fact he had no idea just why they had acted that way or what he should have said instead.

He put the flash back in his pocket and pondered his next move. They had dropped some of their of tools during their panic–stricken retreat. Benton idly picked a couple of them up and looked at them, holding them near a light–creature on the wall so that he could see more detail. One was actually two tools, a large hammer and chisel clipped together, as though both were far too valuable to risk their being separated. Both showed heavy wear. The other was a small pickaxe, but it looked new, hardly used.

The bizarre suspicion that had occurred to Benton earlier came to mind again, but he dismissed it and settled on an alternate explanation. This group he had encountered must be vagrants, ne'er-do-wells, the shiftless waste of Collierite society.

He couldn't remember seeing anything remotely like a slum in the towns he had been in on the planet. There must be very few wastrels on this amazingly rich world. But it was inevitable that there would be some, and apparently a few of them were skulking around down here, hiding from the need to work and their social duties. The strange things they had said didn't quite fit this theory, but he dismissed that as being due simply to his inadequate understanding of their strange dialect.

Benton wondered what they did for food and water. For that matter, he was feeling the need for both himself, and what was he going to do about that? The only reasonable option seemed to be to head off in the general direction those vagabonds had taken, in the hope that he would find either their supplies of food and water or their exit to the surface, assuming they had one.

"Undermen" they had called themselves. Yes, he thought, nodding unconsciously. That fits in with my theory. They recognize that they are at the bottom, the underneath, of their society. Thanks to their irresponsibility, that's exactly where they belong.

He was pleased at his own calmness and confidence as he set off after the undermen.

Some unknown time later, Benton was still stumbling through the tortuous maze of tunnels. Where the hell were the undermen? He had no way of knowing, and he also had no reason to think he was getting any closer to them, or indeed that he was really following them any longer. Undermen they might be, social vermin, dregs of society, but they apparently knew the layout of these tunnels, and he didn't.

He wasn't always sure he was still in the mines. From time to time he stumbled into dark places where there were no light–creatures on the walls. He sensed that those dark spaces were huge. He backed away carefully, terrified that he would be lost in there, away from the faint glow of light.

Often, even though there were light–creatures tied to the wall of a tunnel, there were also needles of rock hanging down from the ceiling and matching spires sticking up from the ground. He stopped once and watched a drop of water form slowly on the tip of a stalactite, hang there for a long time, and then finally fall onto the facing tip of the stalagmite below. Further along, the same tunnel became an impassable forest of rock columns where stalactites and stalagmites had merged and thickened with the continual deposits from the water droplets. He stood staring at the natural pillars, straining his eyes to see into the darkness past where the glow from the light–creatures ended.

How long had it taken for this to happen, he wondered? How long had this tunnel been abandoned?

Or was it not an abandoned tunnel but a natural formation? How much of all of this was really manmade?

Sometimes, despite the presence of light–creatures tied to the walls, he would find his way blocked by a rock fall and would have to turn back and try another turning. Once, he tried to make his way around a large pile of rocks that almost blocked the tunnel. He pushed his way far enough to see a human arm sticking out from under the rocks. It was mostly bones but some flesh still adhered. Light–creatures were picking at the flesh. They raised their claws threateningly at him, and he backed away quickly.

He wondered what the odds were that a slab would tear loose from the tunnel ceiling above him as he traveled and smash him to the ground. If that happened, he thought he would be lucky if the rocks killed him instantly. He hoped that the person whose arm he had glimpsed had died immediately and had not lived long enough to experience being eaten by the light–creatures.

Who had that victim been? An underman? Probably.

Poor bastard. Whatever he was doing down here, whatever kind of man he was, no one should die like that in a place like this.

But I probably will.

The realization made him stop walking. He stood, drooping, hopeless.

Shook himself. Started walking again.

And almost fell down a hole.

He jumped back, his heart hammering. Then he got down on hands and knees and crept closer.

In the dim light, he could only make out the edges of the hole. He estimated it was as wide across as he was tall. Just below the edge, everything was lost in shadows. For all he knew, it was only centimeters deep.

Cautiously, he slid his hand over the edge and down. The

side of the hole seemed to go down vertically for as far as he could reach. The air in the hole seemed cooler than the air in the tunnel, and possibly damper.

He thought he could hear a faint roaring sound coming up from the depths. Voices?

The souls of the damned, he thought. The Garden of Eden is above me and Hell is below. So where am I? In Limbo, of course.

From then on, he watched the ground carefully as he walked.

But he had to watch the ceiling at the same time. Occasionally a tunnel would narrow down, the ceiling gradually approaching the floor, until all that remained was a slit just wide enough for a man to squeeze through. Even though light–creatures were invariably tied invitingly on either side of such slits, Benton would turn away, shuddering, and seek another path. Because of the dim light, he often couldn't tell when the roof was lowering. He'd find out when he hit his head painfully against the tunnel roof. He regretted not having taken an intact helmet from one of the dead men when he first left Borrasca to look for help.

He took to walking in a bent–over, half–stooped position. At first, this made his back ache, but eventually even that faded away into numbness. Everything had become numb, even his mind.

Where was he? These must be abandoned sections of the mines. He must have been wrong about any of this being natural. The machines came in here, he told himself, cut these tunnels, extracted the ore, then moved on. Nothing useful here any more. Just some lost idiot from another planet.

Then why the light–creatures tied to the walls? That was a

mystery. He was having increasing difficulty thinking about mysteries. His mind wasn't working very well. Undermen, he thought. Whoever they are, whatever they are, they do this to give themselves light. But why do they bother? Why do they want to wander around in these areas? Because they're mad. Same reason you came to Colliery.

His hunger and thirst had grown more and more intense and then had faded. He was aware of their effects, though. He was growing steadily weaker, fading as the light from his flash had, but he was different from the flash in that a rest seemed unable to restore his strength. His physical weakness frightened him, and his increasing mental haziness frightened him even more. He slipped and fell with increasing frequency, walked into walls, a few times stumbled too close to a light–creature and received bites and cuts from its claws. Each time he fell, getting up again was harder. Sometimes he stayed on the floor and slept, usually managing no more than nightmare–filled dozing.

He came out of one such doze filled with terror from a nightmare. He jumped up and wandered down a tunnel.

His head smacked against a rock projecting from a wall. The pain was sudden and intense. He sat down, gasping, on the rocky floor. He put his hand up to his head. His hair felt greasy but also wet. He held his hand up in front of his face and stared at it. In the dim light cast by the light–creatures, he couldn't be sure what color the liquid on his palm was except that it was dark. Hesitantly, he put his tongue to it. Salty. A taste he remembered from some childhood injury. And the smell—he recognized that, too. Where was his helmet? He didn't even remember taking it off. Had he knocked it off? Put it on the ground and then forgotten about it? It was broken, he remembered. Split. I left it. That was back at the beginning.

Terror filled him again, but this time it had nothing to do with the imaginary dangers of a nightmare. It was the fuzziness that had enveloped his mind that he feared. He was forgetting everything, losing the ability to think.

Have to keep walking, he thought. Blood circulating. Make my brain work.

He forced himself to his feet again and kept walking.

He was staggering from side to side now, leaning against one wall of the tunnel and then stumbling over to the opposite wall. He feared that more than hunger was at work, that he had injured his brain with that blow against the rock.

He wavered too close to a light creature, and it bit him. This time, instead of jumping back, he reacted with the frenzy of hunger. Overcoming both his revulsion and an unconscious taboo against destroying a source of light, he grabbed the animal with both hands, tore it loose from the wall, and beat it against the floor until it stopped squirming. He ripped off its flexible shell and wolfed down the meat, even while he gagged at its bitterness and stringy texture.

For a few minutes, it helped. He started walking again, feeling stronger. Then the nausea struck.

Within seconds, he was lying on his stomach retching violently, throwing up the creature's flesh and whatever else remained in his stomach. After that he lay in the grip of a brief but violent fever, shivering violently and dreaming that he was helpless on the snows of the ice–cap, naked, freezing to death with no way to summon help.

When that faded at last, he felt far too weak to stand up and go on. He wanted only to stay there and die and thereby escape all this by the only route he now seemed likely to find.

He thought he remembered that during his fever he had heard voices in the distance, the faint sound of words, and even the shuffling of feet along the dirt of the tunnel floor. But perhaps none of that had been real, just a figment of his delirium. Or perhaps the words had been real, but it had been his own voice, mumbling in the depths of fever.

What if it wasn't just an artifact of delirium? Then he might be near rescue, so near, but if he surrendered and stayed here, they would never find him. Fate would have used him as it wished for its own purposes.

Benton struggled to his feet with a groan. He tottered over to the wall and leaned against it, his legs trembling. He breathed deeply and gritted his teeth, willing his knees not to give way. He noticed some remaining pieces of the light–creature's body, faintly lit by the bulb at the end of its tail. The light had started fading as soon as he killed the creature, and now it was almost gone. And it all served no purpose, he thought regretfully. I'm sorry.

His left cheekbone, where he had hit the floor, began to itch suddenly, and he put his hand up to scratch it. To his amazement, he touched hair. He ran his hands over his face quickly. His beard had grown out enough that the hair felt soft instead of prickly. He tried to estimate the passage of time from this. He remembered that on the morning of the underground inspection, he had thought himself in need of a shave, but he had woken up late and so had decided not to bother. Even so, his beard had always grown slowly, so surely it would have required three or four days to reach this stage. Maybe even a week. Was it possible he'd been wandering here for that long?

He forced himself to move on. He had no idea which way to go, but his weakness led him to choose pathways which tended downward. He knew that he should be trying to move upward instead until he reached the surface. Magically reached the surface, he corrected himself. Magic, yes. By now it seemed to him that it would require magic for him to leave these tunnels. A perverse part of him wondered if the upper world even existed, if he had imagined it, if he had always been down here, dreaming of some magical fairyland up above.

He shrugged that irrationality off and told himself that it was important to be moving, covering ground, even though it might be slowly, centimeter by centimeter. At least he was doing something concrete about his situation, making some sort of progress.

His greatest fear was that he would run out of strength or lose consciousness. His second greatest fear was that he would run out light, that the trails marked by the light–creatures would end. Why, after all, should that strange band of vagabonds have marked so many kilometers of tunnels with animals? But he found that the spaces between the light–creatures decreased as he went lower, so that there were more of them all the time. He also occasionally came across some of them crawling free on the ground. He assumed these had somehow managed to wriggle themselves free from the walls. He became aware, too, of a definite increase in the mugginess of the air and of a continuous roaring sound, steadily increasing in volume as he walked.

When he first noticed the sound, he feared it was another terrible gust of air, and he braced himself hopelessly for its impact. When that didn't come, he decided that it must be the sound of a fan and that, by going down, he had nonetheless reached the surface. But he could tell that the movement of air past him had not increased with the sound, so he had to dismiss even that idea.

The tunnel he was walking in, with light-creatures so thick on the ground by now that he had to step carefully around and over them, came to an end. It opened out suddenly into some sort of cavern, filled with the roar he had been hearing for the last hour or two, and echoing deafeningly with its reverberations from distant walls. In the dark, he couldn't tell how large the cavern was, but from the echoes he judged it to be very large.

Near him, the ground was covered by light-creatures, and by their light the surface showed as grainy white sand. Further away, there were more clumps of the creatures. Overcoming a feeling of horror at the presence of so many of them, stepping carefully, he walked slowly into the cavern. As he came closer to one of the large groups of creatures, he could see by their light that they stood at the edge of a body of water, its surface constantly agitated by ripples. Could he possibly be on the surface of Colliery? Surely the darkness overhead was the pitch black of the underground, not the desert night. Even if it were cloudy—unusual enough in the desert—the air of the desert at night had a biting coldness instead of this clammy warmth.

Even at the risk of temporarily blinding himself again, Benton had to know where he was. He took out his flash and pointed it away from him in what was, he hoped, roughly the direction of the center of the cavern, if it was a cavern. Bracing himself, he squeezed his eyes almost closed and flicked on the flash. The light that came out wasn't much brighter than that of the light–creatures. Benton opened his eyes fully with a feeling of relief. Unconsciously, he realized, he had come to think of bright light as a dangerous enemy.

The beam was fading already. The flash must be within seconds of dying completely and forever. At least it was a focused beam and penetrated for some distance. He aimed it in different directions, trying to form a mental picture of his surroundings in the short time remaining before the flash gave out. By the time it finally did fade, he was so astonished by what he had seen that he slid the flash back into his pocket unconsciously, unaware of what he was doing.

He was indeed in a cavern, one so immense that he couldn't see the further walls. The beam of the flash had been unable to reach that far. The cavern seemed to be filled with a vast underground lake or sea. Far away along one of the walls, he had been barely able to see a great waterfall, shooting out of the wall and falling half a kilometer down to the sea. That was the source of the steady, overwhelming roar. The ripples from its impact on the body of water below spread everywhere steadily, lapping on the shore near him like waves.

It all became too much for him to bear. To have seemingly found the Garden of Eden, to then find that garden as much flawed by human failings as any other place, to be lost in a terrifying maze beneath the garden, and then finally to end up at this hidden underground sea, this huge, alien, uncaring body of water—all this overwhelmed him with a sense of total defeat and utter loss of his humanness and his individuality. He was small, insignificant, helpless. Fate would use him as it wished. He was powerless against it.

He lay down and stretched out on the sand, surrendering. Time passed without change, and Benton drifted into a deep and dreamless sleep.

CHAPTER THIRTEEN

Benton woke suddenly to dozens of nibblings and pinches all over his body and the feeling that things were crawling on him. Milky light filled his eyes. All at once he realized that it was the light–creatures. They had discovered his presence and were testing him carefully to see whether he was edible. With a shout of horror, he sprang up and shook the animals off, batting madly at the more determined ones and shouting again and again.

Trembling, he backed away from the jumble of animals on the sand. They crawled over each other aimlessly, struggling and snapping at each other. His legs gave way, and he sat down heavily on the sand. He stared at the creatures in fascinated horror.

Despite their eyes, they were almost blind. Certainly they seemed unable to sense him directly now that he was a few meters distant from them. Probably one of them had found him by accident while he slept and had somehow summoned the others. As long as he stayed reasonably alert, he should have little trouble avoiding them.

How long can you go without sleep, he asked himself.

He sighed in defeat. If he couldn't find food and water soon, sleep wouldn't be a problem.

Food, rather. Water was abundant, assuming the lake was clear water, not salt. He made his way to the water's edge, carefully skirting some groups of light-creatures and guided by the faint, gentle lapping sound he could just make out underneath the waterfall's constant roar.

The water was as warm as the steamy air in the cavern. When he lowered his hand into it, he couldn't tell when his hand penetrated the surface. He raised a handful of water cautiously to his lips and sipped. It had a strange tang. It must have a great many kinds of strange local minerals dissolved in it, he realized. The odd taste was faint enough that he thought he could learn to tolerate it. His caution vanished and he gulped mouthfuls of the water, stopping only when his stomach began to ache and he realized he might be wise to go more slowly.

He sat quietly for a while, monitoring himself. Nothing strange seemed to be happening. He decided he could assume the water wasn't poisonous, or at least not immediately. It might well have substances in it that would kill him in time, but he refused to sit here beside this immense body of seemingly drinkable water and die of thirst because he was afraid to drink. He refused to die of fear.

So the question of which lack would kill him first had apparently been answered. It would be food, rather than water or air.

Idly he watched one of the light-creatures approach the water near to where he sat. It stopped when its front feet felt the water, then it slowly extended its tail far forward over its body and minuscule head until the light-emitting globe at the tip of its tall touched the surface of the water. It pushed the globe gently into the water and let it float there, just below the surface, bobbing up and down on the wavelets. The animal froze in that position.

Too bad you repulsive beasts aren't edible, Benton thought resentfully, watching it. You're so easy to catch.

His gaze drifted to the other spots of white further along the water's edge, continuing in both directions until they were lost in the distance. Other light-creatures doing the same thing this one? Why?

A sudden splash startled him. He looked toward the sound and saw the light-creature he had been watching before scuttling backwards from the water. Its claws were held high in triumph, clutching by the neck a plump, white, snakelike animal almost as long as the light-creature itself. The snake wriggled desperately, trying to free itself, but the light-creature crawled to a space clear of its fellows and, ignoring its victim's struggles, began tearing chunks of snake flesh free with its claws and stuffing them into its mouth. It ate everything, even the snake's slender bones, and when it was done and not a trace of the snake was left, the light-creature, bloated and somehow giving the impression that it was well content, crawled slowly away to the cavern wall and settled down upon the sand. It seemed to go to sleep.

Well, I'll be damned, Benton thought. I should have realized the creatures would have to have some outside food source. They can't survive by eating each other

For whatever reason, the snakes were attracted to the lights on the end of the light-creatures' tails, and the light-creatures therefore used their lights as lures. He should have realized that the lights had some such function. Why else would the virtually blind creatures have evolved them?

Benton's intellectual interest was aroused. For the moment, his mind became alert as he thought about what he had seen.

There were so many light-creatures that there must be a great number of snakes out there in the water. So what was *their* food source? It couldn't be plant life, surely, not underground with no sunlight. Fungi, perhaps. Mushrooms. Could those grow in sufficient quantity to support that much animal life? The roaring of the waterfall, which he had already learned to ignore, to push into the background, now caught his attention again. Could it be that the water came from the surface, carrying with it plants and small water animals? But then, for the two life forms here to have increased so much in number with that outside source as the basis for their food chain, the outside source must have been available to them for a long time. Centuries? Thousands of years? Millions?

He felt frustrated by his own ignorance. If only he'd spent some time reading books on biology and evolution, instead of concentrating so much on computers and their languages and architecture!

The problems kept nagging at him. Surely the only source of this waterfall could be the ice caps and the life-bands. In fact, if the melt from the ice caps was constantly flowing into the life-bands, as must be the case, and then flowing generally across the life-bands, as he believed to be true, it must eventually end up in the desert. A lot of the water in the life-bands probably evaporated, though, forming clouds and then falling back onto the life-bands as rain. Then he remembered that the prevailing winds during the day tended to flow from the poles toward the desert, so the clouds would tend to move that way as well. In any case, a tremendous amount of water must be moving from the polar caps into the desert. A lot of that must be sinking down to this level.

There wouldn't be much evaporation down here. That was probably why the lake water wasn't salty and heavily mineral-laden. That must mean that the water in the lake was draining away further into underground aquifers or other caverns, other lakes like this one. Otherwise, the water would be rising steadily. Eventually it would have to rise, though, wouldn't it? Underground storage wasn't unlimited. Was this lake rising? He had no way of telling.

That's all very fascinating, Professor, he told himself. Food for thought. Now, what about the even more fascinating problem of food for the stomach?

The snakes, of course. He had to face that fact. They might be as inedible as the light-creatures, or even more so. Still, it was worth a try if only because he could think of no alternative beside starvation.

How to go about it? The only way would be to fish as the light-creatures did. Since his flash was definitely dead—and would probably be too bright for this purpose even if it were still alive—that seemed to mean he'd have to borrow one of the light-creatures' tails.

Benton glanced over at the sleeping light-creature he had watched catch the snake. The animal was still sunk in a torpor and would probably be an easy target. But Benton felt a debt of gratitude to the creature for having shown him a possible way to survive, and he decided that it wouldn't be proper to kill that particular one. Honor among troglodytes, he told himself.

Now that he knew what to look for, he could see other torpid light-creatures, swollen from recent meals snatched from the lake. He found a loose rock, crept up on one, and smashed its head. By now, he was so weak that even that effort left him trembling. Perhaps it was really a reaction of a different sort, but he decided not to spend any time or energy dwelling on it.

He returned to the water and held the dead light–creature so that its tail dangled in the water, the bulb floating on the waves, as he had seen it done before. After only a few seconds, there was a sudden splash and he glimpsed a fat body darting along the surface at the light. He grabbed at it and missed, and it swam quickly away in alarm.

Steady, he told himself grimly. You don't have a few eons to evolve this ability. Either you get one of these things, or you starve.

Another snake swam up rapidly. Benton lunged and missed again This time the snake grabbed the tail before Benton could snatch it away, and the whole body of the dead light–creature was snatched from his hand and disappeared into the water.

He killed another light–creature and set himself once again to the task of trying to catch some food. He missed once more, although he was careful this time to yank the tail out of the water before the snake could get it.

The fourth time, he succeeded. He rose to his feet with a snake wriggling furiously in his hand and snapping madly at his wrist. Fortunately he had managed to grab it by the neck, following the light–creature's example. The snake had a large mouth filled with rows of long teeth, and he could guess that a bite from this animal would be genuinely dangerous.

He carried the snake over to the cavern wall and, using the light of his dead light–creature as convenient illumination, smashed the snake's head against the wall until it stopped squirming. Then he sat down with it and prepared to eat.

The snake's body was fat and flexible, and the skin was slippery with water and fluids from the smashed head. More like a giant slug than a snake, he thought, his hunger fading and his stomach churning.

This is a hell of a time to turn finicky, he told himself. He reminded himself of the many stories he'd read of underfed prisoners on various worlds staying alive only because they were willing to pounce on and eat whatever life form wandered into their cells, most of it the sort of thing they would never have eaten in their former lives, not to mention that they had to eat it raw. Manfully, he raised the snake's body to his mouth and bit off a chunk.

Even raw, the meat was tender and flavorful, not unlike the flesh of a certain large bird he had eaten in an expensive restaurant on Farandhazy not long before leaving for Colliery. That bird had been cooked slowly for hours in expensive wines and exotic spices, and the dish had cost him almost a day's pay. He had considered it worth it. Every bite had been heaven. But this—why, even raw this strange, repulsive-looking animal tasted better than that. He looked at his dead light-creature with new respect. "You guys have pretty good taste," he told it, "despite the way you taste."

He wolfed down the rest of the snake, all but the head. The bones were soft and easily chewed.

The meal, despite or perhaps because of his long time without food, left him feeling stuffed. He sat for a long time, letting the effect fade, and then he returned to the water's edge and managed to catch another snake. After eating that one, he felt fully satisfied and even invigorated, although he suspected that feeling would prove to be temporary and he would need a long, restful, well–fed period to recover properly from his days of starvation.

Every time he sat down, he had difficulty finding a completely comfortable position because of the flash in his pocket.

Silly to hold onto it, he thought. Especially since it's dead.

He walked back to the water and heaved the flash as far out into the darkness as he could. As it fell towards the water, the flash came weakly back to life for one last moment, a dim, yellow star sliding down toward the water. The flash rotated slowly. A meter or two above the water, it turned so that it was pointing straight down, reflecting faintly from the dark ripples on the surface. A monstrous shape broke the surface, rose seemingly lazily into the air, and swallowed the flash. With the light cut off, Benton could no longer see whatever it was, but he could hear the great splash it made even over the waterfall's roar. He had had only a glimpse, but he thought the giant head he had seen looked like the head of one of the snake creatures, but fifty times larger. He sat down shakily. So much for going for a swim.

But there was something more, something in the background. He couldn't be sure he had really seen it in that briefest instant.

He had glimpsed the waterfall. Dropping down through it had been a human figure, arms and legs still moving. Something even larger than the monster that had swallowed his flash had been rising up from the water toward that figure, something with a huge mouth gaping open, filled with teeth.

How shallow was the water close to shore? He had to

assume those immense creatures couldn't get close enough to the edge to attack him. He had to assume that because if he assumed otherwise, he'd never eat or drink again.

He had to assume that he had imagined the human figure, or if he had really seen one, that it was a dead body, the limbs being moved by the waterfall. If he didn't assume all of that, he thought he might go mad.

If he stayed out of the water, going only to the edge to drink and catch his food, he could survive here indefinitely. There was no lack of food, water, or air. The only lack, the only reason why indefinite survival down here would not be survival at all, was lack of human company and, far worse, lack of any hope of escape.

He slept and ate and spent long hours staring into the gloom. He had no idea how much time was passing. He was changing, he thought, from a refugee in the cave to a resident of it.

Of course, he didn't have to stay here. He could try once more to find the surface. In a brief exploration, he had found other tunnel exits along the cavern walls. But the thought of entering one of them terrified him. Here he had security, food and water, warmth and safety. The giant cavern was a womb, despite the roar of the waterfall and the danger hiding in the lake.

Sometimes he felt he'd never leave here, that he'd stay here until he died of old age.

CHAPTER FOURTEEN

Benton's stubble had become a beard. The hair on his head was long and lay lank and greasy on his neck. His clothes were torn almost to shreds from his many falls and collisions with tunnel walls, and those shreds were caked with mud. His flimsy shoes had disintegrated long ago, and his feet were filthier than any feet he could remember having seen before in his life. He realized with some distress that he must look much like the members of the band of vagrants he had encountered.

Those vagrants...

He had had a great deal of time to think about that group of men and their presence underground. Indeed, he had had little else to do than think about such things, except for getting food and drink and finding new places where he could sleep without being bothered by the light-creatures. Those tools the vagrants, the undermen, had carried—surely those implied something about what the group of men really were. He knew what it implied, but it struck him as simply too monstrous an idea to accept. It would mean that all the Collierites he had met on the surface, all those pleasant, simple, naïve young people, were astonishingly evil, devils disguised as angels.

But there were those tools, and the vagrants' very presence, and their calling themselves undermen, and the light–creatures tied to the walls, and Galena's concern about a new opening to the surface from the tunnels, and The Jacksonite Corporation's reluctance to let an outsider go underground, and the giant fan that he somehow thought was never turned off... There were all these things, and they kept leading him, inexorably and however unwillingly to the horrifying conclusion that the jacksonite mines of Colliery, far from being the most advanced mines in the Galaxy, were in fact the most primitive—more primitive than mines anywhere else had been since the post–Imperial Dark Ages.

He was sitting down, leaning back as comfortably as he could against a large rock and eating a snake, when he saw a movement near the cavern wall.

He stopped moving and stared, waiting for whatever it was to take shape. Details were hard to make out in the dimness, but he became convinced that he was looking at a human figure standing at a tunnel exit, faintly lit by a group of the light–creatures on the sand in front of it.

He put the snake down and began to move slowly and silently toward whatever it was. He held his breath, afraid that his breathing might be audible despite the constant roar of the waterfall. He lifted his feet carefully and put them down just as carefully, trying not even to create a whisper of disturbed sand. He feared that what he had seen wasn't real and would turn out to be a play of shadows when he reached it. He feared that it was real and would run away if it saw him.

It was real and it didn't run.

As he drew nearer, it resolved into a woman of late middle

age, with filthy grey hair and a tired, defeated face. Her clothes were as reduced to tatters as his own, and the skin that showed was even grimier than his. Benton saw that she was efficiently picking up light-creatures, grasping them high up on their back, just behind the joint where the claws were connected, so they couldn't bite her, and quickly snipping off their claws with a tool she held ready in her other hand. Then she tied a string around their tails and tied the other end of the string around a large metal ring lying nearby in the sand. She kept one foot on the ring so that the growing number of light-creatures tied to it couldn't drag it away.

Benton stood watching her for a while. When he'd first come up, she'd glanced at him quickly, a sharp, up-and-down look, and then she'd returned to her work. After waiting for some time for her to take notice of him again, Benton cleared his throat and said, feeling inane, "Uh, pardon me, ma'am, I'm—"

"Newcomer."

"What?"

"Newcomer. You're a newcomer." Her voice was rough and harsh and seemed even older than the rest of her. She worked steadily while she spoke, not stopping for a moment. "They're rare, but I can always tell them because I was one." She spoke a more recognizable form of English than the undermen did. She had an accent of some kind, but other than that her English was the standard variety spoken everywhere, whether on the surface of Colliery, on Farandhazy, or on Earth itself.

"Yes, I guess I am a newcomer. I need help."

"Sure. Don't we all." By now, the metal ring was heavily loaded with light-creatures. The woman heaved the ring up and put her left arm through it, so that it rested on her shoulder.

Benton was astonished. Even a single light-creature was heavy, and that ring loaded with them must have weighed considerably more than Benton could have managed. She turned and trudged toward the tunnel. "Come on, Newcomer," she called back. "I'll take you to the Big House and get you assigned."

Benton looked after her, and then he looked back at the glowing spots along the softly lapping water's edge.

Leave? Leave his home?

Terror touched him momentarily. The woman had not waited for him, and when he looked in her direction again, she had vanished. The tunnel's mouth still glowed with the light of the bundle of light-creatures she carried, but the glow was fading as she continued up the tunnel. With sudden resolve, he ran into the tunnel entrance and caught up with her.

He walked beside her for a while, waiting to speak until he had regained some measure of calmness and could speak in a level tone. He watched while she stopped occasionally and tied one of her captives to the tunnel wall to replace one that had died and whose light had subsequently faded too much to be useful. He decided that the light-creatures must regenerate their lost claws quickly while they hung on the walls, even without any food. "Why don't you feed them?" he asked her suddenly while watching her at work. "Instead of continually replacing them."

"No reason to bother," she said with a shrug. "With so many of them back there it's easier to just get new ones." She picked up her ring of light-creatures again and began to trudge along the tunnel once more. "We don't have enough food to spare, and no one wants to try to catch lots of those snakes just to feed them. Anyway, mainly I do it because I'm told to. You'd better learn right away to do the job you're told to and nothing else. That's the way it is down here, not at all like up there in Heaven."

She lapsed into silence and seemed likely to remain silent until they reached their destination—the Big house she had mentioned. The name aroused a faint hope in Benton that the place was on the surface, although what she'd said about "down here" as opposed to "up there in Heaven" made him doubt it.

His mind was a jumble of questions. He had the feeling he shouldn't press her, that he should tread carefully. But after having been without the sound of a human voice for so long, Benton couldn't stand the silence now. After a while he broke it by saying, "My name's James Benton."

She stopped walking and stared at him in surprise. Then her face crinkled slowly into a smile. There were gaps where teeth were missing, something Benton had never seen before in his life. "How do you do, Mr. Benton?" she said, her English growing even purer and her voice losing some of its harsh roughness. "I'm Marguerite Borrasca."

He stared back at her. Surely there was no connection! But Borrasca was such an uncommon name. "I, uh, met someone named Borrasca on the surface," he said tentatively. "Harve Borrasca."

Her face changed at the name. The smile disappeared and was replaced by hatred.

"What's the matter?"

"You his friend?" Her voice and accent had deteriorated again, as though she no longer wished to make whatever effort she had been making.

"Well, I thought he was my friend, but now that I'm down

here, I'm not so sure."

"Yeah." She nodded and started walking again. "I used to think he was my son, but now I'm not so sure either. He was a good baby, but he turned mean. Later on, when he turned his father and me in and they put us down here, I decided that my real baby was stolen at the hospital and that thing was left instead."

Benton was too amazed and horrified to say anything, and they trudged on in silence. Finally, he said, "Does your husband do the same work you do? Or did they assign him to something else?"

There was a long pause, during which Marguerite Borrasca replaced another worn-out light-creature. "My husband," she said finally, "was a rebel down here, too. The Headman had him killed."

"That's terrible! I'm sorry."

"I'm not. He was a fool. If it wasn't for him and his son, I'd still be living the good life in Heaven." Her face set in a way that indicated she preferred silence, and it was in silence that they trudged the rest of the way through many twists and turns, stopping only occasionally for Marguerite to do her job with the light-creatures, until they finally reached the Big House.

CHAPTER FIFTEEN

The Big house should have been called the Big Cave. They emerged into it from a tunnel. Marguerite said, "This is it," with a hint of pride in her voice.

Benton's first thought was, So much for being on the surface. But then he looked around and was impressed despite himself.

The cave was large compared to the tunnels, though not when compared to the great cavern enclosing the underground lake. However, it could all be seen, for light-creatures had been tied to the walls everywhere and even along the ceiling. How that had been accomplished, Benton could not even guess, for the ceiling was many meters above his head. People scurried about the cave busily on mysterious errands. This was more people than Benton had seen at one time since leaving the surface. "Who are they all?" he asked. He lowered his voice conspiratorially without realizing he was doing so.

Marguerite said scornfully, "Undermen, all of them. I'm one of the very few who aren't. And you, now. And the Recorder, of course. You'll meet him." Her face contorted with hatred again.

Dim though each individual light-creature's light was, there were so many of them spread throughout the cavern that the great space was relatively well lighted—relative to the tunnels, at any rate. There were ledges running along some of the walls, and other tunnel entrances at various levels. There were holes all over the roof, which Benton realized could also be tunnel entrances. He noticed a pile of stones in the middle of the cave. There were irregular holes in the pile from which still more light glowed. "So much light," Benton muttered in amazement.

"Reminds you of Heaven, doesn't it?" Marguerite said sarcastically. "The Headman wants lots of light here in the Big House and in his own place. That's first priority. Doesn't matter so much about the hands, if they don't have enough light and get killed because the luxes had to be put in the Big House first. No," she shook her head, "doesn't matter to the Headman at all. Less mouths to feed, he says. Less production, too, of course, but all that fool cares about is if there's food and light for him. And for the Recorder, of course." She stopped abruptly, as if deciding she had already said too much. "I've got to distribute these luxes." She waved her free arm and called out loudly, "Thompson!"

A figure rose from the ground in front of the pile of stones and trotted over to them. It was a man, dressed in the seemingly universal tatters and odds and ends of clothing and covered with the inevitable dirt of his strange homeland. Looking at the man and woman as they stood facing each other, Benton realized that they also had in common extreme leanness, almost to the point of emaciation.

"What's up?" the man growled. "And why aren't you both at work?" His accent reminded Benton of that of the group of undermen he had encountered first, seemingly so long ago.

Marguerite raised her hand defensively, as though to ward off an anticipated blow. "He's a newcomer, Thompson," she said quickly. Her posture was submissive and her voice had a whine to it. "I found him down at Lux Lake."

Thompson looked at Benton suspiciously. "Lux Lake! How'd a newcomer get that far?"

"Maybe he came through a no–man's–land."

"Maybe." Thompson still looked suspicious, but he apparently decided to accept the explanation. "Okay, I'll take him to the Headman. You get back to work."

Marguerite returned to the tunnel and disappeared down it. Thompson beckoned to Benton to follow him and he set off back toward the pile of rocks.

As they approached the pile, Benton saw that it was actually a wall, reaching above his head and with a door and windows. These were the holes he had seen from a distance, and they still slowed with light. "What is this?" he asked Thompson.

"Headman's place. Shut up."

Thompson headed for the door but was stopped by a taller, much heavier man who stepped from the doorway and put his hand flat on Thompson's chest. "Where you going?" he barked at the smaller man.

Thompson stepped backward a couple of paces. "Listen, Carnot, I gotta take this newcomer to the Headman."

Carnot shook his head. "Forget it. You stay out here and I'll take the newcomer in."

"But he's mine!" Thompson whined. "I want to do it!"

Carnot stepped forward and slapped Thompson almost casually. It was only a slap, but the two men were so different in weight, and Thompson in particular was so thin and weak, that the smaller man was flung backward and lay for a second on the ground, dazed, before he was able to get slowly to his feet.

"Sorry–sorry, Carnot" he mumbled. "Sorry–sorry."

"I know what you wanted to get in there for," Carnot growled at him. "You wanted to steal some more food, like you did last time. You keep this up, and the Headman'll break you back to hand."

Thompson slouched off to his former position in front of the wall and sat down on a large rock, still mumbling, "Sorry–sorry."

Carnot gestured through the doorway with his thumb and said, "Get inside, Newcomer."

Benton looked the other man up and down quickly and decided not to argue. At this point, he told himself, rationalizing with considerable ease, it was more important to find out how this underground society worked than it was to stand up for his rights and dignity. There'd be time for that later, he assured himself.

Inside, Benton discovered that the wall was one of four, so that the "Headman's place" was actually a fairly large room built within the Big House. There was no roof, which first startled him, until he realized that that was only sensible in an entirely enclosed cavern. Also, that admitted the light from the light-creatures on the ceiling and high on the walls of the cavern.

Luxes, he corrected himself. That seems to be the local name for them.

In addition to this light, many more luxes were tied to the walls inside the room. He had time for a quick glance to right and left, which gave him time to notice guards, also large and broad and lacking the signs of malnutrition he had seen in both Thompson and Marguerite Borrasca. The guards stood at the windows of the room, looking out, keeping watch on the cavern.

Before Benton could examine things any more carefully, Carnot shoved him forward impatiently.

In the middle of the room there was a large boulder, perhaps two meters across and a meter and a half high. The top of this had been painstakingly chiseled flat. A man sat next to it, using another similar but much smaller boulder as his chair and the larger one as a table. He was eating greedily from a pile of something on his primitive table.

The Headman, Benton guessed.

This was the plumpest individual Benton had yet seen underground. Not fat, though. It occurred to Benton that if this society were the primitive dictatorship it appeared to be, the Headman might need to retain his health and strength in order to retain his rule.

Wonderful, Benton thought. I'm back in barbarian times.

The Headman glanced at him and then went back to his food. He concentrated his attention on his food fully, eating steadily, determinedly. Watching him eat, Benton felt overwhelmed with hunger. Most of the pile of food was unrecognizable, but some of it looked like large pieces of meat. Even from his position a few meters away, Benton could smell it. His mouth watered. Raw snake had seemed heavenly when he was starving, but now the smell of cooked meat was maddening.

Almost maddening. Benton already knew or sensed enough about this society to say and do nothing.

He and Carnot stood quietly, watching as the Headman ate his way through the enormous pile of food. When he had had enough, he shoved the remnants—also substantial—aside and motioned to the guards at the windows, who dashed forward and began quarreling over the leftovers. Now the Headman gestured Carnot and Benton to come forward.

Carnot pushed Benton ahead of him. They stopped close to the Headman, who seemed even more enormous from close up.

More than two meters tall, Benton estimated. And solid as a rock, except around the middle. By the Headman's side, an enormous hammer leaned against the table. There were stains on its head that looked uncomfortably like dried blood. For the first time, Benton began to really understand that he faced a power as absolute in this little sphere as The Jacksonite Corporation was in its own realm.

Carnot stepped past Benton and said, "Newcomer, Boss. Marguerite brought him in, and Thompson brought him over here."

The Headman looked shrewdly into Benton's eyes, and Benton received the impression of a brute power that made up for lack of real intelligence with an awesome degree of cunning. The Headman's face was heavy and scarred, and he still chewed slowly, finishing the last shreds of his huge meal. It occurred to Benton that he seemed to keep encountering the same man in different guises, even hidden behind the façade of a corporate entity, no matter where he went: the brute who rules the Galaxy.

Belying his appearance, the Headman's voice was of moderate pitch and mild. "What's your name, Newcomer?"

"What's yours?" Benton shot back, mentally congratulating himself on his quick wit.

Something slammed into his back, and he found himself lying on the ground. A voice from behind said eagerly, "Want me to kill him, Boss?"

The Headman gestured in impatience. "No, you fool. Newcomers have information. Get up, you." When Benton was once more on his feet, weaving a bit, the Headman said, still speaking mildly, "Now, what's your name?"

"James Benton. Sir."

The Headman smiled and leaned back slightly. He put his hammer down. Benton hadn't even been aware of him picking it up. That blow from behind, impulsively administered by a murderous guard, had probably saved his life by making the Headman hesitate with his hammer.

"Now you've got the idea," the Headman said. "You're in my village now. Only you call me 'Boss,' not 'sir.' Okay. Tell me what the latest news is from the Corporation. What are they planning for us?"

Confused, Benton said, "I'm afraid I don't know anything about the Corporation's plans. I don't even work for them. I'm only down here by accident, and I'm trying to get back out."

The Headman burst into loud laughter, and all the guards along the wall and those still stuffing in food at the table duly followed suit. "I've heard that one before," the Headman said. "That's what the Recorder and his wife both said when they came here. Okay," he said, growing dangerously serious again, "if you don't work for them, then who do you work for?"

Benton tried to explain about Contco and its contract and his mission on Colliery, but he quickly got the impression that it was all above his listeners' heads. All but one detail.

"You say you're from off-planet, Benton?" the Headman asked, frowning.

Had that been the wrong thing to say? "Yes, that's right, boss."

The Headman grunted. "Then he really doesn't know anything. Off-planet, just like the Recorder. Take him to the

Recorder and have him assigned to something." He lost interest in Benton and his attention wandered to something else.

Carnot grabbed Benton's shoulder, spun him about, and shoved him toward the door. Guided only by shoves and pokes and an occasional barked command, Benton left the Headman's place, walked toward one of the cavern walls, and climbed slowly up a long, broad ramp that traveled at a shallow angle a third of the way around the cavern's perimeter. At the top of the ramp, he and his guard entered another tunnel, a short one that ended in a cluster of small caves, reminding Benton of a suite of rooms at the end of a hotel corridor. It was all as well lit by captive luxes as the great cavern below.

Benton was pushed into the cave directly at the end of the tunnel. To his amazement, he saw stacks of what looked much like paper. In the middle of the cave, surrounded by such stacks, a man was sitting at a chair and table arrangement much like the Headman's, but smaller, and writing carefully.

"Recorder," Carnot said brusquely. "Got a newcomer here. Headman wants him assigned."

The Recorder waved his hand in a vague dismissal, and Carnot turned and left the cave.

A few moments went by while the Recorder continued to write laboriously. At last he looked up at Benton. "Just a moment." He hunted around for a clean sheet of paper. Benton had the disturbing feeling that he had seen this man before, although without the beard and grubbiness. "All right, now," the Recorder said, spreading a clean sheet of paper carefully in front of him. "Your name?"

Benton sighed wearily. "James Benton."

The Recorder scribbled. "Corporate division?"

"No Corporate division. I'm not even from Colliery."

The Recorder looked up, his mouth open in amazement. "Not from Colliery! How wonderful! Some real company for a change! My wife will be delighted. Never mind your assignment. I'll think of something. I know, I'll make you my assistant."

"Thank you, Recorder," Benton said, intending it to sound sarcastic.

The Recorder jumped up. "Never mind that, my dear fellow. And please don't use that silly title." He stepped forward, his right hand outstretched. "Allow me to introduce myself properly. I am Dr. Benjamin Franklin Coquina. 'Ben' to my friends and relatives."

And Uncle Ben to your niece, Benton thought numbly, automatically holding out his own hand.

CHAPTER SIXTEEN

Coquina took him into a small adjacent cave, one of the cluster Benton had noticed when he was brought to Coquina's cave–office.

"This one is empty," Coquina said. "I'm assigning it to you. I know it lacks the conveniences we were all used to before our, er, fall from grace, but I'm afraid it's the best your new life can offer." He looked Benton over judiciously. "I'll see what can be done in the way of clothing. And I'll have a bowl of water sent up to you so you can refresh yourself. Unfortunately, there are no shavers down here, so you won't be able to shave. Fortunately," he stroked his own face lightly, "one does get accustomed to wearing a long and steadily growing beard. Now I must go to tell my wife the pleasant news. We've just received a food shipment, so there's still meat available. I hope you can join us for supper?"

"My evening seems to be free." Benton wondered how long it would take before he started acting like Coquina.

"Wonderful! May I call you 'Jim'?"

"Please do, Ben."

Beaming, Coquina waddled out.

God, Benton thought, the man's positively fat. Relatively clean, too. Starving serfs, well fed but dirty and brutal masters, and overly well fed, clean scribes. It's like some kind of historical melodrama. Charlie Gabbro always liked those. He should be here instead of me. I wish he were.

Shortly afterwards, a young girl arrived with a metal bowl full of water. She had clothing draped over one arm. Fear was apparent in her movements. She set the bowl and the clothes on the ground, glanced at Benton, then lowered her eyes quickly and fearfully to the ground again. She was as emaciated and dirty as Marguerite Borrasca, and Benton guessed that she'd look as old before long.

When she didn't move, he said, "Thank you very much. Just what I needed."

She looked up at him with sudden hope. "You mean I can leave, sir?"

"Sure. Of course."

"Oh, *thank* you, sir!" She flashed a quick smile at him and darted from the cave.

What the hell?

And then he understood. Now that he was associated with the Recorder, he had become a part of the ruling elite, and he therefore had the right to demand of the girl whatever he might wish.

I don't want to be part of this, he thought.

But he knew he had no choice.

He was filled with resentment against Coquina as the representative of this barbaric little society. Maybe he wouldn't wash after all—just show up dirty and in his ragged clothes and spoil Coquina's pretensions to civilization.

Then he remembered the picture sent him by Augie Syen and the dazzlingly beautiful young blonde woman in the picture with Coquina, and he changed his mind.

He spent some time rubbing off as much of the caked dirt that covered him as he could. Without soap or sonics, there was a limit to what he could do, but at least he felt better for having been able to make even a small improvement. He checked over the pile of clothes. They were also little more than rags, not much better than his own, but they showed evidence of some repair work, and best of all they were clean.

After he had dressed, he felt suddenly silly. From being filthy and dressed in filthy rags, he had changed to being somewhat less filthy and dressed in clean rags. All of that just because he would be having a meal with a beautiful woman—who in all likelihood no longer looked the way she had when the picture was taken.

Coquina showed up shortly afterward to take Benton to his cave for supper. The petite woman who was waiting for them in the Coquina's cave was even more beautiful than she was in the picture.

Benton was sure this impression must be due to the dim lighting provided by the luxes tied to the walls and to his long absence from the company of beautiful women. Nonetheless, when she stepped forward, smiling warmly, took his right hand between both of her hands, and gazed up at him, saying, "I'm Diori Coquina. Ben told me you're from off–planet, too. We'll have so much to talk about," he found he was grinning like a fool.

The dinner table was yet another one of those leveled rocks, although this one was somewhat elongated. It stood near one wall, and there was a ledge on the wall which served as a bench for those seated at the table. The whole arrangement would be awkward, he thought, since one would have to lean forward to eat, unable to put one's legs under the table as with a normal setup. Still, if the alternative was to eat on the floor, this was preferable.

Diori led him to the table. She slid onto the ledge, never releasing his hand, and pulled him insistently down beside her. Somehow, her supple, graceful movements transformed her clothing, no less shabby than his, into the equal of a costly evening gown.

My god, he wondered, what must her body look like underneath that?

Benton forced himself to look away and examine the table instead. It had been set with a few crude implements. The food was on irregularly shaped plates that seemed to be made of leather or thick paper. He felt a rush of amusement. The caveman upper crust! Then he turned his attention to Diori again and was captivated and forgot all feelings of mockery.

Coquina sat down on still another leveled rock on the other side of the table, talking steadily about various things. But Benton, gazing into Diori's large gray eyes, neither saw nor heard him.

Diori's calm voice cut through her husband's monologue. "Darling, I'd rather hear about the outside Galaxy from Jim than have you tell him about underground housekeeping problems. Jim, I'm sorry about this food, but it's the best we can do here. Let's start eating our supper, and whenever you feel like talking, just tell us what's going on in the rest of the universe."

"Well, the price of jacksonite's going up again," he said inanely, transferring his attention from Diori to the food. What a spread, he thought.

There were bread and meat and even some fresh fruit. By the standards he had held to in his previous, aboveground life, it was a strange mixture of different foods, rough and primitive in nature and variety. He would have spurned it before, but his standards had changed. Trying not to be behave too piggishly, he ate a large serving of everything on the table.

"How do you get all this stuff?" he asked in amazement.

"That's our payment for jacksonite," Coquina explained. "We mine the jacksonite and send it up, and the Corporation sends down food in payment. The more ore, the more food and the more varied it is. Less ore, less food. That's why," he said, losing interest in his meal and launching into the subject happily, "the undermen here are so much better fed than elsewhere. Our production is high because of our organization. That's the true importance of my work here—and now your work, too—much more than its contribution to the political organization down here."

Diori interrupted again, this time with a trace of annoyance in her voice. "Where do you come from, Jim?"

"Farandhazy. That's where I've been working for the last few years."

Coquina said, "Now, that's an interesting coincidence. My niece—"

"Yes, I know. I met her there." He hesitated. "A further coincidence."

"And how is dear little Augie?" Diori said sweetly. She had released his hand in order to eat. Now she put her left hand on his right knee and squeezed it gently. The table hid the action completely from Coquina.

"Fine. She's fine."

How was he going to handle this situation? He disapproved of what Diori was doing, but his body was responding despite his beliefs. And for all he knew, given the strange and frightening social structure down here, if he spurned her he could be endangering himself.

He didn't want to talk about Augie Syen, especially not about the nature of his relationship with her. Wanting desperately to change the subject, even if the subject he chose instead might anger Diori, Benton said, "She told me that you had come here to complete work on a process for synthetic jacksonite."

Diori snorted in disgust. "We came here because Ben believed those bastards."

Coquina sighed. "I'm afraid my wife is right. The Jacksonite Corporation brought us here, and they gave me all the facilities and support I could ever want. I believe they've done the same with other men who made similar claims. None of the others proved able to really produce synthetic jacksonite, however, and the Corporation was always understandably happy about that. In my case, after a short while here with their full encouragement and support, I succeeded and produced synthetic jacksonite at a very low cost, even in the experimental stage. With proper commercial application and exploitation, it should be possible, using my process, to produce the synthetic substance for about two or three barnards per gram."

Benton whistled in amazement. "Compared to more than a thousand per gram now. What an effect that would have!"

"Precisely what The Jacksonite Corporation was worried about, as Ben should have realized," Diori said sarcastically.

Her husband was gazing glumly at his food, showing no

inclination to either talk or eat. There was hostility in Diori's voice, but it was directed entirely at her husband. She had shifted slowly closer to Benton so that now her left leg pressed against his right leg, firmly, from hip to ankle.

He didn't return the pressure, but neither did he move away. He was getting more and more aroused by the touch, but despite that, he listened with fascination to the story she was telling of the coming of the Coquinas to this underground world.

"As soon as Ben proved he could do it, they arrested us and destroyed all his work. Then they shipped us to a detention camp in the desert." She shuddered at the memory. "It was awful! They kept us there for I don't know how long. Long enough that we started looking like these undermen, at any rate. After that, they shoved us underground and told us to keep traveling until we found people. We did, eventually—if you can call these creatures people."

"Now, now, dear," Coquina said, in a tone of voice that approached being self-satisfied. "It could have been worse. They might have simply killed us. This way," he explained to Benton, "if we're ever rescued by some miracle, they can claim we stumbled down here by accident, and our story is the result of derangement from being underground for so long. And by the way, do you have any idea how long we've been here? I haven't yet been able to devise any satisfactory way of keeping track of time."

"When I left Farandhazy, Augie said it had been three years since your last letter, just before you went to Colliery."

"Three years!" Diori gasped and put her hand to her mouth.

Her husband looked momentarily depressed, but then he brightened and said, "Cheer up, dear. It was a foolish question for me to have asked. What does it matter how much time has passed? What matters is that we've done a good deal to improve our lot down here and to organize our village, and the future doesn't look all that bad. We'll return some day. It just may take a while."

Diori cast him a poisonous look and then turned to Benton and smiled. "I have to leave now, unfortunately. I'm so glad you're here with us, Jim. It's so nice to have someone from outside to talk to, not just these undermen and the Corporation flunkies who get banished." She took his hand again and squeezed it between hers, then slid from the ledge and left the cave without a glance at her husband.

Benton willed his heart to return to a more regular and slower pattern. Was Coquina going to say something like, "Shall we retire to the smoking room for cigars and brandy while the servants clean up?"

Not quite. Instead, looking unhappily at a metal cup filled with water near his right hand, Coquina said, "I wish they'd send us something better. Wine, perhaps. I've tried to do something with the fruit they send down, but so far without much success."

Now that Diori was gone, Benton realized that there were a great many questions he wanted answered concerning this subterranean world. "There's a lot I don't understand, Ben. You say they send down food from above in return for shipments of jacksonite, and also that you and your wife were put down here to get you out of the way and that Corporation people can get sent here for punishment. In fact," he added, remembering Marguerite Borrasca, "I met one person like that. Does that mean you can't just find an exit shaft and leave?"

Coquina laughed with some bitterness. "Let me give you

some background of which I'm sure you're unaware. Perhaps you knew that this was once an unindustrialized farming planet?"

Benton nodded. "Yes, I did know that. Then jacksonite was found here. The Jacksonite Corporation was formed, and it bought up the farmland for high enough prices that the farmers were glad to sell out."

"Correct so far. The original organizers of the Corporation were local merchants and a few of the wealthier farmers. They had to bring in some outside men to get the really big money, but mostly they were Collierites. Their descendants are the present Board of Directors. Just who sits on the Board is determined by some sort of voting among these ruling families. The rest of the planet's population either left Colliery, starved when their money ran out, or took whatever jobs The Jacksonite Corporation offered them. Some became office workers. The majority, those with real skills beyond tending the soil at a primitive level, were sent underground to mine jacksonite by hand."

"That's barbaric! They could have automated the mines from the very beginning."

Coquina shrugged. "Their way was probably cheaper in terms of initial capital investment. With the Corporation's Galactic monopoly on jacksonite supply and the prices they can consequently demand, they don't have to produce the mineral in vast amounts. The supply is not endless, anyway. They chose labor–intensive techniques because the cheap labor was available. In time, the situation evolved to what we see now. The miners were forced to move underground with their families, perhaps to ensure their fuller devotion to their duties. Food, tools, and clothes were sent down in exchange for what the miners sent up. Guards were posted at the few exits that remained open to make sure no one escaped to resume farming life on the land the Corporation now owned. I would imagine few people on the surface even know about this situation. If they did, I doubt if they would care." He looked carefully at Benton, then smiled. "What's offended more—your sense of humanity or you desire for efficiency?"

Benton chose to ignore his sarcasm. "It *is* inhuman! However, I'm not down here on purpose. I was trapped by accident while I was underground inspecting something. Just show me to an exit and I'll tell the guards who I am. As soon as I get out, I'm getting off this world and going straight to Lark, to tell the government what's going on here."

Coquina laughed. "That is precisely why the guards would never let you out. Whatever reason brought you down here, now that you have seen what the situation is, the Corporation cannot let you leave. These undermen are all citizens of the Republic by hereditary right, no matter that their ancestors foolishly let themselves be made into serfs, and this imprisonment is completely illegal."

"That's why I want to go to the government with this story."

"And that's why you won't be allowed to. Really, your best choice—the safest, wisest one—is to adjust to life underground and make the best of it. Even if you could somehow get out of the mines, you'd never make it off the planet. The Corporation would find you and simply send you back down again. Or they might decide you would escape again and therefore kill you instead. Think of the enormous wealth and power which depend upon this system continuing to operate without disruption. Do you think your freedom or your life count for much when weighed against that?"

Benton thought of Harve Borrasca betraying his parents for their freethinking, and he thought of the treatment he had seen given to the man arrested by Galena and her companion. That man had been betrayed by the woman with whom he'd been living. No, his life counted for little against what the Corporation had to lose. Nor could anyone on the surface be trusted.

There had been societies in the past on many worlds, he knew, not excluding Earth itself, in which children had betrayed revolutionary parents to brutal governments and in which women had betrayed their lovers. This was not a new pattern.

Noticing the signs of Benton's resignation, Coquina said cheerfully, "And it's not as bad down here as you might think. Oh, it was, I grant you, when I first came here, but there have been great changes, rapid strides, during the last... Three years, did you say? Well, well, three years." Coquina sighed and sipped his water slowly, reflectively, as though it was a fine wine and he was pondering well aged memories.

"When I first came underground," he said abruptly, "the undermen were not well organized at all, at least not for high production. You see," he leaned forward, speaking with great intensity, "these people had tried to preserve their rural ways. Villages stayed together and were ruled by councils of old men or by elected leaders. Well, that sort of thing may have been adequate in their previous lives, but they weren't able to produce enough jacksonite to earn themselves reasonable amounts of food. Even worse," he shuddered at the memory, "newcomers were expected to become common laborers, or 'hands' as they call them. To contribute to the tribal welfare, you see. I couldn't imagine myself in that role, and," he laughed, "even less could I imagine Diori working for her survival. Now, at the same time, there have always been groups of outcasts, bands of ruffians who live parasitically upon those who work, violent men who take food by force from those who have earned it rather than working for it themselves."

Benton thought of the group he had first met underground. "I think I know the type."

"Fortunately," Coquina went on, "Diori and I, during our initial wanderings after being cast out by the village we first met, happened to encounter one such group of ruffians whose leader was a man of some intelligence and vision. I fell into a long discussion with him and helped him see how, under my guidance, he could be far better off than he was and could live in far more comfort. His initial interest, I fear, was in Diori rather than in my suggestions, but he was intelligent enough to realize that both had value and that with care he could have all that he wanted."

Puzzled, Benton said "But you're here now, not with that group."

Coquina grinned at him. "Ah, but I'm with both. My first suggestion was that he invade the home cave of the village that had rejected Diori and me and establish himself by force as its ruler. The Headman—you must have met him. His followers became the guards, or police force, who protect him from his not–so–loyal subjects and enforce his decrees."

"Sounds like the Dark Ages."

Coquina looked annoyed. "It's an improvement over the way things were before! Now we have a proper division of tasks, specialization, and we're producing far more jacksonite, and therefore getting more food, than the village ever managed to before we took over. As soon as we can spare the manpower, we plan to train some of the hands to fight and choose the best tools for weapons, and then we can start spreading out and taking over other villages. Why, I've estimated that there may be ten times as many people underground as there are on the surface of Colliery! Think of controlling all of them, just think of it."

Benton hoped his face wore a neutral expression. "And just what is the Recorder's role in all of this?"

Coquina's gaze had drifted to the cave's doorway, and he sat pensively for a moment. He turned back to Benton with a quick, jerky motion. "I'm sorry. I'm very tired. We'll talk about it after sleeping. You know your way back to your place? Good."

Benton left the cave feeling more puzzled than ever. Behind him, Coquina had put his head down on the table and sat that way motionlessly, as if he intended to sleep there.

CHAPTER SEVENTEEN

When he was stumbling through the tunnels after the accident that had trapped him underground, and then when he was living beside Lux Lake, Benton hadn't given a single thought to privacy. He had lain down wherever convenient and slept, and rather than feel any discomfort at the thought that someone might come by while he was defenselessly asleep and exposed, he had hoped that someone *would* show up, some human company. Now, whether it was because he knew humans were all around him in the Big House and he didn't entirely trust them, or because the presence of humans had reawakened the habits he had had in more civilized surroundings, he felt uncomfortable about sleeping in a lighted cave with no door. It made him feel both improper and undefended.

With some trouble, he selected ragged clothes from his pile and tied them together to form a sort of curtain, which he hung on rock projections so that it covered his doorway. The curtain had an unfortunate tendency to fall off the projections when he came or went, but still it was better than nothing. In a similar way, he found he no longer wanted to sleep on the hard, naked floor, and he spread some of the rags over it in one corner to form something of a bed. "Be it ever so humble," he muttered, looking around and feeling suddenly depressed at his rocky and very humble home.

He wondered if he was expected to report for work at a particular time. Surely not, since Coquina had specifically mentioned not having any satisfactory way to keep track of time. That must be a general problem for this supposedly organized empire of the Headman's.

He wasn't going to worry about it. He was dead tired. He would go to sleep and find his way to the Recorder's office when he woke up.

He took his clothes off, lay down upon his makeshift bed and drifted off to sleep.

He couldn't have been asleep for very long when he was awakened by a warm, naked body pressing against him. He was not surprised to discover that Diori was sharing his bed. It occurred to him that the door he had fashioned wouldn't provide much of a barrier to an irate husband. It also occurred to him, forcefully, that he would be violating his principles if he let this go on. In addition to which, Coquina had treated him well.

The situation made Benton feel awkward and uncomfortable. Very soon, however, he began to feel quite wonderful, and he was able to put his doubts and moral qualms aside. A faint and fading inner voice remarked dryly that he had always been able to do that.

Diori's skill was what he should have expected from her skillful way with him during the meal in the Coquina's cave. Benton couldn't help comparing her sexual style with that of her niece, even though he didn't want to remember making love with Augie, not now. While Diori was effortlessly raising both of them to remarkably intense heights of feeling and passion, and finally to an exhausting string of simultaneous climaxes, he kept recalling physical details of Augie's body and moments of their night together. Technically, mechanically, their love-making had been far from as successful as this was, but Augie had been filled with such enthusiasm and appreciation that the details had seemed unimportant.

She was just using me, he reminded himself. She wasn't interested in me for myself. It was all fake.

He drove the memories of Augie away and concentrated on Diori's lovely body and astonishing technique. He knew she planned to use him, too, although he couldn't imagine what use he could be to her, but he told himself that, this time, be was going into it wide-eyed and wouldn't be hurt. Mutual pleasure—at least, he hoped it was mutual—that's all there was to it, and his heart wasn't going to get involved this time.

After their long and strenuous exercise, they lay side by side, panting. Benton leaned over and put his mouth close to Diori's ear and whispered, "Have we been properly introduced?"

Diori burst out with an unexpectedly loud laugh. Then she clapped her hand over her mouth as if to trap the sound. "Ben won't expect me back for some time," she said. "But if he hears me, he might decide to investigate."

He stroked her stomach and legs gently and said, "I'm amazed he doesn't keep you next to him every second, waking and sleeping."

"Hah! As long as it helps keep him alive, he doesn't care where I am."

"Helps keep him alive? I don't understand."

"I've been with that filthy Headman," Diori explained, her voice filled with disgust, "letting him paw and use me. That's my function in this hell–hole." She stared moodily at the ceiling. "Before we came to Colliery, I had lovers and Ben didn't mind that, either. The difference is that those were lovers of my own choosing. I've got half a mind to refuse to go the Headman next time. Then maybe he'll take Ben off my hands."

Benton was felt chilled. "You mean, he'll have Ben killed?"

"Yes. Oh, who am I kidding? I'm a whore. I get paid by not having to work and by getting more and better food than the hands do. That's the real reason I do it, not to keep Ben alive."

They were both silent. Benton tried to think of something to say. He could break the pause, which was growing uncomfortable, by starting to make love to her again, but he thought that wouldn't be well received just then.

Diori ended the pause herself. "At least I don't have to worry about getting pregnant by that animal. Yet. Do you know that these primitives don't even have any kind of contraception? They just hump away in the tunnels, and the women get pregnant, and lots of the babies die. As long as they have enough of them to keep replacing the hands who get killed in accidents, no one seems to care."

She brooded for a while. "You said we'd been gone for about three years. I've been worried about how long it was, since you lose track of all time down here. That means I have about one more year, or a year and a half at the most, before I need to start worrying about getting pregnant. Jim, I've *got* to get out of here before that happens!"

"Ben seemed to think it would be impossible."

"Ben! I don't know whether he's just scared to try or if he's decided he likes it here, being the right–hand man of a petty dictator. Maybe that suits him better than being a well–known academic scientist with no money and no authority." She laughed. "Except over the fates of a few graduate students. Down here, he's the Recorder, and he has real power over lots of people's fates."

She turned to him and pressed against him, burying her face in his neck. "Oh, God, I've just got to get out of here before I go crazy."

At least he knew now what she really wanted from him, and it wasn't sex. But he could hardly be unsympathetic with her desire to escape—with anyone's desire to escape from here. "I'd be glad to help you if I knew of any way to get out," he told her.

She remained motionless for a moment. Then she raised her face to his and kissed him fiercely. "Keep trying to find a way," she said. "Listen, I'm more than the great Dr. Coquina's decorative wife. I was one of his students when he married me. One of his best students. I helped out with the lab work when he was working out his process for synthetic jacksonite. I was the only one he'd trust to get that close to the work. I know where all the notes are, the originals. He just brought copies with him when he came here, and he never told The Jacksonite Corporation that there was another set anywhere. Thank God for that. All he really did here was finish up the process, perfect it. All the underlying science is outlined in those notes. Any competent research team could follow it through to the end, if they had those notes."

He held up his hand to stop her. "Wait a minute. You hardly know me. Why are you trusting me with all this?"

She grinned, then pointed at the clothes he had taken off before going to sleep. On top of the pile was the odd medallion Augie had given him. He had worn it ever since as if it were a good luck charm in truth. "My own judgment in men is lousy and always has been. But I trust little Augie's. She never makes a mistake in judging a man's character. If she gave you that gadget, then she must have trusted you mightily. It's a naval-issue personal field-effect generator, given only to the top ranks of the officer corps so that they'll have a better chance of surviving attacks on their ships. Now, that one belonged to Augie's older brother. He was in an accident of some kind—we never could find out from the navy just what happened—and that little thing didn't do him any good. Anyway, it's the only thing she has left of his, and they were very close. If she gave that to you, then I can trust you."

Feeling very uncomfortable, Benton said, "All right, you can trust me with this information. Since I can't get out of the mines anyway, it wouldn't make any difference even if you couldn't trust me. What am I supposed to do with what you've told me?"

She looked at him thoughtfully. "You know, I've always wondered about my niece by marriage. Is she a sanctimonious, morally self-righteous little twerp in bed, too?"

"No, damn you," he snapped at her. "She was wonderful."

Diori seemed amused by his anger and even triumphant. "Good for her. And you. Now, shut up and listen, and I'll tell you just what you're to do with that information." She paused, gathering her thoughts. "I'll write down for you how to find the notes, and also the name of a man who has the resources you'll need. He's on New Albion. That's where the notes are, too. I'll give you a message to take to him."

"Why didn't you get this man's help before, instead of taking the Corporation's offer?"

She hesitated. "Because he wanted more than just a financial cut. He wanted me, too. I found him repellent. Well, this time, that's what I'll promise him."

"That's a high price."

"We use the coin we have, and we sell what we have to sell. But what I just said was that I'll *promise* him that he can have me. Once you've got the help you need from him, I'll tell him I've changed my mind. I have different plans for my future." Her voice and touch held infinite promise. "Take care of all that, make yourself a multibillionaire from Ben's process, and then come back here and get me."

"You really trust me that far?"

"I really do. Hell, the truth is, I'd do the whole thing myself, except that the Headman keeps his eyes on me to make sure I never go beyond the Big House. It should be easier for you."

"So now all I have to do is accomplish the impossible and get out of the mines."

"Keep thinking of the reward," Diori whispered. She pulled him onto her and they made love again, vigorously and passionately. This time, he was not bothered by memories of Augie.

CHAPTER EIGHTEEN

When Diori left, Benton allowed himself to drift back into sleep, telling himself that he needed and deserved a rest. He woke up still feeling tired in body but inordinately pleased with himself and ready to use his mind for a change.

A bowl of food had been placed outside his doorway while he slept, and he ate it gratefully, finding that he was remarkably hungry.

When he made his way to the Recorder's office shortly thereafter, he found Coquina already there and scribbling busily. Coquina looked up when he entered and smiled in welcome. His mood had brightened considerably since the last time Benton had seen him. "Well, there you are at last! I hope you've had a good sleep."

"Very good. Thank you."

"Fine. Let me show you what I do here, and you can get started right away."

The cave was little more than a large filing system. Sheets of the odd, parchmentlike paper were piled everywhere. Since there was no wind, there was little danger of the papers getting blown about. The papers were covered with row upon row of fine handwriting, except at the top of each page, where a name was written in large block letters. They were, in effect, dossiers on everyone under the Headman's rule. They also recorded position assignments, showing what duty each man, woman, and child was assigned to and how well each performed his duty.

"I can't tell you how much better this is than the chaotic way things were before we took over the village," Coquina said proudly. "I can see almost at a glance who's producing properly and who isn't, and I can punish appropriately and shift people around to improve things. I can tell when someone's recovered from an injury or is not going to recover. It's this approach that has so dramatically increased our production and consequently our food supplies."

Benton skimmed through a few lines on a paper on top of one of the piles. "There seem to be some notations here along political lines, too."

"Oh, yes," Coquina said, beaming around at the piles of paper. "The system lends itself very well to keeping track of loyalty as well as production. Anything said against the Headman—or the Recorder!—gets reported to me eventually and added to the individual's record."

"What about nice things they say about you or the Headman?"

"Come, come, don't be naïve! Kind remarks cannot be trusted. Naturally hands will say such things if they know one of my spies is listening."

"Naturally. It must be hard to rise in this society."

"Oh, yes. You're fortunate to be starting so near the top. There is a lot of social mobility, but you might say that it's sideways rather than upward. We have a fairly high mortality rate, due to the hazardous nature of the work. And health and living conditions, of course. Fortunately, we also have a high birth rate. At first, I suspected that the food being sent down by the Corporation was doctored to keep fertility down, so that the population underground wouldn't increase dangerously, creating pressures for escape attempts. Later I deduced that it was simply the high mortality that kept the population within limits. In addition, under this regime, enemies of the state have a tendency to disappear conveniently. Really, Jim, the longer you're here the more you'll realize how bright our future looks."

Coquina's mention of escape pressures had recalled to Benton the strange usage of the word "Heaven," and especially the fear of the band of vagrants when he had asked them to take him there. "A lot of the undermen seem to refer to the surface as Heaven."

Coquina looked disgusted. "Almost all of them do, except for those, such as the Headman, whom I have educated to know better. I don't know the origin of it. I assume it began some time ago, perhaps not long after the early farm families were thrust underground and forbidden to come out. They can't stand the light at the exits, where some of them must go to deliver the jacksonite and pick up the food. Thus it is the place of the bright and shining light, where sustenance comes from, far up above their heads. It was a natural identification for them to have made. And of course, the dimly seen figures beyond the exit, surrounded by the intolerable light, must be the gods."

Benton laughed. "The Corporation's goons as gods! Wonderful! Then the only way I can ever escape is to die and go to Heaven."

"There's more truth to that than you realize. We send the

bodies of the honored dead out with the Jacksonite—the god-metal, as the undermen call it. An offensive custom, perhaps, but it fits nicely with the older mythology of the good dying and going to Heaven."

"The honored dead?"

"A small percentage of the whole. Most bodies go down a glory hole. You'll see one of those eventually, I'm sure. That was a custom they brought down with them from above."

Benton sighed. "Isn't it amazing how adaptable we humans are?" After a pause, he added, "You or someone else must have told the Headman the truth, because he questioned me about the Corporation when I was taken to him."

"Yes, I told him. To his credit, he believed me immediately. As I said before, he's unusually intelligent for an underman. For the others, the old ideas are still the truth and my revelations have made little headway with them. Come, come, we've talked far too long. I have quite a few new notations to add to these records. I have them memorized from verbal reports, and I must get them set down before I forget any important details. You can help me by finding the papers I need while I write."

For some time, this was the sum total of Benton's duties as the Recorder's assistant. Coquina always seemed to have lengthy additions to make in his cramped handwriting, but usually to only a few of the sheets. Thus Benton had little to do in the meantime but sit watching idly, or sit reading idly.

From his reading of the papers in the many piles, he quickly formed a picture of a petty dictatorship, every bit as brutal and arbitrary as he had guessed at the beginning. Apparently, Coquina didn't believe in pulling papers from the file, even when the subjects no longer existed. Benton found more than one marked "Terminated," with no further entries beyond that one. He was fairly sure what that meant, but his suspicion was confirmed when he found two papers for Borrasca. One was Marguerite's. The other one was for Devon Borrasca, and that one was marked "Terminated."

He kept looking and noticed that the "Terminated" notation almost always followed a notation of a serious injury or a few—often a very few—reports of treasonous remarks. Who, Benton wondered, made the decision to execute an untrustworthy or physically useless citizen of this republic? The Headman, or Ben Coquina?

Without timepieces, they worked until they grew tired of it, ate when they felt hungry, went off to sleep whenever they felt the need for that. Still, Coquina was usually there when Benton arrived and was still at work when he left. The man obviously loved his work.

Benton worried about playing a part in this brutal dictatorship. He told himself that the dictatorship would go on as it was with or without him, and that he was doing very little in any real sense to make it worse. What good would he be doing if he jeopardized his favored position by objecting to what he saw? He would do himself definite harm if he made anyone in power angry at him, but he wouldn't thereby be helping any of the hands.

And there was Diori. He wouldn't do anything to lose Diori. He suspected he might do almost anything to hold onto her.

He would not have thought it possible for him to become addicted to the sexual pleasures a particular woman could provide, no matter how accomplished she might be. And surely knowing, or suspecting strongly, that Diori was doing all this only to induce him to do something for her in return—surely that knowledge should be a strong protection against addiction. That was logical, but logic didn't seem to be involved at all.

He felt guilty every time he saw Ben Coquina. When Diori wasn't there, he berated himself. When she came to his sleeping cave, none of that mattered.

Benton was fully and completely hooked. He had heard and read of addictions to almost every imaginable thing, but this one, he thought, must be the sweetest, most poignant, and most terrible, and it was a habit he had absolutely no desire to kick.

He tried hard to hide from Diori how much he was under her control, but he couldn't tell how successful he was.

Diori had given him the name of the man who could help him and the directions to her husband's original notes, as she'd promised. On more than one occasion, she talked as though she envisioned her future as being with Benton rather than with her husband. "I couldn't live with him any more," she'd say, "not after seeing the side of him he's exposed here. You and I could be so happy together, Jim, if only we could get out of here." And then they'd make love again.

Benton mocked himself, thinking, Not only is my performance so amazing with Diori, it's also the only exercise I get. I need this for my health!

Finally, Coquina asked him to do some of the writing while he dictated. "Remember to write very small," Coquina said. "Paper and ink are so scarce."

Benton nodded, dipped his white, slender, newly pointed pen into the small bowl of brownish ink, and wrote the words down as Coquina spoke them. The paper and ink might be scarce, but their quality was remarkable. As soon as there was a pause, he asked Coquina how he had managed to obtain his stationery supplies.

"I make them," Coquina said proudly. "Or have them made, according to my instructions. Everything you're using. These supplies are the last contribution any citizen can make to the commonwealth. We use the skin, the blood, and the bones of the dead as the basis for our paper, ink, and pens, in that order. One body can go a long way, obviously, so there's little danger of my running out of what I need. There's a large amount of curing, of course, tedious chemical processing. Fortunately, there are chemical deposits of various kinds throughout the mines, so there's more than enough of that to fill my needs. My current projects are to devise a soap substitute and some type of chemical clock. I haven't succeeded yet, but, after all, I have all the time I need."

Benton silently complimented himself on his self-control. There was not the slightest waver evident in the words he had just written, despite the internal jolt he had felt. While Coquina prattled on about his elaborate plans for the future, none involving escape and all presupposing an indefinite continuation of his life underground, Benton argued with himself.

Surely his reaction of horror and his mind's immediate choice of the word "cannibalism" for what Coquina had done were atavistic. Logically, there was nothing at all wrong with using the dead. They had no use for their own bodies any more! Why shouldn't they make one last contribution?

Yes, and by the same logic, he asked himself, why not eat

them? Why not practice real cannibalism? Why does that idea revolt you?

It was scarcely a matter of logic, he knew, but of deeper level reactions. The fact was that he was revolted, sickened, and on the verge of throwing down his pen of bone, even if that splattered blood–ink on skin–paper, and stalking out.

But logic had to rule him now. He had to go along with this madman until there was some chance of getting out. If he cut himself off from the ruling class, he'd end up as just another hand, living the way Marguerite Borrasca did, and there'd be no more private sleeping quarters and therefore no more times with Diori. That last, above all else, was unthinkable.

A few times, Benton raised with Coquina the subject of escape. Perhaps the three of them could manage it together. But Coquina was adamant that it was simply impossible. "The undermen themselves would be against you and would try to stop you. You see, trying to enter Heaven while you're still alive is sacrilegious. They're rather fundamentalist. They would take that very seriously."

Benton knew that was true. He had only to remember the vagrants' anger at his "pretending to be a god." Still, why wouldn't Coquina even try to get out?

"We have so much important work to do down here," Coquina would say, gesturing around him in a way that included at least his office, perhaps the Big House, perhaps all of the underworld. "Why bash our heads against a brick wall? Down here, we can do some real good, and do it in comfort and security. We're powers down here, my boy. We have influence. Soon we'll be extending our influence. And we can use that influence to bring about good changes, both here and in other villages as we bring them under our control."

And always, interspersed among the dreary, tedious, disturbing hours there were the stolen times with Diori, times stolen from both her husband and the Headman and thus dangerous to both the lovers. For different reasons, they were both willing to take the risk.

CHAPTER NINETEEN

"Borrasca," Coquina said, leaning back against the rock wall.

Benton started searching through the alphabetized stacks, then stopped and said, "Going to remove his paper at last?"

"Of course not!" Coquina said impatiently. "I want the other one, the wife."

"All right." This was the first time he had been asked to add anything to Marguerite's file, but when he took it from the stack, he saw that both sides of the sheet were already covered by notations in Coquina's handwriting.

"As I remember," Coquina said, "there isn't much room to add anything more. Just as well, then. Write 'Terminated' on the bottom." While Benton sat unmoving, frozen with shock, Coquina said musingly, "You know, Benton, it's odd, but after all this time, these sheets of paper have come to seem like the real people, rather than those flesh-and-blood creatures out there in the Big House and the tunnels. When I tell you to change someone's assignment, for instance, I think of it as happening when you write it on the paper. That is the real act. I know that some real man or woman is being shifted from chipping out god-metal to helping deliver it to Heaven, say, but that doesn't register. I only know it intellectually, but emotionally it's as if the paper is the real person, the real hand, and your act of writing down some words changes the individual. Similarly, although I know Marguerite Borrasca is already on her way to Heaven with a load of ore, she didn't seem dead until I told you to write 'Terminated' on her paper. Now her file is finished, and only now is *she* finished. Isn't that curious?"

Benton mumbled something in reply and quickly scrawled the grim word on the bottom of the sheet of paper. How silly, he thought. Why should I feel any sort of special kinship with her? She's dead, and that's it. Probably better off now than she was before, anyway, living the kind of life she was being forced to live. Now she's in Heaven, as opposed to this place where I'm still trapped.

Coquina was saying, "Furthermore, it avoids pangs of conscience. The act of changing the nebulous, abstract construct embodied in the words on a sheet of paper causes no feeling of guilt. I can do what I know needs to be done, and rather than burdening myself with worrying about it afterwards, I simply go on to the next task, the next file. Speaking of which, Benton, let's move along. Get out Klon Dawson's file."

Benton was too preoccupied to notice that Coquina had called him by his last name twice already, whereas before he had always called him "Jim." There was also an undertone of hostility that escaped Benton's notice. He went to the stacks for the sheet of paper headed "DAWSON, KLON" but he didn't carry Marguerite Borrasca's file back with him. He set it casually aside instead, intending to look it over carefully as soon as he had the chance.

Later, in his room, he read quickly through Marguerite's file. There seemed nothing of significance, except for the last few entries. For a while before being killed, Marguerite had frequently reported that during her trips to Lux Lake to collect luxes, she had noticed that the lake's level was rising. The last time, she had complained that it was rising fast enough to frighten her, and she insisted the water would soon be up to the tunnel entrances giving into the lake's cavern, and then she would be unable to collect any more luxes. If the water kept rising, some day the Big House and all the jacksonite workings would be flooded. There were no specifically negative reports about her, no evidence of what might be considered treason, so it must be only those claims of rising water that had led to her being eliminated. In the Headman's world as in larger ones, it was dangerous to be the bearer of bad tidings.

Benton recalled his own speculations about water having to drain steadily out of Lux Lake. It could be, he supposed, that the outlet, whatever it was, had become blocked. If that was the case, he hoped that the process would reverse itself just as suddenly and the lake would return to a constant level.

There was another possibility, though. That wildlife documentary he had watched in such fascination had dealt with efforts here on Colliery to save from extinction a native birdlike animal threatened by climatic shift. The contradiction between that self-laudatory program and Borrasca's claim that the climate would not destabilize for thousands of years to come only struck him now. The change must already have started, must be well underway. That must explain why that huge waterfall existed in the first place. There must be other large underground water courses all over the planet. Surely this one couldn't be the only one. The source of so much water would be the melting ice caps, slowly filling up whatever underground storage spaces were available. The water table would rise to levels more like those on other planets. Marguerite Borrasca's fears had been justified.

It was unthinkable to Benton that The Jacksonite Corporation was unaware of all of this. And yet, although they provided new tools occasionally along with the shipments of food, Coquina kept track of tool assignments, and Benton had never seen any notations regarding pumps. That must mean that no pumps were shipped down, that the Corporation didn't care if all the undermen drowned.

Why wasn't Coquina alarmed? Why had he helped silence Marguerite Borrasca when she tried to warn them all? Because, Benton realized, Coquina couldn't face the fact that this underworld empire was doomed and that his petty role in ruling it was therefore doomed as well.

I'd better do some more checking before I go off half-cocked, Benton thought. Maybe some other lux gatherers also reported rising water and were also terminated.

He made his way stealthily back to Coquina's cave and peered around the edge of the entrance. The office was empty. Benton went in and began searching rapidly through the stacks of paper, stopping at those with TERMINATED on them and reading the last few comments quickly. He had not found anything about rising water when he heard a gasp of surprise behind him.

It was Coquina, standing in the entrance and looking at him in amazement. "What are you doing?" Coquina choked.

"Why, hello, Ben," Benton said cheerfully. "I felt like doing something productive, so I thought I'd come in and see what I could contribute. Maybe some organizing."

"Everything is already very well organized," Coquina said coldly. "I'd appreciate it if you'd leave. I want to get some work done. Alone."

Still trying to seem cheerful and amiable, Benton said, "Sure," and strolled out.

Once he was well out of Coquina's sight and hearing, however, he picked up speed and headed in the direction of the Big House. He entered the great cavern and paused for a moment, trying to decide which way to go first. He had been here only twice so far before, once when he had first arrived, and once more when he'd been asked by Coquina to take a message to the Headman. Benton wanted to find some hands who'd worked at various low levels of the mines, to find out whether they'd encountered rising water. From idle speculation of merely intellectual interest when he'd been at Lux Lake himself, the question had now grown to a matter of overwhelming practical importance.

But now he stood at the top of the great sloping ledge that curved around the wall of the cavern and led down to the floor, and he realized that he didn't know whom to contact to find out what he wanted, and that, in any case, he wouldn't know where to find a particular hand.

He stood there irresolutely, watching the figures hurrying across the cavern floor far below and the guards and messengers, including the well-remembered Thompson, lounging about the walls of the Headman's place in the center. Although he was so high above the cavern floor, he was too far away from the center to be able to see over the walls of the Headman's place.

The Headman must be the only one here with real privacy,

Benton thought. You can't see into his house from anywhere. Except from overhead, I suppose. I wonder if those holes in the roof are actually tunnel outlets?

Benton looked up, thinking that perhaps he could tell more about the holes if he stared at them for a while and let his eyes and brain adjust to what he was seeing.

The roof seemed more shadowed than he remembered. Then he realized that quite a few of the luxes tied to the roof had died and faded. In the awkward, distorting shadows, he thought he saw movement, a moving glow lost in the gloom around it. Squinting, concentrating, at last he made out a silhouetted human shape, outlined against the glow of a lux.

At first Benton thought the man was somehow sliding along the cavern roof. Then he made out a rope. The man was crawling along it. Now that he had made out that rope, Benton was able to see others crisscrossing the roof. One of the holes not far away from the moving figure glowed with light. Now Benton understood. The figure was a hand who'd been ordered to replace the dead luxes. He had had to transport a large number of luxes to one of the holes, leave them secured there, and then crawl out along the rope carrying one lux at a time. Benton wondered how many lives had been lost getting those ropes in place and how many were regularly lost replacing dead luxes.

His skin crawled with vicarious fear as he watched the figure moving slowly and painfully across the roof. He was sure the hand would lose his grip and fall to the distant floor. Still, he couldn't tear his eyes from the silhouetted shape.

The hand reached the point he was aiming for, cut the dead lux loose, replaced it with the live one he had carried at such risk, and then edged his way back to the glowing hole, carrying the dead lux with him. Before the hand could emerge again for another trip across the roof, Benton dropped his gaze from the roof and started walking down the ramp.

He was about halfway down when he heard the faint scuffling of footsteps behind him and someone panting. He turned quickly, thinking he was about to be attacked, but it was Diori. She was gasping for breath, her face was flushed and covered with sweat, and her hair, for the first time except when they were making love, was disarrayed. She fell against him, exhausted and unable to speak. He put his arms around her and held her tightly to him. "Diori, what's wrong?'

She pushed herself away from him. "No, don't," she gasped. "The Headman will see."

She struggled for a second, finally gaining enough control to speak. "My husband, he's found out. He's known about us for a while, but he just told me. Get out of here, quickly. I know he's going to try to harm you somehow."

"Why should he care?" Benton said bitterly. "He doesn't object to the Headman."

"That's different, damn it! He objects a lot to you, and he can do something about you. You've got to run away!"

"Run away? There's nowhere to run to. All I'd end up doing is getting lost in the tunnels again."

"But for God's sake, you've got to do something!" She stopped and looked around. "Look, if we're going to argue, let's go back to your quarters and do it there, not out here."

But when they reached the cave which was assigned to Benton, two men were already there waiting for him. He recognized one of them as Carnot, the Headman's guard who had had temporary custody of him upon his arrival in the Big House. The other was a guard he also remembered seeing at the Headman's place.

Benton's stomach knotted in fear when he and Diori entered and found the two guards lounging in the cave, wearing contemptuous expressions, but he tried to brazen it out. "Carnot, this is my place, and you need permission to come in here. Now, take your little friend by the hand and get out."

Carnot was momentarily cowed by this display of defiance. "I'm one of the Headman's guards," he said sullenly. "I can go anywhere I want to. I don't need permission." In spite of his words, he seemed unsure of himself.

"And I'm the Recorder's assistant. I can persuade him to reassign you—change you from a guard into something else."

At these words, to Benton's surprise, Carnot unsureness vanished. He grinned and the other guard gave a short, barking laugh. "Oh, yeah?" Carnot said. "Well, now, that's just why we're here. See, you're not the Recorder's assistant any more. Guess he forgot to tell you. Now you're just a hand."

Behind him, Benton heard Diori mutter a low, despairing moan.

Carnot stooped and picked up something from the floor. Benton saw that it was a tool, a small pick much like the one he'd examined so long ago in the tunnels, when it had been dropped by the fleeing vagrants. "This is yours," Carnot said happily. "You'll get it when we've taken you to your duty station. The other hands'll show you how to use it. They'll show you all you need to know. Move it."

"Wait a minute," Diori said, and Benton could hear the desperation in her voice. "I want to talk this over with my husband."

Carnot shook his head. "The Headman told us to do this, and he said it was because the Recorder asked him to. Benton, we'll even give you a minute to say goodbye," he said, leering at Diori. "And lady, you're going to have to give us some of what you gave this guy, if you don't want the Headman to find out what your husband already knows." The two guards pushed their way past Benton's makeshift door.

Diori threw her arms around Benton's neck and hugged him tightly. She released him, stepped back, and looked at him, her eyes wide with fear. "You've got to survive, Jim," she said fiercely. "Make this your opportunity to escape, and then come back for me." She choked, and they embraced again. "Do you have those directions I gave you?"

"Yes. In my pocket."

"Thank God. You'd better go now, darling. Remember me, Jim."

It was the first time she had ever used any term of endearment with him, and it struck Benton to his heart. "How could I ever forget you?" he said softly. "But you," he said anxiously, "those guards expect—"

"I know what they expect," Diori said scornfully. "Don't worry. I've handled their type before."

There was one last eager embrace and kiss, and then Benton, steeling himself, walked out to the waiting guards.

CHAPTER TWENTY

Later, listening to other hands talk, he would realize how lucky he was to be assigned to Stephan Scheel's crew. Scheel was more intelligent and organized than most of the other foremen. More important, he seemed to really care about his men and to feel responsible for their survival. They were individuals to him, not replaceable parts. Too bad the men who ran Contco weren't more like that, Benton thought. Or, for that matter, the men who ran The Jacksonite Corporation.

He learned that the hole he had almost fallen into during his first hours underground was a fairly common formation, or perhaps a manmade artifact. The hands called them glory holes. They shoved excess rock and dirt down them and dead luxes and tools that were broken beyond repair. Occasionally, they came across dead undermen. If the body was of someone they knew, someone from the Headman's village, they carried it back to the Big House with them so that it could be sent up to Heaven with some future load of ore. If they didn't recognize the dead underman, the body went down a glory hole.

Every time he helped to do this, he remembered his glimpse of the white monster rising from the waters of Lux Lake toward a body sliding down the waterfall, and he wondered if that was where these bodies ended up. Was that also the fate of anyone who fell down a glory hole alive? Had that body he had seen actually been moving, flailing for purchase as it fell?

Benton knew that it made sense not to leave bodies in the tunnels, although he suspected that the luxes would take care of the remains eventually. Throwing them down a glory hole was a quick and efficient way to get rid of them. He hated doing it nonetheless. His fellow hands, though, seemed to see it as a clean and even respectful way of getting rid of the corpses of strangers.

The work was astonishingly hard. He was amazed that the tired, malnourished hands could do it. He was continually astonished that he became able to do it himself. They had only primitive hand tools and spent their days chipping and gouging jacksonite-containing shards from the tunnel walls. Hours of work yielded tiny piles of ore, except on those fortunately rare occasions when large pieces fell unexpectedly from tunnel wall or roof. They carried the ore back to various designated collection points in sacks made from various kinds of cloth. After what he had seen in the Recorder's office, Benton chose not to ask anyone what the cloth was made from.

The work was also horrendously dangerous. There were the glory holes, but they knew where those were and Benton never saw anyone fall down one. The biggest danger was falling rocks. Scheel's crew was relatively lucky, but one of the hands had only one arm and another had a withered leg—both the results of rock falls. At that, those two were lucky to have survived their injuries. Rubel, a fellow hand, told him that when a hand was hurt, they used a tourniquet to stop the bleeding and then carried the man back to the Big House as quickly as they could, where some of the Headman's people functioned as primitive doctors.

"And then?" Benton asked.

Rubel hesitated, then said, "Sometimes he's okay and he comes back to work. Most of the time, we hear that he didn't make it."

"He died?"

"He went up to Heaven." Rubel wouldn't meet his gaze. "The Headman's people let us know."

In other words, Benton thought, if the injury is serious, the hand doesn't get medical care. He goes down a glory hole.

"How long has it been this way? Did this always happen?"

Rubel looked quickly left and right, up and down the tunnel. "Since the Headman and the Recorder showed up. Before that, we used to try more to take care of people. We had a good village."

Now that he thought back, Benton couldn't recall seeing many injured people in the Big House—not people recovering from recent injuries, or cripples with healed wounds. Probably the primitive conditions and medicine ensured that most injured hands really couldn't survive their wounds, but Benton could readily believe that the Headman wasn't likely to expend resources on those who wouldn't be able to contribute by chipping out ore.

"Maybe we should ask the, uh, the gods for medicines and equipment."

Rubel looked uncomprehending. "The gods know best. They give us what we need and only what we need."

"Right. Okay." It was a subject Benton had learned at an early point not to pursue.

"The main thing is," Rubel said, "you have to be careful."

"How can you be careful? There's no way of knowing when some rock will fall on you."

"Or burst out of the wall," Rubel said almost casually.

"What?"

"Oh, yeah. Sometimes it doesn't fall. Sometimes it sort of jumps out of the wall. Explodes. Some newcomer tried to explain it to me a long time ago. He said it was..." He frowned, trying to remember. "Strains, that was what he called it. Forces in the rocks, he said. He said you can break a big slab of rock off in one place, and the strains will come out somewhere else. Makes rocks shoot out of the wall somewhere. I saw a guy's head get smashed that way once. He was working right next to me, and next thing, he didn't have a head. He was just lying on the floor twitching. His body was, I mean..." His voice trailed off. Then he sighed. "That was before Scheel. Some other foreman. He had us put the body down a glory hole. Poor guy."

Rubel coughed and cleared his throat noisily. He stopped walking and breathed heavily for a while. When he had regained some strength, they started walking again.

After a few minutes of silence, Rubel said in an awed tone, "Weird stuff happens. Sometimes, a big rock'll fall in one place, and it forces air through the tunnels for a long way. It can knock you over."

That must be what happened on that first day, Benton realized. That's what caused that accident and got me marooned down here. "How can anyone be careful about any of this stuff?" he asked bitterly. Putting me down here was a death sentence, he thought.

Rubel shrugged. "I guess you can't. Not really. You just have to pray. The gods know what they're doing."

Oh, yes, Benton thought. They certainly do.

Not all corpses went up to Heaven or down a glory hole, though. Some had to remain where they were.

Benton and Rubel were making their way slowly through an unfamiliar tunnel, hoping to find a fresh vein of jacksonite. Scheel's crew had failed to bring in their quota a few times lately, and they were all getting worried about the Headman's reaction. An unworked vein would make a big difference for them all.

Benton was in the lead and saw it first—not the vein they were hoping for, but a wide tunnel entrance in the wall just ahead. There was no light coming from it. He took that to be a good sign. It meant no one had worked that tunnel before.

He pulled one of the luxes from the wall and threw it into the tunnel entrance. Liberated, the lux started crawling away from him as quickly as it could. Then it stopped and slowly settled down onto the tunnel floor. It its faint light, Benton could make out two human figures sitting in the tunnel, leaning back against the wall, one on each side of the entrance, facing each other.

"Hello?" he said.

There was no reply, no movement.

He couldn't see them well enough to tell if he knew them. He stepped forward, about to enter the tunnel. A hand grabbed his shoulder.

"No!" It was Rubel, shouting. "Bad air!"

"What are you talking about?"

"Look at the lux."

The animal's light was already fading. "It's dying," Benton said, surprised. "It was a healthy one."

"Probably already dead. That's a bad tunnel. Those hands, that's as far as they got. Probably felt tired, sat down to rest. Didn't realize what was wrong."

This was something Benton understood. He had modeled ventilation systems in mines before. The software to balance the system—predict the air flow and pressure at every point in the mine—was relatively simple, but the effects of changing a mine's configuration were often odd and surprising. People exhaled unbreathable gases and so did the rocks themselves. Sufficient air flow was required to keep the level of such gases low enough for safety. Even with fans throughout a mine, there were often places where air didn't flow in sufficient quantity and deadly gases collected. Benton hadn't yet encountered a fan underground. If the only ones forcing air through the mines were at the entrances, like the one he had passed on the way into the mine however long ago that was, and if rock falls and steadily growing stalactites and stalagmites kept changing the flow patterns, then it wasn't surprising that unbreathable gases were gathering in various places, including in tunnels that had once been safe to pass through.

"What about their bodies? Shouldn't we try to get them out?"

"Not gonna risk my life for that," Rubel said. "Maybe we could hold our breaths, get in and out with them. Maybe not. I don't think it's anyone we know. Besides, better to leave them there. Makes a good warning. As long as hands see them in time, before they go in there themselves."

They'll never rot, Benton thought, so there'll be no smell to serve as a warning. Nothing lives long enough in there. They don't even look bloated. Maybe the bacteria inside their bodies also died quickly. They'll be there forever, looking just like that, long after I've been killed in some underground accident.

The three hands on the scaffold were irretrievably doomed even before Benton heard the pebble rattling its way down the chimney.

Some long time ago, an underman had made his way painfully and cautiously up the old volcanic remnant, a tube whose sealed top was about 800 meters above the floor where Benton stood now. That anonymous underman had had to reinvent mountain-climbing techniques already ancient on other planets but unknown to him. He had carried with him a lux, hoping vaguely that somewhere in the chimney he'd find a thick vein of jacksonite, unreachable by an easier route, to make his dangerous exploration worthwhile. The jacksonite was there, near the chimney's top, a very thick deposit indeed.

Not that the chimney-climber benefited from it, no more than undermen ever did. All they gained was satisfying their ore quotas and thus getting adequate food and supplies from Heaven. Only The Jacksonite Corporation and the surface dwellers reaped the real rewards.

The climber had wedged a thick hammer handle in the top of the chimney and looped over it one of the few, precious ropes the Corporation sometimes sent down. With mechanical skills transmitted from their farmer ancestors, and using the remnants of worn-out or broken tools, the undermen had devised a scaffold system, drawn up by the rope passing over the now reinforced hammer handle at the top. The rope—a thick, slippery, very strong synthetic—was wound over a crude winch at the bottom. Two hands, and sometimes three, could be slowly hauled up on the scaffold to chip away patiently at the jacksonite.

This time, there were three men on the scaffold. Benton and Rubel had laboriously winched the trio up the chimney, pausing occasionally to look up at the faint glow of the men's luxes, drawing away higher into the darkness. Now the winding rope had finally reached the black mark painted on it that told them the scaffold had reached the jacksonite vein. Benton and Rubel were taking turns keeping watch over the piece of metal—once a chisel—wedged into the winch to keep it from spinning backward and dropping the scaffold. Benton sat idly against the wall, his mind blank, while Rubel watched the makeshift brake.

Rubel coughed again, as he did so frequently now, a deep, wet, hacking cough. Then he cleared his throat and swallowed noisily. Hands who survived long enough, avoiding death from accidental causes, almost always seemed to develop this sort of cough eventually. And eventually, inevitably, they died from it.

Benton found himself trying to sense his own internal signs, waiting with a kind of gloomy resignation for the preliminary tickling in his lungs that would herald the beginning of the ineluctable disease in him.

Or will I make it even that long, he wondered. He had seen so many accidents already, so many different types of violent ending.

As the echoes of Rubel's cough died away, Benton heard the faint rattling sound from high up in the chimney. His first thought was that it was a distress signal of some sort from the men above. Then, as the sound rapidly grew louder and closer, he realized that it was something hard falling, rebounding from wall to wall. Before he could call out a warning, Rubel had heard the sound and stepped around the winch, to the center of the chimney floor, and stood staring upward, his mouth open in dull surprise.

It was a piece of jacksonite the size of a man's fist. One of the hands on the scaffold had carelessly kicked it off and it fell, accelerating steadily, toward Rubel below. The chimney widened slightly near the bottom, and the noise stopped as the jacksonite fragment fell clear the last hundred meters. Still Benton could neither speak nor move as the last fraction of a second, that seemed like an hour, slid by.

Rubel's face exploded into a volcano of red. He collapsed backward onto the winch. As he rolled over it, he dislodged the chisel, and the winch began to turn, slowly at first, then with gathering speed.

Now at last Benton could move. Ignoring Rubel, who was surely dead, he leaped at the winch. But its handle was already a blur, and he snatched his hands back before he touched it.

A noise was growing above him.

He grabbed the rope. Its slick surface, fat and slippery like the snakes in Lux Lake, slid unimpeded through his fingers. He squeezed as hard as he could. For a moment, he thought the rope slowed down, but then he felt enormous heat generated against his palms and searing pain, and he let go again. He suddenly became aware of his own danger, with the loaded scaffold hurtling downwards at him, and he scrambled from the chimney into the wide tunnel beyond.

There he cowered against the far wall, waiting helplessly for the heavy structure to crash to the ground and obliterate the winch and Rubel's motionless body and the three hands on the scaffold.

But it never happened. The noise in the chimney died away. Then, after a breathless pause, tiny chunks, unidentifiable particles, began to rain upon the chimney floor. This went on for some time, until finally that, too, tapered away and all was silent.

Benton waited until he was certain nothing else would fall. Then he crept slowly over to the ominous pile of debris that filled the space at the bottom of the chimney. At first, his mind refused to let him realize what the pile consisted of, but then he caught sight of a feebly waving, still glowing lux tail among the debris, and he knew with a shock that the pile before him was all that was left of the scaffold and the men and equipment on it. They too had rebounded from one jagged wall to another, just like the jacksonite pebble that had started it all. But the men and the scaffold were not as hard as jacksonite, and the effect on them had been to tear them to shreds, to grind them to powder.

Footsteps behind him broke through his daze. He turned to see that a small group of hands, drawn by the noise, had come down the tunnel from their own work to see what had happened. In the front of them was Stephan Scheel. Scheel took in the situation with a quick glance, knowing right away what must have happened. He had seen similar accidents before. "What about Rubel?" he asked Benton.

Benton explained how Rubel had been killed. "He's under there now," he said, pointing a shaking hand at the grisly pile.

Scheel nodded. "If he's not dead, he soon will be. Better off dead than living with his face smashed in." He turned to one of the men behind him. "Gedri, go back to the Big House right away and tell the Recorder about these four being killed. Tell him we'll need more hands to replace them in our group, or he'd better lower our quota."

Gedri walked off, his face showing just how unhappy he was at having to take a pugnacious message to the Recorder.

Scheel pointed at two other men. "You, Breccia and Emery, go find something to carry these men in. I want you to scrape all that together and take it up to the shaft so that it can be sent to Heaven with the next load of god-metal."

The two men nodded and went off to find a container. Their faces were calm. After lifetimes spent underground, they found their assigned task less unpleasant than Gedri found his.

Benton said, "Oh, hell, Stephan, why bother? There's a glory hole just down the tunnel." He regretted his words almost as soon as he had spoken them,

Stephan's face froze. "Listen, I can see you're still upset, so I won't report you for that. Those were my men, those four, and I'm going to make sure they get to Heaven. They were good hands, they worked hard, and they deserve their chance to become gods."

Benton looked from Stephan's coldly angry face to the faces of the other men. Their anger was hotter, less contained, and he suddenly realized what danger he had put himself in. Violence was in the air, almost palpable. He mumbled, "Sorry-sorry, Stephan, sorry-sorry." He hoped that would be enough to defuse the situation.

Stephan waved his hand in dismissal. "Okay. Listen, you go off to the Big House and get some food and a rest. I'll give you a break for a while. I'll put you on shipping the god-metal up to Heaven until you settle down." He stepped closer and spoke to

Benton in a low voice, so that the others couldn't hear. "Maybe it'll give you some real religion, Benton, to see the lights from Heaven and the gods up there. Give you a chance to grow up before you get yourself killed."

Benton had learned a lot about the pointlessness of defiance in certain circumstances. Now he dropped his gaze to the floor, mumbled a vague acquiescence, and shuffled off. He had long ago passed the stage where, after such an incident, he would mentally revile himself for his cowardice.

As he walked back to the Big House, Benton realized that his horror at the accident he had just witnessed had already faded. The only distress he felt now was at his own lack of distress, at the callousness that he detected in himself. He had seen so many hands die horribly—crushed, torn, and in one case on a lower level, drowned—that it simply didn't bother him any more. His reaction to the deaths of Rubel and the three others, he realized now, was not really horror, but more a kind of shock at the bizarreness of the sequence of events.

He had fallen into the lifestyle of a hand in other ways, too, he knew. Here he was, obediently following orders rather than using the knowledge he had gained of the tunnels to try to escape. But he only knew the tunnels controlled by the Headman, and that included only one shaft to Heaven—no, to the surface, damn it!—and two or three access points to Lux Lake.

He wasn't yet prepared to try the exit to the surface. He had been warned that there was always a Headman's guard stationed on the inside of that exit. He had deduced from various reports that there were also Corporation guards on the far side of the exit.

If he left the area entirely and explored other tunnels, he'd soon be as hopelessly lost as he was before he encountered Marguerite Borrasca. At worst, he'd starve. At best, he'd end up as a hand again in some other netherworld dictatorship, a kilometer or two away from the Headman's Big House. There might be some primitive democracies left, as Coquina had told him this village had been before the coming of the Headman's rule, but he doubted it. Even if there were, he doubted even more his chances of finding one. It was much more likely, he thought, that he'd starve, or have a fatal accident, or end up as a serf in another dictatorship, or encounter another group of vagrants and this time get himself murdered.

Food, unsurprisingly, was the real source of the Headman's power, no matter how Coquina might delude himself about his own importance. The Headman's guards supervised the transfer of god-metal to the exit, and they took complete charge of whatever the Corporation sent down in return, taking it to the Big House for storage in the Headman's place. Hands had to return to the Big House regularly and stay in the guards' good graces if they wanted to eat or to get new clothes or tools. They could try striking off on their own—find another exit shaft and exchange jacksonite for food there. But this was an uncertain alternative, even if they could find another opening and contact someone from the Corporation to set the system up. It seemed likely to Benton, though, that every exit was already controlled on this side by some organized group—once again, probably by some other dictatorship. There seemed little point in even trying to escape.

He could go back to Lux Lake and live there in solitude the way he had before, this time knowing enough to avoid any human beings who came by. He'd gain a sort of freedom, and he wouldn't starve—assuming the cavern and the lake still existed, that the water hadn't risen to cover the entrances. He'd heard nothing about that, but he'd been too busy surviving as a hand to think of asking anyone about Lux Lake. Considering Marguerite's fate, he also thought that asking about the level of the lake would be dangerous.

Even if the lake was as he remembered it, he couldn't escape by going there. If he were to disappear, Coquina would surely persuade the Headman to send men out to look for him, and Lux Lake would be one of the first places they'd look. Coquina did not want Benton escaping. Fortunately, he didn't seem to want him killed, either.

He wants me debased and humiliated, Benton thought. Under his control. And where Diori can see what I've been changed into. He'd probably like to do that to the Headman even more than to me, but he'll never get that chance. In the meantime, he'll settle for doing it to me.

It was less than Benton's normal ration. He glanced up at Carnot's evil grin and then looked away again quickly. "I'm supposed to get more, Carnot." He heard the whine in his own voice.

"You said Scheel sent you back before you were finished working."

"But there was a reason—"

"Never mind that!" Carnot shouted. "You didn't finish, right?"

Benton nodded, knowing that, thanks to the peculiar logic of the place, he had already lost.

"Produce less, eat less," Carnot said triumphantly, repeating the basic litany of the underworld. He turned on his heel and walked back into the Headman's place.

Benton sighed and started gathering up his meager rations. Carnot had flung them on the ground. Benton rubbed the dirt off. He'd eat it anyway, of course. Carnot had known that. That was part of the game.

He became aware of someone watching him, and he looked up to see Diori, staring at him with a mixture of amazement and contempt.

"I haven't given up yet," Benton said sullenly.

She looked at him coldly. "Sure you haven't, underman." She brushed past him and into the Headman's place. He wanted to run after her, to grab her and somehow make her look at him in the way she had before his downfall. But he couldn't follow her in there. And he had another job, he reminded himself, one even more intimidating and unpleasant than getting his food from Carnot. He had to go to the Recorder and tell him that Stephan wanted him temporarily assigned to exit–shaft work.

He forced his food down quickly and headed for the long ramp up to the Recorder's office, trying not to think about what was probably happening in the Headman's place at that moment.

This was his first encounter with Coquina since his time as the Recorder's assistant. He expected Coquina to make a great show of his triumph, but Coquina's pleasure seemed instead to come from treating Benton just like any other hand.

Coquina was at his work when Benton strolled in, affecting a casual air, and said, "Hello, Ben."

The older man looked up briefly and then turned his attention again to the paper he was slowly writing on. "Use my title. What are you doing here?"

"Stephan wants me temporarily assigned to handling the jacksonite at the exit."

Without looking up again or pausing in his slow, careful writing, Coquina said, "All right, Benton. You've reported. Now get out of here and go back to where the hands belong."

Benton fought down a brief but powerful impulse to find a rock or a tool and attack Coquina. He left the office feeling curiously and unexpectedly smug. At least there was someone down here he could still feel superior to. But then he paused as he thought that, after all, Coquina had hardly even bothered to look at him. The Recorder must know Benton would feel violent impulses toward him, but he also apparently knew from his years of experience with beaten-down hands that none of them would have the courage to act on such impulses.

Benton's shoulders sagged, and he sighed. Walking in the stooped position of a hand, a habit acquired half because of all the time spent with low ceilings and half because of permanent defeat and fear, he went down the ramp, across the floor of the Big House, and along a tunnel to a dimly lighted gallery that served as a crude dormitory for the hands. He groped his way among the sleeping figures. In the dim light, they looked like scattered piles of discarded rags. He made his way to his favorite, particularly dark, spot, occasionally bumping and disturbing another hand and muttering "Sorry–sorry" when he did so.

He stretched himself out on the dark rocks and fell almost instantly into a heavy sleep. He never dreamed any more. Or, if he did, he never remembered his dreams.

He awoke to the sound of muffled curses and groans. A shadowy figure was making its way across the makeshift dormitory. The figure carried a small lux that glowed faintly. The figure moved slowly, stopping to hold the lux close to the face of each sleeper. It was this that was eliciting the protests from the disturbed hands, most of whom were chronically exhausted and needed desperately whatever sleep they were allowed to get. Benton watched idly, thinking it must be a foreman, like Stephan Scheel, who was searching for one of the hands under his command.

Eventually the searching figure reached Benton, leaned over him to examine his face, and then breathed, "At last. Thank God!" It was Diori.

She flung herself down on the floor and pressed against him violently. "Oh, Jim, I'm so sorry about the way I had to talk to you. They were listening to us, the Headman's guards, and I had to say that." She began to cry softly.

He put his arms about her and held her protectively, whispering ineffectually, "It's all right, Diori, it's all right."

Soon she calmed down and raised her face to his. She kissed him and then began to take her clothes off.

"Wait," he said. "Not now."

"They won't care," Diori said. "They won't even notice."

He knew that was true. The hands sleeping nearby would ignore them. Men and women shared this dormitory and the others like it, and it was common enough for those with enough energy left to couple in the friendly darkness. No one objected, of course. It helped relieve the hands' tensions, and it ensured a new generation of hands. Even now, he could hear occasional grunts from various directions—couplings of many kinds, not all involving only two people or members of opposite sexes. The majority of the hands were sleeping, and they didn't care what their fellows did, so long as they managed to get some sleep themselves.

But as much as Benton wanted that release right now, and as much as he wanted Diori, the thought of grimy skin rubbing against grimy skin suddenly repelled him. Beyond that, his guilt had grown. I've done so much wrong to two members of this family, he thought. I can't keep on doing that. I can't be the one who uses other people for his own pleasure.

Reluctantly at first, Diori settled down in Benton's arms, her face pressed into his shoulder. Suddenly she pulled her face away and shifted upward, so that she could place her mouth next to his ear. "I've missed you so much," she whispered. "I've had to sleep with that foul Headman I don't know how many times."

"I'll try to sleep in the same place here regularly," he told her in a voice as low as hers. "That way you can find me whenever you're able to get away." And I'll hold you, he wanted to add, but that's all I can promise.

"God, that's not good enough!" She lay against him for a moment, breathing heavily while she regained calmness. "I don't want to have to sneak around to see you, darling. I don't want to hump out here like these undermen." The way she spoke it, the name was a curse. "And I don't want to let that animal inside me again. I just want you, and I want to have you in a real bedroom, on some civilized world, without worrying about... about all of this." She hugged him fiercely. "My darling, I want us both free!"

She said more, promising him so much, promising him Paradise, but all Benton heard was that one word, free.

To be free, Benton thought. Yes, that's what I've always wanted. To be a free man, my own man. I've always been a slave.

He had had so little strength and will and freedom to begin with, and he had lost even that little bit underground.

To be free, he thought. To be free...

CHAPTER TWENTY-ONE

This might be his last chance for a long time to come. After they finished loading this pile of jacksonite onto the carts and sent it off to Heaven, he was supposed to return to Stephan's group. He didn't know when he'd be this close to an exit again.

The carts were old, their metal sides much rusted and dented. They ran on tracks through a steeply sloping shaft that turned a sharp corner before it reached the exit. Their movement was controlled from above.

The carts had arrived shortly before, half filled with clothes, tools, and food, payment for jacksonite that had been sent up a few hours earlier. The new load of jacksonite lay on the ground waiting for the carts to be emptied. For once there were no crushed, broken bodies of accident victims to pile on top of the jacksonite for their journey to Heaven.

One of the hands next to Benton looked into the carts and muttered that he thought there should be more food. "That was a big load of god-metal we sent them," he grumbled.

The grumbler was shouldered aside by one of the Headman's guards, angry at the man not because of his words—the guard had been too far away to hear them—but because the hand had infringed upon the guard's powers and privileges by getting so close to the supplies from Heaven. "Get back, you," he growled at the hand. "You don't steal any food while I'm around."

The hand backed off with the obligatory "Sorry–sorry," but the look he cast at the guard's back was pure hatred.

The guards loaded the food and other supplies from the carts into large sacks and tied them shut. This was one job they always did themselves rather than ordering hands to do it for them, perhaps the only hard job of which this was true. When they were done, they ordered some of the hands to lug the sacks back down to the Big House under the supervision of a few of the guards. The remaining hands stared after the disappearing sacks of food hungrily, until the guards who had stayed behind with the jacksonite barked orders for them to start loading the god–metal onto the carts. The hands moved forward wearily to obey.

Benton looked over his fellow hands contemptuously. Why don't they rebel? There are more of them than there are guards, and they could use their tools as weapons.

Not that he was going to lead them in revolt.

Even though the corner protected them from the light shining in through the exit, he could hardly look in that direction. The brightness was intolerable. There were luxes on the walls here, but their glow was invisible in the wash of light flooding around that corner. Benton glanced again at the guards and hands. Both groups were concentrating on the jacksonite, hurrying to get it loaded before the gods took the carts back into their realm. Benton stepped around the waist–high pile of jacksonite on the ground and started walking rapidly up the slope, toward the brilliance.

They must all have been as surprised as he'd hoped they'd be, for they didn't react until he had covered most of the nine or ten meters to the corner of the shaft. Then one of the Headman's guards yelled, "Benton! Stop!"

Benton walked even faster up the steep grade.

The guard's next words were a surprise. "The gods, man, they'll kill you!"

But there were no footsteps. The guards were not pursuing him.

He ran around the corner, gasping for breath, and the light struck him like a physical blow. He fell heavily against the side of the shaft and tried to look at the exit and will his eyes to stay open.

He could see the brilliant opening only through a mist of tears and pain that stabbed through his eyes and filled his head. He would not let himself look away. He stepped out into the center of the shaft and started walking deliberately up the slope toward the exit.

A shadow, a form, appeared in the brilliance ahead. It roared at him with an immense voice. "UNDERMAN! TURN AROUND! RETURN!"

He knew that it was a guard and that the voice was electronically amplified, but despite his knowledge a thrill of superstitious fear shivered through him: Heaven, the gods, and their mighty voices!

"I'm not an underman!" he called back.

He didn't slow or stop, but kept walking steadily upslope. His eyes were already growing accustomed to the light, and he could make the figure out more easily. It took shape as a man with a brilliant glow behind him. The man raised his arms to shoulder height, his elbows jutting sideways, his head ducking slightly.

A gun!

Benton shouted desperately, "I'm an offworlder! I was in an accident!"

Something *pinged* off the wall at head height to his left. Rock splinters burned against his cheek. Benton stood frozen in fear. There was a puff of wind at his left ear and a sudden stinging pain in his earlobe. He knew there'd be a third shot, and this one wouldn't miss. He turned and ran in panic back down the slope. He hit the wall at the curve and stumbled around the corner. Out of sight of the entrance, he collapsed full length on the ground and lay there, his chest heaving. It seemed pitch dark to him.

Benton had entirely forgotten his fellow hands and the Headman's guards. Now he heard feet scuffling in the dirt all around him, and he remembered their existence. An awed voice said, "Look at his ear!" Benton recognized the voice as that of the man who had earlier complained about the amount of food in the carts. "He didn't obey them, and bang! Just like that, they made his ear all bloody."

Benton rose groggily to his feet. The men surrounding him were vague shapes.

Another voice said, "The gods tried to kill him, but he ran away before they could do it."

A third man said angrily, "Don't be a fool, Mikah. They could have killed him easily if they'd really wanted to."

Benton's eyes were recovering at last. The men's faces took form through a haze of dancing sparkles. He saw a mixture of expressions on the hands' faces—awe, uncertainty, sympathy, fear. On the faces of the guards, he saw mostly hostility. Anger arose in him at their stupidity and superstition, and he said, "They wanted to kill me, all right, but their shots missed." His voice sounded harsh in his own ears. The hands looked alarmed at his words, edging away from him. "Damn it," he shouted, "they're not gods at all, they're just men, like you and me, except that they live out on the surface instead of being trapped down here!"

As he spoke, the two groups—hands and guards—coalesced into one. Now all their faces showed hostility mixed with fear. One of them said, "The gods will kill us if we listen to him." Another turned toward the bright corner and bowed, saying, "Sorry–sorry, gods, sorry–sorry."

Benton tried again, but he knew even as he spoke that it was hopeless. He sensed an impenetrable barrier between them and his words, and what he said had no more effect than blades of grass blown against a stone wall. "I know they're men. I came from there myself. I'm only here by accident. Listen to me!"

Their eyes were frantic. A guard shouted, "We'll help you, gods!" Others took up the cry. "Kill him! Kill him!"

They rushed forward. Benton turned to run, but before he could manage more than a step, something—a hammer, some other tool—slammed into the back of his head.

Blinded with agony, he pitched forward, landing on his hands and knees beside one of the partially loaded carts. The undermen rained blows on him, some with bare hands, but a few with tools. Benton tried to rise, to escape, but he couldn't, and he knew as he began to slip into unconsciousness that they would keep on until he was dead.

There was a rattling and clanking from the carts as they

began to move, returning to the surface. Faintly, as if from a great distance, Benton heard one of his attackers yell at the others, "Get him in there. Let the gods have him."

He felt himself grabbed roughly, lifted up, and then dropped. He landed on his back on top of the pile of jacksonite in the cart, with his head lolling backwards on the sloping side of the pile.

He could feel the carts moving, accelerating toward the corner. They swung quickly around the corner and began climbing toward the exit. Filled with pain, unable to move or to open or close his eyes all the way, he stared at the rapidly approaching exit as it grew larger and brighter. He could see the silhouette of the top of the load of jacksonite piled in the first cart. As it passed through the shaft exit, there was a series of flashes, faint many–colored pencils of light lancing into the load of ore. Puffs of dust arose from the surface of the irregular heap of jacksonite wherever the lights struck. Dazed as he was, Benton realized that it was an automated system of particle beams or possibly even Arrastra field generators used to probe for and kill any stowaway undermen who might be hiding under the jacksonite.

He tried desperately to move, to get out of the way and off the cart before he reached the exit, but he could not make his body obey. He lay motionless as the cart he was riding rattled to the exit and through it. He glimpsed the pencils of light striking the ore just in front of his head, then there was an intolerable flash of heat against his chest and everything disappeared.

The carts clattered to a stop inside the hut that covered the exit. The light that had seemed so blinding to Benton was just the artificial light inside the hut. During the daytime, the light in the desert outside was much brighter than this. Now, though, it was night outside.

The two Corporation employees working inside the hut inspected the carts of ore briefly.

"Another goddamned corpse. This one's your turn. Get it out of here."

"We ought to turn off the fans and let them all die. Bring in machines instead. Look at this! Not even a full load of ore this time."

Benton's limp body was dragged from the cart, arms, legs, and head lolling, mouth open, eyes staring sightlessly. He was loaded onto a flat platform tied behind a small floater. The Corporation guard whose turn it was to handle the corpses climbed into the floater and drove out through a cargo door, towing the platform behind. The man who was staying behind called after him maliciously, "Have a nice trip!" but the driver ignored him.

Outside, the larger moon, Rheni, was just rising, looking deceptively large. Her faint, silvery light flooded across the already cold desert floor and shone into Benton's open, sightless eyes. Inside the floater, the driver shivered and tried to concentrate on his navigation instruments. After driving for a couple of kilometers, he reached a wide, shallow pit, an ancient crater in the desert floor about ten meters deep and fifteen times as wide. With the moon still so low and the floater's lights pointed off to one side, the bottom of the pit was a confused jumbled of shadowy bumps and heaps of dirt.

The driver grasped Benton's body by the ankles and dragged it from the platform to the ground, then across the dirt to the edge of the crater. He shoved it off the edge and watched it roll floppily down to the crater floor. He was supposed to get a shovel from the floater and throw dirt down on the body, but he looked around at the lonely desert, the faraway moon, the shadow of desert mountains off in the distance, and the shadows in the undermen's mass grave, and he shivered again and climbed quickly back into his floater and headed back toward his duty station.

The lights of the floater faded into the desert gloom. An occasional breeze stirred the sand. Otherwise, there was no movement at the vast pit filled with the numberless dead of the underworld.

CHAPTER TWENTY-TWO

The morning sun brought feeling and pain and awareness back, and along with those came consciousness of a powerful odor. Benton opened his eyes, then winced at the early morning sunlight and closed them again. He lay still for a while, his eyes squeezed shut, his mind fuzzy. That light—where was he? He put his hand over his face for shade and opened his eyes cautiously.

A face, eyes wide open, stared back at him. It was Marguerite Borrasca.

Benton looked at her in puzzlement for a long time, unable to dredge her name from among his blurred memories. There was something wrong about her being where he was, and her face looked wrinkled and shriveled compared to what he remembered. Her name floated up from the depths of his awareness. "Marguerite?" he mumbled.

There was no response.

He concentrated, and at last he remembered, and at the same time he suddenly recognized the smell. Rotten-sweet and overwhelming, it filled the silent air of the crater. Once, as a child on Earth, Benton had found a litter of dead kittens, dumped under a tree days or weeks before. This smell was the same as that, but far stronger and more concentrated.

He staggered to his feet. Now he could see that only Marguerite's face was left. The back of her head had been crushed. The bones of her legs poked through the withered flesh. Some small desert animal was busily nibbling on one ankle. When Benton moved, it looked up at him in sudden alarm and then scampered away across the pit. Following it with his eyes, he saw a vast field of corpses, some bloated, some mummified by the desert air, others reduced to a scattering of bones.

Gagging, Benton stumbled up the sloping side of the crater to the ground above. Exhausted by the effort, he collapsed on his stomach just beyond the edge of the pit.

A faint breeze was blowing in across the desert, coming from the opposite direction from where the sun was rising. The clean air, still mild from the night–cooled ground, gradually revived him.

He felt a sharp pain in the middle of his chest. He rolled onto his side and craned his neck forward to see the cause of the pain. His ragged clothing was charred in a rough circle perhaps eight or ten centimeters in diameter on his chest.

He pulled at the blackened cloth cautiously. It ripped off easily, revealing a fused lump of metal against his skin. He stared dully at it, finally recognizing it as the remains of the gift from Augie Syen, the field–effect generator that had failed to save her brother's life. Apparently, though, it had saved Benton's. It must have turned on in response to the blue pencils of light at the shaft exit. It had survived long enough to protect him from them, but then it had overloaded somehow and fused. The skin beneath it was badly blistered. And yet, now that he was no longer lying on the chunk of metal, he felt no pain in his chest. It was as if his mind were detached from his body, and there was no pain because something in him had decided to ignore the signals from his nerve endings.

The mental fog lifted, and Benton experienced a degree of clear, crystal intellectual perception that he hadn't known since the accident in the tunnel with Harve Borrasca and the other Corporation men. He understood where he must be and what this place signified. The village he had come from might only send up a few corpses every now and then—the honored dead—but he saw now that there must indeed be many other villages of undermen and that other villages also sent up their dead.

Which was worse—lying out here in the desert, decaying or mummifying, eaten away by small animals, or falling down a glory hole into a dark underground lake, where you were eaten by an overgrown white snake?

It makes no difference to the dead, he thought. And only the living count.

From the number of corpses that he judged to be of relatively recent vintage, he assumed that someone would be returning here soon to dump more of them into the pit. That would give him his chance to escape.

From the desert, first. And then from Colliery.

He took the chain from his neck and sat on the rim of the crater, holding the chain so that the lump of fused metal rested on the ground. His gaze roamed over the corpses in the pit, the exposed bones growing daily whiter in the intense sunlight, the small animals once more scurrying about the crater floor on their gruesome business, and the calm desert beyond. One part of his mind cautioned him that he would soon suffer from thirst and heat, that his white skin, buried underground for so long, would burn and blister just as the skin of his chest had. But with a stoicism and fatalism that would have seemed both alien and repellent to him not long ago, he put those fears aside and sat silently to wait, just another feature of the patient desert. As if foresighted, he had seen what he had to do and would do during the coming weeks, and he was content to follow that path, even determined to do so.

The sun rose higher and higher behind him and to his left. He marked the progress of his shadow, stretching across the crater floor and angling off to his right. He noted the direction in which shadow man's head slid, for that was east. He was obviously in the southern hemisphere, since his shadow was pointing south of east. Or was he perhaps near the equator, in the northern hemisphere, near the time of the northern summer solstice? He had no idea what the date was, so he could not use that as a datum. He knew the planet's axial tilt was slight, and so he chose to ignore it. He decided he had no choice but to assume that he was in the southern hemisphere and that the direction pointed by the shadow's movements was true east. The length of his shadow in the southerly direction seemed to support that conclusion. He must be at a high latitude, too high for him to be in the tropics. Straight south, then, lay the life–band, and it must not be very far away. There he would be able to survive more readily than here, and there he would gain time enough for the next step, escape from Colliery itself. All he needed now was transportation, and he knew that must be on its way.

He waited motionlessly.

A faint hum to his rear alerted Benton that a floater was coming.

Ignoring the protests of his stiff muscles and newly burned skin, he went down on his stomach and crawled away from the crater, edging behind an outlying ripple left from the crater's formation. Here he would be safe from observation unless the floater pilot were actually looking for him, but from this cover Benton would be able to watch the floater.

It was the same floater which had carried Benton to the crater, although of course he didn't know that. Behind it was the platform, this time carrying a load of three dead undermen.

Benton watched while the driver pulled up to the edge of the crater, rolled the three corpses into the pit one by one, and then shoveled a few perfunctory loads of sand down after them. The driver turned back to his floater and found himself face–to–face with Benton.

The driver gasped in shock. "Who—" He looked Benton over quickly, taking in the dirty, long hair and beard and the ragged clothing. "An underman," he said, understanding combining in his voice with contempt. Benton stood unmoving, staring at the driver impassively, unblinking. "You got out alive somehow," the driver said. He grinned, raised his shovel above his head, and said, "I can correct that mistake."

Before the driver could make another move, Benton swung hard, lashing out with the hand which held the chain. The jagged edges of the melted field–effect generator whipped across the driver's eyes. He shrieked, dropped his shovel behind him, and grabbed at his face.

Benton lunged at him, knocking him off his feet. The driver landed on hands and knees, scrabbling desperately for the shovel he could no longer see. Benton jumped onto the man's back, wrapped the chain quickly twice about his neck, and pulled it tight.

Wordlessly, the two men rolled and thrashed about in the sand, the driver clawing at his neck, trying futilely to get his fingers around the thin metal strand that was sinking through his flesh even while it was choking him. Benton held on grimly, making no more sound than the dying man.

At last the struggles of the man beneath him stopped. There was a final quivering, a weak contraction of the torso, and then the driver's body became lax.

Benton's face, hands, and chest were covered with blood. His victim was almost decapitated.

Suddenly filled with horror, Benton sprang away from the body. For a moment, he thought of climbing into the floater and leaving the awful scene as quickly as he could. Prudence prevailed. No, he told himself. I'll hide this body to delay pursuit.

Driven by an indefinable impulse, he pulled the chain from its grisly resting place deep in the dead man's neck and stuffed it into one of his pockets. He dragged the corpse to the crater's edge and shoved it over. When it had rolled to a resting place among the other bodies below, Benton shoveled sand over it. Now from the crater rim it appeared to be just another underman's body. After a day or two in the desert, exposed to the scavengers in the crater and with the effects of both putrefaction and the desert sun and air, the resemblance would be complete.

After some fumbling, Benton managed to unhook the platform from the floater. Then he climbed into the driver's compartment and got the vehicle moving southward.

Time crept by as the floater crawled south over the desert.

There was a small stash of emergency supplies in the floater. Since he didn't know how long it would take him to reach the life-band, Benton tried to use as little at a time as possible of the water and dehydrated food. A day and a night passed, and still the desert seemed unchanged, with no sign that it might soon start giving way to the vegetation that would mark the beginning of the life-band. Twice he thought he saw stands of trees on the horizon, and he changed direction to investigate, but both times he found only strange rock outcroppings, spires with broad, flat, mushroomlike heads keeping their dry watch over the sands.

By noon of the second day, however, he was struck by how low the sun hung behind him.

Now that he felt confident that he was heading in the right direction, he had to start thinking about something he had been deliberately ignoring—the high probability that, sooner or later, he would be pursued.

No one but the dead driver had known of his escape to the surface. By now, however, someone must be wondering about the driver himself. If they decided to search for him and started by going out to the crater, they might or might not think of examining the fresher bodies to see if the driver was among them, but they would certainly find the platform Benton had unhooked and left behind.

Perhaps I should have left it attached, taken it with me.

No, he knew he had been right to leave it. The dial that seemed to show the charge level remaining in the power pack had indicated a low charge from the start. By now, it had dropped almost to zero. He had wanted to reduce the drain as far as possible as well as permitting himself the highest speed the vehicle could attain. The inertia of the platform would have drained the power pack faster and made piloting more difficult.

If the searchers found the platform but not the body, they would probably assume that the driver had taken off on an unauthorized vacation. Benton wasn't sure how the Corporation would react to that, but an employee working at one of the desert stations was privileged with the Corporation's one great secret, and Benton suspected that the Corporation's reaction would be strong. They would pursue the driver.

On the other hand, if they did find the driver's body, they'd know he had been killed and would guess that his killer had taken the floater.

So they would pursue the floater whether they found the driver's body or not.

How would they try to track the floater? By air? By satellite?

Struck by that thought, he stopped the floater and climbed out. As he had feared, it was leaving a trail in the desert. There it was, like a shallow valley a quarter of a meter deep or less, slightly wider than the floater itself, with banks of heaped–up dust, pointing back north arrow–straight.

Given time, the desert winds would eliminate it.

Given time.

He crawled up onto the top of the floater. Ignoring the fierce heat baking up at him from the metal roof and penetrating his callused soles, he shaded his eyes and stared at the southern horizon. The rippling, dancing heat waves rising from the desert floor made it impossible to be certain of the details, but he convinced himself that there were trees on the horizon.

He knew that it could turn out to be yet another pile of rocks. Given the low energy level remaining in the floater's power pack, an unsuccessful side trip entailed a risk.

Thanks to the trail he was leaving in the desert, so did continuing on his present path.

He clambered back into the artificial coolness of the floater and sat for a while, recovering from the heat and weighing the risks. Even such a relatively short time outside the floater at the height of the day had sucked moisture from him. Walking in that would be impossible.

Earlier, he had searched the compartment for maps, but with no success. Even the navigation instruments were minimal, limited to a directional compass and a gauge to show speed and distance traveled. Perhaps this was due to the Corporation's penchant for secrecy, perhaps due to the lack of settlements in the desert. On a more heavily settled planet, he would have expected any vehicle designed for long trips to display his correct position on a dashboard map and to keep that position updated by regular, frequent automatic queries to ground navigation beacons and navigation satellites. Obviously that was not to be expected on Colliery.

Which was something to be thankful for, he realized. If the floater had been communicating with a navigation satellite all this time, the Corporation would have been able to listen in on the communication and would have known exactly where he was.

Think like the man you killed, he ordered himself. A Corporation guard, stationed out in the desert, well paid but bored. And now you've gone AWOL. What would you do? Where would you go? That's the kind of thought process the

Corporation will be trying to duplicate right now.

Was that compass magnetic? If so, how far off would it be here on Colliery and at this longitude? Geology, geography—he should have read more on those subjects!

Well, maybe the guard wouldn't have known the answer either.

Suppose, still playing the guard, he'd decided he was off course on his way to whatever illicit fun he might have arranged. What would the guard do?

Benton couldn't guess. He couldn't really be sure what the guard would have done in his circumstances. All he could really do was come up with something the guard might do, something believable to any pursuers. Fooling the pursuers was what really mattered.

He changed the vehicle's heading until the compass indicated he was aiming twenty degrees west of south.

Benton's original intention had been to set off south on foot while the floater continued unmanned on its slightly angled course. Now he reconsidered. When the pursuers found the empty floater, they would backtrack it to this point, where the floater had changed course, and would naturally assume that he had left on foot from here. That would make him too easy to catch. Also, he already knew from his few moments on the floater's roof that he would have to travel during the night.

He started the floater moving again at top speed and kept it at that steady rate for hours, until the sun had slid down the sky almost to the horizon. Then he cut the speed to about a walking pace.

While the sun moved past the horizon at a shallow angle and the desert night closed in—much more sudden than in the life-bands, but still slowed by the high latitude—Benton made a small package out of the dehydrated food and added to that package one small container of water. It wasn't much, it might even prove to be not enough, but he didn't see how he could carry more than that.

As soon as he thought it was dark enough, he slid over to the left–hand door of the floater, opened it, and stepped out at a walk. Without stopping, he walked rapidly off at what he hoped was about a twenty–degree angle to the floater's route. The door of the floater was still open and he could see the lights of the driver's compartment, keeping pace with him and slowly drawing further and further away to the right. It was strangely fascinating to watch, and it provided a rough directional guide for him. At last, after what seemed like hours of walking, the lights had drawn so far away, dwindled and faded so much, that he could no longer see them.

From the start, he had chosen a star just above the horizon that seemed to lie directly in front of him. Now he focussed his full attention on it and walked directly toward it, trying to ignore the steadily more penetrating cold.

The distance of the star above the horizon seemed to have increased slightly. Benton knew that this meant either that the star was not truly to the south and was rising with Colliery's revolution, or that it was indeed a southern polar star and it had risen because he had traveled that much further south. He reassured himself that it must be the latter and kept walking as steadily as fatigue, cold, and occasionally uneven terrain permitted.

From time to time he thought about the identity of the pursuers. Would they be guards from the mine? No, more likely the Corporation would send out some of its policemen.

Benton thought of Galena and shivered, not entirely with fear.

CHAPTER TWENTY-THREE

So far, day was just a faint glow outlining the horizon beyond his left shoulder, but Benton was already wondering what he would do for shelter during the coming hours of fierce heat. His thoughts were growing blurry from the combined effects of exertion, sleeplessness, and the blows he had received underground. Was it his imagination, or perhaps his fatigue, or was the ground now actually pulling at his feet, holding on to them at each step?

The breeze had lost its biting edge and felt softer. How nice it would be to lie down and drift away....

He shook his head and cursed himself. He couldn't stop yet.

Benton realized that his walk had slowed to a stop and that he was swaying, his sense of balance slipping from him. He fell to his knees and then forward onto his hands, his head hanging down. He stayed in that position, hoping vaguely that the rush of extra blood would help clear his mind. It did, at least enough for him to become aware that his fingers were sinking into what looked like mud.

In the middle of the desert? He must be hallucinating. But if so, it was a remarkably complete, detailed hallucination, for he could even feel the cool moisture soaking through the cloth covering his knees. He pulled his hands from the ooze, which let go with a reluctant, sucking noise. The shock had cleared his mind even more, and he slid his hands delicately over the mud's slippery surface, hoping and yet trying not to hope. He found what he had hoped for—low, stubbly vegetation living on firmer islands within the mud. It was no hallucination, then. He had found moisture. It was the beginning of the life-band.

But why a swamp? Why mud, instead of isolated clumps of vegetation in the midst of sand?

He realized that somewhere ahead of him must lie a small stream, a river from the life-band. It petered out in the desert, creating this mud flat with its straggling vegetation. And below him, he knew, the water filtered steadily downward through the sand and cracks in the rocks beneath until it joined with underground rivers, perhaps even making its way to join the roaring waterfall he had seen at Lux Lake.

He forced himself to his feet again and slogged on through the mud. Eventually, he hoped, he'd find the stream itself, and he could then follow that back into the life-band. Along the way, it would also solve a problem he had been worrying about, that he would run out of water and hence also be unable to use his food supply. With the river water available, he should have no problem making it well into the life-band. Once there, he knew he could survive indefinitely.

The sky was brightening. Benton toyed with the idea of stopping at this point and waiting for night. He could cover himself with mud to stave off dehydration and lessen the chances of detection from the air. But surely those were trees ahead—the real thing, this time. He couldn't stop this close to his goal.

He forced himself to move, walking with increasing difficulty through the deepening mud. The sun rose slowly, a huge, mild, red ball at first, but growing smaller, brighter, and hotter as it rose. What he had thought were distant trees looked even more like trees as he drew closer. Small, stunted, twisted outposts on the desert, only slightly taller than he was, they struck him nonetheless as supernaturally beautiful. He leaned against one of them, embracing it.

The mud had given way to firm riverbanks covered with grassy vegetation. The banks were wide, but the water that ran between them was slow moving and shallow, with the riverbed exposed in many places, so that the river was more like a collection of small separate streams twisting back and forth over each other in the space between the banks. There must have been much more water in the past, and not too long ago.

Gratefully, Benton prepared himself some of the dehydrated food, using up the last of the water he had brought from the floater. After eating, he lay down in the trees' meager shade and slept.

The driver who did not return was named John Biot. The guards at the shaft exits worked in pairs, and his partner and friend, Phil Skarn, waited until his shift was over and he'd been relieved before reluctantly reporting Biot's disappearance.

Skarn knew what this would do to Biot's career. Biot had left his post in the desert without authorization twice before, and the second time he'd been warned that he'd get no more chances, that the third time would mean demotion or even firing—a grim fate on Colliery. For a time, it had looked as if Biot was taking the warning seriously and had reformed his ways.

He'd become almost as diligent a worker as Skarn himself. But now he'd pulled this.

Skarn shook his head. He liked John, but there was a limit to friendship. It wouldn't be safe for one man to guard the shaft alone, and if he didn't report Biot's absence quickly so that the work schedule could be rearranged to make up for the missing worker, then Skarn would find himself working alone every time his shift came up, until Biot chose to wander back in again.

It was midmorning and the heat was already fierce. Skarn hurried across the open square of beaten–down sand into the welcome cool of the foreman's office. "Mr. Green," he said, "John Biot went out last night with a body for the crater and never came back."

Green slammed one hand against the desktop. "Damn that man!" He stood up and stalked over to a window. After a moment, he said without turning around, "Okay, Phil. Thanks. I'll take care of it."

Green stared morosely out the window at the featureless kilometers of blazing sand while he listened to the sound of Skarn leaving. Wonderful goddamned scenery we have in this goddamned place, he thought. He could understand Biot's being sick of it. Every man here was. The difference was that the other men stuck it out for the sake of their careers and families. Biot had been warned of the consequences before, but Green had received an even sterner warning from his own superiors. "Keep your men in line, Green," they'd said, "or we'll put someone in there who can." This time, they might carry out their threat.

What to do? If it had been any other employee, Green would have assumed that the man's floater had broken down and Green would have sent out a rescue party. With Biot, though, he knew that would be a waste of time. And it would reduce his now limited manpower even more. If it really was a floater breakdown and Biot was innocent—Well, Green thought, looking out at the yellow-white sands with a kind of gloomy satisfaction, let the bastard walk back anyway. He deserves it for the last two times.

He wouldn't file a verbal report. That would be too sure to attract the kind of upper-echelon attention to Biot's latest escapade that Green most certainly did not want. He sat down at his desk again and with great care and deliberation composed as innocuous a report on his employee's disappearance as he could dream up. With luck—and he felt he deserved some for a change—this report would grind its way slowly up the lines of communication until it reached some bored personnel clerk who'd file it away without comment. In the end, Biot might even escape being punished by Corporation officialdom, if not by Green, when he floated back. Far more important, Green's own job and career would be undamaged. With real luck, this time Biot would decide not to return at all, and no one would ever have any reason to open the man's personnel file and confront Green with the misdeeds of one of his men.

Meanwhile, John Biot's body lay in the crater beneath its coating of sand, sightless eyes staring at nothing. Already the organisms that lived within the body were doing their destructive work. Attack would soon begin from the outside as well, for the crater's small scavengers were working their way toward the body. Not much time would be needed before John Biot would be unrecognizable to the men he had worked so closely with for the last two years.

The floater trail leading away from the crater had already been obliterated by the unusually strong morning breezes of desert springtime. Further south, the trail persisted, but its edges were blurring as the sand that formed its banks dribbled back into the central depression. Long before Green's report came to anyone's attention, the trail would have attenuated so completely that not even the most sensitive of heat or chemical sensors would be able to tell it apart from the surrounding sand of the desert.

Still further south, the unmanned floater drifted slowly to a stop and, with a sound much like a sigh, settled down onto the sand. The lights in the compartment faded one by one and blinked out. Now the floater was as dead as the guard who had once driven it. Unlike the escapee from the underground who had commandeered it, the floater hadn't quite managed to reach the fringes of the life–band.

The escapee himself was on the move again, following the river in the upstream direction.

The volume of water in the river increased constantly as Benton traveled south. Vegetation increased and the sand disappeared. The desert blended slowly and steadily into the life–band. Small animals appeared before his food supply ran out, tame enough that he had no trouble capturing them when he needed to.

He knew the worst was over now. He had no idea how to start a fire and so ate his meat raw, hoping that these wild animals had no diseases that could threaten him. He had eaten the water snakes from Lux Lake raw, and those hadn't harmed him. If he had come up with a way to make fire, he would not have done so, for fire would have increased the risk of detection.

Even raw, after his long time in the mines on underman rations, the food was pure Heaven.

But after all, he reminded himself, I am in the Garden of Eden.

With adequate food, water, rest, and the exercise of walking, Benton's strength increased rapidly. He wandered aimlessly, observing the plant and animal life and the weather patterns of the life-band.

There was frequent rain, usually brief showers but sometimes great storms with lightning, thunder, strong winds, and heavy downpours. Consistently, it seemed to him, the storms moved to the north—from the pole toward the desert. The streams he encountered tended to flow in the same direction. The air was mild most of the time, but there were occasional unexpected cold breezes. Sometimes these came with the storms, but at other times they seemed to spring up from nowhere and then fade away just as quickly. The sky was rarely cloudless, and even when there were no thunderstorms visible, Benton could always see high, thin cirrus clouds moving surprisingly quickly, always from south to north.

After about ten days of this, Benton felt ready at last to make his next move.

So far, he had seen no one, whether policeman or vacationer, and he had been happy with that fact. Now the time had come to start actively looking for other human beings.

CHAPTER TWENTY-FOUR

It took him days to find anyone, but Benton knew from his own past experiences with Borrasca that there were many vacationers and Corporation-provided cabins in the life-band. If he roamed for long enough, he'd find them eventually.

By chance, he seemed to have hit upon a part of the life-band where vacationers were rare. Finally, prompted by the memory of the campfire he and Borrasca had built, Benton took to climbing partway up the taller, thicker trees to look for smoke.

That there were so many huge trees and so much wildlife suddenly struck him as odd. Hadn't there been extensive farming in the life-bands before the discovery of jacksonite? Surely the wilderness couldn't have recovered so quickly. Or was the plant and animal life of Colliery given to unusually fast growth and adaptation?

Near sunset, when he was about to give up searching for that day, Benton saw what he was seeking: a thin, blue-grey column of smoke rising above the tops of the intervening trees and floating high into the still air. It was an atypically clear day, and the smoke rose straight against the richer blue of the sky, improbably high without dissipating, until it reached the winds of the higher altitudes and vanished. He clambered down the tree quickly and headed off in that direction. Once on the ground, he could no longer see the smoke. Occasionally he climbed again to check his direction.

It was a party of four, two young couples seated around a fire in a small clearing, laughing and joking, eating and drinking—not water—and enjoying themselves with innocent noisiness. They might have been any of the young people he had partied with during his first days on Colliery. He could almost have imagined that they and the world they knew were the true reality and that he had been wandering lost in the life-band, hallucinating, dreaming up the mines and the undermen.

There was no vehicle in the clearing. He would surely have heard or seen a flyer from some distance. They must have walked to this point.

He had learned more while living off the wilderness than he had been aware of at the time. He crept silently along the edge of the clearing, just hidden from the four vacationers, scarcely moving the grass and branches as he passed. He examined the ground and the vegetation carefully as he went, thankful for the long, slow twilight. The trail the four had made on their way to the clearing was very easy to spot—a pathway of crushed grass, scuffed dirt, and broken branches as definite as that left by a small herd of animals. Benton was unaware of any irony in his feeling of contempt at their lack of care.

Moving swiftly, he followed their trail backward through the forest and across an open meadow. By the time he reached the trees on the other side of the field, although the trail was still well-marked, the light was fading. Benton vacillated, finally decided that the group would surely sleep late. They had walked many kilometers before reaching their present camp site, and their fatigue, combined with the effects of all the food and drink he had seen them consuming and whatever games they planned for the nighttime hours, would keep them from making an early start. He quelled his impatience, found himself a comfortable spot in the branches of a nearby tree just in case someone did come by during the night, and slept.

As soon as the light returned, he was on the move again. About midday, he found another campsite and, not many kilometers further, yet another. The trail he was now following was therefore presumably three days old. Still he persisted, looking carefully for the fading signs. Instinct told him that this trail would take him where he needed to go.

By then, it was twilight again. Rather than stop, Benton pushed himself even more, moved even faster. There was no forest here, only rolling fields, grassland that retained well the trail of the clumsy hikers. Suddenly desperate, Benton ran, ignoring the startled animals and birds that fled to either side. He breasted a hill and stopped short. He had almost lost faith in his instinct, but now that intuition was proved triumphantly correct.

In a small valley below him, situated next to a small stream, stood one of The Jacksonite Corporation's vacation cabins. A small flyer was parked in front of it.

The scene had a waiting, inviting look, as if it were ready for the return of the two couples—or for him.

There might still be someone in there, he warned himself.

Hell with that, he thought.

Throwing caution to the winds, exhilarated, he raced down the hillside. Would the door be locked? Not in the Garden of

Eden.

The cabin door was not locked.

Once inside, he stopped in momentary confusion. What to do first? Surely, first priority should be to check out the flyer, looking for maps and making sure the power supply was adequate, and then leave for the nearest city.

However, he couldn't go to a city looking like an underman.

He knew that was seductively appealing logic. The comforts of civilization, even though represented here in simplified, toned–down form, were exerting an irresistible appeal. How long had it been since he'd looked and felt like a civilized urban man? Weeks, even years? He had no idea how much time had passed since he'd gone underground. The two couples would certainly not be back for days yet. He could even treat himself to the luxury of a bed, if he wished, after all that time of sleeping on hard rocks, hard ground, hard tree branches.

No. What came first was undoubtedly the longest shower of his life.

He stood happily in the gush of water from the showerhead, marveling at the dirtiness of the water as it ran off him. He blessed the Collierites for their decadence in providing running hot water even out here in the wilderness. He soaped himself over and over again, vaguely surprised that there was still pink skin beneath the grime. Once he'd washed them, his hair and beard seemed even longer than they had before, when they'd been so snarled and tangled with grease and filth.

Benton stepped from the shower and, for the first time, caught sight of himself in the bathroom's full–length mirror. It was a stranger who stared back at him, an underman. A clean underman, admittedly, and therefore unique, but still an underman.

Eyes and nose were the only facial features visible through the shaggy tangle of hair. The body he remembered as slightly plump was now extremely lean but with hard, wiry muscles visible everywhere. For a long moment, he stared at himself in mixed puzzlement and amusement. Combined with those feelings, though, was a tinge of fear. He didn't know himself any more, and he felt slightly frightened of this wild-eyed stranger, who looked capable of any sort of violence if he was interfered with.

Who had already killed one man he hadn't even known.

The memory would haunt him, he knew, no matter how much he rationalized the necessity of killing the guard at the crater.

Were there pictures of him scattered around Colliery, saying WANTED FOR MURDER? Pictures of an underman or of the real James Benton.

Whichever one was the real James Benton...

Any pictures would surely be of a generic underman. Which meant he had to get rid of the long hair and beard. For that matter, he couldn't remember having seen any other man with beard or long hair on Colliery, so to look the way he did now would only make him more conspicuous.

One of the men in the party had left a shaver in the bathroom. Benton played it over his face, removing the beard and vaporizing it at the same time. The shaver had some problems dealing with such a quantity of hair at one time. Doubtless it had never been called on for such heavy duty before and wasn't designed for shaving off full beards. Shavers also weren't designed to give haircuts, but Benton persevered and improvised and managed at last to achieve a somewhat ragged and very short cut.

A bit more, and he'd be bald. He considered that for a moment. That would also help disguise him, but it would also render him conspicuous, for he didn't think he'd noticed any uncorrected baldness on Colliery.

The planet of the happy medium, he thought. No man bald, no man's hair too long. Everything happy and innocent and aboveboard. Except for what's below the boards.

Benton studied his face in the mirror. It, at least, was still recognizable, although there were subtle changes. He couldn't pinpoint them, but he could see the overall change in the impression his face gave. He had always thought his face looked easygoing and amiable, if a bit withdrawn. Now the expression was one of wariness and impenetrability. This was an uncompromising face, strong and with hard edges. The strange, fierce man staring out of his own face disturbed him even more than the changes in his body.

Enough of this, he told himself impatiently. What you don't need is more introspection.

Of the clothing left in the cabin by the two men, one set was considerably too large for Benton, and the other set was slightly too small. After a moment's hesitation, Benton chose some of the smaller clothing. He returned to the bathroom and picked up the ragged clothes he had taken off before showering. He stuffed them into the toilet and pushed the button three times, feeling reasonably certain after that that the last thread had been obliterated.

The vacationers would be able to tell someone had been in here, especially since he had taken some clothing and planned to take the flyer, and they would presumably report the incident to the police. However, surely no one would guess that the burglar had been an escaped underman.

It occurred to Benton that Collierites seemed to lock their doors in town but leave things unlocked when vacationing in the life-bands. Personal property in town, but Corporation property out here? Perhaps that was it—that they cared about the former but not the latter. Or perhaps even criminals were too frightened of the Corporation to commit crimes against its property. He hoped the pattern held and the flyer door was unlocked.

Benton went out to the flyer. The door was indeed unlocked. He was relieved to see that it was a public vehicle assigned to the vacation trade, and he would be able to start the vehicle up and operate it without first having to give his hand or eye prints to an onboard computer.

There was one map in the flyer. It covered the cabin and the surrounding area, with the location of the cabin circled in red. Near the edge of the map, just beyond the fringe of the life-band, there was a fair-sized city. Benton took the machine off the ground and headed in that direction.

It was dark by now, and he had at least an hour of flying time ahead of him. He could take a brief nap, if he wished. But his heart was pumping with sudden excitement, his adrenaline level was high, and he knew sleep would be impossible.

CHAPTER TWENTY-FIVE

It was the middle of the night. The city was a brilliant cluster of jewels below and ahead of him, lights of every color, blinking, moving, lines of them marking streets and dark spaces marking residential areas and parks. Benton headed for one of the dark places near the fringe of the city and came down almost to ground level on a quiet country road.

Keeping the flyer less than a meter above the ground, he drifted toward the city. The flyer was not much larger than a typical floater. To any observer at a police scope in the city, his vehicle should look like just another floater carrying its occupant back home.

The number of shadowy buildings beside the road kept increasing, indicating that he was well into the fringes of the city. Benton began to worry that the chances of detection were also increasing. At last he saw the pale glow of a roadside public comm kiosk. In the dark, it looked unsettlingly like the glow of a lux in an underground tunnel. At least Colliery had such public comms, thanks to their odd system of fixed comms and lack of portable ones. Primitive technology was not always a bad thing.

He landed beside it and walked quickly to the half-enclosed terminal. He had used these kiosks occasionally before, but he still found them strange, exotic, and intimidating. Unlike the systems on other worlds, Colliery's comms weren't equipped for voice input. The user had to type everything—a particularly slow and painful process for anyone who had grown up using more advanced technology and therefore didn't know how to type.

At least the most common functions had dedicated buttons. He pressed the one labeled INFORMATION.

As he did so, it occurred to Benton that this primitive system had a big advantage. Voice recognition would have meant that his voice might have been recognized as that of James Benton.

The screen displayed the message TYPE IN REQUESTED NAME—LAST, FIRST. A rectangular array of alphabet letters appeared on the screen.

Benton shook his head in annoyance. Searching for each letter, he slowly entered BORRASCA, HARVE.

There was a long pause. Finally a comm code appeared on the screen. The system added the information that the comm code he had entered was in Pearlight.

Where the hell is that? Benton wondered.

He considered trying to ask the comm system, but he quickly discarded that idea. It was quite likely that any native would know where Pearlight was. His asking about it might trigger an alarm.

I'm getting paranoid, he thought. On Colliery, though, paranoia was the better part of wisdom. It was a survival trait.

He signed off and returned to his flyer. He searched the vehicle quickly, but there were no maps beside the one he had already used, and that showed only this city. There was nothing named Pearlight on it.

If only there were some sort of intercity public transport on Colliery! Then he would have been able to use his palmprint for the fare and travel to Pearlight, no matter where it was. Collierites used private vehicles for intercity travel, a consequence of wealth and a low-density population.

Perhaps he could get the current time in Pearlight from the comm system. That might also expose him as a non-native, if a native would know the time in the other city. But it would look reasonable at first glance. Perhaps he just wanted to know the time before comming his friend in case it was nighttime at the other end. The time would give him a rough idea of the longitude separation between here and Pearlight. There weren't many cities on Colliery, and they were all situated along the edges of the life-bands, so he would then know about how far to fly east or west. The flyer's power pack was still almost fully charged, so he could surely reach Pearlight, assuming it was no more than a couple of thousand kilometers away.

Oh, I'm not doing anything, officer. Just looking for a city. You haven't seen one around here, have you?

No, on second thought, that was a silly idea. Longitude wouldn't be enough. Pearlight could be near the *northern* life-band, maybe 15,000 kilometers north of him.

The system had told him the comm code was in Pearlight. On any other world, the most the system could have told him was where the comm for which he had entered the code was currently located. Benton wondered if the system of fixed comms meant that codes were assigned on some sort of geographical basis on this peculiar world. It seemed worth a try.

During his previous experiences with these kiosks, he had

learned to navigate through an absurdly bewildering array of menus and options to get the system to display street maps of the city the kiosk was located in. That too would have been a simpler task on, say, Farandhazy, where a few simple voice commands would have done the trick. In spite of the clumsiness of the local system, though, he had found the mapping capability invaluable during his walks around the city where he had spent those first days on Colliery. Now he gritted his teeth and attacked the cumbersome software, persevering until he reached a screen display that let him display maps by comm code.

He started with the first four digits to get the largest possible area displayed. Pearlight was marked on it, and there was also a red X elsewhere on the map that he assumed displayed his present position. He noted the distance and direction—directly northeast, about five hundred kilometers, which meant that Pearlight had the unusual advantage of being situated fairly deep in the life–band. Four hours of flying, he guessed. Then more searching for Borrasca when he got there, but he could use a comm kiosk in Pearlight for that search, too. Really, in the end none of this was all that different from what he'd done on other worlds. His grand, once–in–a–lifetime adventure was suddenly turning oddly humdrum.

Harve Borrasca was on his way home from work. He was walking.

Almost half a year had passed since his demotion, but he still wasn't used to his new job or reconciled to his new status. Instead of being invigorated and pleased with himself, as he had felt before in his old position, now he felt tired and pessimistic at the end of each day. He used to willingly continue his work on his own time, but with this job he tried his best to leave it behind him at quitting time.

Today, though, the messy problem he'd been given in the morning wouldn't stay behind in the office. It was more than a somewhat unusual disciplinary matter. He had the strange hunch that it involved him personally.

After the underground disaster, the blame had fallen on Borrasca for letting the Contco man wander away into the mines. It was absurd to blame him, but he was a convenient scapegoat, and so he had been demoted from his minor but promising policy-making position to a job in which he investigated employee discipline and morale problems. He had been assured this wasn't a dead-end position and that after a few years of diligent work he'd begin moving back up the ladder. He hadn't entirely believed that when he was told it, and his doubts had kept growing. He had once had hopes of some day rising high enough in the Corporation to be able to socialize with members of the Board families and then eventually to marry into one of those families. That would have given him real protection when the shutdown finally came, along with immense wealth. But now, all because of that son of a bitch—what was his name? Benton. Now, because of Benton, that was looking impossible. Now he couldn't realistically hope to get that high in time.

He tried to do his new job conscientiously, but the fact was that it bored him silly. The trivial problems of technicians and secretaries—it lacked that wonderful feeling of power his old job had had, the sense of playing a part in the world's and the Corporation's destiny, and the almost certain knowledge that he was headed rapidly higher, to much greater power and importance and to a position of real security when things on Colliery became insecure.

He sighed. The good old days, he thought bitterly.

Thunder muttered in the distance. Borrasca could see storm clouds piling up on the eastern horizon. The air was heavy and still. A breeze touched his face at last, but it was chilly and made him shiver. The weather was better in the old days, too. It was getting strange lately.

From time to time he thought that he should have refused the demeaning job they'd offered him. He should have been brave and stood up to the bastards. He could have tried to get into the Corporation police force instead. He had the background for it. Hell, in his previous job, he'd almost been a sort of police administrator already. But the idea of joining the police always brought to mind another thought, one that made him shudder, and that was that Galena was in the police, and rising steadily and quickly through their ranks. If he got himself in, it would surely be at a low level, and then he might end up with Galena as his boss. That thought alone, even without the consequences of defying the Corporation's job-assignment orders, was enough to make him settle down into his new, dull job with at least outward docility.

This thing with the floater and the missing guard from the desert outpost was almost interesting. The man, John Biot, had what most would consider a good job. True, his duties must have been unpleasant: guarding an exit shaft, spending all his time out in the desert, occasionally having to take care of underman corpses. But if he had stuck it out until his tour of duty ended, then he'd have been given some plush job in a town.

It wasn't a route to the top Borrasca would have cared to go through himself, but for a man of Biot's low social origins, it was about the only route available. And it *was* such a route, that was the real point. Having been given such an opportunity, why had the idiot worked so hard to foul it up, to destroy his career?

Biot might think he had disappeared, but on a world with such a small population, and that so well under surveillance, he'd be found eventually. On Colliery, no one could stay underground indefinitely.

In hiding, Borrasca corrected himself quickly.

The man had apparently made a clean escape for the moment, though. Borrasca had to grant him that. The police had found the floater during a routine check, but there had been no traces of the driver getting out of it—no human traces in the surrounding sand. They'd traced the vehicle's path back as far as possible, but that wasn't very far after the wind had had a few days to do its work. Biot was obviously clever, but the puzzling part was that he seemed to have been heading for the life-band, not for a town. On his previous two escapades, according to his file, he'd flown off to a town for a meeting with his girlfriend. Of course, there was that report of a missing flyer, presumed stolen. But that was kilometers away from where the floater had been found. Surely Biot couldn't have made that on foot!

Biot's floater had run out of charge. Perhaps the man had miscalculated, and now he was just a dried-up husk somewhere in the desert. The image and the phrase tickled Borrasca's sense of humor, and he felt suddenly, and unusually, filled with good spirits. "A dried-up husk in the desert!" he repeated to himself with delight. He chuckled, and his step took on a new bounce and spring as he walked briskly along the last block to his house.

He felt so energetic and lighthearted all of a sudden that his slight limp, last remaining legacy of that dreadful day underground, almost disappeared.

He wasn't used to this small house, either. Tiny damned place, in Borrasca's eyes. Forcing him to move here from his previous place, which he had loved even while he had been looking forward to moving into some place grander, had struck him as a gratuitous bit of nastiness. But that was the way the Corporation operated. He understood the principle well enough. Some day, with any luck, he'd again be in a position himself to exercise such gratuitous nastiness toward subordinates.

It wasn't until Borrasca had unlocked the front door and gone inside that the unconscious knowledge that someone had been walking behind him for the last few meters suddenly made itself conscious. He turned quickly to shut the door, but the man had already entered behind him, and now it was too late. The door slipped from Borrasca's suddenly weak hand and shut by itself, locking with a loud *click.* It was programmed to prefer the closed and locked position. Borrasca had programmed it that way himself.

"Good evening, Harve," the unwanted visitor said, smiling a smile that had no trace of friendship or amiability in it.

Borrasca stumbled backward until his knees hit the edge of a chair and he sat down in it heavily. His face was as white as the glow of a lux or the face of an underman. "Oh, my God," he whispered. "Benton."

Unable to say any more, he stared at this ghost from the past, and Benton, standing in front of the door, stared back unblinkingly with that frightening smile still on his face.

CHAPTER TWENTY-SIX

Borrasca tried to work up an outward show of cheerful friendliness and enthusiasm. His attempt at a grin ended up as a grimace that displayed his fear as much as it did his teeth. His first name, he thought desperately. What the hell is his first name? The grin froze on his face. Then the name came back to him at last. "Jim! I'm glad you survived! Where have you been all this time?"

Suddenly he felt genuinely glad to see Benton. The man's reappearance could be useful. Maybe Borrasca's career could be salvaged now, after all, and he could get his life back on track.

Benton's eyes never left Borrasca's face, and Borrasca had the unpleasant impression that the offworlder could read his thoughts. "Seeing how the other half lives. Or is it the other nine-tenths? You know, the undermen."

"Maybe you shouldn't have told me that."

Benton laughed. He strolled over to a chair and fell into it. "A soft chair, and it even has arms. That's a real change for me. Would you have believed me if I'd claimed, say, that I was on the surface all this time, suffering from amnesia?"

"You know I'm not a fool," Borrasca said scornfully. His earlier physical tension continued to ease. He began to feel he could regain control of the situation, despite the inexplicable fear Benton's appearance had engendered. It was just a matter of stalling the man until he could think of a way to call the police. With Benton's capture to his credit, he could begin to work on the rehabilitation of his career.

Benton looked at him carefully. "I used to think you were, but then I learned better. You told me your parents 'weren't around any more.' Remember that?"

Benton's habit of suddenly changing the topic was unnerving. "Yeah, I remember," Borrasca snapped. "So what?"

"I met your mother." Benton nodded toward the floor. "Way down there. Your father was murdered underground some time ago. Before I got there."

"So what?" Borrasca repeated, this time speaking through gritted teeth.

"I thought you might want to know," Benton said mildly. "Oh yes, I almost forgot. Your mother was murdered while I was down there. Of course," he mused, "one could raise the philosophical point that they were both killed in a sense when they were first sent underground. In which sense, you're really their murderer. Yes, I think I'd agree with that interpretation."

He still spoke in a mild, conversational tone. The effect on Borrasca was just what Benton wanted. The growing hint of cockiness, Borrasca's feeling that he was in charge after all, had evaporated. Now Borrasca stared at the floor, muttering to himself, but too softly for Benton to hear the words.

Benton added, "I'm sorry I can't tell you what happened to your father's corpse, although I can make a very educated guess. In your mother's case, however, I do happen to know for sure where she is now. Mostly rotted away. Legs eaten to the bone by scavengers, head crushed in. Her face was undamaged when I saw it, though. In a big crater in the desert, filled with undermen bodies. Fascinating place. Educational, for someone like you."

Borrasca groaned and covered his face with his hands. When he spoke, his words came out as a choking sound. "What do you want from me?"

Benton smiled slowly. "I want you to get me off this planet and on my way back to Farandhazy."

Borrasca raised his head and stared at Benton in amazement. "You're crazy! Why would I do that?"

"Because, if you don't, I'll let you call the police. As I'm sure you'd like to do."

Borrasca looked at him blankly.

"And when they get here," Benton continued, "I'll tell them that you helped me escape from underground and were planning to get me off the planet. And then you'll find out first hand how your parents lived during their last years. That would be educational, too."

"Why, that's ridiculous!" Borrasca blustered. "Why should they believe what you tell them? I'll tell them you're lying."

But Benton only laughed at this, and Borrasca knew with sinking heart that the police would ignore anything he said, once Benton had told his story. They were a brutal group of men—and women, he reminded himself, remembering the example of his own cousin—and they liked nothing better than an excuse to beat a man up and send him down among the undermen. He'd insulted some of them, not least his cousin, when he'd been in such a strong position that he thought he had nothing to fear from them. Now that he was reduced to this impotent social level, they'd love it if someone handed them the chance to get their revenge.

Making one last attempt at taking control of the situation, Borrasca said, "They'd put you back down there along with me."

Benton nodded. "Yes, they would. And I'd hate that. But I'd survive it. I've already been there."

"I'll see what I can do," Borrasca muttered.

Benton shook his head. "You'll do what I've told you to do."

It was not until he was actually on his way out of the system that Benton was entirely sure Borrasca would be able to do what he had demanded of him.

He spent three days hidden in Borrasca's house and watched Borrasca age five years. He never asked Borrasca how he obtained the money, fake documents, and passenger ticket that he had ordered him to get. In truth, Benton didn't care. All that mattered to him was that Borrasca should remain sufficiently frightened and cowed to follow his orders while not daring to turn him in or attack him. That last possibility was the one Benton worried about most. Borrasca's safest course of action would be to obtain a gun, kill Benton with it, and then tell the police any story he wanted, without fear of being contradicted

Borrasca actually did think of doing just that, and it was only a fortuitous conversation that made him drop the idea.

The disappearance of John Biot and the feeling that it concerned him directly would not leave Borrasca's mind, despite the more immediate and pressing problem of Benton's presence and getting rid of him. One evening, Borrasca asked his unwanted guest, "Do you know what happened to John Biot?"

Benton looked uninterested. "Another friend of yours?"

"No. He was a guard at one of the desert outposts, where they take care of the exit shafts. He disappeared a few weeks ago, and his floater was found with a dead power pack in the desert near the perimeter of the southern life–band."

"John Biot," Benton murmured. "Maybe I do know, after all. I took a floater from a man in the desert, near that crater I told you about, and I left it near the edge of the life–band."

Borrasca tensed, anticipating the answer even before he asked his question. "What happened to the man?"

Benton smiled faintly. "He's keeping your mother company on the crater floor."

Case closed, then, Borrasca thought, feeling numb. At least he knew what had happened to Biot, although he could never tell his superiors that, for then he would have to tell them how he knew. What really mattered to him, though, was that this ghost, this imposition from his past, had just taken on the aspect of a very live and very dangerous cold–blooded killer. An attempt at violence against him had now become unthinkable. Now all Borrasca wanted was to get Benton off the planet and then to forget all about him and everything connected with him. He didn't really want to have to deal with the police anyway. He wasn't sure if he'd be able to convince them that he was an innocent in all of this. If Galena got involved, he was sure he wouldn't be able to convince them.

Borrasca told his superiors he would be using some of his vacation time on Winze. It was an unusual spot for a vacation, but certainly not unheard of. To make sure they wouldn't be suspicious, he told them that he had reason to believe the missing guard, John Biot, might be on Winze waiting to get onboard a passenger liner due there soon. Borrasca would be combining his vacation with his duties. He told them everything could be handled quietly and without alarming the employees on Winze or involving the police. Thus all credit for the capture of Biot would devolve upon them. Because of Biot's sensitive knowledge, the possibility of his leaving the system while in a rebellious, anti–Corporation frame of mind was enough for them to quickly approve of Borrasca's request for leave and a passage to Winze. He took care of passage for Benton by saying he was a minor Corporation employee who had known Biot and could identify him, hopefully even if Biot were disguised.

In fact, Borrasca would have greatly preferred not to go to Winze with Benton. He would have preferred it if Benton had left Colliery by himself, passing out of sight and mind forever. Benton had insisted that Borrasca accompany him, though. He wanted Borrasca in his sight until the last possible moment.

The passenger ship in question was stopping at Winze to let off some high–level Corporation executives who were returning from a contract–renegotiation trip necessitated by the latest jacksonite price increase. There were a few customers who were big enough purchasers of the mineral that The Jacksonite Corporation, despite its monopoly of supply, traditionally gave them a special price for their bulk purchases. With the new price, the quantities involved in such purchases and the price breaks had had to be redefined.

By a chance that Benton found amusing, the ship was the same one which had brought him to Winze in the first place. This time, it was on the opposite leg of its schedule, with a planned stop at Farandhazy

Borrasca and Benton were waiting in the shuttle when the

Corporation executives and their secretaries, assistants, and sycophants disembarked. They were an expensively dressed group, talking busily to each other, and they brushed past the two waiting men as if they didn't exist.

Borrasca watched them sourly, thinking that with this little adventure he was throwing away whatever small chance might yet have remained to him of one day being one of them. The lies he'd told during the last few days, the false computer records he'd created, the papers he'd forged for Benton's use—he feared it would all catch up with him eventually. If Benton had accused him as he'd threatened to do, Borrasca would certainly have ended up in the mines. He was beginning to think he'd end up there anyway. "You've ruined me, you know that?" he snarled at Benton.

Benton shook his head. "You ruined yourself, Harve, long before I met you."

The boarding call came over the speakers, and Benton stood up. "Goodbye, and thanks for a wonderful vacation on lovely Colliery."

Borrasca gritted his teeth. "Just get the hell out of my life."

Benton stepped into the shuttle's airlock. Behind him, the door began to slide shut, hiding Borrasca's angry, frightened face. Benton turned and, just before the door closed all the way, called out, "I'll be back some day, Harve. Sweet dreams."

CHAPTER TWENTY-SEVEN

After a few days of the journey, Benton realized that he'd been drinking too much ever since the Arrastra Drive had been turned on. Annoyed with himself, he decided to abstain from that point on.

Something might happen. The Drive might malfunction in one of the ways no one yet understood, causing him to disappear as his parents had. Perhaps they were trapped in some strange dimension, suffering unimaginably and forever. Perhaps their ship had blown up, vaporized, along with all its passengers. In any case, such things were beyond his control. Alcohol wouldn't change the odds of it happening. More to the point, he was his own master, and he couldn't let fear take control of him.

He also realized that he had been halfway expecting Sadie Hornsfels, Brook Plasser, and the rest of the unsavory bunch of passengers from his first trip to appear this time as well.

The ultimate users, he thought. That's what that bunch was. But this is a different trip, with a different collection of passengers.

Although when he looked around at his fellow passengers, it seemed to him that this group was really little different from that other one. My fellow human beings, he thought, deciding not to abstain after all and beckoning a waiter to bring him a refill. Maybe, he told himself, you don't really want to save the Galaxy. Just don't drink enough to interfere with what you need to do.

There were two things he needed to do on Farandhazy.

One was to withdraw the savings which had been accumulating for the last few years. He wanted to be able to use the money when and where he needed to. Instinct told him to carry it with him rather than asking his bank on Farandhazy to transfer it to a bank on another world. That instinct suggested it would be unwise to leave such an easy trail. It was the presence of that instinct that made Benton realize how much he had changed since leaving Farandhazy.

The other thing Benton had to do was resign from Contco. He could have done it by letter or comm, but he wanted very much to do it in person, to see Charlie Gabbro's face when he told him.

Nothing had changed at Contco, except that the new offices he'd rented for the Colliery project were now being used by another company. Had they closed the project down?

In the old building, the same people sat at the same desks—probably still working on the same tasks. Benton entered the place as if he were arriving to start work on any typical morning. His presence seemed scarcely to register on his coworkers. This amused Benton until he realized that what had not registered was not his sudden reappearance but his long absence.

Benton strolled down the hallway to Charlie Gabbro's

office. Charlie was already at work, sweating behind his undersized desk in the cramped room. He didn't look up until Benton dropped into the chair facing the desk and said, "Good morning, Charlie."

Gabbro looked up and his mouth drooped open. "Benton! My God, they told us you'd been killed in some sort of underground accident. More than half a year ago."

"Who's been handling the project?" Benton said casually, steering the conversation away from what had happened underground.

"No one. The Jacksonite Corporation told us to suspend the whole thing until they gave us further instructions, but they haven't said a word since then."

Benton shook his head. "Tsk, tsk. Ten billion barnards down the drain."

Charlie jumped to his feet. "Don't say that! Now that you're back, we can get things going again. Come on!" Without waiting to see whether Benton was following, Gabbro dashed from the room and down the hallway to the large, desk–filled room where most of his subordinates worked.

This suited Benton's wishes, for he thought it would be more amusing to make his announcement before the other employees than in the privacy of Gabbro's office. He followed Charlie at a leisurely pace.

When he caught up with him in the large room, Gabbro was jittering about impatiently. "Benton!" he bellowed in annoyance. "Jamie, me boy! You gotta get yourself back in harness again. You gotta learn how to *move* again! Now, let's go, boy. We're gonna get this project ay–live again."

Benton glanced around to be sure they had the full

attention of everyone in the room. Gabbro's loudness had assured that. "Up your rosy red rectum, Charlie," he said pleasantly, but in a carrying voice.

For a moment, there was no sound but the sigh of a dozen people gasping simultaneously.

Gabbro stared at Benton in astonishment, then recovered enough to growl, "What the hell is this, Benton?"

"This is my resignation, effective immediately."

Gabbro's eyes narrowed. "I get it, I get it. Some other company offered you a bundle to jump over to them. They think they can steal the Colliery contract from us. Well, let me tell you something, fella—" Benton was shaking his head, but Gabbro rushed on heedlessly, his face flushed with anger. "It won't work. We've got all the rights to the product and we've got an in with The Jacksonite Corporation. We'll talk to them about it right away." His face grew redder still. "And I'm going to see to it that you're blacklisted, you bastard. I don't care what they offered you. Without the Colliery contract, they won't want you any more, and neither will anyone else. You'll never get another job." He ran out of breath at last and stood panting, glaring at Benton.

"Charlie, Charlie. You're so impetuous. You can keep that contract for as long as The Jacksonite Corporation survives, for all I care. I'm quitting in order to become one of the richest men in the Galaxy. Doesn't that sound like more fun than working for Contco?"

Gabbro sneered. "You? Fat chance. You're an inept fool, Benton, you know that?"

The retort he had been formulating died on Benton's lips. He looked at the furious Gabbro and the embarrassed but very attentive workers and realized how silly the whole incident had become. He had been planning this for days on the passenger liner, writing scripts in his mind, reveling in anticipation. Hell, in reality he'd been planning it for years. But now that he had made his point, it seemed puerile to continue. It was not that it was an empty victory to humiliate Charlie Gabbro in front of his subordinates. Rather, it was no victory at all.

Benton turned away from the group, ignoring whatever it was Charlie was saying now, and walked rapidly from the building.

Benton had deliberately left enough credit in his account to cover about two weeks' worth of rent, food, and transportation. He planned to leave Farandhazy much sooner—that afternoon or the following morning, if possible—but the extra two weeks should cause anyone trying to trace him at least a bit of delay. He hoped they would assume that he was planning a short period of relaxation on Farandhazy before going job hunting again. He wasn't sure there would be any "they" trying to trace him, but when Contco contacted The Jacksonite Corporation, as Gabbro had said they would, and told them about Benton's reappearance, the Corporation would surely realize how much he must know—even if Borrasca had been wise enough to keep his mouth shut—and would set about trying to silence him.

There was something he had to take care of before be left the planet, something of overwhelming importance. He must make an attempt to see Augie Syen.

Benton had sold his floater before leaving Farandhazy. That was something he'd been thinking about doing anyway, and his assignment on Colliery had spurred him to take care of it. Now, after leaving the Contco building, he walked to a restaurant near his apartment for an early lunch. It amazed him that before he would have considered this distance of just under five kilometers impossibly far to walk and would have certainly gone by floater.

He ate slowly and watched a news broadcast on the restaurant's vidscreen.

There seemed to be yet another crisis in parliament. The same parliamentary leaders were making the same speeches as a half a year ago, or so it seemed to Benton. Once again, the cause of the crisis was a newly announced price hike for jacksonite. The more things change, he thought cynically.

But he sat up and listened when the newsman mentioned the concurrent announcement from The Jacksonite Corporation that the production rate for jacksonite would be reduced gradually throughout the following year.

Why? Benton wondered. Rising water?

Benton finished his meal quickly, paid, and left. The time might be much shorter than he had realized.

Benton walked quickly to his apartment and set about throwing out whatever he could. When he had left for Colliery, he'd been depressed by the shallowness of the roots he'd set down on Farandhazy after five years of living and working there. This time, seeing how much he could throw away and how little in the apartment was of real and lasting value to him, he was aware of the shallowness of those roots again, but he was elated rather than depressed. It gave him a feeling of new beginnings, limitless horizons, freedom of action.

Working swiftly, he packed one small travel bag and, looking around at the suddenly sterile, impersonal rooms, felt he was ready.

He made a quick trip on public transport to the spaceport located just east of the city and bought a ticket on a liner leaving the following morning for New Albion. He paid cash so there was no record of his identity. He had considered clouding his trail still further by taking a roundabout route from Farandhazy to New Albion, buying a ticket for the next leg at each stop, but time was too pressing for that. As it was, the journey would take more than three days going direct, and he resented even that much delay.

Much as his new mood of urgency made him chafe at any delay, Benton knew there was no point in dashing over to Augie Syen's apartment immediately. She wouldn't be home from work yet. Instead he took public transport back into the city, getting off about ten kilometers from Augie's apartment and setting off on foot the rest of the way. He should get there shortly after she returned, he calculated, and he hoped that the walk would help calm the knot of tension that had suddenly appeared in his stomach.

Augie opened the door. Even though seeing his face in the small screen beside the door had given her a few seconds' preparation, she still looked stunned when the door slid aside and they stood face-to-face. She was unable to speak, staring up at him with a face as pale as an underman's.

Mentally, he kicked himself. Well, what did you expect after the way you treated her? Open arms?

At last she managed to speak. "I—I talked with someone at Contco." Her lips felt suddenly extremely dry, and she licked them quickly. "They said you'd died on Colliery."

Benton smiled faintly. "I came close a few times." He dug

into his pocket and brought out the chain with the fused chunk of metal at the end. "This saved me twice. I know about your brother, and I thought you'd want it back." She took it automatically, and he said awkwardly, "I won't bother you any more. Goodbye, Augie."

Before he could move, she clutched his arm. "For God's sake, Jim, please come inside."

He allowed himself to be drawn into the apartment, and Augie shut the door behind him. The light was brighter than outside in the hallway, and he could see shadows under her eyes, a new gauntness in her face, and a slow weariness in her movements. What had been natural slenderness now looked more like the effects of illness or a long wearing–down. Her hair was still its natural black color, long, straight, and unadorned, but it was dull and lifeless. Her intense, direct stare was gone. Now she avoided his gaze and looked weakened and vulnerable. His heart went out to her. He wanted to put his arms around her and protect her.

She licked her lips again and, looking at the floor, said, "Until I heard... that you were dead, I hoped we'd be able to straighten things out when you came back." She looked up at him hesitantly, uncertainly.

Quickly, he said, "It's my fault there's anything to straighten out." Speaking gently, he added, "I want to apologize for the way I behaved before I left."

To his surprise, and perhaps to her own, Augie stepped forward, flung her arms about his waist, and pressed her face to his chest. He stroked her hair and her back, feeling rather than hearing her sobs, and trying to comfort her. Her voice muffled against him, she said, "I'm so glad you're back."

Benton's rush of affection and tenderness astonished him. I hardly know this girl, he reminded himself. And I'm supposed to go back to Diori. Confused, he lowered his face to her hair and whispered, "Yes, I'm back."

CHAPTER TWENY-EIGHT

Much later that night, as they lay against each other pleasantly exhausted and drifting off to sleep again, Augie raised herself on her elbows abruptly and said, "How did you know anything about my brother? I didn't tell you when I sent his field-effect generator to you."

"Your aunt told me. On Colliery."

Augie gasped and put one hand over her mouth. She stared at him wide-eyed. "You saw her! And my uncle?"

"They're both there, on Colliery. Both alive and unharmed."

"Why didn't you tell me earlier?"

Because I didn't want to talk about either of them. "I'm sorry. I should have."

"Well, when are they going to leave? To come home?"

"They can't leave. They're... they're not able to."

Augie was horrified. "You mean the bastards have them in prison, don't you?"

"Not exactly, but they are trapped. Listen, Augie, I can't tell you the details. For your own sake. I'm trying to help them."

"But you got away from Colliery!" she protested. "So why can't they?"

"I got away partly by accident. Honestly, I can't tell you any details without placing you in danger. Oh hell, I'm probably doing that just by staying here so long."

She drew away from him. "What're you saying? After disappearing for so long, you're spending another night with me, and then you're going to vanish again?"

And that, he realized sadly, was just about the truth. He reached out to her and pulled her gently toward him. She resisted at first, then sighed and moved against him.

"I escaped by accident," he repeated. "Your aunt and uncle are still trapped. So are... well, an enormous number of people. I'm going to get them out, all of them, but it's going to be a slow and arduous process. And roundabout. And it's likely that The Jacksonite Corporation will try to stop me. With violence, I mean. I have the best chance of avoiding them and succeeding if I'm alone."

In other words, you're a lamb in a world of wolves. If you had the armor of Diori or the brutality of Galena, perhaps it would be different.

Augie felt empty. "So you'll be leaving again. When?"

"In the morning. I'd better not even tell you where, or anything else, just in case. And I can't communicate with you until it's all over, for the same reason."

Intending to be sarcastic, she said, "You're on a secret mission. It's dangerous. Vicious people are trying to kill you. This means you'll have to slip away, and I'm not supposed to try to contact you. You can't tell me any more for my own protection." She wanted to add, "Do you expect me to fall for a ridiculous line like that?"

"Yes, I guess that sums it up."

And she believed him.

She moved her head to his shoulder and laid her arm across his chest. "I have to get some sleep," she murmured. "Please wake me before you leave." After a while, her breathing became slow and even.

Benton didn't know if she was really sleeping or just wanted him to think so. He lay wide awake, watching the time displayed on the ceiling, glowing red digits that changed with silent regularity.

At three a.m., Benton decided, with far more regret than he could have anticipated, that it was time for him to leave. He wanted at least an hour of darkness to allow him time to return to his apartment, collect his travel bag, and leave for the spaceport, all before sunrise.

Not that darkness would be any barrier to an experienced and determined observer, but he hoped that they—the nameless, faceless "they"—wouldn't be expecting him to do anything at night. He hoped they would assume that, like anyone else, he would come and go in the daylight.

He kissed the top of Augie's head softly. She responded so quickly that he thought she must have been awake after all. She reached up, put her arms around his neck, and pressed against him, her mouth seeking his. On his part, their lovemaking was tender and gentle, but he could feel her barely restrained desperation and emotional hunger.

Afterwards, she held him tightly. "I have to leave," he said. They had left the lights on in the room, turned down very low. Perhaps it was the dimness—and his eyes still seemed to be unusually able to see in such dim light—but he thought some of the fatigue and soul-weariness he had seen in her face the evening before was gone.

"Yes," she said calmly. "I know you do. I will hear from you again, won't I?"

He promised that she would, kissed her again, dressed, and left. He hadn't meant to mislead her, to lie to her. He realized with diminishing surprise that her importance to him was much greater than he had known.

And yet he had made a commitment to Diori, and even if things went as well as they possibly could, his next communication with Augie would probably be a message telling her that Diori had divorced her mad, aged husband and would be marrying him.

There were planets where marriage was not the rule, others where multiple spouses were common, but the thought of Augie and Diori in such an arrangement was almost comical.

It was still fairly dark when he reached his apartment, but he could make out a pale light along the eastern horizon. He hurried down the hallway to his door and reached out for the palm plate beside the door. Just before his band touched the plate, a thrill of alarm coursed through him, an intuition of danger. He shook the feeling off, telling himself he couldn't afford to live by instinct. He pressed his palm to the plate, and as soon as the door had slid aside he stepped into the apartment.

The lights were off in the apartment, but he didn't bother with them. The door was still open, and by the light from the hallway, a brilliant shaft of white penetrating the gloom of the apartment, he could see the travel bag ready for him on the floor in the center of the room. He stepped toward.

Something dug into his back. A voice said quietly in his ear, "Glad you're all packed. You're making a quick trip back to

Colliery."

Benton moaned "Nooo!" in a voice filled with terror. His knees buckled. He pitched forward.

Behind him, someone cursed.

Benton lay half on his left side, immobile as if in a dead faint. Through slitted eyes, he could see the other man as a silhouette against the open hallway door.

The shadow leaned forward, perhaps to slap Benton back awake.

Benton's right foot whipped up against the shadow's head. The man collapsed and Benton leaped to his feet and grabbed his travel bag.

The man on the floor, lying in the shaft of light from the open door, shook himself and tried to raise what looked like a gun. Benton kicked again, missing the head and instead hitting the hand with the gun. The weapon slapped against the man's head and jerked. Benton's assailant jerked at the same time and then sprawled lifeless on the floor. His head was misshapen. Blood flowed from the top of it.

Clutching his bag, Benton stepped into the hallway, pulling the door closed behind him. He stopped and looked both ways. There was no sign of anyone. The incident had probably taken less than a minute. Benton leaned back against the wall, panting more from terror than from exertion.

God, he thought, they found me that quickly!

Then he realized that it hadn't been that hard a thing for them to do. They could have simply come to Farandhazy and looked up his address.

But the fact remained that this agent must have found out about his escape and left Colliery not long after Benton had left himself. And the man had gotten into his apartment, which was supposed to be impossible.

Had they also followed him to Augie's apartment? Did they know about her?

He could ask her to come with him. But then she'd be in even more danger. Once he left the planet, she should be safe. He had to hope so. There was no way he could protect her even if he changed his plans and stayed on Farandhazy. When he left, the agents of The Jacksonite Corporation would lose interest in her.

Would they be able to follow him to New Albion? Only if they knew ahead of time that that was his destination. Or if they had someone watching for him at the spaceport and knew which liner he boarded. He'd take that chance. It was certain that he couldn't stay here in this apartment until departure time.

Outside, the sky was lightening with alarming speed. It seemed likeliest that a Corporation agent would be watching for him at the transit interchange nearest his apartment, waiting for him to arrive or leave. He took a deep breath and, holding his travel bag in what he hoped was a casual, inconspicuous way, walked off in the direction opposite to that which would have led him to the nearest transit interchange. He walked for some distance—perhaps three or four kilometers—before he felt it was safe to try a different interchange.

There were only a handful of other people waiting, and all of them got on a coach headed for the business district. Workers going in early, that was all. Nothing more sinister than that.

A coach headed for the spaceport came along, and he got in it. As it happened, it passed through the interchange nearest his apartment, stopping there for a few short moments. He glanced out the window and saw a tall, broad–shouldered man, his back to Benton, watching the stairs that led up from street level.

Benton sat frozen, unable to duck out of sight. At last the coach started moving again, picked up speed, and slid away from the station.

There were three more stops scheduled before the spaceport. Benton realized that there might also be someone watching at the exit for the spaceport itself. He checked his watch and the route map on the wall of the coach and decided he had time to walk from the third stop, rather than going all the way.

By the time he reached the spaceport's pedestrian entrance, he was beginning to feel a bit worried about the time. He had only an hour left before the ship lifted off—time enough normally, but not if he had to spend time eluding Corporation goons. Then there was the pedestrian entrance itself to worry about. Wouldn't they be watching that?

He shrugged and headed for the double glass doors. He was suddenly tired of the whole pretense, and even more tired of his own cowardice, or at least of behavior that struck him as cowardice.

You've dealt with those people a few times already, he reminded himself, and each time you won. Two of them are dead because they tried to stop you.

There seemed to be no one at the pedestrian entrance except a few spaceport employees who had every reason to be there.

They're as spoiled by floaters and flyers on Colliery as they are here, he realized. They can't imagine I might choose to walk.

He was in without any trouble. Now he had only to make

his way to the New Albion liner without being noticed and kill almost an hour before liftoff.

Like spaceports everywhere and in all ages, this one had an overabundance of restaurants, snack shops, gift shops, book shops, and barbershops. He went to one of the latter and requested a quick dye job for his light hair. "Jet black," he told the professionally unsurprised barber, "but make sure it looks real and dries in about a minute."

"Certainly, sir," the man murmured. "This will take no time at all." It hardly did take any time.

Looking satisfactorily dark, Benton paid and left. Next stop was a gift shop, which included the sort of cheaply made false moustaches and beards that had delighted children since time immemorial. Benton picked out a trim moustache and beard that he thought matched his new hair and should be convincing from a distance. Fortunately, facial hair was becoming fashionable at the moment on Farandhazy. Had the fashions been as uniform as on Colliery, disguise beyond his new hair color would have been impossible.

After leaving the gift shop, Benton went to a restroom, shut himself into a stall, and applied the moustache and beard. He pressed them repeatedly onto his skin until he thought the glue backing had taken. Then he leaned against the wall and breathed deeply and repeatedly, trying to calm himself down. He checked the time frequently until he saw at last that only minutes remained before his ship left. Only then did he head for it, walking rapidly enough to make it in time but not fast enough to attract attention.

Curiosity about whether or not broad-shouldered, low-browed Corporation goons were patrolling the spaceport looking for him was almost overpowering, but he controlled himself and didn't look to either side as he walked briskly and aggressively along. He kept his eyes fixed before him, trying to look like an important man with important business on his mind.

He stalked through the waiting and reception areas and down the flexible tube into the spaceship. Impatiently, as though he felt that he of all men shouldn't have to be bothered with such trivia, he handed his ticket to the waiting attendant and bustled off into the bowels of the ship. He found his stateroom with little trouble, put away his travel bag, and collapsed into the armchair, listening to the distant, beginning rumble of the engines with enormous relief. He didn't leave his room until the ship was well underway. By that time, he had removed the beard and moustache and seen them disintegrated by the stateroom's toilet.

CHAPTER TWENTY-NINE

Every tree looked the same. Or so it seemed to Benton, strolling around the verdant Alun University campus on New Albion. Some of these were probably descended from seeds brought from Earth ages ago, he suspected. Others were probably native species that occupied the same ecological niches as trees did on Earth and thus were superficially similar. In any case, they all looked the exactly same to him.

He gave up and entered the large building in which Ben Coquina had had his office. The office itself had already been reassigned, unsurprisingly. Benton walked in without knocking and then stopped in embarrassment, staring puzzledly at the young academic behind the desk. The young man looked at him with annoyance poorly disguised as polite helpfulness. "Oh," Benton said in a soft voice. "I'm so sorry. I thought this was the office of my old friend Ben Coquina."

At this evidence that Benton had some sort of academic status and even a connection with a famous man in his field, the other man thawed and became almost affable. "Well, it still is, officially. It's been assigned to me for now."

"While Ben's away, you mean?"

"Right, right. While he's... Yes, right, while he's away."

"I was hoping he'd returned." How long before they drop him from the faculty, Benton wondered. And what euphemism would they use? He walked around the desk to the large window looking out over the campus. "He told me about the fine view from here." He pointed. "That's east, isn't it?"

"Yes. Right." The other man's friendly façade was thinning. "Um, is there some way I can help you?"

Benton was staring at a large tree with a thick trunk a few meters outside the window. The trunk forked about a meter and a half above the ground. "No, I don't think so." He turned around and smiled disarmingly. "I'm only on the planet for a short time, and I thought I'd take the opportunity to look up an old friend. Perhaps on my next trip he'll be here. Goodbye, now."

Outside, he went to the tree he had been looking at through the window. It had to be the one Diori had described. In the fork, where the two branches of the trunk met, the wood was smooth. This was not the way she had described it. She had said there was a small opening in there, and she had put the metal box he was looking for in it. Had someone found the box and removed it?

Time had passed, probably more than she had anticipated. Everything grew quickly in this climate and soil. He could only hope that was the explanation. Otherwise, it was all over and all his plans were dust.

He walked rapidly away.

An hour later, he was back with a small, sharp knife. He looked around, made sure no one was watching him, and began to dig into the wood in the crotch of the fork.

The wood was hard and resistant. In a way, this was like digging jacksonite out of the hard rocks beneath the surface of

Colliery. He concentrated on this task in the same way he had learned to concentrate on that one, shutting out external distractions, forcing himself to be unaware even of his fatigue. Students passing by saw him and occasionally stopped to watch for a few minutes, wondering what this strange man was doing. Benton saw none of that. All that existed for him now was the tree, the hard chips falling away, the wood giving up its treasure. All that mattered was the goal.

Eventually the knife hit something hard. He redoubled his efforts.

Metal glinted.

The box was small, perhaps ten centimeters on a side and only two or three thick. Benton attacked the tree furiously. Chips of wood flew. Why, this was much easier than digging out jacksonite!

He had the box free and was gone. Two campus policemen, summoned by the only student of all those who saw Benton who had been alarmed, arrived minutes later. They looked at the hole gouged in the tree and the wood chips on the ground, debated with each other for a while, then shrugged their shoulders and wandered off.

Back in his hotel room, Benton opened the box. Diori had assured him it was not booby trapped, and he believed her and didn't bother to take precautions. The most precious secret in the Galaxy, he thought in wonder, entirely unprotected, put in a tree where anyone could find it. What if the tree had died and had been removed? What if it had been struck by lightning and destroyed?

What if I had died underground on Colliery, he asked himself. What if Diori had? What if I had never gone there in the first place?

What if I had never met Augie? That struck him as the most unnerving what–if of all.

He had expected to find some kind of recording wafer or chip inside the box. Instead, the box contained a few sheets of paper covered with the neat, small handwriting Benton recognized from his days as the Recorder's assistant. Looking at it now gave him a queasy feeling.

Beneath the pages with Coquina's handwriting were a few others. The handwriting on these he didn't recognize.

He looked through them quickly. They were a record of Augie Syen's indiscretions.

According to the notes, when Augie was still a teenager, she had had an affair with a young colleague of Coquina's, a man Coquina hated, a professional rival he feared. Augie had confided in her aunt, looking for understanding and support and for intercession with her uncle, her surrogate father. The notes were quite detailed. Benton felt as though he were snooping, prying into the intimate details of someone else's life. He found it hard to stop, though.

Some of the notes were written in first person, and it was clear they had been written by Diori. It was also clear to Benton that Diori's reasons for keeping this record had nothing to do with helping Augie. Surely she planned to use them some day to cause a rift between uncle and niece, to her own benefit.

Without hesitation, without qualm, Benton destroyed those pages.

He had the papers that counted, Coquina's notes. Now he was ready to approach Fowler Silurian.

Fowler Silurian, President, Chairman of the Board, and majority (90%) stockholder of Euclase Chemicals, also on New Albion, was the man Diori had told him to see.

He was not an easy man to see.

Benton was an unknown outsider with no business connection to Silurian or Euclase. His casual clothes were a mark against him in the eyes of the glossy, self–important young front men in their well tailored, conspicuously expensive business suits. There were layer upon layer of such front men to pass through. As calmly as he could, Benton repeated the phrase "a message from Diori Coquina." He did his best to project sanity and appear non–threatening. He told every questioner that the phrase would mean something to Silurian, and that the great man would want to hear more.

Benton thought it might take hours. Instead, it took days. Finally, some version of the phrase he kept repeating reached Silurian's ears. After that, it only took minutes.

Silurian's office was enormous and expensively furnished. Three of the walls were completely transparent, offering a magnificent view of the city. Silurian himself was a slender, wiry man of indeterminate age with thinning hair. Few men, even the poorest, allowed baldness to progress that far without having it corrected. Benton decided that the fact that Silurian did nothing about his own head must either be an affectation or a proclamation of his power and a declaration of how little he valued the world's opinion.

Silurian had a slender, bony face with a long, prominent nose and shrewd eyes. He transfixed Benton with a sharp stare as the latter entered his office and, skipping the usual hollow pleasantries, got right to the point. "Benton, right? Listen,

Benton, I only let you up here because Diori Coquina is an old friend of mine and I've been worried about what happened to her. But I'm also a busy man. You've been saying you have a message from Diori. Give."

Benton chose a comfortable chair well away from Silurian's immense desk and dropped into it. The distance, he felt, would diminish the intended intimidating effect of the desk. "Your solicitude is overwhelming. If Diori knew, I'm sure she'd say the same. She's in trouble. You can help her by helping me. Her message is that if you help me, she will give you what you told her you wanted for helping her husband. I think that would probably be enough for most men, but in addition, you'll gain such wealth and power that what you now have will be nothing by comparison."

Silurian laughed. "Except for the part about Diori, you sound like all the kooks who try to get in here with a process that'll make me *really* rich, and all I'm supposed to do is back them with research facilities and cash. What's *your* secret discovery?"

"Synthetic jacksonite. But it's Ben Coquina's discovery, not mine. He completed his project, the one you knew about. He proved it can be done. Unfortunately, that was on Colliery, and now he can't leave. So the last stages of his work will have to be repeated here."

"So you aren't just a kook. How do you know where Ben and Diori are and what their situation is?"

Dangerous territory, Benton thought. He could trust Silurian's business instincts and his rapacity. He certainly wouldn't trust him with information that could put Benton in peril. "Irrelevant."

Silurian nodded. "All right."

His skepticism had disappeared, and in its place a wily, cunning look had crept into his face. Benton watched him formulating some cautious, subtle remarks, opening moves in a long and complex chain of negotiations. Time was too pressing for that. Benton said abruptly, "First, final, only offer. Euclase Chemicals absorbs all costs of research, development, marketing, et cetera. Ten percent will be tacked on for profit, of which you'll get one percent and I'll get the remaining nine."

Silurian turned red. "That's preposterous."

"No, that's still more profit in a few weeks than you make in a year. The Jacksonite Corporation sells its jacksonite at more than a thousand barnards per gram, and they sell an immense amount even at that price—maybe a couple of million kilograms a year. They've just announced a ten percent increase, and that probably won't decrease their sales at all. No one has a choice. There's no substitute for jacksonite, and there's no alternate supplier. They've also announced a production decrease, so the supply will get a lot tighter. Using Coquina's process, you'd be able to offer a substitute for less than three barnards per gram, and you'd be able to produce as much of it as needed to meet demand."

Silurian whistled softly. "We'd corner the market, all right," he muttered. "Wait a minute, though." He frowned for a moment. "That's still only around sixty million barnards profit a year for us. Not very much. Over five hundred million for you. This doesn't sound like the kind of wealth you've been promising. It's considerably less than Euclase makes in a year from its current business. Why should I go along with this?"

"That sixty million is only the beginning. There are stagnant technologies waiting to come alive but stymied because of the price of jacksonite, which they all need. At the price you'll charge, the market will quickly increase a hundredfold, a thousandfold, even more. And you can buy into the new technologies in advance, before you announce the new product. From being a fourth–rate chemical supply company, you'll become one of the major economic powers in the Galaxy."

Silurian smiled thinly. "I've encountered that sort of enthusiasm before when someone wanted to sell me something." But despite his protests, Benton could tell he was hooked. Silurian asked, "Do you have power of attorney to act for Ben Coquina?"

Benton laughed. "I've got all his research notes, and that's even better. I'll sign in my own name."

Silurian vacillated. "There might be legal difficulties over that some day."

"You've got expensive, top–level lawyers, and I've got Diori's promise that she'll fulfill her part of the bargain. Now, take my offer as is, or I'll go elsewhere. Diori gave me a couple of other names to whom I can make the same offer. All of the offer."

Hastily, Silurian spoke into his desk comm unit and summoned the firm's head legal counsel to his office. The technical legal details of setting up the agreement and the organizational details of getting the research work underway were accomplished with remarkable dispatch.

It's all a matter, Benton told himself smugly, of finding the right buttons to push. Silurian's button is labeled "Diori." With his wealth and position, he could surely get other beautiful women. If he's so eager for Diori, it probably means he's already sampled the wares. Poor sucker. I've sampled the wares too, and I can sympathize, but I have top priority with her.

One of Benton's buttons was also labeled "Diori."

Benton's impatience couldn't speed things up. He decided matters would proceed more rapidly at Euclase if he wasn't there to stare over their collective shoulder and make them collectively nervous. After making as sure as he could that the agreements, duly signed and deposited with New Albion's courts, would protect his interests without his being there in person to keep watch over those interests, Benton spent another large part of his savings to book passage to Earth.

This was not a nostalgic trip to the haunts of his almost youth. Rather, it was a research trip for information that could most easily be found on the old Imperial capital, in the dusty archives that carried the records of decades and centuries of Imperial exploration of new worlds.

CHAPTER THIRTY

Benton raised his eyes from the screen in which he'd been absorbed for hours to the lofty, shadowed ceiling of the long room. He put his hands behind his head, fingers interlaced, and mulled over the picture he'd put together from the collection of centuries-old survey reports.

Throughout Republican times, Colliery had been a settled planet. It had been dominated by The Jacksonite Corporation for a good deal of that time. Climatic records on Colliery itself would have been collected and stored under the aegis of the Corporation. They were therefore unavailable to him. The Republican government had no such records, for weather was a matter within the purview of a planetary government, and the member worlds of the Republic were notoriously prickly about any central government infringements upon their rights. Colliery, however, had been first discovered and opened up for settlement during the Empire's later stages. Benton had hoped that some of those ancient records would still be available on Earth. They had not been easy to find, but they were there and he had them now.

Benton had only the faintest memories of his childhood on Earth. The litter of dead kittens was one of the few things he remembered. During his three years of college on Earth, Benton had been as insular, as focused on campus life, as most of his fellow students. He had had little interest in what was going on on the rest of the planet. He had been left with the impression that Earth was much like any other world.

He had a very different impression now.

Earth struck him as markedly different from anywhere else. It was an introverted, insular world. At times it struck him as old and deteriorated, its society mirroring its faded glory and lost importance. At other times it seemed to him provincial, naïve, and surprisingly underpopulated, as though it were a youthful, primitive outpost of the new civilization centered on Lark. The cities that had once administered a vast empire were now largely abandoned as Earth's population built anew on reclaimed lands. The huge buildings that had housed the Imperial government were reduced to the status of museums and libraries, of interest only to visiting scholars from other worlds, and ignored by the sparse numbers who passed by daily on their way to or from work.

The present government of Earth hadn't the time, money, manpower, patience, or inclination to care for those old buildings or the dead archives they contained. The government agencies that had generated the material and taken care of it had vanished with the Empire itself. In some cases, municipal governments had commandeered the vacant buildings for their own use, removing and destroying whatever got in their way. Centuries of Earth's history had been incinerated to make way for maps of sewage systems or records of tax payments—history in their own way, but of a much less stirring variety. Even the papers that were destroyed had been a small fraction of the original, mere random printouts, a sampling of the enormous storehouse of computerized data that had vanished as a result of the attack that had precipitated the Empire's collapse.

What still survived was nowadays maintained only through the efforts and money of volunteer preservation societies and the rare local government with a taste for the past. Fortunately for Benton's purposes, one of those societies had managed to take possession of the buildings and files of the Imperial Survey Commission. It had taken days of searching, visiting, and comm calls before Benton had finally been directed to the right place, but he had been successful in the end. Now he sat in what had been the Commission's viewing room, in those days accessible only to those with proper credentials, but now available to anyone who could find it and was willing to make a small donation for the building's upkeep.

The Imperial surveyors had done their usual thorough job on Colliery, recommending it for limited settlement. Their words and pictures depicted a world covered with forest and meadows, as if the life–bands Benton knew had covered the entire surface. There was no sign of a desert anywhere on the planet and no large bodies of water. The old surveyors had remarked upon the smallness of the southern ice cap and the virtual nonexistence of any cap in the North. Axial tilt was slight. They painted a picture of a generally equable and temperate climate. Groundwater supplies appeared extensive. A broad band on either side of the equator was too hot for human comfort, but plant life thrived there. In short, a good prospect for colonization.

A report from another group in the original team, however,

indicated some disturbing activity deep within the star Colliery orbited. The survey team and their ship's computer were both inadequate for a full investigation of the phenomenon, but the two astrophysics men on the ship hazarded the guess, contained in an appendix to the group's report, that the primary's total energy output was cyclical, with a period of roughly only five hundred Earth years. Visible light would not change so that the human eye could notice it, but the change in overall energy striking Colliery would severely affect the planet's plant life both directly and indirectly. Currently, the appendix concluded, the cycle was approaching its peak. Half a cycle later—another 250 years—and much of the planet's water would be bound up in thick, wide ice caps at both poles. Most of the planet's surface would become desert and remain so until the cycle reversed itself. The change from one phase to the other would come quickly.

The joint commanders of the survey team took the astrophysicists' guesswork seriously enough to recommend only limited colonization at that time. Clearly, in its desert phase Colliery would only be able to support a much smaller population than in its present, optimum phase. They also recommended a lengthy and detailed follow-up survey by a much more extensively equipped team.

If such a follow-up had ever taken place, Benton could find no record of it. Quite possibly it had never happened, for at the time of that original survey, the shockingly sudden collapse of the Empire, precipitated by the calamitous loss of computer ability, had already started. Within a year, the links of administration and communication that had bound the Empire together and defined it had dissolved. In all likelihood, Benton knew, the settlers hastily shipped to Colliery during the Empire's death throes weren't even told about the climatic cycle. Their descendants must have found out about it the hard way once the change began 250 years later.

Borrasca had even mentioned the cycle. But he had said it lasted thousands of years, not hundreds. He had also implied that the change wasn't due until well after his lifetime and that even then it would be a mild one, nothing like the drastic effects these old reports predicted. Could the Imperial survey team have been that far off? Or was The Jacksonite Corporation, speaking through Borrasca, simply lying?

As far as Benton could correlate the dates, the discovery of jacksonite and the subsequent creation of The Jacksonite Corporation must have happened during the desert phase, and that phase must now be ending suddenly. Such a change would explain much, from the vidscreen documentary he'd seen on Winze about the birdlike species endangered by climatic shift to Marguerite Borrasca's observations of the rising level of Lux Lake.

And if all that were true and the Imperial team's conclusions had been correct, then he couldn't imagine that The Jacksonite Corporation didn't know what was happening to Colliery's climate. That seemed borne out by their announcement that they would be reducing the production rates for jacksonite. Without the constant sale of the mineral, much of the Corporation's business would have to be shut down—for 250 years, anyway! Just what were they planning? To seal off the shafts and let the undermen die?

Was the work still on schedule at Euclase? From what he'd been told before he left New Albion, it would be another five or six weeks before Euclase would be ready to announce publicly the availability of synthetic jacksonite. Benton had no idea how short a research and development cycle that represented for something so major. It seemed to him that it should all have happened within a matter of days. If he had paid more attention to the details involved, perhaps he would not have been surprised. All he could think about, though, was how many more undermen would die in five or six more weeks, killed in accidents or murdered by the guards of the Headman or other headmen like him. How fast would the water rise in the workings all over the planet? How many of the places he had known were already under water?

If there was one thing Earth still did better than anyone else, it was provide endless fascination for tourists with a bent for history. This excellence was not due to any greater effort Earth made to preserve its past. On the contrary, many far younger worlds took far more trouble. Rather it was that Earth simply had so much more history than any other world and that every human being, no matter where in the Galaxy he might live, knew that his ancestors had played a part in that history, had perhaps walked these streets or been in these rooms. Benton threw himself into the tourist role in a frenzy.

He flew around the planet to various historical sites and great museums, and he strolled through cities, some ancient and deserted, some still populated, many of which had themselves once been the capitals of empires.

The idea of an empire restricted to just part of the surface of one planet fascinated him. Even the greatest of all of Earth's old empires, the one centered in a small island in the Atlantic, which had grown to cover a third of the planet's land surface and had included continents, parts of continents, and islands large and small all over the planet—even that one, so amazing to the people who had lived on Earth during its time, was utterly insignificant compared to the interstellar empire that had come into existence centuries later. And yet there was a grandeur to these more ancient monuments that entranced and captivated him. There was a sense of great battles and feats of daring on frontiers of empire spread all over the planet that appealed to the boy in him in a way that Imperial survey teams charting unpopulated planets never had.

The most amazing thing of all to him was the lack of attention the current inhabitants of Earth paid to all of this. It was as if they felt less connection with the Earth's past than he, an offworlder, did. He wondered whether their attitude was simply the contempt born of familiarity or an indication of dullness of imagination and meanness of spirit.

In more than one museum, Benton saw models, reconstructions, paintings, and in a few cases actual artifacts, of the first mechanical clocks. To him, a clock had always been glowing digits projected against a wall or ceiling or suspended in the air. Now he saw devices which used pointers to indicate the time. In some cases, the pointers moved in a circular motion, while the numbers were inscribed on a circular backing. In other cases, the pointer remained fixed and the numbers moved. What interested him most, however, was the variety of ingenious methods the ancients had devised to power the clocks—before electricity, he realized with a faint shock. Some were driven by water, some by weights on cords. Later ones used wound springs.

Coquina had complained about the lack of timekeeping underground. Couldn't he have duplicated this ancient technology? There were used tools and supplies to provide the raw materials, and there were the mechanical abilities and ingenuity of the undermen to take care of the details. Coquina, with his genius and presumed erudition, should have been able to come up with something like this. Not the wound spring version, perhaps, but a clock driven by weights or by the waterfall at Lux Lake.

Perhaps Coquina simply hadn't chanced to think of it or knew no more about this ancient technology than Benton had before coming here. Perhaps Coquina couldn't think of any workable timepiece, despite his stated desire to do so, because of his peculiar blind spots. Coquina's contempt for the undermen, his need to believe himself infinitely their superior, and his preferred role of arbiter of their fate would have prevented his seeking their help for anything. Most of all, Benton suspected, Coquina didn't really want any kind of clock. He might say he wanted a way to keep track of time. He might even think he wanted it. Certainly it would be useful for further organizing the hands. However, it would also show Coquina that time was passing underground just as it had above, that he was aging and so was his beautiful young wife, that the inevitable end was approaching no matter how many kilometers of rock hid him.

Time, Benton thought. It's time for me to go back to New Albion.

CHAPTER THIRTY-ONE

Silurian seemed displeased to see him.

Hoping I'd just disappear and leave everything to him, Benton thought. All the profits at whatever price he wanted to charge. I'd better keep watching my back.

Matters had, however, been moving smoothly in Benton's absence. Given the work Coquina had already done and his notes about what he felt remained to be done, the researchers put to work on the problem at the Euclase headquarters had taken it to its conclusion without serious difficulty. Marketing arrangements were already underway. Euclase's first approaches to such major consumers of jacksonite as the larger manufacturers of Arrastra Drive vehicles had been met with wild enthusiasm and huge orders.

"And that's true," Silurian pointed out, "even at the higher price."

Benton nodded. Silurian had already told him that the final costs, at production levels, would run over ten barnards a gram. Coquina had either miscalculated or been hopelessly overly optimistic. Benton strongly suspected that the truth was that Fowler Silurian was lying through his teeth and intended to absorb the extra profit himself under the heading of some vague, catchall cost or other.

Benton could insist on a complete breakdown of the money spent on the project, and perhaps Silurian would even provide the numbers. They would mean nothing to Benton, but he could hire accountants to audit the books. He really didn't want to bother, though. His visit to Earth, to those silent, ancient, timeless historical sites, had, to his own surprise, given him a detached, ironic view of such short-term or immediate problems. His original reason for keeping down the price of synthetic jacksonite had been philanthropic. This new higher price Silurian claimed they had to charge was still a great reduction compared to the current price of the mineral. There seemed no really good reason to force the issue. And the higher price would mean higher income for him and therefore more power to help the undermen—even though he hadn't yet formulated with any precision just how he was going to do that.

"I won't argue about the price," Benton said, "but there's one factor you'd better remember. I know from personal experience that The Jacksonite Corporation's real costs are very low. They could lower what they charge quite a bit without feeling much pain. Price our stuff too high, and we'll lose our edge over them,"

Silurian smiled. "I'll remember that." So we reach an understanding, Silurian thought. Benton doesn't mind making more money, either.

"You got payment in advance for those orders, I hope?"

"Of course. They know they can trust me. That's the basis of my success and always will be."

"How very exciting. I'll take my share right now."

Silurian opened his mouth to protest, then saw it would be

pointless. He shrugged. "If you insist." He hesitated for a moment, then said, "You know, Benton, you're trusting me further than a wise businessman would."

Benton smiled slightly. "Copies of Coquina's notes are safely stored in various places. Under certain appropriate circumstances, they will be transmitted to a number of major chemical firms, some here and others on other worlds. You'd find yourself with competition from companies charging much less than ten barnards per gram. The big ones could undersell you by so much and for so long that you'd eventually either fold or drop out of the synthetic jacksonite market. That's how much I trust you."

"That would violate our agreement."

"You could sue. Eventually you'd win, if you could stay in business for long enough. Those other companies also have packs of competent lawyers on staff."

Silurian glared at him. "I think we'd better not meet in person again."

Benton laughed. "I wasn't planning to come here again. Just keep transferring my profits to my account with each and every sale. Don't get greedy, Silurian, or you'll end up cutting yourself out of a very good thing."

In fact, what he'd told Silurian about the copies of Coquina's notes was a lie. It was a precaution he certainly should have taken, but it had only occurred to him at that moment in Silurian's office. Benton had kept a copy of the notes for himself, and that was still in his hotel room, easy pickings for a burglar in Silurian's employ. Benton hoped that Silurian's greed would keep him from seeing through the bravado—at least until Benton had a chance to make some copies of the notes and set up precisely the sort of arrangement he had claimed was already in existence.

Benton's dwindling bank account had swelled again with his share of the advance orders for Euclase's synthetic jacksonite. For the next few days, he watched newscasts for The Jacksonite Corporation's reaction. There wasn't one.

This must mean, Benton thought, that the Corporation hadn't yet realized its customers were switching to another source. Those customers must be playing it close to their chests. That made sense. The new product might prove to be inadequate, and if they then had to go running back to The Jacksonite Corporation hat in hand, they wouldn't want the Corporation regarding them as its enemy. As orders were not renewed, The Jacksonite Corporation would notice what was going on eventually, but that might take many weeks.

Benton didn't want to wait. He decided to do some advertising and publicity work of his own.

He went to the local bureau of one of the four major Galactic news services and told his story to the bureau chief—the only reporter employed there, an indication of New Albion's ranking in the eyes of the news–gathering profession.

The response was cynical. "Synthetic jacksonite at one per cent of The Jacksonite Corporation's price, huh? Gee, you must be only the tenth person to pull that off this week."

"Oh, I didn't do it. The achievement is Ben Coquina's. Check out that name. You'll see he's legitimate. And the product is already being marketed by Euclase Chemicals."

Perhaps the reporter had heard of Coquina's name before. Locally, Coquina was relatively famous. Certainly the reporter had heard of Euclase Chemicals, one of the planet's major corporations. Possibly Benton's behavior was sufficiently calm and rational that he took him a bit more seriously than he might otherwise have. In any case, his cynicism faded somewhat and Benton left with the impression that the story would be followed up.

The story broke a couple of days later. It was accompanied by one new detail that was of great interest to Benton. The reporter—or someone else in the news service—had done a good job on background work, detailing both Coquina's reputation and the economic role played by The Jacksonite Corporation and its expensive product.

Benton hadn't given his own name to the reporter, so no mention was made of him. The news story concentrated on the difference between the price asked in the past by The Jacksonite Corporation and that being asked by Euclase. That much hardly went beyond what Benton had told the man at the news service bureau. What was really news in Benton's opinion was that The Jacksonite Corporation had already reacted by announcing a twenty-five per cent cut in their price and a temporary increase in production.

Benton shook his head. That won't be enough to impress anyone, he thought. They'll have to fight back harder than that.

The angry call from Silurian came just as the broadcast ended. "What the hell are you up to, Benton? I know you leaked that story. We're being swamped!"

"With more orders, you mean?"

"With calls from reporters and politicians. And new orders," Silurian added grudgingly.

"I'm sure you can meet them."

"I can meet them. But I wanted to go slowly. I don't want to have to make a major conversion of our facilities."

"Fine. Don't. I'll contact some other company—someone who isn't afraid of making money."

Silurian cursed him and broke the connection. Benton sighed. He would never have expected this sort of timidity from a man like Silurian. He hoped that the momentum of the events now developing around synthetic jacksonite and the money pouring in from the flood of orders would carry Silurian along with them in spite of whatever misgivings he might be feeling.

The first news The Jacksonite Company had of the threat to their monopoly came when a reporter contacted the public relations office on Colliery to ask what reaction the Corporation had to the synthetic jacksonite situation. The P.R. man's jaw dropped, then he recovered his professional composure and told the reporter he'd call him back. He passed the matter up the ladder quickly, having no wish to hold onto this very hot potato.

The matter rose up through the public relations hierarchy swiftly and ended up within hours on the desk of the chief of public relations for the Corporation, Gyp Kaolin, "Clay" to his superiors and "Mr. Kaolin" to his subordinates.

Kaolin called up the Board member under whose control the public relations department operated and asked for advice. "Mr. Enno, we've got to tell this guy something, and I don't know what's the right thing to say." There was always a whine in his voice when he spoke to Enno. He was aware of it, but he always ignored it, convinced that it endeared him to those above him.

"Let's see now, Clay," Cal Enno rumbled, thinking aloud.

"One hundredth of our price, eh? If it's true, that's... well, it's bad. It's very bad. We could certainly come down a bit. Maybe as much as twenty five per cent. And boost production for a while. For as long as it takes to settle this thing, anyway. Make something up, Clay. Just keep them satisfied. I'd better call a Board meeting right away. Don't worry about a thing. We'll be able to take care of this."

As Kaolin's grateful face faded away, Enno punched the comm code for another member of the Board. "Another supposed synthetic jacksonite process," he muttered as he waited for the connection to be made. "Wonder how this one got past us. Wonder how serious it is."

After ending his call to Enno, Kaolin called in his own underling and told him importantly, "I've just discussed this problem with the Board of Directors. This is what we've decided to do. Call that reporter back and tell him we're cutting the price of jacksonite by twenty–five percent and temporarily increasing production."

"Thank you, Mr. Kaolin," the underling replied, relieved at not having to accept any responsibility himself. He scuttled out to deliver the message to the news service reporter.

A meeting of the full Board of Directors took place that afternoon in a conference room with dark wood paneling and furnished with comfortable chairs and a long, dark table. The eight members of the Board sat widely spaced along the two sides of the table and stared at each other wordlessly. They all knew why they were there, and each of them understood the magnitude of this possible threat, but no one seemed to want to begin.

At last Kyan Silman rose and walked gracefully to the head of the table. He was a tall, slender, handsome, greying old man, and he did everything with a grace that disguised his political power. "Since no one else seems willing," he said calmly, "I'll open this meeting. By now, you all know the basic problem. Someone is marketing synthetic jacksonite, something we've all been afraid would happen eventually, and this time we have to take it seriously. The reporter who contacted Cal's P.R. man said the process had been developed by a man named Coquina."

Enno glared at the speaker. He'd long suspected that Silman's police were tapping the comm lines of the departments under his control, and this seemed to verify it.

"Now, you may not remember that name," Silman continued, "but I do. A few years ago, we lured him here and sent him down into the mines. When he came here, his work was incomplete, and we had reason to believe he brought all his research notes with him. So how did the present situation develop? According to information obtained by an extraordinary young woman in my police, Galena Hess, another offworlder named James Benton, who was also confined in the mines, escaped with the help of one of our own employees and started this problem."

He looked around the table. "Don't any of you recognize that name? James Benton?" He saw blank stares. "Contco?"

"Oh, yes," Enno said. "That."

Silman nodded. "Yes. The young man who gave us that interesting demonstration. And then insisted he be taken underground, was involved in an accident, wandered off, apparently joined one of the villages, met Coquina, and ended up escaping, taking with him knowledge of Coquina's process. So our decision about Contco has, in a sense, led to our own destruction. It's poetic justice, isn't it? And yet, as people say, it seemed like a good idea at the time."

It had seemed like a very good idea, he remembered. Contco's work, they all hoped, would give them useful information about what was happening underground and would enable them to prevent any natural leader among the undermen from organizing the villages and leading the revolt the directors had always feared. Eventually, building on what Contco had done, they'd be able to automate the mines in preparation for the next climate cycle. To do that would require killing off the undermen by shutting down the ventilation. But they couldn't do it all at once and thus cut off the flow of jacksonite entirely. Contco's software and sensors would show them how to safely kill everyone in one section of the vast mines at a time. Automation could then proceed, also a section at a time.

Contco was the perfect company for the job, too. Large and competent enough to do the job well, small enough so that it and its employees could be eliminated once the job was done without causing too much fuss or attracting too much attention. That remarkable Hess woman would have been in charge of that part of the project. Silman had had great plans for her.

He sighed. "Too bad for Hess," he said. "She would have had a brilliant career in the police had things not changed this way."

Enno snapped, "Kyan! What's the point of all this?"

Silman smiled faintly at him. "The point, Cal, is that I wanted all of you to realize just how serious this one is. We let Coquina complete his work here under our observation, so that we could see what further action was indicated. We ended up placing him and his wife in the mines because—and here is the point—his process worked superbly, yielding pure jacksonite at even less than this one percent of our price the reporter mentioned."

Enno forgot his hostility and sat back in his chair. He felt as though there were no strength left in any of his muscles. "Damn! That's it, then."

Silman nodded. "That's it." He might have his running battles with Enno, but he did like this about him, that he was the only other Board member with any real intelligence, the only one who could catch Silman's meaning so quickly. He had often wondered if that was why they fought each other so bitterly. Each was the other's only worthwhile opponent on the Board. There was something cozy and familiar in their attacks on each other. Their war had added interest to Silman's life for decades. He felt sad that it was all about to end.

"We probably should have switched to the synthetic product ourselves right away, as soon as Coquina finished his work," Enno said quietly, as though speaking to himself.

"Yes," Silman agreed, "we probably should have. At the time, though, that seemed like the wrong choice. The way we were doing it seemed better, and now it's too late. You see what I mean, don't you, Cal?"

"Of course. We'll have to close down and... well, and leave, I suppose."

At last the meaning of their dialogue sank in. The other Board members realized they were being told to close down the jacksonite mines and end the way of life that had been so pleasant for them and their ancestors. Cries of protest arose from five of the other six.

The one who didn't protest was Dumortier, always a loyal

supporter of Kyan Silman. Dumortier was far from intelligent, and Kyan's devious doings and subtle arguments always left him confused, but his devotion to his leader was unquestioning. Silman, once he'd discovered this fact, saw to it that Dumortier remained on the Board. With Dumortier's vote, he thus had an automatic twenty five per cent say in any Board decision.

Usually, Enno led the opposition, and the Board would polarize around the two men. This time, though, Enno stood up and shouted for quiet, and then announced his complete agreement with Silman. Even if their surprise at this unlikely alliance hadn't been enough to calm the Board down, Silman now had three votes and only needed to sway two more members to achieve a majority.

When Borrasca had explained to Benton how the voting system on Colliery worked, he had thought he was telling the truth. Borrasca didn't know, however, that in truly important matters, such as the one presently under discussion, there was no public vote of the type he'd described. Such matters were decided privately by the eight Board members.

"Let me sum up the difficulty," Silman said with quiet sarcasm. "We've been starting the process of shutting things down anyway, simply because of the climatic change and the resulting flooding of the mines. We've all known from the start that this was coming. We expected to use our stored supplies of already mined jacksonite to carry the Corporation and its customers through the next two or three hundred years. But the point is that we, personally, would not be around by then, or even in another hundred years. Our planning was all for our descendants, who would be in charge of the Corporation when the next cycle began and the mines could be reopened. All Enno and I are recommending is that we close down without any plans to reopen in two or three centuries. Our personal futures will be no different than they would have been. We all have more than enough money to take care of us no matter what happens with the mines. It now appears that because of this synthetic substitute there will never be any point in reopening the mines. In another century or so, there might well be other synthetic substitutes available at even lower prices."

"But what about our descendants?" one of the other members protested. "I never had to worry about—oh, about investments, and so on. There was always so much coming in as my share of the Corporation's profits."

His neighbor sneered. "Then you've been a fool, Vannad. But what bothers me," he continued, turning his attention to Silman, "is why I should leave Colliery. This is still the most pleasant place in the Galaxy for a rich man."

Enno answered him. "You can stay if you want to. I'm leaving, and I'm sure Silman plans to as well. This world will be full of hundreds of thousands of unemployed and starving office workers, a whole planet gone bust, and it won't take them long to figure out who's to blame and who's got the money they no longer have. The idea doesn't appeal to me."

"Moreover," Silman said, "as long as you have any money to play with—and even Vannad must still have a lot—you can use it to invest wisely in industries on other planets and become even wealthier. You can reestablish yourselves, your fortunes, and your families on other worlds where there's opportunity. There won't be any opportunity on Colliery. Vannad, you'll have to acquire the business knowledge you never needed here and your ancestors never needed either. I imagine a lot of you are in

Vannad's position. Well, it's a new age, a new era, and we'll have to live in it or fail. The rules have changed, and you must accept that. I find it exciting, I must say."

"You know," Enno said reflectively, "maybe it's just as well all this happened when it did. I've always had my doubts about our original plans. We thought we could simply shut down the mines when the climate changed and let the undermen die down there. Everyone else would have been thrown out of work and would have learned to live as farmers again, like their ancestors. Something along those lines, anyway. We would have left for our own safety. Then eventually, in two or three hundred years, our descendants were supposed to return, exercise our dormant property rights, take over, and reopen the mines. Do you really think that would have happened? How many of them would have chosen to return? And those who did, what chance would they have of taking over again and make the populace into undermen again? I think this new plan will give our descendants a better chance. We are the Galaxy's natural ruling class, after all."

Silman and most of the others nodded their agreement, now that the initial shock was fading. There were a couple of exceptions to the general mood of agreement, though. Vannad was one of them. He slumped in his chair, looking broken and foreseeing a bleak future for himself and his posterity.

Enno and Silman both glanced at him at the same moment. Then they exchanged looks filled with cynical understanding. Vannad was far inferior to that ancestor of his who had led the fight to create The Jacksonite Corporation generations before. The blood had run thin, and now Vannad and the rest of his clan would sink back down to their natural level.

Silman, still dominating the meeting, proposed the wording of the official announcement, and it was approved by the Board by a vote of six to zero, with two abstentions.

As the members all stood up and left the room, each wrapped up in his own thoughts, Enno realized for the first time that this was the last Board meeting. He felt momentarily depressed at the sudden end of institutions which had been on Colliery since before his birth, but then he became exhilarated. He would never have to put up with these fools again. He could start up businesses on other worlds and run them all by himself without these endless, pointless discussions. Like Silman, he was excited by this new future.

Habit took the edge off his excitement for a moment when he returned to his office and ran through the most recent offworld news reports concerning the Corporation and discovered what Kaolin had done with his casually uttered words.

That idiot! he thought angrily. I should send him into the mines for this. Good God, why did I put that nitwit in charge of the public relations department in the first place?

Then he realized that his reaction was no longer appropriate in view of the suddenly changed situation on Colliery. Circumstances themselves would take care of Kaolin's punishment. He relaxed and smiled, his earlier ebullience returning at the thought of pompous, nattily dressed Gyp Kaolin being forced to grub in the dirt for his survival while Kaolin's erstwhile superior continued his life of luxury and power on another planet.

All day long, the newscasts had been mentioning rumors that

some major change was underway in The Jacksonite Corporation. The news readers' excitement kept growing with each repetition of the rumor, but vague rumor was all they had. It wasn't until evening that Benton finally saw a newscast with solid information on the subject.

The Jacksonite Corporation had just announced, the news reader said excitedly, that they were suspending all operations for an indefinite period—in effect, going out of business. This, the news reader added, was presumably connected with the announcement only hours ago that a company on New Albion was now marketing synthetic jacksonite at a very reduced price.

Benton booked passage for Colliery immediately. He would be able to leave in less than two days, and the trip would take almost five. One short week, and he'd be back on Colliery.

As soon as business hours began the next day, he visited his New Albion bank and arranged for a new account to be created in Ben Coquina's name and for half of all money transferred to Benton's account by Euclase Chemicals from then on to be shifted over immediately to the Coquina account.

As he left the bank, the smug feeling that he had been noble and honest despite a strong temptation to be otherwise warred with a strong intuition that he had been abysmally stupid.

CHAPTER THIRTY-TWO

For no real reason, Benton had expected Winze to be deserted. While enduring the days of the journey from New Albion, pacing about the ship nervously and wondering what was happening on Colliery, he had unconsciously formed a background mental image of the Corporation withdrawing to Colliery like a tortoise retreating into its shell, abandoning such outposts as Winze. The opposite proved to be the case.

Benton was the only passenger the shuttle from Winze picked up from the passenger liner. However, as he watched the shuttle drawing near through a porthole, he realized it was considerably larger than the shuttle he had ridden in to and from Winze before. It also turned out to be unusually crammed with people—more than Benton thought safety regulations probably permitted. They were all boarding the liner, leaving Colliery.

He stood beside the lock until all the new passengers had entered. The crowd pushed past him, men, women, and children. The children looked tired and confused. The adults looked tired, confused, and bitter.

This was no crowd of Corporation employees off on a vacation. If anything, despite—or partly because of—their uniformly expensive and fashionable clothing, they made Benton think of vidscreen newscasts he'd seen of ruling-class refugees fleeing the violent revolution on Scandium some years before. Is that it? he wondered. The ship is sinking, and these are the rats?

Benton had the feeling that someone was staring at him. He looked over the crowd of arriving passengers and his eyes met those of an older man, tall, slender, ascetic, and greying, who was looking at him with interest and frowning slightly, as though trying to decide something.

Finally the older man pushed his way through the crowd and came up to Benton. "You're James Benton, aren't you?"

Benton tensed, straining his senses to try to tell if someone was coming up behind him as well. Should I say I'm someone else? Probably too late for that. He nodded.

"Yes, I thought so, although you've changed considerably." He looked Benton up and down quickly, then smiled slightly. "You don't look the part at all. Not the type to have done all this damage." He shrugged and returned to his group.

A crewman gestured to Benton. He picked up his luggage—a single small bag—and pushed past the group of refugees on his way into the shuttle. The older man didn't look at him as he passed, and no one else in the group seemed to consider him worth noticing.

On Winze, in the building to which the shuttle attached itself, another crowd was waiting, pressing into the tube so quickly that Benton could hardly get out of it. They had the same look about them as the previous group, but with the addition of an air of desperation.

Benton had no trouble finding passage to Colliery itself.

Three Corporation–owned vessels were ferrying regularly between Colliery and Winze, heavily loaded on the outward leg but with no one but the crews for the return trips to Colliery. Benton was allowed onboard without any questions being asked. He found this more than a little amusing when he compared it to his previous nerve–wracking trip under an alias on a similar vessel.

The scene on Colliery was similar to that on Winze. Benton and the tired ship's crew, who were being relieved, were the only arrivals, but large crowds were waiting their chance to get away. There were no spaceport officials this time to hurry him through. All organization or governmental effort seemed to have been abandoned. Benton remembered Borrasca saying that there was no government on Colliery, that The Jacksonite Corporation was the government.

And now there was no Corporation.

That couldn't be quite true. There must still be enough of the Corporation functioning to keep the ships operating between Colliery and Winze and to maintain the facilities on Winze while they were still needed.

While they're still needed, he repeated to himself.

The thought brought with it a sudden chill.

Everything will close down once the Corporation's top brass has left, he thought. Their underlings probably think they'll be taken care of. Once they realize they've been abandoned, there'll be real chaos. Some of them may be able to afford to leave, but most of them probably can't pay the price of a ticket. I've got to find Diori and get us both off the planet while that's still possible. Otherwise, we'll be trapped on a world in collapse.

Carrying his bag, he walked rapidly toward the exit.

Because he'd gone straight from the ship through a landing tube into the spaceport, he'd not yet been outside. From a clock on the spaceport wall, he knew it was still early morning here. As he passed through the building's exit, he unconsciously braced himself for the already fierce heat of the desert. He stepped outside and stopped in astonishment at the cool, damp air that washed over him.

The sky was grey instead of the harsh blue he'd anticipated and a slow, steady rain was falling. The street was glistening and water ran steadily past in slender rivulets. The rain must have been falling for some time. Beyond, the desert sand was dark with the water it had already absorbed, and in places he could see the tell–tale green of new plant life.

As far as he could see, there were no more refugees arriving outside the building at the moment. What he had seen inside and on Winze must have been the tail end of the flow. Flyers and floaters were scattered helter–skelter along the road leading to the spaceport. Clearly they had been abandoned there by the refugees, who had no intention of returning to this world. Their dedication was not to Colliery, the planet which had given them their wealth and enabled them to lead such pleasant, luxurious lives, but rather to that wealth itself and to that pleasantness and luxury.

Parasites, he thought scornfully. Not even rats. Tapeworms.

Benton found a large flyer that had a full charge and, like those in the life–bands, could be started without any palm identification. He threw his bag into it and then walked down the straggling line of abandoned, unlocked vehicles and searched each one methodically for maps, food, and spare power packs. When he had assembled what he thought he'd need, he took it all back to the flyer he had chosen, climbed in and closed the door, and settled down to plan his course.

The spaceport building had its name painted on the outside in large letters. He found the name on one of the maps without much trouble. Spaceports, cities, and life-band recreation spots were the places most clearly marked of all. He was near the northern life-band. He glanced out the window at the steady rain and the new vegetation. It looked even denser and greener than when he'd first seen it just a short time before. He realized that "life-band" would soon be an obsolete term.

He remembered the name of the city in the south to which he'd gone in his first stolen flyer, after escaping from the mines and the desert. He unfolded more maps and finally found the city on one. The exit shaft and the crater in which undermen bodies had been dumped were of course unmarked. Everything connected with the actual operation of the mines had been ignored as if it didn't exist. On all the maps he could find, the desert was a blank, a white area beginning beyond the ring of cities and extending to the edges of the map. New maps, he thought. That's another problem Colliery will have to deal with now. Glad it isn't my problem.

He studied the maps of the southern life-band for a while, trying to estimate as best he could from his memories of his desert trip and subsequent wandering in the life-band just where the exit shaft might be. He knew that his final guess might well be off by a hundred kilometers or more, but he had to do something. Hadn't he come all this way, done all this work, simply for the purpose of rescuing Diori Coquina and taking her away with him? Yes, that was why he was here.

What about rescuing Ben Coquina, source of Benton's wealth, the man Diori had pledged herself to? Ben Coquina was evil. Benton must keep reminding himself of that. Ben Coquina's evil outweighed everything else and eliminated Benton's debt. He was almost sure of that.

As best he could tell, if he kept to a heading about thirty degrees west of south and kept the flyer at top speed all the time, within something like forty hours he should be in the vicinity of the exit shaft. How he would know it from the air, he couldn't guess, but he hoped there'd be some sign he could detect.

A geographical sign at any rate. A landmark. Moral guideposts were too much to ask for. No one made maps containing those.

He started the flyer and climbed to altitude, well above the low–lying cloud cover. He could see nothing beneath him but the rumpled white surface of the clouds. The ground was completely hidden. There might have been no world down there, no people, no society, no rules or restrictions.

He typed in his course and speed. As the vehicle rocketed away from the vicinity of the spaceport, Benton put his hands behind his head and leaned back in the pilot's chair seeking a comfortable position, pondering both his future and Colliery's.

As Benton sped toward the exit shaft at a steady altitude of ten kilometers, much was happening some kilometers below the surface of Colliery. As the polar ice caps melted, the rivers emptying into what had been the desert swelled, the constant rainfall became more widespread, and underground water levels rose catastrophically.

Because of differing water pressures and different rock and soil porosities, the water spread through various channels at different rates. In more than one part of the mines, it happened that there were pockets of hard, nonporous rock filled with veins of jacksonite and riddled with the tunnels and living spaces of the undermen. Where the orientation of the tunnels was just right, the water soaked the softer soil surrounding the rock pocket without intruding into the tunnels. Then, when it had risen high enough and came across a tunnel opening leading down into the rock, the water made its entrance, first slowly and then in a flood. The clans of undermen who worked those tunnels and lived in them had no chance to escape to higher places, for their first warning of danger was the roar of water pouring down on them from above.

In other places, it was the sheer weight of the water that brought disaster. The melting of the ice caps and the accumulation of water in the desert where there had been none for centuries caused earthquakes which seemed small and insignificant to the surface dwellers but which spelled death to the undermen. Tunnels that had seemed utterly secure for generations of undermen suddenly gave way under the weight of water soaking through the earth and under the vibrations from the earthquakes. The walls collapsed inwards, sending hurricanes of displaced air shrieking through the tunnels and caverns, smashing human bodies to pulp and causing still more collapses.

Air flow had never been adequate. The only significant force moving air through the tunnels had always been the enormous fans at the shaft exits. Now the guards, learning that there was to be no more pay or other reward, were leaving their posts. Power was interrupted. Machinery failed and was not repaired. One by one, the fans stopped. The newly fallen rocks and the swiftly spreading water blocked what air flow there still was. Carbon dioxide began to gather in the great natural caverns where most of the undermen lived. Other gases, released from pockets in the rocks and no longer dissipated by moving air, accumulated in tunnels and caverns. Groups of undermen trying to escape from inrushing water blundered into tunnels filled with invisible gas that killed them all in seconds.

No one would ever be able to determine how many undermen—hundreds of thousands, millions?—were drowned, crushed, or suffocated and entombed forever under kilometers of rock, dirt, and water.

The village centered around the Big House and still ruled by the Headman was luckier than most. Lux Lake had continued to rise, flooding the lower tunnels and cutting off access to most of the places where the clan had chopped out jacksonite. As their production of jacksonite fell, they received less food from Heaven.

The rising waters were preceded by waves of luxes, crawling up the tunnels with surprising and menacing speed. Their feeding patterns had been badly disrupted, and the luxes were starving. They snapped viciously at anything that came within their reach. Where the water was high enough, the luxes, floating unhappily on it, were able to reach their clawless brothers tied to the walls, and they made quick meals of them.

Perhaps because so many of the tunnels were now dark, the undermen didn't notice that luxes floating on the rising water would suddenly disappear in a flurry of splashes and struggles. Some undermen tried to wade waist-high or chest-high or even deeper in the flooded tunnels, hoping to get some jacksonite from known veins. They too disappeared with hopeless struggles. The larger water snakes, their feeding patterns also disrupted, were moving up the tunnels after the luxes as the lake spread.

The miseries of hunger, bewilderment, and fear, even combined with the torment of snapping luxes and the terror of ferocious water snakes, were not quite enough to cause revolt. More would be required before the undermen broke out of their old habits of subservience. The Headman and his guards—and the Recorder and his wife—had first call on what food still came down, so that the disparity in strength between the hands and their rulers increased. A watch was posted on all the entrances to the Big House to kill any luxes that tried to enter. For those who bowed to the Headman's wishes and followed all his orders, the Big House was still a place of refuge and safety, light and food. The reduced village huddled in the great cavern, still well lit by the luxes along its ceiling and walls, and listened, trembling, to each new report of blocked tunnels, rising water, and oozing walls.

"Why are the gods doing this to us?" they moaned, but no one knew the answer. "We've always been faithful."

Someone suggested that a delegation should approach Heaven and ask for help, but that was too frightening an idea. When the Headman ordered the hands to go back to work, this time to search the higher, older tunnels for veins of god-metal overlooked by their ancestors, they quivered with fear at the thought of leaving the Big House. But under the Headman's glowered threats and the upraised weapons of his guards, they left.

The revolution finally came because of three more burdens. The air began to grow stale. At the same time, nervous hands reported no response at the gate of Heaven. No carts came down, either to pick up god–metal or to deliver food. No food? And yet the undermen were playing their parts in the grand scheme as well as they could under these new and trying circumstances. Why weren't the gods responding in kind? The constant roar of sound and rush of fresh air from Heaven, moving from the exit down into the tunnels—that had stopped too, and that must explain the staleness of the air in the Big House.

And then, most frightening of all, it began to rain in the Big House.

When the soft drizzle started, no one knew what was happening. Then someone noticed that water was dribbling in through some of the many holes in the roof, the tunnel exits through one of which Benton had once watched a hand crawl in order to replace dead luxes on the roof. The water fell as a light rain near the center of the cavern. At one of the sides, it ran down the wall. The undermen stared up at this phenomenon in amazement but not, at first, in fear.

The flow increased. At this, their pent–up terror exploded into confused yells.

Soon the water was collecting in pools across the floor of the Big House and making parts of the ramp along the edge of the cavern dangerously slippery. This was the ramp that led up to the Recorder's office and apartments, and he appeared at the top of the ramp to see what all the noise was about. He held a sheet of paper clutched in one hand and a bone pen in the other, and he glared down at the frightened crowd. "Be quiet!" he shrieked at them. "You're making me forget what I was going to write!" But his voice, never very penetrating, had grown noticeably weaker of later, and none of the crowd heard him.

The Headman and Diori, both disheveled, emerged from the Headman's place to confront the crowd as well. Water had begun falling on them from the ceiling at a very critical moment, and the Headman was in no mood for further disturbance. He bellowed at the crowd, his powerful voice cutting through the babble and echoing from the cavern walls. When he had their attention, he yelled at them to get back to work. "Get out there and find more god-metal!" he boomed. "Then the gods will make everything normal again."

Stephan Scheel and his men had just returned to the Big House. They were in time to hear the Headman's words. Scheel's self-imposed subservience deserted him. He pushed his way to the front of the crowd, his face flushed and angry. The crowd parted for him, taking in the dampness of his clothes, wet from the waist down.

By now, the water from the ceiling had increased to a hard rain. It made a constant rushing noise as it struck the deepening puddles everywhere. It was running steadily from most of the holes in the ceiling.

Scheel dropped the head of his heavy pick to the floor and leaned on the end of the handle. He had bossed a gang of hands for long enough to have developed a voice even louder and more penetrating than the Headman's. "There's no more god-metal to find, Bort. The water's everywhere. Tunnels are collapsing. We've got to go to Heaven and speak to the gods directly."

Scheel had used the Headman's name, remembered from the days before Bort had been thrown out of the village. It had been years since anyone had called him by name instead of addressing him as "Boss." The significance of Scheel's doing so was not lost on the crowd or on the Headman himself. His eyes flickered toward his guards, waiting tensely on either side, and he nodded in Scheel's direction.

The guards understood him perfectly. They began to close in on Scheel from both directions, raising their weapons. The crowd fell back quickly out of their way, leaving Scheel alone.

Scheel knew the guards were already too close for him to turn his back on them and leave. There were a dozen of them, men all too used to killing hands at the Headman's command. He raised his pick to shoulder height before him and waited calmly. The guards assessed Scheel's evident strength, for he looked more like one of them than a hand, and the deadly weapon the pick had suddenly become, and they hesitated.

Scheel's gang of hands, who felt for him something approaching loyalty, raised their own weapons and began to move toward the guards, timorously at first, but then with increasing courage. They splashed through the standing water, a grim bunch of starving, fatigued, half–crazed hands, and the crowd began to mill about and then to coalesce behind them.

There was a sudden burst of yelling at one of the lower entrances to the Big House. The men stationed there to keep the luxes out came running into the cavern shouting incoherently. But no one needed to understand their words. The water gushing out of the tunnel behind them told everyone what had happened. Lux Lake had at last reached the Big House.

At the top of the ramp, Coquina stepped forward to see what was happening. His feet shot out from under him and he found himself skidding on his back down the wet surface of the ramp. He bounced against the cavern wall on one side and then caromed off at an angle, skidding across the ramp until he flew off the edge and fell to the cavern floor.

He landed on a clump of undermen, hurting them far more than himself. He staggered to his feet, still clutching his pen and paper, and stared about wildly. He headed for the foot of the ramp, splashing through the knee–deep water, oblivious to the snakes and luxes which had at last made their way into the cavern.

Coquina scrambled desperately, but the ramp was so slippery that he could get no more than a couple of meters along it before his feet flew out behind him and he landed on his face and slid back down into the water at the bottom. He stood up again and stared up the ramp. "My files!" he moaned.

The water flooding across the cavern had broken up the confrontation in front of the Headman's place. The crowd of undermen stumbled about aimlessly, knee deep in the water and soon thigh and waist deep. The snakes were attacking furiously. Only small snakes so far, even though there were great numbers of them, but the larger snakes would reach the cavern as soon as they too sensed the existence of this new food source. Screams of terror and agony arose throughout the cavern.

Stephan Scheel shouted to his gang to follow him. He headed resolutely for the cavern's higher ground and the exits there. His purposefulness infected the other undermen, and they began to push their way through the water after him. The Headman's guards hesitated only a moment. Then they cast away their weapons and splashed after the others, ignoring Bort's furious shouts.

The Headman's place was raised sufficiently high above the general level of the cavern floor that the water hadn't yet got above Bort's and Diori's ankles, and so the snakes hadn't yet discovered them. But it was rising even faster now. It was as though the lake were sentient and wished to satisfy its ravenous hunger now that it had discovered this great, open, unfilled place.

Bort stopped shouting. It was clear to him that his authority had just vanished. It was also clear that he would soon be almost alone in the cavern with the rising water, the ominous white shapes leaping from it, and the floating corpses of the less fortunate undermen. He grabbed Diori's arm, and headed across the cavern after his erstwhile subjects, dragging Diori behind him.

She looked back as Bort dragged her off. Her husband was still trying to climb the ramp, but he was tiring and making less progress with each attempt. "Ben!" she shouted. "Come on, you idiot!"

Coquina looked in her direction, his eyes glassy, then back again at the ramp. "But my files," he whispered. "The ink..." He took a step after his wife, then a step toward the ramp, then stood still, not knowing which way to move.

As the vanguard of the refugees from the Big House finally reached the gate of Heaven, they straggled to a stop, frightened and awed by something they had never seen before. They had never expected to see it. It filled them with even greater fear than the monster-filled water behind them, with an even greater sense of loss than the knowledge that their home cave was gone forever.

Heaven had gone dark.

It wasn't completely dark. It glowed with a faint grey light that was about as bright as the milky shine of the luxes the undermen had known all their lives. But Heaven had always been so bright with the light of the gods that no underman could even look at the exit to Heaven without being blinded for his blasphemy. The now-drowned Big House had been brighter than this!

Stephan Scheel was at the front. He turned to the others and said, "The gods have left Heaven and gone away from us. But smell the air. They left that for us."

Hesitantly, they stepped forward and sniffed. It was twilight out in the desert beyond the exit, and as the air outside cooled it drifted down into the tunnel, chilly, clean, and fresh compared to the ever staler air they had been breathing.

"Follow me!" Scheel cried, and he headed up the shaft toward the exit. The others hung back fearfully. Scheel trudged forward without them, heading fearlessly toward the dimmed light of Heaven.

He had no way of knowing how great his fortune was. When the guards deserted their place, the foreman, Green, had been the last to leave, hanging on in the desperate hope that things would somehow return to normal. When he'd finally had to admit that that was not going to happen, Green had left too. First, however, he'd cut power to the huge fan. He wanted to be sure that all the undermen would die. But his hands-on experience with the hardware was years in the past, predating his supervisory appointment, and he had thrown the wrong switches. The fan had slowed and stopped, satisfying Green, and the bright lights had died too, but the beam defense system that would otherwise have killed Scheel instantly had also been killed.

Scheel walked through into Heaven.

Rather than in a place of glory, he found himself in a large building filled with machines. The machines were strange and unidentifiable, but they looked like the sort of thing men might build and use. So did the place itself.

Scheel reminded himself that the gods looked like men, had made men in their image, and therefore would quite probably use machines like those of men. He walked past the machines to the building's open door. He stood looking out at the darkening expanse of desert. He was bewildered by what he saw, unable to comprehend it. His eyes and brain were so unused to such distances that he couldn't quite interpret what he saw. He shrugged and turned away. He was a practical man and would deal with the strange sight later.

There was no movement in the building except for the breeze coming through the door from the desert. Scheel returned to the shaft opening and called down it, "There's no danger. The gods have left. The air is clean, and there's no one here. Come on."

It was not his words that convinced them but his survival. The gods seemed willing to permit this invasion.

Slowly and hesitantly at first, then more eagerly as they smelled the air beyond the exit and as those behind saw the ones in front enter Heaven without being harmed, the undermen emerged onto the surface of Colliery.

CHAPTER THIRTY–THREE

When Benton's flyer first left the vicinity of the spaceport, nothing was visible above him but blue sky and nothing below but the white of cloud cover. As the spaceport receded invisibly behind him, the ship that had brought Benton from Winze broke through the clouds, once more fully loaded with refugees, and shot up into the sky.

How many more trips, Benton wondered, before everything closes down?

Breaks began to appear in the cloud cover as he drew ever further from the life–band. Below, through those breaks, Benton caught glimpses of green dusting the sand. He saw glints of reflected light, evidence of new rivers and of standing water beginning to collect in low lying places, new lakes being born. Occasionally he had to land to replace a drained power pack, and he was astonished anew each time at how what had been desert sand squelched underfoot.

Benton wracked his brains trying to remember something about water tables. Didn't the standing water mean that the ground was so saturated that the water table had risen higher than the bottoms of those low spots? If so, it would surely stay that high or go even higher, unless the rain stopped, and what did that mean for the mines?

He flew steadily. Hours dragged by and kilometers slid by below. He ate and napped irregularly as he felt the need. He felt suspended in a timeless, motionless world, with nothing recognizable but the steadily, slowly moving sun.

Assuming he could find the shaft, and assuming that Diori was still alive and that he managed to find and rescue her, what happened then?

He tried to imagine himself leaving here with Diori, going to some civilized world like New Albion, and spending the rest of his life with her in wealthy indolence—assuming they'd stay together that long, assuming that she would still find him interesting even after the novelty wore off and she was exposed to so many other men who weren't undermen, assuming that his guilt about Ben Coquina and Augie Syen didn't destroy him.

Too many assumptions, he thought gloomily.

Each year he would be far wealthier, one year older, and with no accomplishments to chalk up for that year. He tried to imagine this future in detail, but his mind rebelled and settled instead upon other things. He'd been essentially goalless all his life, and his childhood and later the loss of his parents had combined to make him rootless. Perhaps all he'd done since escaping from Colliery had been somehow—subconsciously—intended to perpetuate just those qualities of his life, just the ones that had always made him feel dissatisfied beneath his placid exterior.

Maybe there really is some sort of god or gods arranging everything after all, he thought, filled with sadness, and it's my fate to always live this way.

Benton crossed the equator early the next morning. Along the equator, and for hundreds of kilometers on either side of it, there were virtually no clouds, no rain, no sign of green on the desert floor, and the sand was bright yellow–white. He landed, replaced the power pack, walked around the flyer a few times to stretch his muscles, felt the sand crunching under his shoes, felt the dry air sucking moisture from his face, and then took off again.

As he drew further south and the equator dropped away behind him, the clouds and rain began again, and soon he was once again suspended between the silent white below and the infinite blue above.

He was afraid that if he kept flying, he'd pass over the area he was looking for during the night. Some time after dark he landed cautiously and spent the night on the ground.

He slept little. His imagination kept approaching the subject of his future, dreaming up various scenarios, and he couldn't make it stop and quiet down.

By early afternoon of the next day, Benton thought he must be approaching the general area of the exit shaft. Because of the almost constant cloud cover, even thicker and with fewer breaks as he approached what had been the northern life–band, he knew he had virtually no chance of seeing anything from the air. He dropped down below the clouds and continued on the same heading at a reduced speed. He saw kilometer after kilometer of the new carpet of green, broken occasionally by stretches of water and even less frequently by glimpses of the darkened desert sand.

When he was sure he must already have gone too far, he

entered a new course, a spiral. This would be time consuming, but after a few turns around the center he would have covered an enormous area of desert, and if the shaft were anywhere in the area covered, he would have to see something.

On the second turn of his spiral, he spotted a new lake that was so nearly circular that he slowed his motion and hovered over it, puzzled. That could not be natural, he was sure.

Unless, he thought with sudden excitement, it's an old meteorite or volcano crater.

He hovered just above the surface of the water, staring down at it as though by sheer intensity of gaze he could penetrate its opacity and see the dead undermen heaped on the bottom of the crater. He gave that up at last and looked at the horizon, trying to remember if it was the same scene he remembered.

He thought it was, despite the softened green outline of what had been harsh contours. On that assumption he headed in the direction he remembered the floater having come from so long ago.

Benton first saw the buildings that had been the living quarters and offices for the guard emplacement. As he drew nearer, he saw the clump of ragged figures standing aimlessly near the door of the largest building of all.

They heard the noise of the flyer and watched motionlessly as he landed on the open ground a few meters from them. Then they broke with cries of terror and vanished inside the building.

Benton jumped from the flyer as soon as it had stopped moving and yelled, "Hey! Come out! I'm not going to hurt you."

Long moments passed without movement. Then a figure emerged from the doorway and walked cautiously forward. As it drew nearer, Benton thought it looked familiar, but his primary reaction was revulsion at the ragged clothing, the grimy skin and dirty, unkempt hair and beard, and most of all the powerful smell.

The underman stopped in front of Benton and said in a timid voice, "Sorry–sorry, god, sorry–sorry, but we were dying down there."

"God!" Benton laughed harshly. "I'm no god. I'm a man." He peered at the underman's face, and suddenly he recognized him. "Stephen—Stephan Scheel! I'm James Benton. Don't you remember me?"

"They said they killed you and sent you to Heaven. I mean, to here. And now you look like a god, like people who go to Heaven are supposed to."

Benton gestured impatiently. "Look, I can't explain it to you now. Eventually you'll understand everything. I don't even have time to listen to how you got out alive. Did most of the others escape, too?"

"No," Scheel shook his head with a bitter expression. "Most of them didn't." He turned toward the doorway of the large building. In the darkness of the interior, the frightened faces of the other survivors were barely visible as they watched Scheel brave the god's wrath. "Come out here!" Scheel yelled. "It's not a god at all. It's only Benton."

They pushed warily out into the open. A ragged figure shoved them aside and came running across the intervening apace.

"Jim!" It was Diori. She flung herself at him, almost knocking him off his feet. "My God, I thought they'd killed you! I'm so glad you're alive. For God's sake, come on, let's get off this planet."

"Wait a minute," he smiled, gently pushing her back. "Calm down. We'll leave, but not just yet." He looked at her, trying not to let his shock show on his face.

Was this the woman who had so fascinated him, who had seemed as beautiful, as sensuous, as captivating as any courtesan in history? It was bad enough that she was filthy and in rags. That could be taken care of easily enough. But despite her words, he sensed an utter lack of any real feeling for him. He had the same sense as he had felt underground that she saw him only as a vehicle, a means to her own escape and return to civilization. Then he had been able to ignore that feeling. He couldn't do so now, not in light of the uncomfortable self–questioning he'd been undergoing during the last two days.

"Something needs to be done about these people," he said.

"Undermen!" she spat. "For God's sake, who cares?"

As the crowd of undermen drew near, still hesitantly, Scheel, who was looking beyond them at the building they'd come from, suddenly pointed at the door and cried out, "Look! Someone else made it."

An underman was in the doorway, leaning against one side of the opening as if in the last stages of exhaustion, his ragged clothing dripping wet and one sleeve red up to the elbow. The crowd, including Benton, hurried back to help him.

The first survivor to reach the man stopped and turned away. "It's the Recorder," he said in a voice choked with both anger and disappointment. "Let him die."

Coquina stared blankly at Diori and Benton, apparently unable to take anything in. His right hand was missing, bitten off by a snake as cleanly as if it had been removed surgically. He must have had some presence of mind still when it had happened, for a tourniquet of rags torn from his clothing had been tied about his arm between the elbow and wrist. He collapsed on the ground between Diori and Benton.

The two looked at each other over Coquina's prone form. Diori startled Benton by saying, "Tell me what the situation is with synthetic jacksonite and money."

Benton bent over Coquina and examined him briefly. Just as briefly, he told Diori what had happened on New Albion.

She looked at him in amazement. "In Ben's name?" she asked. "Half the money is in his name, instead of all in yours?"

Benton nodded.

Diori pursed her lips thoughtfully. "I thought you were more intelligent than that," she said. "This is... unfortunate." She shrugged, then bent down and tugged at her husband's body. "Help me get him in the flyer."

Benton picked Coquina up himself and slung him over a shoulder. He was astonished at how light the older man was. Insubstantial, he thought. Insignificant.

He carried him to the flyer and placed him in the back, in the roomy passenger compartment. "There's a good emergency aid kit in these machines," he told Diori. "Why don't you see what you can do for him, especially for the loss of blood."

Diori climbed in beside her husband without speaking.

Benton returned to the group of survivors. They still stood near the doorway where he had left them. He called Stephan Scheel over. "Stephan, come with me. I want to make a quick investigation of these buildings." Benton felt vaguely guilty spending any time at this while Diori and her injured husband waited for him to take them to safety, but he also felt too much kinship and sympathy for these survivors to simply leave them to fend entirely for themselves.

The two men found living and working accommodations. To Benton, his tastes already readjusted to the standards of civilization, they seemed Spartan. To Scheel, however, it was all so splendid that it was almost proof that this was Heaven after all. Everything seemed wonderful to Scheel, the tools perhaps most of all.

Scheel had lost his pickaxe during the escape. In one of the workrooms, he found a substitute that he seized on with delight. It was actually a large crowbar. Benton suspected it was intended for use in manipulating large chunks of ore when the carts were being unloaded. He thought he should explain to Scheel that no tools of that sort would be of use in the undermen's new life. What they needed now were farming tools. But the glee on Scheel's face silenced him. He held onto the crowbar as if he intended to keep it next to him forever.

Fortunately, the living quarters were equipped with an independent power system of their own, and no one had turned that off. Benton had no idea how long it would last, but it would at least give the survivors a fighting chance for the immediate future.

He showed Scheel where the food was stored and how to use the automated kitchens to convert it to edible form. "You see," he told him, "this was what your so-called gods did before they sent the stuff down to you. Now that you're going to be living in the gods' quarters, you might as well learn how to live like them. In fact, let me show you something else." He took Scheel into a bathroom and demonstrated how the equipment worked. "Believe it or not," he told him, "you'll find that you like cleanliness after you get used to it. You'll also like wearing those clothes we found back there."

He waited for Scheel to protest that using these buildings themselves would be blasphemous, but the underman said nothing. He was already learning, Benton thought with approval.

As they returned to the outside, Benton said, "The food here won't last indefinitely, and I don't know about the power and the water supplies. It's just a base, a starting point. Someone will have to come out here and help you get going on some new footing. Farming, perhaps, like your ancestors. There's no point in going to the towns. There'll be chaos there for some time to come, I imagine. I'll take the Recorder and his wife away, and then I'll try to round up some help, send someone out here to help you, before I leave the planet."

"You're leaving?" Scheel said in sudden alarm.

Benton looked at him in surprise. "What did you think?"

"I thought," Scheel licked his lips, "I thought maybe you'd be staying with us and helping us. Leading us."

"Leading you? Oh, no, Stephan, you're going to be their leader. I have to get to a spaceport quickly, while there's still a chance to get off Colliery."

"Maybe I'll be their leader," Scheel muttered. "Look." He pointed at the cluster of survivors.

A new figure had joined them and was yelling at them and waving his arms. Even at this distance, Benton could recognize the Headman.

Bort looked in their direction and came loping toward them. He stopped in front of them, a far less terrifying figure than Benton remembered. He peered at Benton uncertainly for a moment, as unable to recognize him as all the other undermen had been. Finally Bort realized who this was, and he drew back his lips in a silent snarl. "You've been making trouble here, Benton. Go away."

"You have no more authority," Benton told him. "Scheel is the leader now."

Bort laughed. "Not if he's dead, he isn't. But you come first." He lunged forward, his fingers reaching for Benton's throat.

Before Benton could move, Scheel's crowbar swung up, catching Bort on the chin.

The Headman staggered back, his arms flailing as he tried to catch his balance. He fell, landing heavily on his back. Before Bort could get up, Scheel lifted the crowbar over his head and brought the sharp blade down with full force on Bort's face.

Bort twitched on the sand, his face covered with a pink froth of blood. He gurgled, as though still trying to intimidate his former subjects. Benton was glad he couldn't see any more than the covering of froth. He wished he couldn't hear anything, either.

At last Bort stopped moving.

Scheel pulled the crowbar free and stepped away. He raised the tool and examined the bloody blade with interest. "This is wonderful!" he said. "The gods never sent anything this good down to us." He glanced at the Headman's body. Only now did he seem to really understand what had just happened. "I guess I *am* the leader, after all."

Already he seemed straighter and more confident, less subservient toward Benton, less in awe of Heaven—more aware, perhaps, of just how far this was from any kind of Heaven.

Manhood through murder, Benton thought. Nothing new there.

He looked at Bort, then quickly looked away again. He supposed that if anyone deserved to die, Bort was a fine candidate. Power struggles resolved by killing weren't surprising in these circumstances. There would almost surely be more of them as the undermen shook off the subservience of underground and adjusted to their new world. Others would die, and not necessarily only those who deserved to. The moral issue involved in whether or not anyone deserved to die, and if so whether anyone else was qualified to decide who, let alone to carry out the sentence, was one Benton couldn't bear to deal with now. He could only hope that Scheel and the others he had grown to like survived.

"The people will be in good hands now, Stephan. Please be careful. Protect yourself." But not the way the Headman did, I hope. "I have to leave now."

They said goodbye. Scheel made no effort to stop him. Benton knew that was a good sign, even though a small part of him was disappointed. He hurried toward the flyer and climbed quickly into the pilot's seat. He leaned back and called through the narrow entrance into the passenger compartment, "Diori, are you both ready? I'm taking off."

"Both ready, Jim."

Benton started the engine. At its hum, starting low and then rising in volume, Scheel and other undermen backed away nervously. Scheel might be feeling more confident, but the others looked at Benton longingly. He leaned out the door and called out, "Someone will come back to help you. Don't leave this area."

He closed the door and took off rapidly, hoping the acceleration wouldn't aggravate Coquina's wound, but desperate to escape the faintly accusatory feelings of loss, aloneness, and desertion he thought he could sense emanating from the huddled group of undermen.

CHAPTER THIRTY-FOUR

Once they were in the air with the flyer on course toward a spaceport shown on one of the maps, Benton went back to the passenger compartment.

Diori was nowhere to be seen. After a momentary panic during which Benton thought he must have left her behind, he realized that she must be using the small bathroom at the back to clean up. Her husband was there, on a couch that had been set back to full horizontal extension to form a serviceable bed. He was well strapped in and still unconscious.

Benton checked him quickly. Coquina seemed no worse. Thanks to the blood substitute in the emergency aid kit, he'd reach the spaceport alive, and there should be medical help available there.

There was a paper clutched in Coquina's remaining hand. Benton extracted it with some difficulty. Even though he was unconscious, Coquina held it as tightly as he could.

It was one of the sheets of skin-paper Coquina had used in the mines, the writing almost completely washed off. Benton threw it from him in revulsion.

Diori emerged from the back transformed. She was once again the beautiful woman of the picture. She had done more than wash away the cavern grime which even she had not been able to avoid completely. She had also found some clothes and makeup, probably left behind in the haste to escape. Inevitably, the clothes she had found were too large, but that seemed insignificant because of the comparison with the rags she had been wearing before.

"There now," she said in satisfaction. "Not as good as I used to be, but it's the best I could do with what's available."

Benton remembered to breathe again. "You're... lovely."

Diori smiled. "Ben isn't going to wake up until a doctor gives him something. I've already seen to that. We could make one of those other couches into a bed. Much better than the floor of a cave."

The suddenness and intensity of his desire jolted Benton. Part of him cried out for her, for that small, strong, supple, infinitely capable body, but another part of him shouted even louder that if they made love he'd become her slave. Again. Whatever major decision he made about his future—and he knew that he would have to make one very soon—it must be made rationally, with some degree of detachment, and not because he was addicted to the pleasure this amazing woman could give him. That pleasure meant control. That's the way it was with Diori.

Perhaps all those thoughts showed on his face. When he said, "No, there's been a lot of air traffic. It wouldn't be safe for me to stay out of the pilot's compartment," she didn't object or press him, even though she probably knew that the flyer's computer could handle the job better than any human being could.

She pursed her lips. "Hmm. Yes, I suppose you're right. I'd

better try to find some clothes for Ben and clean him up. They probably wouldn't want an underman on one of their nice, clean spaceships."

About an hour later, Diori came into the pilot's compartment and sat down in the seat next to Benton's. "There, it's done at last," she said, pushing a stray hair from her forehead. "You'd be surprised how hard it is to wash and dress an unconscious adult."

"Why didn't you call me? I'd have helped you."

She looked out the window by her side, away from him, at the uniform cloud cover below. "Because it wouldn't have been safe. You said yourself that you have to stay here to watch for other traffic."

There was a long and prickly silence. Diori finally broke it by asking, "How much longer to the spaceport?"

"Two or three hours, I think. Although those clouds mean we'll have to drop down and search, so maybe longer."

"Time enough. Tell me again, just so I'm sure. Half the money is in Ben's name, not even jointly in his and mine, and the other half is in yours."

"Right."

Diori sighed. "You really surprise me. Don't tell me you didn't even take credit for the synthetic jacksonite process."

"I had nothing to do with the process! It was Ben's achievement. Of course I gave him full credit for it. The news services know all about him and what he accomplished. He'll be a hero when he gets back. Good god, Diori, what kind of man do you think I am?"

She glanced at him, then looked straight ahead. "A foolish

one. Also young, naïve, and overly romantic. Think ahead. I don't think you've been doing that. I like fame and the social life it brings. I'll have that if I stay with Ben. I like great wealth and what it brings. The way you've set it up, I'll have to remain Ben's wife to have that. No, wait." She held up her hand imperiously, sensing that he was about to speak. "There is an advantage to the situation. On New Albion, widows inherit everything, except in exceptional circumstances, so I'll get the money eventually. Ben never was strong. Now his mind's gone, and with that injury to undermine him further, I don't think he'll last long. In a year or two, I'll be a widow, extremely rich and getting steadily richer, and still young and very, very beautiful. Come to see me then, and we'll discuss some sort of arrangement to combine our fortunes."

"Yes, of course," he said, having no intention of ever seeing her again.

The silence returned, thicker than before. Eventually, Diori got up and returned to the passenger compartment to take care of her husband, whose life she intended to preserve until she was properly reestablished on New Albion.

Benton had been trying for some time to pick something up on the flyer's receiver, some sign that he was near the spaceport he was looking for. There was nothing but a faint, faraway hiss. Already, then, the deterioration had progressed far.

A long, dark shape curved from the sky and penetrated the clouds about twenty kilometers to his right. That must be where the spaceport was. Hastily, Benton cut his speed, dropped below the clouds, and turned the flyer ninety degrees to the right. He found the port visually, feeling lucky even at that.

He set the flyer down outside the entrance to the main building. The scene outside the building was a repetition of the one where he had found his flyer after arriving from Winze. Abandoned flyers and floaters were scattered all over the space in front of the building, their owners having left them behind with their other abandoned possessions and their abandoned planet.

Benton told Diori to wait in the flyer with her husband while he went for help. He was able to track down an emergency aid team in the spaceport. Two men came back with him, bringing a stretcher, and took Ben Coquina into their charge.

Watching their efficiency and willingness to help, Benton wondered again what promises had been made to such Corporation employees to keep them working during these final hours and how they would feel and react when they finally realized that the promises would not be kept.

Diori and Benton followed the two workers and the stretcher with Coquina in it skimming along the ground between them. They went into the spaceport. The crowd of refugees had dwindled considerably here. Watching the refugees who remained, Benton experienced an even greater feeling of disgust than he had at the other spaceport. "Look at them," he said to Diori. "After all they've done to this planet, to the undermen, rather than making some attempt to make up for it, they just take their money and leave."

Diori shrugged. "That's human nature. When you grow up, you'll understand that."

The flood of refugees had ebbed so much that only one more ship was scheduled to leave for Winze that day. There would be one more the following morning, and then nothing more was scheduled at all.

Benton was able to book passage to Winze for Diori and her husband with no trouble. The ship would be leaving half empty as it was. Further passage for the two through to New Albion took slightly longer to arrange, but finally that was done too. Benton paid for all of it from his account on New Albion, also paying for the high–speed transmission needed to verify the existence of the account and to transfer funds for this purchase. Even all of that made only a negligible dent in his now enormous balance.

Coquina had been taken to the port's small infirmary for treatment. He would be transferred directly from there to the ship. Benton turned to Diori, who had been standing next to him during all of this. "You'll need your account code when you get there," he said. He gave her the number.

She raised her eyebrows. "You didn't book passage for yourself?"

"There's that other ship tomorrow," he said evasively. "I have to try to arrange some help for Stephan and the others. And anyway, it's...it's better this way,"

Suddenly and unexpectedly, Diori laughed. "You're probably right. I think perhaps I've underestimated you. So. Goodbye, Mr. Benton." With a faintly mocking smile, she held out her hand, and Benton took it automatically. "Do remember what I said about seeing me in a year or two," she said.

"Yes. Yes, certainly," Benton said mechanically. He drew his hand from hers, turned, and walked rapidly away. When he was at last outside the building, he breathed a deep sigh of relief, feeling that he'd escaped from something immensely powerful that had threatened him in a way he'd never been threatened before.

He found his flyer, changed the power pack, and took off, heading for Pearlight.

He had half feared Pearlight would be deserted, but it was not. Some traffic still moved on the streets. It seemed to be random, just individual floaters on individual errands, rather than the pattern one expected to see in a busy city at dawn.

Now that he was here, he realized he hadn't thought about what to do next. It had seemed logical to come here. He had gained the impression from Borrasca, during his unwelcome stay in Harve's house, that this was as close to an administrative center as the Corporation, and hence the planet, had. He doubted if Borrasca was still here, and he didn't care one way or the other. But he did hope that he could find someone here who still had the authority and resources to do something for the undermen.

He drifted slowly over the city, headed toward the center. Was there a single building, or a single complex of buildings, where the administrative center was located? Would he have a chance of recognizing it from the air?

Benton shook his head. Perhaps the best thing would be for him to book passage out right away and leave the planet. His wish to help the undermen was strong, but there seemed to be no way for him to actually do anything for them. Even if he found the corporate center, what was the chance that it was still operating? And even if it was, surely the people still manning it would be most concerned now about their own survival and would not be likely to concern themselves with food and other aid for a bunch of undermen.

He told himself that whatever organization still existed on Colliery would probably crumble in another week or two. There'll be little local dictatorships springing up, he thought. Back to the Dark Ages.

But the undermen are hereditary Republican citizens! I wonder if the Republic would be willing to do something to help them. And send in some forces to keep order here while they're at it. But there's no one here who would officially request that, and the Republican government isn't likely to step in without a request from someone in authority. Authority which no longer exists. Round and round.

As he approached the downtown area, he began to notice occasional small groups of people. Some of them were just standing and talking, but others were moving with a purpose he sensed was aggressive. He wondered if this was the beginning of anarchy and riot.

He was hovering indecisively over one of the moving groups when the man who seemed to be in charge suddenly raised his hand and pointed up at the flyer. Benton heard no sound over the hum of the flyer's engine, but a small hole appeared in the window near his head. He shot up to a higher altitude and skimmed off well out of range.

For the first time he regretted that the Headman was dead. Bort would been at home in this new order—perhaps even a force for organization in it.

Again he dropped lower.

He was now over one of the city's main business sections, but here it was completely deserted. The trash littering the sidewalks showed why. Looters had already taken everything worth taking.

Or perhaps not quite everything. A flyer, even larger than his, sat in the street in front of a building whose door had been broken in.

Curious enough about this detail of a society's breakdown to ignore the probable danger, Benton landed just behind the other flyer and waited. A few minutes passed, and then a man appeared in the doorway, backing out, struggling with his end of a wide, long, and apparently very heavy box. That tall, beefy, blond-haired figure looked familiar, even from the back.

Good Lord, Benton thought. It's Borrasca.

Benton climbed out of his flyer and walked quietly toward the doorway. Borrasca, sweating and panting, his attention focused on the box, didn't notice him.

"Having trouble, Harve?"

Borrasca jumped at the sound of Benton's voice. The end of the box slipped from his hands and crashed heavily to the ground. He spun around to face Benton, dropping into a defensive crouch. "What the hell—! Benton!" He straightened "God damn you, when will you stop turning up?"

"When you stop being so entertaining. What are you doing?"

"Cleaning out my office," Borrasca snarled.

The person at the other end of the load appeared in the doorway. Benton was unsurprised to see that it was Galena Hess. She had walked out cautiously, prepared for trouble, a gun in her hand. Now she took the situation in at a glance. She put her gun away in a small holster on her belt with a smooth, practiced movement and told her cousin in a commanding tone, "Harve, go to the flyer and make room for this box. And stay there until I call you."

Borrasca looked back and forth between his cousin and Benton, and any protest he might have been intending to make died on his lips. His shoulders slumped and he trudged off toward the flyer.

When Borrasca had climbed into the flyer and closed the door, Galena said, "So you came back to see just how much damage you had done."

"You know better than that," Benton said mildly. "All of this would have happened without me."

"Yeah, sure." Bitterly, she said, "I should have killed you when it would still have done some good. Strangled you." She smiled. "In bed."

The old air of tension and suppressed violence was there again. Absurdly and to his own annoyance, Benton found that he was responding to it, as he had before, with sexual arousal.

Galena's aggressive posture relaxed subtly and she said, "Maybe you're right. The old way has died. That's all that really matters. We have to deal with the way things are. And we will. We'll manage."

"We?" Did she want to resume the relationship with him? The prospect excited him, eliciting memories of strenuous, combative sex, of fighting hard and wanting to lose, of submitting to Galena's will and strength. But that would be as much a trap as life with Diori. In both cases, he would be under someone else's control. There was a choice to be made about his future, and he had to be the one to make it.

"Harve and I." She grinned at his astonishment. "At one time, you were more what I had in mind. However," she looked him up and down, "you've changed, and not in ways I care for. Now that the Corporation's gone, there are no more stupid laws about cousins. I can do what I want. And with Harve, I will."

"Sounds like Heaven," Benton said sarcastically.

"To each his own. We'll be happy. Well, I'll be happy. We've got enough supplies collected now to take care of ourselves for a long time, just the two of us."

"Correction, then. Not Heaven, the Garden of Eden. It sounds like a dull future."

She grimaced. "It's better than this." She gestured toward the trash on the street and sidewalk from earlier looting. Benton understood her gesture to take in the scattered, shattered state of her world.

"Why not stay here and try to help people reorganize?" he asked. "Help them rebuild."

Galena snorted. "Because they're all weaklings, worthless trash. Most of them will be dead of starvation or disease or violence within a year."

"That only shows how much they need leadership. Here, I'll help you with this box. Let's spare Harve's flabby muscles. I have a feeling he'll need what strength he has later." They picked up the box between them and carried it toward the flyer.

Borrasca opened the door as they approached and stood aside, glowering, while they heaved and wrestled the box into place. Benton got out of the flyer again, and Galena jumped down lightly immediately behind him.

"You know you caused all of this," she told him. "If you're so concerned about the poor, starving fools, then you do something to help them." She laughed. "And when you need policemen again, come and get me."

Benton said nothing. Her laugh had affected him physically in the same powerful way as when he'd first met her, and he felt momentarily unable to speak. Her words had struck him, too, with their truth.

Galena stepped close and put her hands on his shoulders. She stared down into his face. "You've changed a lot," she said thoughtfully. "There's much more to you, now. Harve is still more to my taste for the long haul, but every now and then..." She bent forward and gave Benton a long, deep, passionate kiss. "Now and then, it could be interesting."

She turned away, climbed into the flyer, and closed the door. Benton, stunned, stood unmoving as the sudden gusts of air swirled around him and the flyer hummed into the air and shot away to the north.

But if Galena, watching him through her window in the pilot's compartment, thought with pleasure that it was her kiss and his memories of her that had so stunned him, she was only partially correct. In the end, her words had had a greater effect, bringing to consciousness and coalescence the threads of internal argument that had been filling Benton's unconscious for days and weeks, denying him rest and peace.

CHAPTER THIRTY–FIVE

At the end of one of the worst days she'd had in the last year, Augie Syen trudged slowly home from the public transit interchange. Everything had gone wrong at work from the moment of her arrival in the morning until quitting time. What made it worse was that she knew it was more than just a bad day, more than just an isolated stretch of time during which, by coincidence, many things had been unusually dissatisfying. Rather, it was merely the worst of a series of bad days, each worse than the last. At this rate, tomorrow would be worse yet, and then the day after that, and the day after that...

To her right was a long, featureless building wall. To her left was a street, a relatively quiet, suburban street, but even here the traffic roared by constantly. The wind from the traffic whipped fine dust against her face, arms, and bare legs. The wind and the constant noise set her nerves on edge. Perhaps she should give in at last and buy a floater, use it to go to and from work rather than walking this short stretch morning and evening just in order to use public transit. But no, that would be a final surrender to the way everyone around her lived, a lifestyle that had always seemed sentient and sinister in its bland insistence that she adopt it.

Ahead of her, in a gap between buildings, the sun fell huge and red toward the brown haze that hid the horizon.

Augie stopped at the door of her apartment building to watch the sun fade and die as it sank into the thick layer. The haze turned first grey, then black as it swallowed the sun.

The fact was, she admitted to herself reluctantly, that she hated Farandhazy. The further trouble was, as she well knew, if she got a job elsewhere, things would be the same—the same work, the same kind of people, on a world virtually interchangeable with Farandhazy, even down to the sunsets. It looked just like this everywhere else, because everywhere else was just like this.

Once she was inside her apartment with the door safely locked, she fixed herself a drink. It was an indulgence that had become a daily habit during the last year—a habit usually repeated two or three times in an evening. Then she relaxed in her most comfortable chair and idly watched the news. The reports concerning the closing down of The Jacksonite Corporation had virtually disappeared, but she still watched, hoping there'd be something about her aunt and uncle, or even, well, yes, even about James Benton. Especially about James Benton.

When the first news had appeared about synthetic jacksonite, Augie had acted on a hunch and contacted the company mentioned in the broadcast, Euclase Chemicals on New Albion, paying more than she could really afford to send the high-speed message. She had addressed it to James Benton. She had never received a reply.

That's funny, Augie, she told herself in bitter mockery, usually you give up when a man says goodbye once. This one did it twice, and you're still trying.

Later, when her aunt and uncle returned home to an eager press and Galaxy–wide acclaim, she had watched reports of the event with a lack of real interest or relief that had made her feel guilty. She supposed she still loved her uncle and felt grateful to him, but from the first she had despised Diori, whom he'd married while Augie was still living in his home on New Albion. A couple of years later, Augie had left New Albion and gone off to her first job. She had been escaping her lover and her aunt, and she still wasn't sure which motivation had been more powerful. Now, years later, her feelings for her uncle struck her as pallid and a matter of duty rather than real emotion.

It was easy to recognize real emotion, she thought. Sometimes, anyway.

After two drinks, she began to feel drowsy. Drunk, she corrected herself.

Rather than giving in to the temptation to fall asleep where she was, she forced herself to her feet and set about making a meal. While she waited for the *ping* from the food center that would announce the meal's readiness, she decided she might as well check to see if she had received any messages. She'd been neglecting this for long stretches lately, not expecting any communications and not really caring whether or not there were any. Most of the messages she did get were of no importance. Maybe if she could dredge up the energy—and courage—to reactivate her social life, that would change

There were quite a few messages waiting, the earliest one dated a week ago. How could that much time have passed since she'd checked? She was surprised, but also disturbed at the realization that she had been letting time slide by unnoticed.

Almost all of the messages were totally unimportant, mass messages sent automatically by various advertisers and others to virtually every comm unit on the planet. She was able to kill and discard these after the first couple of lines had appeared on her screen. A couple were invitations to parties. After a momentary hesitation, she discarded these as well, without bothering to send replies. A few were bills, which she paid with her mind preoccupied.

Now there were two messages left.

The first, dated the day before, was from New Albion.

Augie sat forward in shock, her heart beating faster. From Jim?

It was an audio message, with no picture. She sat back again happily to listen, anticipating that voice she had missed. But the voice which came from the small speaker was not Benton's. It was her aunt's.

"Dearest Augie," Diori said with a degree of syrupy sweetness that Augie's stomach, full of alcohol and empty of food, could hardly take, "by now you've probably seen the news reports about our escape. We're back on New Albion at last. Your uncle is very ill from our ordeal, but he really wants to see you, and I know you'll want to see him as soon as possible. I have so much to tell you about our time on Colliery and the fascinating people I got to know there. One of them in particular. It's all quite unbelievable. Please come as soon as possible and plan to stay for a long time. We have lots of money now, thanks to Ben's brilliance, so we can pay your way this time and take care of you while you're here. Message us at the following code." The number appeared on the screen.

Augie made a face and wondered what reply to send. Again

she felt guilty for not feeling more pleasure at the Coquinas' escape and safety or excitement at the prospect of visiting them. Her concern for them, expressed so frantically to Benton when they'd first met, now in retrospect seemed to her more the duty owed by blood than genuine feeling. Again she found herself thinking about other, deeper, more important feelings which had superseded those familial ones, and she forced her mind away from that topic.

She ordered up the next message. Dated that morning, it was from Colliery.

She caught her breath, suspended between fear and hope. Another audio message. She waited for the voice, almost afraid to hear it.

"Hello, Augie. I imagine you're surprised to hear from me finally. I hope it's a pleasant surprise." It was Benton's voice, but stronger, firmer, more self-confident than she remembered.

"As you can tell, I'm on Colliery again. Or still. A great deal has happened here, and I don't know how much of it has been reported in the news. I suppose that now that The Jacksonite Corporation's gone, the news services have lost interest in us.

"Maybe that's just as well. We have an enormous amount of work facing us here."

There was a longish pause, as though he were gathering his thoughts, or possibly even reading notes. Augie waited, all her usual impatience when listening to comm messages gone.

"Everything has collapsed on Colliery," the voice continued. "The world's in a desperate state. We know for sure that there are a couple of hundred thousand people in locations known to us, and as far as we can guess, there might be many hundreds of thousands more scattered around in places we don't know about, lost, starving, ignorant, and terrified. It's too complicated to explain how all this came about. If I tried to, you probably wouldn't believe it. You have to be here to see it for yourself, not only to believe the background, but even to get some grasp of the magnitude of what we face.

"You've probably noticed that I've been saying 'us' and 'we.' When The Jacksonite Corporation collapsed, its ruling elite fled the planet. Since they ran the place, everything dissolved in chaos. The Corporation was the only government, and it was also all industry and commerce. It also provided the people who knew how to keep things functioning. Those people are still here, but their bosses left, and the underlings are mostly the sort who don't know what to do without someone to give them orders. So here we have a populated world that used to import virtually everything, including much of its food, suddenly with no way to pay for those imports. They were facing mass starvation, disease, riots, civil war—who knows what else. I couldn't just leave, knowing what was going to happen, and knowing that I was at least partially responsible for the situation."

There was another, shorter pause. When Benton's voice came again, it was even firmer than before.

"I'm staying here. I've organized a kind of ruling council with me at the head. Collierites are so dependent on following orders that they've accepted us as the top dogs so far, and at least so far, we're holding things together. The Corporation's ruling families took as much of their wealth with them as they could, or got it transferred to other planets, but a fair amount of it was left behind in the rush. We've been able to freeze that. We're working on getting back some of what they took with them. Fortunately for us, a lot of other worlds still harbor resentment against The Jacksonite Corporation because they were under its thumb for so long, and those governments have cooperated with us. And also, of course, there's my share of the proceeds from synthetic jacksonite, although I'm sure Fowler Silurian is already working on trying to break that agreement. He'll get help from your uncle, no doubt. Maybe from Diori, too. But that's even more complicated than the history of Colliery, so I won't go into it any further.

"The point is that with these sources of wealth, we're able to scrape by for the immediate future, but maybe for no more than a year or two. In that time, we have to rebuild this world, organize people to manufacture our own goods to replace imports, and most of all—and hardest of all—build up agriculture on a large scale among people who know virtually nothing about it. All this in the middle of a continuing planet–wide climatic change. When I think of it in those terms, instead of in terms of all the little day–to–day tasks, it seems impossible and I feel that we can't possibly make it in time. But we're trying, everyone's trying, together, with remarkably few malcontents. Most of all, I'm trying. I spend my time working, organizing, flying around the planet visiting settlements and solving problems. On and off, I find time to sleep and eat. I keep telling myself that I'm a dictator, ruler of a whole planet, but somehow, at the end of the day it doesn't feel much that way."

His next words resonated with a different sort of intensity. "Augie, I'm happier than I've ever been in my life. I could go on and on about the work and my satisfaction with what I'm doing with my life. Something meaningful for a change. You can probably hear them in the background, yelling impatiently for me to come and solve the latest crisis!"

He gave a little laugh. Augie could hear the joy in it. She realized that she had heard such a laugh, so pure and spontaneous, from very few adults in her life.

There was the muffled sound of a short dialogue. Then Benton's voice continued. "I just told them to give me a couple of minutes. This is the hardest part of all for me to say, so it's just as well I have to hurry myself and spit it out. There's a lifetime of work to be done here, purposeful work. I think you'd enjoy it as much as I'm enjoying it."

Augie saw that her right hand, the one holding the now unheeded glass, was trembling slightly. She set the glass down next to the comm, waiting for the next words, trying to master her breathing, which was now very far from normal speed.

"I'm trying to ask you to come here and join me, Augie. I mean, in whatever capacity you choose. After the way I behaved on Farandhazy, you'd be justified in discarding this message and never replying. Or you probably have someone else more reliable by now. In that case, why don't you both come here for a visit? We can use your tourist barnards!

No! she wanted to shout. No, there's no one else!

"You might even both decide to stay. We're not really trying to get immigrants, since we're having enough problems just taking care of the people we've got, but if Colliery's dictator can't make exceptions for special people, then what's the point of being a dictator?"

He waited as though he were expecting, hoping for, an immediate reply. After a moment, he said, "Well, that was what I wanted to say, although I'd planned to use much more elegant and subtle phraseology. Never works out that way, does it? Yes,

yes, I'm coming! Sorry, Augie. I'll be waiting hopefully for your reply. Goodbye...dear."

There was a faint click, and MESSAGE END appeared on her screen.

"Good God!" Augie said aloud.

She sat up and paced nervously about the room. What in heaven's name was she going to do now? Stay where she was, go to New Albion, go to Colliery? How could she trust her feelings, which urged her so strongly to leave immediately for Colliery? What could she trust—or whom, for that matter?

Preoccupied, she composed a noncommittal reply to Diori. Before transmitting it, she played it back on her screen and was astonished to see that she had told Diori she'd send her a more definite message, not "in a few days," as she'd intended to say, but "from Colliery."

Oh, my tricky unconscious, she thought.

The food preparation unit chimed at her insistently. The chimes meant that this was the third time it had signaled, and she realized that she had been ignoring its previous summonses.

"Damn!" she said aloud. She hated overdone food of any kind. This was very overdone. The blackened mess was obviously inedible. She threw it out and decided to skip supper. She could hardly eat, anyway, in the midst of this tension and indecisiveness.

She laughed aloud. "Augie Syen," she told herself, "don't be such a fool. You're not undecided at all!"

Filled with an almost overwhelming mixture of fear and excitement, and with a sense of suddenly wider, almost limitless horizons, she sat down again and began to compose her reply to Benton. She searched as he had for elegant and subtle phrases. Not finding them, she spoke instead from the heart.

About the Author

David Dvorkin was born in 1943 in England. His family moved to South Africa after World Two and then to the United States when David was a teenager. After attending college in Indiana, he worked in Houston at NASA on the Apollo program and then in Denver as an aerospace engineer, software developer, and technical writer. He and his wife, Leonore, have lived in Denver since 1971.

In addition to non–fiction, David has published a number of science fiction, horror, mystery, and Star Trek novels. He has also coauthored two science fiction novels with his son, Daniel. For details, as well as quite a bit of non–fiction reading material, please see David's Web site, *http://www.dvorkin.com*.

www.ingramcontent.com/pod-product-compliance
Lightning Source LLC
Chambersburg PA
CBHW060553310726
48982CB00008B/1115/J

* 9 7 8 1 7 3 4 5 6 3 6 2 7 *